THE

LIFE AND CAREER

OF A

LONDON ERRAND BOY

BY

JOHN BENNETT

AUTHOR OF "NIGHT AND DAY;" "FAMILY MYSTERIES;" "CAREER OF AN ARTFUL DODGER;"
"TOM FOX;" "WAYS AND MEANS;" "REVELATIONS OF A SLY PARROT;" "THE
ORPHAN SISTERS;" "THE EMIGRANT'S DAUGHTER;" ETC., ETC.

"Boys often become tyrants from a mistaken notion of its being grand and manly."
"I would take off my hat in admiration of any boy who did his best."—DR. ARNOLD.

WITH TWENTY ORIGINAL ILLUSTRATIONS

LONDON
PUBLISHED BY HENRY VICKERS, STRAND
AND SOLD BY ALL BOOKSELLERS
MDCCCLXV

CONTENTS.

LIST OF ILLUSTRATIONS.

LIFE AND CAREER
OF A
LONDON ERRAND BOY.

THE GOOD MOTHER PREPARES HER BOY FOR HIS FIRST SITUATION.

CHAPTER I.

A MAD GAMBLER.—A DESPAIRING WIFE.—
DEATH IN A FOG.—THE LONDON ERRAND BOY
LEAVES HOME FOR HIS FIRST SITUATION.

IT was a dark, cold, comfortless morning in
January of the past year when Mrs. Brown
after a sleepless, anxious night arose from her
bed, hastily threw around her an old black gown,
and as hastily lit a fire in the little room. No
sooner did the kettle begin to sing his merry
notes over the crackling spitfire wood, than a
grave old cat came forth from the cupboard and
took up her accustomed place on the hearth, and
a yellow black-nosed puppy began to bark and
gambol about. Mrs. Brown cast her eyes to the
clock hung on the wall, and finding it was six,

she became more active in the preparation of the early breakfast. The bellows was brought into the service, and she puffed rapidly away until the kettle was buried in blazes, and the darkness of the room was killed by the reflection of the cheerful flame.

Never in her life, perhaps, was she so glad as when the kettle boiled on this morning, big with the fate of her little son Tom Brown, who still slept on in the bed on the floor, behind the chintz furniture hung across a line, to convert this one room in reality into two practically.

The black tray was now set on the table, and quickly filled with odd cups saucers; then the loaf and bit of butter were brought forth—the latter luxury got especially for Tom's breakfast, in honour of this his first morning at his first place.

During her morning's labours, Mrs. Brown heaved many a sigh; and as she looked upon her husband—(who slept and seemed to scowl while he slept—his eyelashes pulled down so low that they almost covered the closed lids, his massive, wiry beard of many colours and hues resting on the turned-out sheet)—she clasped her hands as if in prayer, and raised her tearful eyes to the smoke-dyed ceiling.

Something terrible at that moment passed through the woman's mind.

She now pulled aside the pinned-up blind at the window and looked forth upon the morning —she saw nothing but a black fog, which stood between heaven and earth like an impenetrable wall.

She dropped the blind, and then cut a slice from the loaf, and resting her feet on the fender, kindly made her sleeping boy some toast, and then the repast was ready for Tom's reception.

Unwilling to rouse her son a minute earlier than necessary, she looked once more upon the clock, and found the time had come when she must awake him. This, as in all her operations of the morning, she did in the quietest possible manner, for she was anxious not to disturb her wild-looking husband.

Softly she stole across the apartment, lifted the chintz furniture which divided the room and the beds, and for a minute stood by the lowly bed of her little boy, who was this morning to make his first start in the battle of life.

With her long brown hair streaming down over her black stuff gown behind, she knelt down and pillowed her head by the side of her genteel, intelligent boy, and sobbed—

"I had hoped better things for you, than the life of an errand boy! But God's will be done!"

Tom awoke, and grieved to see his mother thus, said—

"Whatever is the matter with you, mother?"

Her only answer was a loving kiss on Tom's open brow. She then said—

"It is time now, dear Tom, for you to get up. I have got the breakfast all ready for you, and I will black your boots while you dress."

"No, mother, you shan't. I can do that. Is father awake?" he inquired, as he rose from his pallet.

Had her pale lips given expression to her heart, she would have replied—

"Oh! that he would awake no more!"

But she restrained her outraged feelings, and simply said—

"No, Tom, and I hope he will not awake until you are off to your new place."

She took her son's ill-conditioned boots from the floor, and returned to the fireplace, and made them bright.

Tom now stepped forth to the breakfast table, his face ruddy-red with the cold-water washing he had just given it, and his light hair tastefully combed back from his brow. He was a genteel-looking boy of about thirteen years of age, and somewhat tall. His kindly-officious mother would do that for her only child which he was quite capable and willing enough to do for himself, and she took the clean collar from his hand and neatly pinned it around his neck.

The father now turned in his bed, groaned heavily, and grasped his hair. Tom looked upon him, and the wife trembled.

"Oh! what a misfortune for us, my boy!" exclaimed Mrs. Brown, "that you should have such a father! Tom, remember your mother's words on your first going into life—let your father's example warn you! you are the only person in the world that your mother now has to depend upon."

"And you *may* depend upon me, mother," said Tom in sincere, unaffected tones.

Mrs. Brown poured out his tea, and pressed him to make a good breakfast.

"How can I, and see you so wretched?"

"I shall be better, no doubt, when I become more reconciled to this poverty. But it is no use to say otherwise, my boy, than that I deeply feel the wrongs your misguided father has heaped on us. Squandered my fortune and his own—left us without a penny, and himself without a character!—and to see you taken from a good school, in order that your little hands might be pushed abroad to earn a trifle—Oh! it is enough to break a woman's heart!"

"But we may get up in the world again, mother," said Tom, encouragingly, taking the playful puppy on his lap, and feeding him with bread.

"Never through your father. He did not fall through misfortune, or honest speculations in trade, but through his bad habits. And now he has fallen, despair has seized him, and he is oftener mad than otherwise. God only knows what the end of him will be—or myself either. But come, my boy, I must not detain you longer, though it is a relief to my poor heart to pour out its troubles to you. Selfish, no doubt to make you share my troubles, but I cannot help it."

"It's seven o'clock, mother, I must be off," said Tom, rising from the table.

"It is so dark with the fog, that I hardly know how you will find your way to your place. But tell me, Tom, you don't feel afraid to go among strangers?"

"No, mother—it is no more than going to a new school. I shall soon get used to everybody, and everybody will soon get used to me. Give me a couple of slices of bread and butter, and that will last me until I leave off work and get home. I shall be very glad when Saturday night comes, to bring you home some money, mother."

"Good son!" exclaimed Mrs. Brown, encircling Tom with her arms.

"I tell you what I have been thinking I should like to do with my first wages."

"What?" asked the mother.

"Why that I would buy you a nice new pair of boots that you want so badly."

"Boots, indeed! It must go for the rent of this horrid room—which we are obliged to call our home."

"But it don't matter much what my money goes in, so long as it makes us more comfortable.

But being my first earnings, I should like to buy you something with it for yourself. For I cannot forget—nor ever shall forget—that you have been a good mother to me. And I mean to be a good son to you—see if I don't, mother."

"I have no fear of that, Tom," said Mrs. Brown.

"And I tell you more, mother," said Tom, enthusiastically, "I this morning begin life as an errand boy, and I don't mean to be content until I become master."

Tom said this more to cheer up his distressed mother than from any other motive.

Mr. Brown here sat up in his bed, and loudly raved—

"Six thousand to one on the favourite!"

Then he looked wildly around as if he were in a place he did not recognise, or as if he had awoke from a dreadful dream. The alarm or fright soon vanished from his swarthy face, and he turned on his side, dug his elbow in the pillow, threw his head on his clenched hand, and fixed his discontented eye on his wife and son, just as the former was enveloping Tom's throat in an expansive woollen comforter.

Not many months ago Mr. Brown stood as high in credit and esteem as any merchant in the City of London—and now he is little better than a pauper. He began business with good capital as a wine-merchant. For some time he went on well and flourishingly. But unfortunately for him his trade lay a good deal with men of the turf, by whom he was continually being fleeced and drawn into ruinous speculations. Never a Derby passed but what Mr. Brown was at the races, and he went after the most expensive fashion. He was the liberal "crow," amongst a number of second-class sporting men, and well they plucked him. A coach and four with hampers of the most expensive wines, and other viands of the most extravagant kind, was the usual manner in which he went down the road on these occasions, and he was always good-natured enough—and some said "green" enough—to invite as many friends (sponges would have been the better term)—as the coach would hold.

Mr. Brown was a good coachman—and a bold one, too—and he was proud to be considered both. When the coach and four of the best "tits" he could hire, were at the door, and the hampers, and his hangers-on each seated with their cigars—then smack went the whip, off went the horses, and Mr. Brown, wine-merchant, made it a point and kept it too, that nothing passed him on the way to Epsom races.

Mrs. Brown, although once or twice she accompanied her husband in a quiet manner to Ascot, never knew—never dreamt—that her husband was a reckless spendthrift. Never for a moment suspected that he lived beyond the fair earnings of his business. He was not a drunkard—nor did he keep late hours—nor was he the slave of women—but he was an inveterate gambler! For gambling he had quite a thirst—a passion! The glass of wine he held to his lips must have been won or lost by gambling. From the best "two out of three" for a glass of ale to unlimited loo—and from unlimited loo to betting long odds on dog-fights, boat-races, horse-races, running, fighting, walking, and boxing, Mr. Brown's days were passed, although to the eyes of his friends, creditors, and wife, he seemed a steady attentive man of business.

Mr. Brown was weak-minded, and the dupe of any cunning rascal that got hold of him. He would freely lend money to worthless people, discount worthless bills, and made bets that none but a fool would have done.

"Tom, my boy, I want you to do a bit of stiff for me, and I will then put you up to a good thing on the Derby,"—was the customary way Mr. Brown's sporting friends had of drawing him of his money. The "bit of stiff" our readers will please to understand is the slang term amongst low tradesmen for a bill of exchange which they hawk about until they can find some one silly enough to give them cash for it. Mr. Brown was always silly enough to do that kind of thing for any one who got the weak or blind side of him, which it was not difficult to do. He had a cash-box full of dishonoured bills, and yet he never had the courage to refuse a friend.

At length Mr. Brown found himself in commercial difficulties from which he vainly endeavoured to extricate himself by borrowing—selling his wines at less than cost price—and creating fictitious bills and discounting them with his bankers.

He raved just now "six thousand to one on the favourite!" It was taken—the race came off —and the "favourite" was no where! And where was Mr. Brown! Lost! ruined! mad! In less than a month from that fatal race he was in the Gazette—his stock-in-trade and furniture in the hands of his creditors—himself and heart-broken wife doomed to the miserable room in which we first find them—and their little son driven from a good school, and compelled for a living to take service as a London errand boy.

Tom was much bewildered while his father raved, and seemed to look in his mother's face for an explanation of the meaning of "six thousand to one."

"Some other time I will tell you about that and other matters of your unfortunate father's history. You must go now."

"Go where?" exclaimed Mr. Brown.

No one replied. The mother took Tom by the hand, and as she led him from the room—

"Go where?" Mr. Brown again exclaimed.

"What interest can you have to know either about our child or myself," replied Mrs. Brown, holding Tom by one hand while she opened the room door with the other.

"That is not a proper answer for a wife to make to her husband."

"You have been no husband to me— no father to your child," bitterly replied Mrs. Brown.

"Indeed! what then have I been?"

"Our curse!"

The wretched man deeply felt his wife's charge, and with a deep groan sank back in his bed. grasped his thick beard, and turned his face to the wall.

Outside the door, on the dark landing, Mrs. Brown embraced her son, begged him to be a good boy and come home straight from his place, for she would be anxious to know how he liked it.

Down the rotten stairs groped mother and son, when the former had reached the bottom she drew back the rusty bolts of a dirty dilapidated door—then one more kiss—one more admonition to be good and hasten home—and little Tom Brown, with as cheerful a heart as the circumstances allowed, and his bread and butter dinner in his hand, made but a step or two from his mother's gaze before he seemed swallowed up by the great fog.

CHAPTER II.

THE NEW SHOP.—A COLD RECEPTION.—THE GAY CLERK.—FORTUNE-HUNTING.—A MAN OF MYSTERY.

ALTHOUGH Tom had not far to go, it was a perilous way in so dark a morning. He heard the rattle of carts and horses, and the sound of voices, but he could see little. Here and there was a coffee-house or tavern with gas burning in the windows, but there was light from little else. Even had the street lamps been lit they would have been of little service in the thick wet fog that now hung over the metropolis.

The boy was making his way from Sun Street, Finsbury, to Fleet Street, and had got into the middle of Barbican, when he was startled by a loud scream from a poor woman struggling under the legs of a horse by whom, while crossing the street, she had been knocked down. The sudden scream of death caused the traffic to pause, and comparative stillness reigned. Policemen with their bull's-eye lanterns rushed to the spot opposite a baker's shop—extricated the unfortunate and bleeding woman, borrowed a shutter from the baker's, placed the corpse—(the woman was dead)—upon it—and hurried with it to St. Bartholomew's hospital.

"One victim to the fog!" exclaimed a pale-faced workman smoking his short pipe.

"It makes me that sick," said another, "that I must turn in here and have a drop of gin."

"There won't be no grief for somebody, will there, mates?" said a carpenter, with his basket of tools slung across his back. "She seemed a poor woman by that rag of a bonnet that she had on."

"Her feelings were none the less for being poor, I suppose," said a half-starved revolutionary looking man closely buttoned to the throat, and his hands sheltered in his pockets from the cold.

"And who said they were?" inquired the carpenter.

"I did'nt say you did—did I? But some people think no more of a poor person being trod to death than a dog!" exclaimed the other, with an eye of fire, and deep emphasis.

"All bosh! don't believe it!" retorted the hardy carpenter. "There's as much feeling for the poor as for the rich."

"But there ought to be no poor!" exclaimed the man with the buttoned-up coat, drawing himself up to his full height, and extending one hand while he thrust the other in his bosom, with all the airs of an orator. "British workmen have only to move as one man, and the social and political horizon would assume a sunnier aspect."

The carpenter smiled and said—

"British workmen have only to mind their own business—turn their backs upon the public houses—give less attention to praters and idlers —to make themselves better off."

"The Eternal God intended better things for a man than to be a slave!" exclaimed the enthusiast.

"Depend upon it, you would find yourself a happier man if you worked a little harder than I suspect you do."

"You know nothing about me, sir. I am a great mental worker. I have proposed to myself to make all mankind happy—"

"You had better get up a company—the task you propose is too much for one individual," said the carpenter with a laugh. "But I will tell you something better than all,—take a hammer and chisel and saw, same as you see in my basket, and work with them, and my life upon it you will get more happiness out of them than all your schemes.

"The Eternal God—."

"Now, then, move on," said a policeman, making his way through the crowd which had gathered about the scene of the accident. The honest carpenter "moved on" without a word—so did the crowd generally; but the orator slipped away into the fog, muttering something about the "cursed myrmidons of the law."

After the poor woman's scream had rent the air, Tom Brown's progress to his new place was somewhat retarded by the crowd of the idle and curious, who rushed from all quarters to the scene of the accident.

Tom went his way forward in the best manner the fog and growing crowd would let him, for much as the scream terrified him, and for the moment transfixed him, he was determined to be in time at his place.

Had he tarried longer he would have seen, without knowing it, in that excited socialist who had just been authoritatively told to "move on" by a stern policeman, his new master's son, whose name was Bonthron, or "Mad Bonthron," as he was more generally called.

Altogether it was an inauspicious morning for Tom's entrance into business life, and although his courage sustained him under it, his heart nevertheless felt it—especially the grief of his mother and the wretched situation of his father, who, with all his faults, Tom was not ungrateful enough to forget had been very kind to him.

As he got into Smithfield, the black fog curtain was withdrawn by unseen hands, and Tom stood face to face with the bold red sun. As he cast his eye upon its mighty splendour his soul was cheered, he mended his pace, pulled himself together as it were, and mentally prepared himself for his new position.

The old cattle-pens still remaining in Smithfield, were now alive with the shoutings, demon-like whistling through the fingers and hollowing of boys and young men from the numerous adjacent workshops. Here they spent their time allotted for breakfast, dinner, and tea. Here every species of mischief and wickedness was now to be seen. It was a fiend's pantomime. While Tom cast his eyes in passing upon the pitch and toss, fighting, bonnetting, caps flying in the air, leaping from pen to pen, his ears were assailed with dreadful oaths, and no harmless passer by was safe from insult and indecent "chaff."

Tom himself, although moving briskly onwards, was marked by two young daredevils in dirty cotton jackets, with short pipes in their ill-looking mouths; over the pens they came, and attacked him like a couple of footpads. Tom had plenty of pluck as well as goodness, but he was so suddenly attacked, and his arms held, that he had no defence to make.

"How dare you!" exclaimed Tom, and he was going on further to remonstrate, when one of his low assailants pulled his cap over his eyes and mouth, and replied:—

"None o' your cheek, young un', or we'll soon put you on your back."

"Cowards!" cried Tom, struggling; but

while he struggled his paper parcel of bread and butter fell from under his arm. He was now released, and the boys who attacked him scrambled for the parcel.

Tom's face was red with rage, whilst his bread and butter spinned in the air; he was deeply hurt by the cowardice of the transaction, and his fingers itched to try his strength with his tormentors. But just now discretion was the better part of valour with Tom. Want of time alone kept him from an encounter with the gaol-birds. He was not prohibited by fear that he might get the worst of it;—Tom Brown, young as he was, was always ready to fight for truth, and right, and justice. He had an heroic nature.

But now he was on his way to win his mother's bread, and he dare not sacrifice his mother's interest for the sake of his feelings, and he reluctantly moved on, telling the young scoundrels who stood by sporting with his poor dinner—

"That he would find out where they worked, and the first opportunity report their conduct to their master."

"Go on, curly-headed crocodile!" cried one, while the other put his fingers to his nose.

For a short while Tom, as he hastened on, chafed under the assault, but as he drew nearer his place of business, his mind became occupied with things of more importance.

"I wonder how Mr. Bonthron will like me!" he mentally mused. "I wonder how I shall like Mr. Bonthron! I know that I will do my best to please, and to advance myself. I had rather have stopped at school, though. But never mind —I can read, write, and figure better than most errand boys, and I ought to push on, and mean to push on. Father has brought us down—I must bring us up! Some of our Lord Mayors, I have read, began as London errand boys."

And the Lord Mayor's carriage already seemed realised by the enthusiastic and determined boy.

Tom Brown at length reached the shop where he was to make his first essay in life. It was situated in one of the many courts that intersect Fleet Street. To a minute of his appointed time the boy stood before an unopened green-shuttered shop, over the dingy top of which might be read in bold black letters, "Bonthron and Son, Rag Merchants."

Tom leant against the shutters, and looked up the court and down the court, his eye in search of some one to open the shop. A few minutes after eight, two men emerged from a public house in the court, and one dangled two large keys in his hand, and the other lamely walked by his side. Tom thought it early that men should visit public houses so early in the morning —but Tom was "green," and knew but little of life in London.

The man who held possession of the keys had a comic cast of countenance, produced by a defect in his left eye. He was in all his Monday morning's cleanliness; the remains of the Sunday polish still reflected on his boots, and his wife's clear-starching was not quite obliterated from his Sunday shirt and collar.

But these glories—cheap as they were—Mr. Swift did not maintain through the week; therefore Mr. Swift was a very different man in appearance during the latter part of the week to what he was at the beginning. Boots and shoes will lose their splendour, and shirts and collars their starchiness. Very well, let them; it was quite trouble enough for Mr. Swift to be clean one day in the week, and he was so far a Sabbatarian to elect Sunday for the purpose. Mr. Swift considered himself quite slave enough to "Bonthron and Son," without being a slave also to boots and shoes, or shaving or shirts. Mr. Swift was a married man too, but it must be confessed, she was a poor housewife, and had but little energy, and was slothful enough to neglect her husband as much as he neglected himself. Mr. Swift liked his pipe and cribbage till late at night, and his breakfast in bed in the morning, and he had neither time nor inclination to rob these luxuries of one minute to bestow on cleanliness. And as for Mrs. Swift, she would not give up her attention to other people's affairs, and her dawdling through the day, for all the husbands in the world.

"Hullo!" exclaimed Mr Swift, in an uncouth accent, as he came up to "Bonthron and Son's" door, against which leant Tom Brown, "are you the new boy?"

"Yes, sir," replied Tom.

"Then I'm sorry for yer!" exclaimed Mr. Swift.

"Sorry!" reiterated the bewildered boy. "What for, sir?"

"Why this place will kill you in a week. God knows you look sickly enough now."

"Oh, I'm very well, thank you, sir.."

"Then take my advice, keep so. If your mother—I s'pose you got a mother!"

"Yes, sir," said Tom, "and a good mother."

"Then if she knew as much as I do, she would't like you to be here."

"But tell me why, sir?" said Tom, somewhat alarmed.

"Ask the last boy that was here—he could tell you a tale," said the mysterious Mr. Swift, commencing to take down the shutters. "You go and light the shop fire and counting-house fire—we shall want 'em, and no mistake. Such a mornin' as this will try some of the hasmatick and weak-chisted. Old Bonthron will nap it this mornin'—but that don't matter."

Tom Brown ever and anon cast his light blue eye on the rambling speaker, who, part of the time, seemed more talking to himself than to him. However, Tom had heard quite enough to make him thoughtful and miserable. He wished Mr. Swift had spoken plainer, or not at all. It had made him nervous and uncomfortable; and, somehow or other, he could not get the fire to burn. Tom felt that he was bungling, and trusted Mr. Swift would not notice it. But Mr. Swift was a man of the keenest observation, and without seeming to be so. While he dusted desks and counters, and lifted sacks of rags from one place to another, he kept his eye on Tom, and quickly discovered that he had not been used to fire-lighting.

"It strikes me, young 'un, that I shall friz afore you light them fires," said the satirical Mr. Swift. "And I certainly would not like to be you if old Bonthron comes before his fire is lit and his room prepared.

Tom's inefficiency was found out, and he smarted under it, and felt ashamed at his stupidity; but he was not disposed to throw the blame on the wood or the coals, and he frankly replied—

"That he never could light a fire; but that he was willing to do his best."

"Out of the way," said Mr. Swift, falling on his knees, and arranging sticks, coals, and cinders, and quickly kindled a cheerful fire; and as he looked at his masterpiece, he hummed "I wish I was a daisy."

"I tell you what I've been thinking, young 'un,—shall I?" interrogated Mr. Swift.

"If you please," said poor Tom.

"That you're a duffer—now you know it," said Mr. Swift.

"I don't know what you mean, sir," said Tom, reddening to the eyes.

"Don't know what I mean by a 'duffer?' That's a good 'un! Well, then, you are a cure!"

Tom felt that some insult to him was intended by Mr. Swift's polite observations, but they were still too much of a riddle for him to make formal reply to, and he still looked confused.

"Well, then, you're a fool! is that plain enough."

There was now no mistaking Mr. Swift's meaning, and Tom for the moment felt over-powered by the man's unkindness and insolence.

"And why a fool, sir?" he inquired.

"Because you can't light a fire. Why I could light a fire, bile a kettle, get a breakfast, and eat it too, afore I was five years old. But boys now-a-days are brought up to do nothing, and that they don't do well—ha! ha!"

Mr. Swift's laughter showed that he was on good terms with his last observation, which he considered a good joke. He little thought or cared about the sensitive spirit he was wounding by his coarse, unmanly speech. It was nothing to him whom he hurt or offended.

Tom felt that he could have annihilated him. He did not feel himself a "fool," and he did not care to be called one, yet he did not know how to resent it. Had it not been for his mother, he would have resumed his cap and comforter and left the place. He secretly chafed under the brutish reception he had met with from Mr. Swift.

"Now then, young 'un," said the porter, "move that 'ere sack of rags from that corner to the yonder one."

Tom looked at the sack in surprise, and then at the man, who pointed to it with extended fingers.

"I can't" said Tom. "It is too heavy, sir."

"Well, I'm blest!" exclaimed Mr. Swift, "Why my boy who left afore you came, would have done it in a jiffy, and thought nothing of it. Yet he couldn't please Mr. Bonthron. But what have you come here to do?"

"To do my best," said Tom. "I'm not a strong boy, sir—nor a fool!"

"Well I don't care what you are—but I know I'm not going to do your work, and so I shall tell the guv'nor when he comes."

"Perhaps, sir," said Tom, who was very much perplexed to know what course to take with Mr. Swift, "you will have a little more consideration for me when I tell you that this is the first place I have been at—that my father was a wine-merchant and failed—and then I was taken from school that I might earn a few shillings to help support him and my mother."

Mr. Swift ruminated for a while over what Tom revealed to him.

"Brown? Brown, wine-merchant?" he half-muttered to himself. "He was a bankrupt, was'nt he?"

"Yes, sir."

"And was'nt he sent to prison?"

"How dare you, sir?" cried Tom.

"There, you needn't jump up and never come down again, young 'un. Didn't your father live in Cross Street?"

"Well?"

"Then I say if my memory serves me right, there was something queer about your father's affairs. If he wasn't sent to prison, he ought to have been—or something of that kind. But that's no business of mine, or your's either. You can't help what your father did."

"My father was the victim of swindlers—"

"One tale is very good until the other's told," interrupted Mr. Swift.

Tom replied with indignation.

"Why are you so ferocious with me?" he said. "You have insulted me every way—and now you dare to have a hit at my father!"

"Well, I'm blest!" exclaimed Mr. Swift, startled at Tom's attitude. "Dare! That's good! An errand boy to dare me! I shan't forget that in a hurry. I and you, young 'un, shan't agree—and that don't take me long to see. There's some rhyme for you. And I'll give you some more!—young 'un, on your memory, book it—he who dares me will have to hook it. That's through reading Shikspeare—he made a poet on me. But, mind yer, I'm in earnest."

"And I'm in earnest too, sir, when I dare any one to speak of my father as a common thief!"

"P'rhaps he was an uncommon one," retorted Mr. Swift. "And p'rhaps you mean to do nothing at all this morning? P'rhaps the shop 'aint to be swept? and the counting-house dusted? —and those ere shutters taken into the cellar?"

"I am here," said Tom Brown, "to do what I can; and what I can do, I will do willingly."

"And what you can't I s'pose I must. You have pitched a nice tale to Mr. Bonthron, or I don't know why he should have engaged you."

"The only tale I pitched," retorted Tom, "was that I saw a bill in the window, Wanted an Active Lad—"

"And wasn't it a tale to call yourself an active lad?" interrupted Mr. Swift.

"Well, never mind," said Tom, "I got the place, you see, and if doing one's duty will keep it, I shall not lose it. I shall do all I can to please my master—"

"I'm your master," said Mr. Swift, drawing himself up an inch or two higher.

"I have not much hope of it," said the chivalrous boy, "but I will even try to please you."

"Move them ere shutters into the cellar," said Swift.

"I can't," said Tom.

"Move them ere sacks," said Swift.

"I can't," again replied Tom.

"Well, I'm blest!" exclaimed the porter. "You can speak plain if you can do nothing else. Now I tell you candidly what it is, young 'un," added Swift, in confidential tones—

"Well?" said Tom inquiringly.

"You are not big enough, nor strong enough, for the place."

"Perhaps not," said the boy, regretfully. "And if Mr. Bonthron thinks so, I must find another situation."

"Didn't I tell you Mr. Bonthron has not nothing to do with it? I am master of the errand boys."

"Then tell me what to do, sir."

"Sweep the shop," said Swift, "if you are not too respectable. Do you know it seems to me you ought to have been a junior clerk."

"I hope to become one," said Tom.

Mr. Swift laughed outright at the boy's ambition, and then said—

"Why, junior clerks are nothing more than shirt, show, and stoopidity! Ha! ha! Made up of mock jewellery, cravat, and turned-down collars. Better be an errand boy, any day, than a junior clerk. Sort them ere rags—the whites from the coloureds."

Tom set himself in earnest to the work that Mr. Swift directed him to do, and felt relieved at having a little steady employment.

What time will Mr. Bonthron be here?" inquired the boy.

"Too early for me," said Swift, who was engaged in polishing a large metal inkstand. "Always glad to hear when he's laid up with the gout. I feel myself a man when he's away, and a slave when he's here. Pity such an old grumbler should be so rich."

"Is he rich?" exclaimed Tom. "Why, then, does he keep on business?"

"Because he's rich and greedy. Here he comes, rain or shine, ill or well. The hand of that ere clock never goes over ten before his hand is on the brass handle of the door, and he comes in puffing and blowing, without never a ' Good morning,' Mr Swift,—hurry and skurry to his desk —do this, do that, and do 'tother thing—and expects 'em done almost afore he's told you!"

"What about his son, Mr. Swift? Is he such a disagreeable gentleman?"

"Gentleman! Ugh! He owes me not a few shillings to keep himself from starving. He's a mad socialist!"

"What's that?" inquired Tom, still attending to the task Mr. Swift had set him.

"Why, he believes that he has as much right to what I've got, as I have to what he's got. Ugh! Now, as he has got nothing and I have, I dont seem to see it!"

"I should think not," said Tom, who was now getting to feel a little more at home with Mr. Swift, his assumed master. "But isn't he a partner?"

"He was—but he isn't. His father kicked him bang out of the consarn. They were a couple of Kilkenny cats, and no mistake. I've often seen them at that ere old desk threatening each other's life—one with the ruler and the other the large inkstand. Oh! didn't the young 'un go on about the Eternal justice, and the Eternal God! the old 'un calling the young 'un all the scamps and fools under the sun. I had to call a peeler in once. Such a lark! to hear them give each other in charge. The peeler stared, and I laughed. But I and Mr. Yapp, our clerk, got the young 'un out, and I, and him, and the peeler went and had a drop of gin, and the old 'un went home to his country house and his fat deaf wife. But aint she a dresser! and aint she got a stunning daughter! Miss Bonthron is a booty, and no mistake! Quite a treat to see her in her finery come up this ere court. I say, young 'un, push on with them ere rags; they'll be wanted to send off to the paper mills to-day. Half arter nine—our Mr. Yapp will be here directly—or he ought. He's only particular about leaving off, never about coming!"

At this instant the grim office door opened, and a genteel, good-looking young man, of about twenty-two entered. He was well wrapped up in a fur great-coat, with a snow-white handkerchief peeping out from a side pocket, a handsome scarf round his throat, and his long legs encased in knickerbockers. He had a fine colour on his cheeks, a dark gipsey-looking eye, and a small dark moustache, his light hair was scrupulously brushed and parted in the middle; he carried a stout cane with a bone handle, and he had a fragment of a fragant cigar in his mouth.

But ah! those thin red lips! They seemed only made for tender vows, and saying sweet nothings to the ladies. Those eyes, again—they seemed full of falsehood, and sparkled in their sockets only to betray!

It was somewhat remarkable that a young man who was never early to bed, and never early to rise—and who liked the cup that cheered but which *did* inebriate—who every day went the "pace" and despised all the physiological rules of life—should carry the freshness and healthiness of a garden in his face.

It was remarkable, too, where he could find time for such careful attention to his person—for it was from business to pleasure, and pleasure to business, and no one but himself could properly know where he found the time for such a becoming "make up" as he was always to be seen in.

It was no mere accident—no mere going to the opera, to an evening party, or keeping an assignation with a young lady—that Mr. Yapp was to be found so becomingly attired—so exquisitely clean—so well arranged his hair—even his eyebrows bearing witness of comb and brush. Oh, no; he was *always* to be found in first-rate style —well appointed from top to toe. In dress he was faultless—he loved it, and studied it; he would rather die than live to be ill dressed.

The fear of debt never stood between him and a suit of clothes—never between him and finery. He rarely had a farthing of his own— his seventy-five pounds a year from Messrs. Bonthron and Son, paid monthly, was always anticipated. He was a debtor to every one he knew—indeed he thought it the only charm of having acquaintances that he might borrow from them. Even the decrepit old woman—a mystery she was—who rented the garret over Mr. Bonthron's rag warehouse was a creditor of Mr. Yapp's to the extent of sixpence.

The ingenuity Mr. Yapp displayed in meeting the demands of his numerous creditors was very comical. But he never let himself down in his poverty. Not he; he was too clever for that. He made his poverty the very means to exalt himself in the eyes of his creditors. True, he couldn't pay—because he had just bought a share in a yacht—or because he had just had to pay a loan for a friend he had been answerable for—or because he was just furnishing a house for a lady of large fortune that he was going to marry.

Then Mr. Yapp was so pleasant—so confidential—so affable—dressed so fashionably—looked so gentlemanly—and told his lie in such a plausible manner—that every one felt proud to be Mr. Yapp's creditor.

Friends he met were always in the most pleasant manner asked to have a glass of ale with him, and which he invariably made the occasion of borrowing, as—

"Bye the bye, before you go you haven't a shilling or two about you that you could lend me till the morning?"

The money was generally lent—but the repayment in the morning—not a bit of it.

"Never did sun that morrow see."

"Morning, Swift!" patronisingly exclaimed Mr. Yapp, pitching the end of his cigar into the court, then divesting himself of his fashionable fur coat, handsome scarf, and his well-fitting gloves. "Ha! is this our new fag?"—fixing his eyes on Tom Brown, who stood on a stool before two high sacks of rags.

"Fag!" reiterated Swift, with a satirical glance, "master more likely. He wants to be a junior clerk, Mr. Yapp. That's what the rising generation have come to."

"The devil! Bettah drown, boy," said Mr. Yapp, adjusting the horse-shoe pattern pin—loud in colour and dimensions—properly in his gold-striped black satin neck-tie. The pin arranged, his hair next met with scrupulous attention before a small glass in the corner of Bonthron and Son's rough and murky little counting-house. While Mr. Yapp conducted these operations—more interesting to his devoted self than any one else, Tom Brown cast many a sly glance on the clerk, and could not help the thought, that Bonthron & Son must pay him well or he could not keep up such a rich personal appearance.

Tom said nothing, but he certainly wished now more than before to be a clerk—not that he might dress like Mr. Yapp, but that he might be in the receipt of Mr. Yapp's salary to assist his father and mother. He was not so much dazzled by Mr. Yapp's jewellery—he was familiar with that, for it was not very long ago that his father and mother wore rings, and gold chains, and watches; but they were down, down in the world now, and were almost glad of bread. The little heart of Tom panted to raise them again, and he was determined to do everything that was honest to achieve his desire.

Mr. Yapp's toilet finished, he pulled himself together for business. He unlocked his desk, pulled forth the well-worn ledger and waste-book, and turned over the leaves to the tune of "Sweet spirit, hear my prayer!"

Then he lifted the lid of his desk again, and rested it on his head while he rummaged to the farthest dusty corner of it, and drew forth a brass-clasped vellum-bound account book, and turned to a page therein, meditated awhile and murmured to himself "That's ugly!" and shook his head.

Swift the warehouseman, here came to his side, looked in his face and significantly smiled. Mr. Yapp changed colour. There was a great deal conveyed in that roguish smile to the mind of Mr. Yapp, who hastily threw the book back to the dusty corner, and quietly closed the desk and said—"Well, Swift, what is it? spit it out, old boy."

Swift made no reply, but tortured Yapp with a still more significant smile. Could the fellow have wormed himself into Mr. Yapp's secret?

"Whew!" said Swift, pursing up his lips as if about to whistle.

"Whew!" reiterated Mr. Yapp. "Well, I am not the wiser for that. What would you say, Swift? Don't speak loud—that boy yonder has a sharp eye, and a sharp ear, I can see."

"And a sharp tongue too, I can tell yer," added Swift, regaling himself with a pinch of snuff, and Mr. Yapp took a pinch with him, for Swift was polite enough to offer one. "He is dangerous, that boy, that's my belief, and we must get him the sack."

"Now, then, Swift, what have you to say to me?"

"I s'posè I didn't see nothing yesterday, did I?" replied Swift, still keeping up the mystery. "I didn't see Mr. Yapp, not I, in a dashing trap, with a dashing young woman? Whew!"

"Oh! oh!" exclaimed Mr. Yapp, laughing. "Gad, where could my eyes have been not to have seen you?"

"When a young man has got a young woman, he has no eyes for any one but her—that's my experience. She did you credit, Mr. Yapp, there is no mistake about it."

"She was a beauty, was she not, Swift?"

"That she was. And talk about finery—she whopped everything I ever saw. My old wum-mum said to me, as you druv past, that the whole turn-out must have cost a tidy penny. Money makes the mare to go."

"Between ourselves, Swift, don't breathe a word what you saw."

"Mum!" said Swift. "It's no business o' mine, you know. But you really need not nowise be ashamed on her, for she was a booty and no 'flies.'"

"I am flattered by your opinion, Mr. Swift—still I do not wish it to be known. Many people have honoured me, as you know, by reposing in my credit—you amongst others."

"Don't mention it, Mr. Yapp; you are quite welcome to all you owe me."

"Thanks, Swift," said Mr. Yapp, grasping him by the shoulder; "your good nature will not go long unrewarded. That young lady you have just been speaking of has lots of tin, my boy, as well as beauty. And if things are only kept dark for a little while, I flattah myself that I shall be the owner of her tin and her beauty. Understand, Swift, she thinks I am more than what I am, that is to say, I have pitched my tale to her in a very high key indeed."

"Just what you are wery able to do, Mr. Yapp," said Swift with a grin.

"To begin with, she cannot fail to see that I am a gentleman."

"Impossible!" exclaimed Swift.

"Nor can she be blind to my accomplishments. I can sing, play, and dance well—as you know. Besides, I am well up in business. Few fellows could keep Bonthron and Son's books, eh?"

"Daresay not, Mr. Yapp," said the good-natured Swift.

"And I don't think I'm a bad-looking fellow, eh, Swift?" said Mr. Yapp more in earnest than jest.

"I have seen wery much worse," said Swift.

"Very well, then," said Mr. Yapp, "now comes the point. My difficulty is, how to impress her with my social position. It would not do for her to know that I was a clerk in a vile hole like this,"—looking round the small counting-house with great contempt.

"Aint it a hole!" responded Swift.

"Fortunately for me the young lady is of a romantic turn of mind."

"And you can ro-mance a little," said Swift, with a laugh.

"You think so, do you? Well I mean to get up my ro-mance as you call it, on this occasion, and no mistake. To her I am a mysterious man—and don't she love mystery. I have told her that I am the son of somebody, I don't know who, but that I have every reason to believe that I am the son of an Earl, who dares not at present acknowledge me, but who regularly supplies me with money through a solicitor."

Swift laughed outright, struck the desk with the ruler, and exclaimed—

"That's a good 'un; the best I've heerd for many a day!"

The warehouse door was thrown back, and to the surprise of Messrs. Yapp and Swift, Miss Bonthron made her appearance, most seasonably and fashionably dressed; a gold chain adorned a rich black velvet cape, and her well-gloved hands were further protected from the bitter cold by an expensive muff. Her dark grey hat and feather sat proudly over as beautiful a face as it was possible to conceive; rich chesnut curls hung down each red, round, rosy cheek, and the

SWIFT BRUTALLY SPRANG UPON TOM, AND SHOOK HIM VIOLENTLY.

everlasting smile that dallied with her arched lips was killing indeed to those who came in contact with her.

Mr. Yapp, after he had recovered his surprise, stepped forward with the best grace he could command at so short a notice, bowed, and waited the young lady's errand. Swift stood by anxiously hoping for a word from his gay and youthful mistress.

"Pa asked me to call as I was coming into the City, and say that he was too unwell to be in business to-day."

"Truly sorry to hear it, ma'am," said Mr. Yapp. "The old enemy, I suppose?"

"Yes—the gout. Is it not disagreeable weather?"

"Nothing could be worse, ma'am. Our office, I regret to say, does not afford much accommodation for the comfort of ladies, but if you would condescend to take a seat by the fiah—"

"Oh, dear no! thank you, Mr. Yapp; I am on a very painful errand, or, I can assure you, I should not be abroad in such miserable weather as this. And how do you do, Swift?"

Swift left his dusting, and proudly stepped into the foreground. Oh! how pleased he looked, and how awkwardly he showed it! he smiled like the clown in a pantomime—it came all over his face, and eventually settled into a grin. Making an elephantine bow, while he held in his hand a large duster, he replied to Miss Bonthron's kind inquiry—

"That he was as well as hard work and a small hincome would let him be."

"Ah, well," sympathisingly replied Miss Bonthron; "poor and hard-worked are misfortunes enough; but you haven't got a brother that is mad, have you, Swift?"

"Well, not exakly mum; but I'm almost mad myself sometimes."

"You should know, Miss Bonthron," said Mr. Yapp, with a pleasing smile, "that Swift's chief pleasure in life is to complain."

"I don't see it, Mr. Yapp," said Swift.

"A thorough Englishman for grumbling," observed Mr. Yapp, stirring the fire into a blaze.

"Ha, ho, hi! I dare say you know all about it," said Swift, at a loss how to reply. "Few men as I knows have seen more trouble than I have. To begin with, I married young, and she turned out a nagger."

"I dare say you gave Mrs. Swift a good deal to nag about," remarked Miss Bonthron. "One tale is all very well until the other is told."

"Precisely so, ma'am," chimed in Mr. Yapp, shaking out his perfumed handkerchief; "I can bear testimony to Mrs. Swift's worth as an industrious, attentive wife."

"That was always my opinion of her; but, of course, I have not had much opportunity of judging," said Miss Bonthron, examining her ivory card-case.

"No, mum, that's it," said Swift; "but had you known her as much as I do you'd have judged her quite a different article—another pattern altogether. Then see the heaps of crockery she smashes in her tantrums. She makes nothing in chucking a chayney-plate at a man's head!"

Tom Brown, who had been for a long time silent, but not unobservant, could not resist laughing outright at Mr. Swift's notions of trouble, and his eccentric pronunciation. The loquacious warehouseman was very indignant to find his troubles made sport of, and as he could not resent it with Mr. Yapp or Miss Bonthron, he made a cowardly assault upon Tom.

"There's a clout in the ear for you, young 'un!" he exclaimed, suiting the action to the word. "Herrand boys have no business to laugh, anyhow."

The blow roused Tom's monkey; he turned red and white, and while his ear tingled with pain and his soul with humiliation, regardless of the presence of his young mistress, he caught up a rusty two-pound weight and retaliated on the brutal Mr. Swift. The weight was thrown with too much passion to do serious mischief; Tom meant it for the miscreant's head, but, fortunately for Mr. Swift, the missile had more respect for his head than his foot, on which it descended with more force than pleasure.

After many exclamations of pain, and writhings of agony, Swift looked with passion and contempt on poor Tom; then he limped round by the sacks where the boy was engaged, seized him with both hands by the collar, and cried between his teeth—

"You 'orrid little willain!"

"Hands off, Swift, that's a good fellah," interposed Mr. Yapp. "Remembah the boy is no match for you."

"He should not have been imperent, then. I wouldn't stand to be laughed at by a man, much less a herrand boy."

"Believe me, Swift, you struck first," said Mr. Yapp.

"Indeed you did," said Miss Bonthron, "and I thought it was very ill-natured of you to strike a poor little fellow like that. Here is sixpence for you, boy, and think no more about it."

"I can assure you, ma'am," said Tom, "that the blow is the smallest thing that I have borne from that man this morning. He seems to have taken a great dislike to me—for why, I cannot tell."

Swift writhed with the pain in his foot; but that was comparatively small to the hatred he felt when he found that the boy enlisted Miss Bonthron's sympathy. His jealousy aroused, he exclaimed—

"You artful willain! Oh! you *werry* artful willain! I'll sarve you out, or my name is not Swift!"

Then he turned to Mr. Yapp, and said—

"I'm downright surprised that a gentleman like you, Mr. Yapp, should see an old servant like me run down by a herrand boy!"

"Come here to me, my little man," said Miss Bonthron; "tell me now what is it you have been doing to put Mr. Swift so much out of temper?"

"I cannot tell, ma'am," said Tom, with emotion. "I am but a stranger to him. I have not been in the place more than two hours."

Swift looked unutterable things. He never thought before that he should live to be braved by a London Errand Boy who couldn't light a fire, and the boy to be supported by his mistress.

"Is he a new boy, Mr. Yapp?" inquired Miss Bonthron.

"Perfectly so, ma'am. Permit me to say that I exceedingly regret the occurrence of such a scene before you, Miss Bonthron, especially as you favour us so rarely with your society. But we have so little to interest the ladies here, that we feel grateful for their angel visits—few and far between though they be."

"Thank you, Mr. Yapp. But now I am come let it be my pleasure to play the peacemaker. Go, boy, to Mr. Swift, and ask him to be friends with you."

Tom was about to carry out his instructions, when Mr. Swift exclaimed—

"Stand hoff!"

"Come, I say, Swift, old fellah, remembah what's due to Miss Bonthron," said Mr. Yapp. "It is her wish that you be friends with the boy."

"Friends with a herrand boy! I feel ashamed on yer, Mr. Yapp! How can you expect order in this 'ere office if sooperiors are to be friends with hinferiors? That won't do for Mr. Swift. I know my dooty to you; you know your dooty to the gov'ner; and I'll take good care that that 'ere boy knows his dooty to me! He has been imperent to me, and I struck him; and, as William says, in Black-eyed Susan, 'had he been first lord of the hadmiralty, I'd have done the same!'"

"'Pon honour, Swift, I feel a little ashamed of you," said Mr. Yapp. "Miss Bonthron will conclude that we are a lot of savages."

Swift sulkily turned away, and buried himself among the sacks of rags.

"Dear me, Mr. Yapp," said Miss Bonthron, "I had almost forgotten to tell you Pa desires that you will write a peremptory letter to Mr. Hart for the settlement of his account."

"Hart!" reiterated Mr. Yapp, turning very pale. "Did you say Hart, ma'am?"

"Oh, yes; I'm sure Pa said Hart. Why do you doubt?"

"Only that Mr. Hart has been so long a good customer to us, and one who has always paid so well. Pardon me, but I think it ill-advised on the part of Mr. Bonthron to write to him about his account."

"Perhaps you had better defer it, Mr. Yapp, until Pa returns to business. I have many calls to make now I am in the City, and must bid you good morning."

"Can I be of any service to you, Miss Bonthron; I should be most happy if I could?"

"You are very kind; none in the least, thank you. By-the-bye, a friend of ours was telling Pa that he saw you yesterday driving out a very handsome young lady."

"Indeed!" said Mr. Yapp, more in confusion than pleasure.

"Yes, indeed," Miss Bonthron reiterated, with a smile. "Pa seemed deeply interested, I thought, by the questions he put to our friend."

"What questions, Miss Bonthron?" inquired Mr. Yapp, in evident alarm.

"Well, he asked about the colour of the horse, the style of the chaise, and even—I'm almost ashamed to say—how the young lady was dressed."

"The devil! He suspects me!" mentally ejaculated Mr. Yapp. "I'll fly! I'll hang! I'll drown!"

Then to Miss Bonthron he stammered—

"He *was* particular, was he not, Miss Bonthron?"

"I could not help thinking so. But it was very wrong my telling you."

"Might I ask who it was that saw me?" gently asked Mr. Yapp.

"Mr. Whitehead. I don't think you know him—quite a private friend of Pa's; he is a young gentleman, and he spoke so enraptured of the lady that I ventured to tell him he was envious of you."

Mr. Yapp affected a smile, and said—

"When the mattah comes to be explained it is all very simple enough, Miss Bonthron: my landlady has a friend who has a friend who is a livery-stable keepah, and the father of the young lady I was driving; he was kind enough to lend me the trap for the day, and his daughter was kind enough to accompany me for a little ride in the country."

"Oh, I am sure it is all simple enough, and I have no doubt will have a simple ending," said Miss Bonthron, with a smile.

"How, Miss Bonthron? In what way a simple ending? I fail to understand."

"Time will show. Good morning."

Miss Bonthron drew her ample skirt around her and withdrew, leaving the well-dressed Mr. Yapp in the greatest perplexity and anxiety.

"Demn it!" he exclaimed to himself; "I did my best not to be seen by a soul in the world, and, by jove, all the world has seen me. I must have managed demned bad, or have been demned unlucky. It don't mattah which; I have been seen, and that's enough to feed the suspicion of suspicious people, who have a habit of putting that and that togethah and coming to conclusions, not always pleasant and advantageous to a

fellah's charactah. I feel a little terrah; still I think my ingenuity will carry me through it."

"By your leave, Mr. Yapp," said Swift, "I'm that excited that I'll go and get a two of gin."

"As you like, Swift," said the obliging clerk, deeply thinking of something else.

"Would you like to jine me?"

"Rathah too early—don't you think so?"

"Never too early for me. As our old buffer's away I don't mean to be over busy; it's all too cold for me, too. A drop o' dog's nose wouldn't do me nor you any harm. If you like to jine me I'll stand it. I want your advice about a little affair."

"All right, Swift; on you go, and I'll follow. The boy can keep watch, Swift."

"Oh, yes; there's no one will be here; and if there are, boy, you'll find us over at the Lion, at the corner of the court. But I don't hexpect no one."

Tom nodded assent, and small as the office was that he had to perform, he began to feel proud that he had so onerous a task as to keep watch over his master's possessions in the absence of the other servants.

"Why it rains, and snows, and hails!" exclaimed Mr. Yapp, pausing in the doorway, and hesitating in what manner he should get to the Lion.

"It don't matter to me if it thunders and lightens, it wouldn't prevent my getting a drop of dog's nose. Do as I do, Mr. Yapp, throw an old sack over your shoulders"—here Swift suited the action to the word, and so snugly enveloped himself in the sack that you could see very little of him more than his eyes and nose.

That style of thing would not suit the exquisite Mr. Yapp, and he did not care for the trouble of putting on his handsome fur coat; so he sheltered himself under an umbrella, and picking his dainty way through the wet and slush of the dark court, he was in a minute making himself agreeable at the little bar of the Lion, and drinking, at Mr. Swift's recommendation and expense, some dog's nose, and making a few brilliant remarks (at least Swift thought so) on the curl-papers of a sleepy-eyed, fat-faced barmaid, the landlord's daughter.

"How much I wish I had the good fortune to be one of those bits of papah to be attached to those luxuriant tresses. There I could be happy for evah, Swift."

"I've known you before to day, Mr. Yapp," said the girl, grating the ginger into the smoking gin and beer.

"I hope you don't regret it, Miss Bowers," said Yapp.

"Impossible!" exclaimed Miss Bowers. "You are the most agreeable gentleman I know."

As she laughed and coquetted about the little bar, the ample skirt of her morning gown swept two glasses to the floor, while neither of them broke.

"By jupitah!" exclaimed Yapp. "That's the most remarkable thing I evah saw. There's a token in that, Miss Bowers."

"I hope a good one. What is it a token of?"

The ready-witted clerk soon replied—

"That every event in your life will happen in pairs; you will be married in pairs; have children in pairs; have fortunes in pairs; die in pairs——"

"And buy my gloves, stockings, and shoes in pairs?" interrupted Miss Bowers.

"A werry good wind up," said Swift. "And here's your werry good health, Miss Bowers."

"Bowers! ah! what a sweet name," said

Yapp. "I never think of it but love and roses fill my memory."

"And I never think of it but the taste of gin comes into my mouth; and I'm off to the Lion," said Swift.

"You are a good fellah; but no poet."

"I don't know so much about that. I have made up a good deal of rhyme in my time."

"Bosh! there may be poetry without rhyme, and rhyme without poetry. Listen to what Otway says of women:—

"'There's in them all that we believe of heaven,
Amazing brightness, purity and truth,
Eternal joy and everlasting love!'"

"Hotway wouldn't have written that had he known my old 'oman," said Swift. "A chayney plate at his head wouldn't have put him much in mind of heaven."

"What do you think of this, Swift? An impromptu."

"What's that? I never heard of him afore."

"An impromptu is a thing said or done on the instant—a piece made off hand—an extemporaneous——"

"There, there, you are fogging me again. Trumperysaveus! these long words were made for stronger jaws than mine."

"And wiser heads, eh, Swift?"

"That I shan't allow. But the poetry, Mr. Yapp, out with it."

Mr. Yapp poured out two more glasses of the steaming frothy dog's nose, drank, then stretched forth his hand, and half said, half sung the following doggrel—

"Och! Miss Bowahs,
By the powahs
Ye have a bright and sparkling eye;
I'll bet a crown,
And put it down,
Ye'll be married by and bye!

"There, Swift, that's what we in the classics call an impromptu."

"I call it impudence," said Miss Bowers, coquettishly. "It'll be a long by-and-bye before I get married; indeed, no one would have me."

"Oh! but what about the bright and sparkling eye, Miss Bowers?" said Yapp.

"That it is the grossest flattery I ever heard," said the good tempered barmaid; "and had your young lady——"

"What young lady?" inquired Mr. Yapp.

"How simple we are this cold morning to be sure. I know I should like some one to drive me out in such style. Mr. Giles said it was well to be Mr. Yapp to be able to do it so splendidly."

"Oh, deah, what exaggeration!" exclaimed Yapp. "Why had I been living in a country village it could not have been more talked about. A young fellah driving out a young lady in a humdrum horse and trap lent by a relative! What a crime, to be sure."

The gay clerk had to tell so many lies that his memory was continually at fault.

While this little bantering was going on between Miss Bowers and Mr. Yapp, Swift was silent, and appeared in a brown study, which was soon explained. He did not mean to be outdone by Mr. Yapp in poetry—or by anyone else. He had been thinking over an impromptu, and waiting his opportunity to deliver himself of it.

There was a pause. Swift took the short pipe from his mouth, and without one word of introduction, abruptly broke out with—

"Let 'em talk of the rose,
But I like my dog's nose,
Well ginger'd, and season'd, and hot;
It is very good lap,
So come Mr. Yapp,
Let us toss for another full pot."

"Devilish funny, Swift!" exclaimed Yapp, patting him on the shoulder. "And did you really spin that out of your own head?"

"Quite as good as yours, Mr. Yapp," said Miss Bowers.

"You are ungrateful," said Yapp, smoothing his moustache, and fancying that he had a beard. "Swift said nothing about 'bright and sparkling eyes.' His muse rose no higher than a pot of dog's nose,—ha! ha!—while mine aspired to the regions of beauty!"

"And a beautiful mess you made of it," said the tantalising barmaid.

"It certainly was not up to my theme, Miss Bowers. But come, I'll accept your challenge, Swift, and give a fling for a pot—no, no, a pint, we dare not have more or the business of Bonthron and Son will go to blue blazes for this day!"

"As the school boy said, 'Hurrah! another holiday, master's ill!' Here goes for a pint!" said Swift, spinning a penny on the counter and covering it with his hand, distinguished only for dirty nails; while Mr. Yapp flung his coin (a rare thing for him to have one) to the ceiling, caught it in his hand, and cried "Head!"

It proved a "tail," and Swift laughed, and showed his large, yellow teeth in a broad grin.

"It's a good job for you that it warn't a pot, Mr. Yapp," said Swift, twirling his coin once more on the pewter counter."

"Don't know that—haven't lost yet," replied Yapp, again spinning his coin to the smoke-dyed ceiling. Swift was at fault this time, and Yapp exulted.

"The last fling does it," said Swift, "and I'll have a woman."

"Lucky dog, Swift; woman it is," said Yapp. "And now, Miss Bowers," catching the young lady by her stout wrist, as she was wiping down the counter, "I must ask you to concoct for us one more pint of dog's nose, and put it down to my already extensive score."

"Father says you must be a favourite of mine for allowing the score to be so extensive."

"I hope your father's solution is a correct one."

This sentiment he whispered in a not unwilling ear.

At this inopportune moment the burly landlord Mr. Bowers—or Joe Bowers as he was more frequently called amongst his customers—entered the bar; he had but a poor crop of reddish hair on his enormous head, and his cheeks hung down over a red-spotted neckerchief.

"Hullo! I say there! what are you arter? Love-making so early in the morning! Now, Bess, gal, get those glasses washed up, and see how the draught of fourpenny ale stands. Morning, Swift."

"Morning, Joe," said Swift, offering the landlord his pint to drink from.

"Nothing can be nicer than dog's nose this cold weather," said Joe, drinking.

"One pint to be scored to Mr. Yapp," said Miss Bowers, who, in a very business like manner, set to work amongst the jingling glasses according to her father Joe's directions.

Miss Bowers, after the manner of many young ladies at public-house bars, might coquette with the young men customers (she was tutored to do so), but let it be said that she was never disobedient to her father; and for the father it must also be said he was always kind and affectionate to her.

"I shall be very glad when your quarter comes round, Mr. Yapp," said Joe Bowers, taking down an enormous slate of scores, "for there's hardly room to put down any more."

"All right, Joe," said Mr. Yapp, "with the quartah all will be squared."

"I'd sooner have a clean slate than the name of a bad customer on it," said Joe Bowers, tying his apron round his beer-barrel waist.

"The ready-money customer is the best, and that's me," said Swift, swinging his head to and fro, and thrusting his hands in his pockets, and showing other airs more independent than graceful.

Mr. Yapp here gave a scream of affright. The cellar-man, in a long leather apron, with a flaming candle fastened to the end of a stick in one hand, and a rusty iron cage, in which was imprisoned a fat, brown rat, in the other. The long, thick tail of the alarmed creature hung out through the bars, while his eyes sparkled defiance over his long white whiskers. The obtuse Mr. Swift pulled the animal by his tail, while he stood by admiring his size and beauty.

Mr. Yapp had a great antipathy to rats, and declared that he would rather be attacked by a lion.

"Why you must be a baby, Mr. Yapp, excuse me," said Swift. "I could fondle the hannimal in my bosom," here he sprinkled the rat's head with a few crumbs of biscuit.

Joe Bowers, with his arms folded on the counter, looked with much pleasure on the cellar-man's trophy, while Mr. Yapp's alarm gave great fun to his daughter by his side.

"So we've caught the——"

"Hush! father, no swearing," said Miss Bowers. "Poor mother never could bear that."

"All right, gal," said the softened landlord; "and I promised her I would leave it off; but I feel so rejoiced at the capture of that thief," bending his stout fist at the crouching thing in the cage, "that I could hardly help swearing, and that's the truth."

"But there are other and better ways of showing joy than swearing, father."

"Don't preach, Bessie. People in the public line shouldn't preach. What are you going to do with him, Jem?"

"Let me try my dog with him," said Swift. "I was going to take him round the corner to Mr. James's little bitch terrier. He'll stand a tanner for him, I know."

"I'll tell you what, Jem," said the landlord. "Get the dogs here, and let 'em have a turn with the rat in the cellar. He has given us so much trouble that I should like to see the death of him. That's the little bitch that would have tackled him, and no mistake," pointing to a wiry stuffed terrier in a glass-case, fastened underneath the bar clock.

"You are right," said Swift. "I like sport;" taking the candle from Jem's hand and burning the tip of the rat's tail until the poor thing loudly squeaked with pain, at which Swift heartily chuckled.

"I shall retiah," said Mr. Yapp, putting up his hand to his averted head, "if there is not a little more respect paid to one's antipathies."

"La! rats are harmless enough," said the barmaid.

"No doubt, to those who think so, Miss Bowers; but I am one whose nerves are strong for every fate, but the presence of a rat. I loathe the creatures! Would to heaven that all of them in the universe were collected together in one heap and crushed out of existence!"

"I say the same of black beetles," observed the barmaid. "I can't abear them."

"There it is, you see. Now I don't care one fig about them," said Mr. Yapp. "They may crawl all over me——"

Miss Bowers shrugged her shoulders in disgust, and interrupted the clerk with——

"Oh, the nasty things! I can't abear them!"

"As to that we have all our likes and dislikes," said the philosophic landlord, drawing a pot of beer for a customer, "except money—no one dislikes that."

"But some like it too well," said Miss Bowers. "Misers hoard and worship it; while others will lose a good name by stealing it."

"What's the guv'nor not in business to-day?" said Joe Bowers.

"No, thank God," said Swift. "He's got the gout, and the holiday fever has broke out all over us."

Swift took the cellar-man and the rat on one side, and after a slight conference, and the passing of twopence from the hands of the former to the latter, Jem returned to the dark regions below with his terrible guest.

When the rat had disappeared from view Mr. Yapp became himself again——

"'I feel much relieved,' as the debtah said, when his creditah declared he would call no more."

"The fog gets thicker, don't you think so, father?" said Miss Bowers.

"Yes; it is a case of gas all day to-day, take my word for that," said the landlord.

Swift whispered to Mr. Yapp, and the words—— "No; it is a secret," were plainly heard by Miss Bowers and her father. Then Swift took up the pint, and he and Yapp adjourned to the snug little parlour.

Just, however, as Yapp was following on the heels of Swift, Mr. Bowers beckoned him back, and said on one side to him——

"Friday has passed."

"What about Friday?" said Yapp, failing to see the landlord's meaning.

"The crown I lent you."

"Oh, yes, I remembah. How demned stupid of me to forget that to be sure! It ran in my head that there was something! If there is one thing I am more particular about than anothah it is prompt payment of borrowed money. I beg pardon, Joe. Demn it! I had the tin on Friday, and now I haven't. Well, there's one blessing, Joe, I can lay my hand upon my heart" (suiting the action to the word) "and say that you are my only creditah."

"Then you don't owe much," said Mr. Bowers.

"Not much, is it, Joe?" said Yapp, confidentially. "In truth it would be a great convenience to me if you would allow me to owe you a little more. Look here, Joe, I am making up to a young lady with considerable property, and it is rather an expensive time with me, for I must keep up appearances, or it would spoil everything. Lend me five shillings upon my I O U until quartah day—eh?"

Joe Bowers did not seem to like it; but after a little hesitation, complied, and Mr. Yapp, a richer, therefore, a happier man, tripped after Swift to the parlour, to hear his secret communication.

———

CHAPTER III.

A MYSTERIOUS WOMAN.—A MOTHER'S GRIEF.—
A MOONLIGHT MEETING IN ST. PAULS.—

AFTER the two bad servants—Messrs. Yapp and Swift—had left the warehouse in charge of Tom Brown, he did not relax in his duties, but went on sorting the rags as indefatigably as if the eye of the master had been over him. The day was yet young, but it had seemed a week to him. He longed for the night that he might again meet his heart-broken mother; not that he had any good news to bring her, only he knew that she would be deeply anxious to hear how he had got through his first day at his new place.

The postman, well wrapped up against the cold and dismal weather, came in with a letter for "Bonthron & Son, Rag Merchants."

"Tuppence to pay," said the postman, throwing down a somewhat heavy letter. "Over weight, and under paid."

"No one in," said Tom.

"And haven't you got tuppence?"

"I haven't," said Tom.

"Where is Mr. Yapp?"

"Close by. I'll fetch him if you like," said Tom.

"Can't wait," said the man of letters. "Mind, tuppence to pay. Oughtn't to leave it. What's your name?"

"Thomas Brown."

"The other boy gone?"

"Yes."

"What for?" said the postman

"That's more than I know."

"Where's Swift?"

"With Mr. Yapp," replied Tom.

"That's not business. Can't wait. Mind, tuppence to pay."

"I'll mind," said Tom, placing the letter on Mr. Yapp's desk, first observing the post-mark upon it; then he stirred the fire, put on more coals, and resumed his work at the sacks.

Not long, however, was he left in his loneliness.

The shop door was thrown back, and a woman, with a remnant of beauty in her face, entered.

She was Bonthron & Son's attic tenant, and a mystery to all who knew her. She was tall, thin, and not scrupulously clean; her grizzled hair was bound up behind, and fastened with a comb, that stood conspicuously high above her head. There was considerable wildness in her eye and manner, but withal a commanding dignity.

The first impression Tom had of her was that she was a mad woman. Her face seemed lined and elongated with pent-up grief and trouble.

She visited no one, no one visited her. She rarely went out but in the dark of the evening, and then only for the bare necessaries of subsistence. All her actions betokened that she was under hiding—that she was double dealing with the world, and playing the part of a poor recluse, not from necessity but from some secret cause.

Every Monday morning, as true as the clock struck twelve, she thus made her appearance with her half-a-crown for the rent. This it was observed she never missed.

She was not more than forty-five, but had it not been for her burning black eye, the beholder might have been excused for saying she was sixty. Time had not aged her—nor whitened her hair—nor wrinkled her broad brow—nor furrowed her cheeks—nor lengthened her features; it was the fury of her mind that did all this.

She walked about and abroad like a tempest. The poor family who dwelt below the attic were often disturbed at night by her stately striding to and fro her garret for hours together. The other tenants of the house made many kindly advances to her, but they were indignantly repelled.

None knew her right name, but she was spoken of, by the other tenants, as LADY BLAZE, a name no doubt suggested by the fierceness of her character, and her undoubted respectability.

She had on a much-faded, brown silk dress, with a broad, black stripe; around her waist was a long, black tape, attached to which were two keys, one for the attic-door, which she always locked after her if she only left for a minute, the other belonging to a great hair trunk, which she rarely opened, and which served her as a footstool when she sat over her garret fire.

Tom was awe-struck at her appearance, and for the minute could not speak. She looked up the shop and down the shop, and as she was about to walk into the counting-house, the boy ventured to ask—

"What she wanted?"

"Not you," was her brief reply. "Where is your master?" familiarly walking into the counting-house, and glancing at the letter the postman left with "tuppence" to pay.

"Which master do you mean, ma'am?"

"Have you so many, boy?" she asked, in a hollow, tragic voice.

"I have three:—Mr. Bonthron, Mr. Yapp, and Mr. Swift," said Tom.

"And which of the three do you like the best? There, don't hesitate—you need not say if you would rather not."

"I like Mr. Yapp best," at length said the boy.

"Dear me! do you indeed?" exclaimed Lady Blaze, in the most unintelligible manner.

"But I have not yet seen Mr. Bonthron," said Tom, hardly knowing the woman's drift.

"And when you do see him, you see nothing but a vulgar, well-to-do tradesman," said the woman, with ineffable contempt, while grasping the jingling keys by her side. "But Mr. Yapp, what is he?"

"A clerk," readily replied Tom.

"A clerk! He is a gentleman!" exclaimed Lady Blaze, most emphatically.

"Oh, yes, ma'am, quite a gentleman," rejoined Tom, and so unwilling was he to disagree with this singular woman that had she said Mr. Yapp was a lady he would not have disputed it, but suffered her to enjoy her own opinions. He believed her to be a dangerous woman, and he would much rather have had her room than her company.

One thing the boy discovered, that she took a great interest in the fop of a clerk; others had discovered this also, without being able to divine the reason why.

Mr. Yapp himself seemed conscious that she was always on his track, but he took little notice of the circumstance; treated it as accidental and free from design. For years he had known her, and wherever he went she would contrive to take lodgings in the same house or very near. At his last place there was Lady Blaze, and she came when he came; and when he left for Bonthron & Son's, Lady Blaze took the garret there.

Mr. Yapp was not sorry for this, for he rather liked her acquaintance, as she was always good to loan a little silver from when he was short (which was of daily occurrence), or his other friends failed him.

One summer moonlight night, on his homeward way, he met Lady Blaze walking sad and melancholy within the shadow of St. Paul's, and he accosted her by saying—

"How strange it is that I and you—excuse me, but I don't know your name?"

"You will *one* day, and until that day arrives it is better that you should not, Mr. William Yapp."

"You seem to have *mine* pat enough, though," said the young clerk, twisting his silver-headed cane round and round his finger.

The woman frowned, then cast her eyes for a moment to the moon. Mr. Yapp decided that she was a lunatic. How could he come to any other decision?

"You said something about strange. *What* is strange?" she demanded.

"Oh, I was only going to observe——" he checked himself, she looked at him so piercingly that he hesitated to proceed.

"*What* is strange?" she again demanded, while her light, black shawl fluttered in the breeze that played about the corners of the great cathedral, troubled the trees, and made music in corners and crevices. "What is strange?"

"That I and you should live at Bonthron & Son's, and at my last situation."

"I suppose I may live where I please!" she offendedly rejoined; and then in tones of the deepest pathos she added—"Live! can such a life as mine be called living? A living-death—death!"

Mr. Yapp, as we have before remarked, decided that the woman was mad, and, therefore, while he took little or no heed of her incoherent speech, he felt as much as his surface nature was capable of feeling for her mental condition. He would like to have said something consoling to her, but he knew not what. Consolatory language suited not the genius of his speech. Had Mr. Yapp been asked to descant upon the opera, races, good dinners, fashion, gambling, cigars, or the law of I O U's, he would not have been found wanting.

He was so unacquainted with grief that he had not the art of approaching it. Had he believed the woman's sorrow to be a reality, and *not* an emanation from a diseased brain, he could command no language of pity—he had no balm for grief or wounded souls. He tried his best, and his best was to exclaim, taking his cigar from his mouth—

"What's the mattah with you, old gal?"

She looked upon him darker than the darkest night. If looks could kill, the dashing young clerk must have been a victim to them, and fallen a corpse at the feet of Lady Blaze.

The anger that mantled her face, and lit up her eye, soon consumed itself, and the softening influence of a tear stole down her cheek. Mr. Yapp, while he stood looking on, beating his cane against his well-fitting trousers, was fairly puzzled at the woman's mysterious conduct, and very much repented speaking to her. He was glad when she moved away, holding the back of her black straw bonnet, which was threatened by the gusts of wind that blew sharply round the corners and through the gateways of the great cathedral.

Mr. Yapp looked after her and said—

"Good night."

She spoke not a word, but slowly went her way, keeping close to the wall of the church and avoiding the pavement. As she faced Ludgate-hill, the cathedral bell struck ten. She paused by the black statue of Queen Anne, on which the moon poured down a flood of light, and listened with intense admiration to the tones of the clock.

"A grand sound!" she muttered to herself—"A solemn sound!" She waited for the last echo, then, like a spirit, fled.

The whole scene quickly passed out of Mr. Yapp's mind. He treated it as an interview with a mad woman, and so he spoke of it to Swift and others in the morning, and while he related it, laughed heartily, and cleverly mimicked Lady Blaze.

It was not long before she reached her gloomy residence in the gloomy court where Bonthron & Son carried on their rag business. Quickly she ascended the broad old staircase, with their large knobbed balastres of the Dr. Johnson period.

As she passed the doors on the many floors of the tall house, the inmates made strange remarks to each other.

"There goes Lady Blaze, as if the devil was at her heels," said a tenant to his wife, as he sat smoking his pipe over an empty but rusty grate.

"Never knew her so long out before since she's been here," observed the wife.

"Something up," said the man, filling another pipe. "She's a mystery, and no mistake. A good-looking woman, too."

"But disagreeably proud. Passes by one like dirt," said the wife, contemptuously, working assiduously at her husband's stocking. "Come, old man, you'll drink all that beer; and I'm sure I'm not going out for more this time of night."

"Don't trouble," said the husband; "if we want more I'll fetch it. This ain't half out yet."

"But it soon will be while you keep on swig swig at it," said the ill-tempered wife, readjusting the brass spectacles on her dumpy nose.

"Why don't you swig yourself? Dear me, the pot's as near you as me!" said the husband, getting a bit angry.

"I like *my* beer with *my* supper, and I don't mean to have *my* supper until I've finished *my* stocking!"

Both were startled from their quiet snarling by a scream that echoed up and down the old staircase. They came from their room, and heard a heavy fall, with words that pierced all hearers—

"My baby's dead!—my baby's dead!"

Husband and wife went quickly up the stairs to the floor above, where, on the landing, lay an outstretched woman. Oh! so white!—so faint!

Lady Blaze was there as quickly as they. She had scarcely unlocked her garret door, and relieved herself of her bonnet, when that scream—that fall—had also met her ear. Soon the landing was crowded with aroused tenants—some had hastily risen from their beds, while others had been preparing for them.

Old Mrs. Benbow, in her flippitty-floppitty night-cap, flannel-petticoat, and short bedgown; and Grandfather Grimes (as he was called by the children of the house, out of sugar-stick fondness, and who looked every inch a grandfather) just with his trousers on, and his braces hanging down behind, stood differing on the best method of restoring the afflicted woman, and while she lay moaning they stood by disputing which was best—water, vinegar, or brandy—to "bring her round."

"Stand back ye prating do-nothings!" exclaimed Lady Blaze, "and give the creature air. Get a pillow, some of you, while I raise her head. How cold she is! Here," giving a useless bystander a shilling, "get some brandy *immediately!* and you see that a kettle of boiling water is ready." The latter direction was given to the husband who lived below, and he was very glad to have a job that should take him from a scene which pained his feelings, and where he felt himself to be in the way.

He went below, and in the most fussy manner kicked the cat out of the way, kindled a fire, put on a large iron kettle, and blew with the bellows in a most furious manner; but never mind his manner—what he did he did with a cheerful heart, and did his best, which cannot be said of many persons.

Almost before the brandy came the good man (he was only a working tailor,) had got boiling water, and he met the messenger with the shilling's-worth of brandy, which required a microscope to discover which part of the large bottle it was concealed in.

"Where's the brandy?" he inquired.

"Here! don't you see it?" said the young-man messenger, who had slipped on a ragged great coat, instead of his ordinary one, holding up a quart wine bottle.

"I see the bottle, certainly," said the tailor, "but I must get my old woman's glasses to see the brandy. And do you really call that a shilling's worth?"

"I don't—but the landlord does. But this is no time to discuss the price of brandy, let it be mixed with the water and given to Lady Blaze for poor Mrs. Mullins. She feels the loss of her baby more than I should. I'm not sorry it's gone, it suffered a good bit; and waked me up o' nights with it's crying."

"Pain—it was all the cries of pain, poor little soul," said the tender-hearted tailor, mixing the brandy, and grating some ginger into it. "I'm not sorry its's gone either, for it never could have recovered. There, what do you think of that?" handing the young man in the great coat the mixture to taste, after the tailor himself had sipped it.

"Devilish good. Let us take it upstairs, or we shall taste it all away."

When the men reached the landing with the strong-smelling brandy, they found Lady Blaze kindly bathing the poor mother's face and temples with cold water and a flannel, while old Grandfather Grimes knelt and half supported her in his arms as she lay on the floor.

The distressed mother scarcely moaned, but still gave signs of restoration. "Dear babe!—Dear child!" she ever and anon feebly muttered through her clenched teeth and lips.

When the brandy was brought it became difficult to administer it, her white lips were so compressed. Lady Blaze moistened those lips with a feather and brandy.

"What is her name?" inquired the mysterious tenant of the garret, who knew nothing of any one present.

"Mullins, mum," replied Mrs. Benbow, surprised, as were the other bystanders, at the kind and business-like manner of Lady Blaze; indeed this was the first time she had given evidence of her humanity, or of her having a heart at all. But now she commanded the respect of every one, and her great superiority shone conspicuously.

"Take a little brandy, Mrs. Mullins," she said, placing the glass against her pallid lips.

The tender invitation failed, but not so the ingenuity and determination of Lady Blaze, who had a teaspoon brought her, and while the young man who fetched the brandy held the glass, she gently forced a spoonful of the restorative down the woman's throat.

She gave a deep-drawn sigh, opened her eyes, and muttered—

"Bring me my babe!"

"Baby's in a better world, Mrs. Mullins," said Mrs. Benbow, abruptly; and the mother suddenly broke out into a passionate fit of sobs and tears.

Lady Blaze here administered a further spoonful of brandy-and-water, and then another. This seemed to do its work, and bring back animation, for Grandfather Grimes felt less of a weight in his shirt-sleeved arms.

"Do take a little brandy, Mrs. Mullins," said Lady Blaze, with more success; for the woman was sufficiently restored to drink from the glass. "Where is her husband?"

"Oh, my poor husband!" moaned Mrs. Mullins. "My dear babe!"

"Mr. Mullins is a sailor, Mum; and he is on the seas," said Mrs. Benbow. "This was her first baby."

"And it is dead! Oh! my darling is dead!" interrupted the mother, weakly bringing her hand to her clammy brow. "Oh, take me to my babe!"

The young man and "Grandfather" helped her to her feeble feet, and slowly led her to the room "where lay the lovely child."

Spare us a moment—we are in a room with death? Who dares call him grim after beholding that baby Mullins! Oh, mother, you should not weep—you should not faint—for you never saw your darling with such a countenance before. Smiling—ah! that smile made mockery of the ghastly little bones that pierced the skin; it irradiated the whole room, and fascinated all eyes.

The candle had burned out while the mother lost herself in her great grief, and the room had no other light than the beams of the moon that bathed the resting, smiling, peaceful face of the sailor's baby.

The sight of the little corpse, as it lay on its back in the middle of a lowly bed, hushed every tongue, and melted every heart. A tear glistened in "Grandfather's" eye; and while the hapless mother moaned and hugged her breast, moving her body to and fro, the others stood round the bed spell-bound by that infant's smile. Heaven had never before been made so plain to them.

Happy baby! the more thy mourners wept the more thou seemed to smile!

Restless Lady Blaze moved to and fro the room, but still kept her burning eye on the dead baby.

"How long had your child been ill, Mrs. Mullins?" she inquired.

"A month this very day, ma'am," said the still weeping mother. "Not an hour ago I thought it better; went to sleep; woke up, and found the little dear dead! Its father will break his heart when he hears of it!"

"Oh, dear no, Mrs. Mullins," said Lady Blaze. "Men and sailors don't care so much about these things as women."

"My husband has a tender heart, ma'am, and will grieve as much as I do," said the distressed mother.

"No one ought to grieve at a sight like that, Mrs. Mullins," said Lady Blaze, stretching forth her finger to the child. "I see the likeness of God there. A sight like that should reconcile you to your loss."

"I cannot bear to lose it, ma'am," said the uncomforted mother. "I'm glad to see it out of pain, though."

"And it has suffered," said old Mrs. Benbow, smoothing back a stray lock of long silken hair from the baby's marble brow. "Its bones are through its skin, I declare."

TOM STRUCK OUT, AND KNOCKED HIS CHURLISH OPPONENT DOWN.

"I see no bones—no flesh—I see nothing but that smile, and nothing in that smile but an assurance of heaven that we shall live again," said Lady Blaze, who spoke so emphatically, so oracularly, and so reprovingly, that she astonished those who heard her, and they looked upon her with the same awe as the poor worshippers at church look upon a great preacher.

For the m ment, all eyes were taken from the infant, who lay there with her

Little eyes closed,
Little hands crossed,
Like a drooping rose in Summer,—

to the august Lady Blaze, who stood apart from the rest. They felt her superiority, although she was not better dressed than they were, and lived in the garret.

She stood from the bed, but still within view of the spiritualised child. With one arm resting on a smoke-dyed mantelpiece, her hands cloked together, her fine profile was only disclosed while her face was turned to the moon, which shone in at the window.

Above her head were many trophies that had been rescued by baby's sailor-father from the roaring sea, and a poor portrait of the honest man, in seaman's habiliments, his short hair scrupulously combed on one side, and his tarpaulin hat held by his side. 'Twas but a daub, but the unskilful painter had not failed to convey to the beholder the face of a downright sun-dyed, storm-beaten, honest tar.

The poor mother thought it would be a relief to her if they would all kneel and pray for her babe.

"Aye, come now, do, Lady Blaze, if you please——"

"That's not my name," she sternly replied, interrupting old Mrs. Benbow.

"Well, I'm sure then I beg your pardon, ma'am," said the old woman. "But do ye, ma'am, if you please, pray for the dear child!"

"I'll pray no more," said the stern inexorable woman. "No prayer of mine was yet heard."

"Well, then, I'll just offer up a bit of a something of my own, just for the poor mother's sake," said Mrs. Benbow, falling heavily on her knees, and burying her head, nightcap and all, in her hands and bedclothes. The young man in the ragged great coat followed, and then Grandfather Grimes knelt beside that lowly bed as well as his stiff old joints would let him.

The young mother, who had previously been kneeling, moaned and sobbed, while Mrs. Benbow collected her thoughts on what she should say. It was a grotesque scene, but it was all reverentially done, and the little child's heavenly smile hallowed it.

The mother, Mrs. Mullins, entreated Lady Blaze to kneel with them, but she resisted, and coldly replied—

"I have no faith. God is not moved by our prayers. Besides, what is it you pray for?"

"For the peace of my darling's soul," said the mother, all tears.

"What greater assurance can you have of that than what you have got?" demanded Lady Blaze. "Look on your child. Heaven has anticipated all you could wish."

"Don't argify, good folks," said Grandfather Grimes, with his braces trailing on the floor as he knelt, "you stop Mrs. Benbow from her prayers."

"Four times have I been going to lift up my voice," said Mrs. Benbow, in rather snuffy tones, raising her head from the side of the bed, and looking sternly towards Lady Blaze, "and your palaver with Mrs. Mullins has taken all the bootiful words out of my mind. I feel for you, Mrs. Mullins, but I cannot pray. And p'raps, after all, a drop of gin and hot water would do you most good."

Lady Blaze disdained to reply to so much vulgarity, and silently left the room, and returned to her garret.

———

CHAPTER IV.

FIGHT—A ROBBERY PROPOSED—A THIEF DISCOVERED.

TOM BROWN, as we have already seen, did not much like the visit of Lady Blaze, and he was sorely puzzled how to deal with her. He prayed for the return of Messrs. Yapp & Swift, and ventured to ask the mysterious woman, who stood with her back to the door, as if keeping guard over it to prevent Tom's escape, if he should run and fetch them.

"They are only over the way at the 'Lion,' ma'am; if you like, I will go for them."

"Go," said Lady Blaze.

"Who shall I say wants them?" inquired Tom, placing his cap on his head.

"Say the woman who lives in the garret has called with her rent. That is all they know of me, or possibly care to know."

As Tom was going, she stopped him.

"Mind, I don't want to see that vulgar fellow, Swift. You think him vulgar, don't you?"

"Worse than that, ma'am, I think him cruel; at least, he has been cruel to me."

"Ah, that is because you have taken the place here of his son—the young reprobate!"

"That was not my fault," said Tom.

"But it was mine," said Lady Blaze. "He was insolent to me. I complained to Mr. Bonthron, and he dismissed him. I tell you that for your warning. I allow no one to be insolent to me because I live in a garret. When I have fulfilled my purpose, I may live in a palace, or sleep in a grave."

As Lady Blaze spoke, her noble nose dilated at the nostrils, and the faded colour on her somewhat long cheeks came and went with her deep, loud respiration, and the heaving up and down of her well-formed bosom.

She grasped the two keys by her side as though she had a neck to strangle; and her looks, as she pronounced—"When I have fulfilled my purpose," indicated that she was capable of such an act.

Tom pulled back the black door of the warehouse, and made a quick exit, leaving Lady Blaze in full possession of the place and all it contained.

An old wooden chair was by the fire, and the tenant of the garret sat down in it, folding her arms, and casting her fervid black eyes on the rag-strewn floor.

She had no sooner seated herself, and became buried in her own mysterious thoughts, than a witch of a large yellow cat leaped into her lap. Lady Blaze jumped up with horror. She had as much terror of cats as Mr. Yapp of rats. Poor puss—a great favourite with Swift—could not tell what to make of the woman's alarm, gave one look at her, and stole away among the sacks.

Thus unpleasantly disturbed, the "woman with the rent" during Tom's absence paced to and fro the small space of the warehouse that was free from articles of merchandise.

Tom Brown, very cold as it was, felt delighted and relieved when he got once more from the hated atmosphere of Messrs. Bonthron & Son's. He had met with such an evil reception from the porter, Swift, who, as the latter affirmed, was to be his master, that the thought flashed across his mind while on his short journey to the "Lion" never to return.

"Is this the 'Lion?'" he asked of another errand-boy, who was making his way through the court, with a tea-kettle in one hand and a pitcher in the other, to the parish pump, for water, the pipes in his master's house close by being frozen.

The boy who was addressed by Tom stared at him with great surprise.

"Well, you are a greenhorn!" he exclaimed, laughing. "Can't you see it's the 'Lion?'" pointing to a flaring daub of a lion over the low doorway. "And if you can't see, can't you read?" inquired the young wiseacre, who considered it the height of ignorance of any one not knowing the "Lion" in his court.

Tom Brown thought all the world against him. Nothing but wretchedness at home, he had as yet met with neither civility nor kindness abroad.

He smothered his wounded feelings, however, and sharply replied to the "knowing" boy, who stood by measuring him from top to toe, as if he was the greatest curiosity he had ever seen in his life—

"Thank you, I can both see and read."

"Don't think you can," said the other. "Ugh! who do you want?"

"That cannot matter to you," said Tom, with pluck.

"Ugh!" said the other, dropping his pitcher and kettle, and sparring up to Tom, "P'raps you want to fight?"

"And perhaps I don't," said Tom, taken by surprise at the pugilistic attitude of the young Hector. "I am on an errand."

"So am I," said the other; "but I don't care for that."

"I do, though," said Tom.

"You—you're a cur!" and he gave Tom a push.

Tom would not endure this, and he returned the push with such force that his assailant fell over the pitcher he had left behind him, and he measured his length on the wet and slippery pavement amongst the broken pieces of the stone vessel, and seriously cut his head.

The crash and noise brought spectators from the "Lion," amongst whom were Messrs. Yapp & Swift, while Miss Bowers got on a stool, and her curl-papered head might be seen looking over inverted wine-glasses with lemons placed on them.

The boy on his way to the pump soon got up from the unpleasant position Tom had placed him in, and amidst the laughter of those who looked on, furiously went at Tom, who well stood his ground.

Miss Bowers entreated Mr. Yapp to go and part them.

"Oh, dear no; let them fight on and be demned—'twill warm them this cold morning," said Mr. Yapp, who stood leaning by the porch of the doorway, his hands in his pockets, his hat on one side his head, and showing other indications of the effects of the "dog's-nose" that he and Swift had consumed.

"Why, I'm jiggered if it ain't our new boy!" exclaimed Swift, in great surprise, taking the pipe from his mouth.

"Gad! so it is, Swift. Didn't think there was so much stuff in the fellah."

"Well, arter this," said Swift, pulling the sack over his shoulders—"arter this, I shan't judge any more by appearances, Mr. Yapp. I thought that 'ere boy of ours was a sop, and would have stood anything from anybody. But he's a trump—a reg'ler trump—and no flies."

Joe Bowers, the landlord, and his tall cellarman, here showed their heads over the shoulders of Yapp & Swift, and the little court was getting inconveniently full of people.

Tom was giving the other little bully a sound and serious thrashing. Fortunately for the latter, a policeman in his rounds came by, and parted them. Tom was very little damaged, while the other, with his head bleeding, was well marked in some parts of his face, that would take a week's time to remove. The policeman gave him his kettle and led him away to a chemist's,

to have his head dressed, for the pitcher had made a serious gash in it.

When Tom revealed the cause of the encounter, and it was made plain that he was not the transgressor, a loud cheer was given for him, and Mr. Yapp took him into the parlour, and gave him some "dog's-nose" for his pluck and courage. Even the surly Swift, who returned to the parlour with Mr. Yapp, and whose heart was no doubt softened by the influence of the dog's-nose, did not fail to bestow a word or two of vulgar praise upon Tom, who, though inwardly pleased with his triumph and the notice it attracted from his masters, was sorry that he had been provoked to fight.

"And where were you going, boy?" inquired Yapp, leaning back in his chair by the fire, crossing his legs and sending up his smoky incense to the ceiling.

"Ah, that's what I want to know," said Swift, taking a chair opposite his superior, and dislodging the rag sack from his shoulders, and filling his short pipe. "I'spose you know it aint right to leave a place you are left in charge on?"

"I came for Mr. Yapp," said Tom, after the moral Swift had finished his lecture.

"Ha! who wants me, pray?" inquired Yapp. "The govnah has not come, I hope."

"Not likely," said Swift.

"No, Sir," said Tom. "The woman in the garret has called with her rent."

Yapp and Swift smiled significantly at each other, but neither for the moment spoke. Yapp drank and passed the pint to his companion; Swift drank and passed it to Tom, who took a little more and laid the pint on the round table between Yapp and Swift.

"Aint it funny, though?" said the latter.

"What?" said Yapp

"That we should have forgotten about her coming with the rent this morning, when we have been talking about her"—

"Hush!" exclaimed Yapp, in a suppressed whisper. "Don't be a fool and show it!"

Swift readily saw the import of Yapp's meaning, and appreciated it.

"Let her wait, boy," said Mr. Yapp. "I'm not going to be disturbed from my beeah for a hag like Lady Blaze."

"She is a hag," said Swift. "She got my boy out of his situation, and I'll——".

"Demn it, Swift! have a little caution."

"Shall I run across and see her?" said Swift.

"She said she wouldn't see you," said Tom.

"Curse her!" exclaimed Swift, rising from the wooden chair in great passion. "That seems to please you, young un! I'spose she's a friend of yours, and got you my boy's situation."

"Never saw her in my life before, Mr. Swift," said Tom.

"Let me tell you, young gentleman, it is not good manners to stand before me and Mr. Yapp with your cap on."

Tom withdrew his cap from his head, and held it by his side, silently waiting what more the ill-natured Swift had to say.

"Take my word for it, Mr. Yapp, that malicious woman won't be satisfied until she has got me and you out of our situations," said Swift.

"She seemed," said Tom, with hesitation, "she seemed to like Mr. Yapp."

"Would you say, boy, that she had fallen in love with me?" said Yapp, with ineffable contempt, smoothing his moustache. "Tell her I am not here."

Swift, who was getting slightly "beery," staggered to Mr. Yapp's shoulder and whispered in his ear—

"Aint that strange now! Didn't I tell you afore she seemed to have some hex-tra-ordinary feeling like towards you? Even that stoopid boy notices it."

"Rubbish, Swift, rubbish!" said Yapp, aloud, laughing; while Swift still held possession of his ear, and continued—

"I'll take my oath on it, that the portrait on ivory which I saw in her hand is as like you as two peas. There's the mystery that I can't make out." Mr. Yapp laughed more heartily still.

"Sit down, that's a good fellah," he said, when his laughter allowed him to speak. "The deuce take it! Would you have me believe that Lady Blaze is my mothah?"

"There's the mystery!" said Swift, resuming his chair, and his pipe. "Time works wonders, Mr. Yapp."

"I hope I may never live to see the time that discovers Lady Blaze to be my mothah," said Mr. Yapp, throwing himself back in the wooden arm chair, and blowing a curling cloud from his cigar to the ceiling.

"She may be a Countess—what then?"

"Why, then," said Yapp, smiling, "I should be a lud! The Countess Blaze, and my Lud Yapp. Good! Ha, ha, go it Swift!"

"Look here, Mr. Yapp," said Swift, pulling the bell for more dog's nose; "if you will leave off joking and reason this matter out, I'm sure you will see more in it."

"Go on, Swift, reason away, but don't reason away my reason."

"Fust and foremost—you don't know who your mother is—do you?"

"No."

"Nor your father?"

"Admitted."

"Then, again," said Swift, "Lady Blaze is always a follerin' you about?"

"That may be accidental," said Yapp.

"Gammon," said Swift.

"Your next point, old boy?"

"That 'ere picture," said Swift, mysteriously.

"A fog of your fancy," said Mr. Yapp, paring his exquisite nails with a pocket knife.

"Fancy!" exclaimed Swift; "I never had a fancy! I take my oath that ivory picture that I saw in the old woman's trunk with the jewellery was your image! There's no mistake about it. But that don't say that Lady Blaze is your mother; but I do say that she has a picture hoarded in her box which is as like you as two peas; and as long as oak and ash grow I shall believe no other. Then, again, what did she say to you when you met her in St. Paul's, the night Mrs. Mullins's child died?"

"That Lady Blaze was not her name."

"To be sure she did, Mr. Yapp! Well, I say, if you put that and that together, you will make——"

"Nothing of it," said Mr. Yapp, interrupting Swift in his sentence. "You have found a mare's nest. The woman is mad."

"Well, it don't matter to me, you know," said Swift, hurt at the clerk's incredulity. "I know who my mother and father is, and good old folks they are, and both on 'em would enjoy this dog's nose above a bit, and I wish they were here to have some."

"I wish, Swift, that I could speak so well of my fathah and mothah. Not very parental to leave me to the mercy of the world. Demn it! I don't think I should be a disgrace to any one, eh, Swift?"

"Certingly not," said Swift. "You are every hinch a gentleman! You must have come of a haristocratick stock—first-class breed, no doubt. Then look you here—Lady Blaze is no common woman—she carries it high, though she rents our garret."

"A superior woman, I must allow—but she's got a tile off."

"Trouble's done that," said Swift. "A lady, p'raps, that's had a child on the sly!"

"And you think this child," said Mr. Yapp, pointing to himself, "is the child on the sly?"

"Well, I'm d——d if I don't!" exclaimed Swift. "There, now you have my mind."

"And it is my belief that your mind is not worth having. Ha! ha! ha! Look here, Swift—look here, old boy. You have the key of her room—"

"There it is," said Swift, holding it up; "and I mean to keep it."

"And you have a key to the trunk?"

"Ditto—ditto," said Swift, holding up another key. "But these are secrets, and we are speaking too loud, and too open. Our affairs—"

"What affairs, Swift?"

"Why, the affairs we've been speaking on—the picture—the jewellery—"

Swift stopped. Miss Bowers entered with another steaming pint of dog's nose, her hair still packed up in broad pieces of the "Times" newspaper, and so radiant with smiles that her pearly teeth showed to great advantage above her double chin.

"Jewellery, eh, Mr. Swift!" she playfully exclaimed, just catching the warehouseman's last word. "Are you going to make me a present of a diamond ring?"

"'Pon my word I should like to, Miss Bowers; but what would my old woman say?"

"Old woman, indeed! No woman is old, let me tell you. How disrespectfully you men speak of your wives! I hope you will know better, Mr. Yapp." Influenced by the dog's nose, and the coquettishness of Miss Bowers, Mr. Yapp sprang from his chair and encircled his arm round her substantial but tightly-laced waist; the while he gazed in her blushing face, and exclaimed—in Romeo tones—

"Ah, love, were I your husband, in my eyes you would never be old, and I would tend and watch you as constantly as the stars the earth."

"Indeed! would you really? I should expect my husband to be a little more constant than the stars."

"They always shine somewhere, love," said Yapp.

"Somewhere wouldn't do for me," said the landlord's daughter. "If they gave me no light I shouldn't care a fig for their shining elsewhere."

"Well, then, I would be as constant to you as a dun to a debtor," said Mr. Yapp, releasing his charmer.

"Ah, now you speak of something like constancy—don't you? But it is too early in the morning to be love making. I must to business."

"No more business for me to-day," said Mr. Yapp, resuming his seat, and idly stretching out his arms and legs.

"I shall only just get them 'ere rags off to the wharf," said Swift, "then I shall hook it."

"Happy men!" said Miss Bowers, turning the gas a little more on, then making her exit singing a ballad air from an opera; and Messrs. Yapp and Swift started off on the same suit.

"Once more, Swift, we are alone—now for your secret communication"

"You've had a bit of it," said Swift, rising and seeing that the parlour door was as fast as it well could be. "Now, no joking—but listen."

"Attention!" cried Yapp, in military accents

"Now then, look here—what d'ye say to that, eh?" said Swift, holding up to the eyes of the enamoured clerk (whose god was jewellery) a diamond ring that literally blazed with sparkles as the light from the fire fell upon it. "Ah! what d'ye say to that?"

After the clerk had turned it round and round, and held it to his eye and from his eye, examined the jewel indeed from every point of view as an artist would a picture, he exclaimed—

"Say to it, Swift! that I never saw such a beautiful ring in my life before. First-watah gem! Worth a hundred at least! Couldn't be a more beautiful diamond!" Here he placed it on his finger, and reflected on it in great admiration. He could not keep his eyes from it—"Grand! glorious! charming! exquisite!"

"Would you like to have a share in it?" said Swift, touching the clerk on the shoulder.

"Do you mean a share in a raffle?"

"Raffle be ——!" exclaimed the warehouseman. "Would you like to go halves in it?"

"How?" interrupted the astonished clerk.

"What would you risk for it?"

"Demn it!" exclaimed the still admiring clerk, "I would risk my neck for it. Never saw such a ring in my life before!"

"I know where to get hundreds of them," said Swift, in an emphatic whisper.

"Hundreds!" exclaimed the clerk, jumping from his chair, full of wonder.

"Not so loud, I tell yer," said Swift. "Now for the secret!"

"I'm amazed, Swift!" exclaimed the clerk, polishing the gold of the ring with a finger of his glove. "Good enough for a duke, by Jove! However and wherever did you get it, Swift?"

"First of all, just hand it over here, and let me see how it would look on my finger."

"Can't part with it, 'pon my soul, Swift," said Yapp. "I'll give you a hundred for it, if you will let me owe you the money."

"Don't see it," said Swift. "I can get that for it ready-money."

"Have you tried?" inquired the anxious clerk, again gazing with greedy eyes on the lustrous jewel.

"That ain't the point, Mr. Yapp. You shall have half if you will go in the risk."

"What risk?" inquired the clerk.

"Hand over the ring and I will tell you.'

With reluctance the clerk did as Swift requested; and when the latter got the jewel back he did not attempt to make a display of it on his dirty brown finger, but he returned it to the paper, and put it in his pocket.

"I have told you about Lady Blaze's jewellery," said Swift, keeping his eye on the door, and leaning forward with his arms on his knees to get as close as he could to the clerk without rising.

"Well?" said Yapp.

"That ring I brought away as hevidence of the wonderful heap of property that old woman has stowed away in her trunk."

"You surprise me!" exclaimed Yapp.

"Lord! it would have taken your breath away if you had seen what I have."

"But what if she misses it?"

"Why then she won't find it—ugh! ugh! But there's no fear of her missing it, she has too many for that. Hark! I certainly heard the rustle of

a woman's dress," he said, springing up, and opening the parlour-door.

"I heard nothing," said Yapp, as Swift returned.

"Well, I see no one," said Swift. "It would spoil our little game if we were overheard."

"Our little game!" exclaimed Yapp. "I have had nothing to do with the stealing of the ring."

"Too honest for that, I s'pose, Mr. Yapp," said the ironical porter.

"I hope that is your opinion of me, Mr. Swift," said Yapp.

"Well, it don't happen to be, Mr. Yapp," said Swift, with confidence.

"Ha! how so?" exclaimed the clerk, in surprise.

"Now, you don't s'pose, Mr. Yapp, that if I didn't know a great many things, I should have been foolish enough to have asked you to jine me in this little affair? I'm a bit green, but not green enough for that."

"And pray, Mr. Swift, what do you know about me that would lead you to propose a robbery to me?"

"Don't be hindignant with me, Mr. Yapp, for it won't do."

"You forget yourself, Mr. Swift. You are talking to a gentleman, sir."

"That's right, keep it up, Mr. Yapp. I like to hear you talk. You *can* talk, you can! And you can hact, too. You should have been a hactor, Mr. Yapp."

"I really fail to understand whether you are in jest or earnest," said Mr. Yapp, his guilty mind evidently disturbed. "If in jest, allow me to say that the subject of a man's honesty is not a becoming one; if in earnest you call me a thief, I'll throttle you! Demn it! I'm poor—I owe money—but I'm honest!"

Swift smiled defiantly, drew the sack over his shoulders, looked steadily in the face of Mr. Yapp, who sat before him with a reddened face and a scowling countenance, furiously puffing the smoke from his mouth.

"I could transport you, I could," at length said Swift.

"You'll transport me with rage, Swift, if you don't cease this farce."

"Oh, no, it ain't a farce, nor a comedy, but a downright tragedy, in which one Mr. Hart will be a principal character."

"Ha!" exclaimed Yapp, who was now quite satisfied that his co-worker knew that which he thought only known to himself.

"There now, all the steam is taken out of yer, Mr. Yapp. You see I know all about it. But I shan't split, so you needn't be alarmed."

The clerk bit his nails with shame and deep chagrin. The game seemed up with him, for he did not care to have such a partner in his guilt as Swift. But for the moment he saw no way out of it.

The mention of the name of Mr. Hart was quite evidence enough that Mr. Swift was in unmistakeable possession of that knowledge which, were it divulged to his employers, would inevitably, as Swift had the plainness; to say, transport him.

"Pass the pint, Mr. Yapp," said Swift. "I'm rather dry after so much conwersation. And you seem troubled—drink yourself."

"And what do you know about Mr. Hart?" at length spoke the discomfited clerk.

"There now, don't try it on any longer with me, Mr. Yapp. I'm a wery clever but wery quiet man."

"Stuff! What do you *know* ?"

"You want chapter and werse, do yer ? Well, then," said Swift, throwing aside the sack from his shoulders, and producing from the side-pocket of his coat a crammed, creased, dirty memorandum book, which he had evidently manufactured himself, and stitched in brown paper, "Well, then," —turning over leaf after leaf, to find the place he wanted—" on the thirtieth day of March, in the year of our Lord one thousand eight hundred and sixty-three, you, William Yapp, did receive the sum of ninety pounds from Mr. Hart, whole-sale stationer, and that——"

"I borrowed twenty pounds of it," interrupted Mr. Yapp, whose gaiety had now deserted him.

"Borrowed! ugh! ugh! I'm thinking the guv'ner would find a huglier word for it. Let's see, what do lawyers call it—felony or embezzlement ?"

"You won't alarm me, my dear fellah," said Yapp, with an assumed nonchalance. "I shall pay it all back to-morrow."

"Too late—too late," said Swift. "You have fiddled with the books."

"Ha! how do you know that ?"

"Oh, I know *more* than that. I know a little about the petty cash."

Yapp winced, every muscle of his face perceptibly jerked. He exclaimed—

"You have been a complete spy upon me !"

"Well, I do like to know the pecooliarities of those I work with," rejoined Swift, coolly smoking his pipe, and showing evident pleasure that he had got Mr. Yapp in his power.

The clerk at length made acquaintance with his position; and while he despised and hated the dangerous customer he had found in Swift, saw that it was his policy to conciliate him before he discovered another game to play.

"Look here, Swift," he said; "I wanted money demned bad——"

"No doubt, Mr. Yapp," interrupted Swift. "How could you dress as you do—keep traps and gals——"

"Come, I say, draw it mild, old fellah," said Yapp, smiling. "Your hand, Swift."

The warehouseman gave his hand to Yapp with a smack that echoed within and without the room in which they sat, and when he grasped it, the clerk's milk-white, delicately-formed member felt itself in a vice.

"Now that we have the pleasure of understanding each other——"

"We've been a long time about it," interrupted Swift. "But I think we have made a friendship that will last."

"Ye-e-s—unfortunately," said Yapp; the last word he muttered to himself, or "aside"—to use stage phraseology. "Do I at all seem altered to you, Swift ?" he abruptly added.

"Not in the least. Why do you ask ?"

"Only that I feel so strange to myself. I seem shrunk, and my very clothes appear to hang loosely about me. And as for *you*——." He hesitated.

"Well, what about *me* ?" demanded Swift.

"You seem a very devil !"

"Well, I never! What a thing the fancy is !" said Swift, laughing. "There is nothing cloven there," putting out his dirty foot.

"Oh, no, it is in your *face* that I discover it. Maybe it is only a reflection of my own; for I feel a devil now, Swift; ripe for anything—murder, if you will !"

He spoke excitedly, drank deep, and paced to nd fro the small dimensions of the little sanded parlour, and where chairs impeded his progress they were hurled out of the way.

"To be a thief, and know it, is one thing; but to be a thief, and others know it, is not so pleasant."

He wildly pushed his hand through his well-arranged hair; he was regardless now of appearances. Swift quietly smoked his pipe, and seemed amused, rather than anything else, at his friend's frantic display.

"You can't mean all this, Mr. Yapp. It must be put on. I thought I should have had your blessing for introdoocing you to a good thing."

"A very good thing, indeed, is it not, to be made a slave of ?" exclaimed the clerk.

"A slave! what *do* yer mean, Mr. Yapp ?"

"Yes, a slave! I feel already the chains and fetters you have forged for me about my hands and feet. A *slave*, Swift—*your* slave !"

"Nonsense, Mr. Yapp. I want to row in the same boat with yer."

"I am at your command, Mr. Swift," said Yapp, in tones of an inferior to a superior.

"You do me proud," said Swift, smiling, thoroughly feeling that Yapp was in his power.

Mr. Yapp caught up his hat, and was about to make a rapid exit; but Swift quickly rose, caught him by the arm, and said—

"You don't go until this business is settled one way or the other. I am your friend, Mr. Yapp. I might have gone to the guv'ner and transported you."

Yapp gave a groan, then exclaimed—

"And why not Her Majesty's fetters as well as yours ?"

"Well, I don't think they would suit you as well. That beautiful head of hair of yours—you wouldn't like to lose it, would yer, Mr. Yapp ? You wouldn't look well either in prison grey. Nor does Her Majesty allow her prisoners to drive out pretty girls on a Sunday. And the divil a drop o' dog's nose is to be had, nor even the smell of a full-flavoured cigar. Those beautiful white hands o' yours, Mr. Yapp, would soon be spoilt in Her Majesty's transport service."

This humourous, but forcible appeal, to Mr. Yapp, fully confirmed him in the seriousness of his position.

"What would you have, Swift ?" he sternly asked.

"Have both on us rich,—there, won't that please you ? In for a penny, in for a pound. Sit down five minutes longer, and I'll tell you my plans. *You* can't be worse off, you know."

"True," said Yapp, slowly; and with a pale face and a changed countenance he resumed his seat.

"D—d if I didn't hear some one at the door !" exclaimed Swift, pulling it back quickly and widely—but not quick enough to discover Joe Bowers and his daughter, who had been the deliberate listeners to all that had passed between Messrs. Yapp & Swift that morning in the parlour.

The "rustle" that Mr. Swift had been once or twice alarmed by was caused by Miss Bowers' heavy curl-papers coming too near the door when she bowed her head and bent her ear to the keyhole.

Instantly that Mr. Swift made his advance to the door, Joe popped round to the adjoining tap-room, and his daughter, like a flash of lightning, whipped round the bar, the entrance to which faced the parlour-door, and appeared busy with the beer-engine—looking *so* innocent, did the curl-papered creature !

"More dog's nose, Mr. Swift?" she inquired, when he opened the parlour-door, and looked on the bar.

"Not just yet, Miss Bowers," said Swift. "I thought I heard some one at the door."

"And so you did, Mr. Swift," said the playful young barmaid.

"Ha! Who?" asked Swift, somewhat alarmed.

"The old tom-cat," said Miss Bowers.

She laughed loudly— Swift joined in the chorus —and Joe Bowers shuffled out of the taproom, and his long, red, hanging cheeks were also set in motion with laughter, though he hardly knew what about.

"The old tom-cat—that's a good un, Miss Powers," said Swift. "You may make I and my friend Yapp another pint after that. Joe, your daughter is worth a jew's eye, if you know what that is."

"Don't exackly, Swift," said the burly land-lord.

"Nor I either," said Swift.

"I've heerd of a jew's harp," said Joe, pretending to play upon one that he held between his teeth, which was the occasion of another chorus of laughter.

While Swift stood laughing at the doorway, poor Yapp sat moodily with outstretched legs, one hand supporting his head, and the other thrust between his buttoned-up coat and his breast. Swift found him thus when he returned with the new pint of dog's nose.

"Drink, and cheer up, boy," said Swift.

"It would take an ocean of drink to make me cheer up," said the gloomy clerk.

"Go in with this swim of mine, and we'll have a merry time of it either in this country or another. My old woman will find me scarce, I know; she may get somebody else to fling chayney plates at. Now, business, Mr. Yapp," he added, producing the glittering ring. "Are you in or not? That's the question, as Hamlet says."

"Had your question been put to Hamlet he would have soon decided," replied Mr. Yapp, taciturnly.

"Hamlet might have done worse though—and he did do worse," said Swift. "He broke Ofeelyer's heart and killed her father. He was a nice kettle of fish, he was! But he's not here now, and if he was I shouldn't give him so good a chance as to go shares in a thousand pound s worth of an old woman's jewellery. Nor I'm not going to persuade you any more, Mr. Yapp. In or not? You are in already on a chandler's shop scale, you know, so you can't harm by going into the wholesale trade under the firm of Yapp and Swift. Don't be squeamish—it's a fine chance for a nice young man."

"I don't like the partnership," said Yapp.

"Don't you indeed! Want it all to yourself I'spose, eh?"

"Well, it would have been more agreeable, Swift. But as we are so thoroughly known to each other—why—ye-e-s—better go on with the harmony and a fig for the discord!" he exclaimed, snapping his fingers as if some good thought unknown to Swift had suddenly occurred to him.

"Richard's himself again!" exclaimed Swift.

"Hurrah!" cried Yapp. "As well be hung for a sheep as a lamb, you know, Swift."

"Isn't that what I've been saying to yer all the morning. In short judge, jury, and public think more of the man who steals the sheep than he who steals the lamb. Pettifoggers in anything are now looked down upon——"

"While men, like Robson and Redpath, are extolled for the magnitude of their transactions," said Yapp, completing the purpose of Swift's sentence.

"Now, before I reveal my plans," said Swift, drawing his chair close to Yapp's, the two men of mischief now sitting side by side and facing the fire—"before I tell you anything, there must be a little freemasonry between us—you must swear to be faithful to me."

"Good," said Yapp. "What shall I swear?"

"Take my hand, and say after me. 'I, William Yapp, swear to you, Jeremiah Swift, by the God who made me—(hold up your eyes to the ceiling)—that living or dying—whether we are friends or enemies—rich or poor—living together or apart——'"

"Look here, Swift," said Yapp, taking his eyes from the ceiling, tired of Swift's tedious terms of oath, which he saw no end to—"I swear to you that under any circumstances I will not betray your confidence."

"Well, there, I'll trust yer," said Swift; "but its hardly solemn enough. You ought to have brought in something about heaven or hell. Yes—say this—that if you do betray me may you be cast into the bottomless pit."

Mr. Yapp complied; and the heavy terms of betrayal settled, Mr. Swift went on to say—and Joe Bowers and his daughter Bessie heard him say it—

"That he had the keys of Lady Blaze's trunk, and the key of her room-door."

"But how did you first learn that Lady Blaze was possessed of this jewellery?"

"That hardly matters to you. But this is how it was. You remember Mrs. Goodenough, that lived in our second-story back?"

"Yes—the woman who died."

"She told my boy, and my boy told me, that she had seen the jewellery, and that she was sure Lady Blaze was some great lady under hiding. It is no use asking me how Mrs. Goodenough knew what she told my boy, because I couldn't tell yer. I'm not fond of asking questions. But I can tell yer that when I heard about her wealth, I couldn't rest content until I had satisfied these eyes"—pointing to his ugly visual organs, with which he stared at Yapp, "that what I had heard was true. Every time she went out I tried the garret door with all the keys I could find; at last, the old cellar key proved my friend."

"How about the trunk?" inquired Mr. Yapp.

"I borrowed a heavy bunch of keys from the locksmith's in Fetter-lane, and almost the first key I tried was the Open Sesame—and I saw a sight, Mr. Yapp, that my eyes will never forget. A whole jeweller's shop was before my eyes! I couldn't help thinking that she must be a great thief or a great lady. It was dazzling to behold! When I turned my eyes away for a minute everything seemed quite dark. Fancy a whole trunk full of things like these, Mr. Yapp, better than these!" added Swift, holding up the diamond ring, like a "Cheap Jack" selling his Brummagem wares.

"Stuff, Swift!" said the unbelieving clerk.

"I tell yer its true," said the cunning porter. "Go into this matter with your whole heart, and ye needn't tinker any more with Bonthron and Son's petty cash-book——"

"Shut up, Swift!" exclaimed Yapp, waving his hand offendedly. "I shall pay all that back—"

"With Lady Blaze's jewellery," interrupted the porter.

"I had other plans," said Mr. Yapp.

"One of which was to pay back when convenient. That's thieves' law, eh?"

"How dare you, Swift!" exclaimed Yapp, who was far from reconciled to his unenviable position. "I'll go no further in this business. You pursue it with too much indelicacy for me!"

"La! I only said that between ourselves. I'm just like you in feeling, and would knock any one down who called me a thief."

"Our time is up, Swift," said Mr. Yapp, tired of the business, and now hating the very man he was so seriously linked with. "Your plans?"

"Are these," said Swift. "I thought one night that we should both return late when all the lodgers were asleep, and that I would keep watch below while you went to the garret—let yourself in—and if the old woman stirred or resisted, that you should—should—"

"What?" inquired Yapp.

"Strangle her!" said Swift.

"Thank you. But I decidedly decline that office," said Yapp.

"Then you shall keep watch, and I'll do the other little business."

"You are mad, Swift! Think you I would be a party to a murder?"

"What is the life of a hag like that worth?"

"Well, I value my own at something, at all events," said Yapp; "even if a portion of it should be destined to be passed in other and less agreeable lands."

"Now you know my plans, let us hear yours," said Swift.

"I have hardly thought the matter out; to tell you the truth, it has taken me by surprise. I thought you were an honest man, Swift."

"Just as honest as my neighbours," said Swift, "no honester! We are all honest till we are tempted. Why a bishop would become thief to get Lady Blaze's jewels."

"Why not take the first opportunity when Lady Blaze goes out, and then you attack the trunk?"

"And what would you do?"

"Watch," said Yapp; "and if she returned whip up the stairs and give you warning."

"Her going out and her coming in is so uncertain, that's the worst on it," said Swift. "But as you like—hit or miss—luck's all! I say, don't let there be any chicken-heartedness in the matter, or we shall be done."

"And when we have the jewellery safe, what then?"

"Leave that to me and my friend, the Jew," said Swift.

"And when we have converted it into money, what then?"

"How green we are!" said Swift. "Why, spend it, to be sure."

"But not in England?"

"In England, if you likes. But for myself, I means to make a tower of Amerikee, where a man is a man, liquor cheap, and good pay for little work. But there, I shan't want no more work, nor you either, Mr. Yapp. We shall have no end of wealth; and I'm sure it will do us and the commoonity more service than locked up in an old hair trunk."

"You may be deceived; it may not yield as much as you imagine," said Yapp.

"Then my name's not Swift!" he exclaimed, smacking his hands together, the sound of which reverberated through bar and parlour; indeed, the "dog's-nose" began to tell on his brain, and he became excited with his splendid prospects.

"Ain't it a booty!" holding up the ring, which Yapp extended his hand to take. "Not as I knows it, Mr. Yapp. This don't go from me till we have the whole swag, and then we'll sell to my friend Moses, and divide to a farthing. 'Honour among thieves,' that's—hic-cup—my motter."

"Well, the sooner the better, that's what I say," said Yapp.

"Oh, to-night, if you like," said Swift, attempting to stir the fire, and he only succeeded so far as to scatter the burning coals over the room, while the clerk sat like one who was heaping coals of fire on his head. He sat with a gloomy but ever-changing countenance, and occasionally, unperceived by Swift, a half-suppressed "Demn it!" would escape his pallid lips.

"Well, have we anything more to talk about?" he said to Swift.

"Nothing to talk about, but plenty to do," was the ruffian's reply.

"Then we had better go," said the clerk—but where now was his pluck and gaiety?

"I'm off now to the wharf with a load of rags," said Swift; "and if you don't see me—hic-cup—any more to-day, don't be alarmed. We quite now understand each other—hic-cup—eh, don't we?"

"All right," said the clerk, the liquor entirely failing to have any effect on his troubled mind.

Swift staggered out into the court, drew the sack over his head and shoulders, and was soon in Bonthron & Son's warehouse. Mr. Yapp bade a good morning to Joe Bowers and his daughter, and moodily made his way to the same destination as Swift.

On opening the warehouse-door, both were much surprised to find Tom Brown bound hand and foot, stretched out on the top of the sacks of rags, screaming "Mur—der!"

CHAPTER V.

TOM'S LIFE IMPERILLED BY A MANIAC—SAVED BY A POLICEMAN—A SAD HISTORY.

WHILE the two men, Yapp & Swift, had been boozing and planning a robbery of Lady Blaze's jewels, Tom Brown's life had been seriously imperilled by the mad son of Mr. Bonthron.

The boy had no sooner returned to Lady Blaze, who waited with her rent, and informed her, according to his lying instructions, that Mr. Yapp was not at the "Lion," and that she with a hateful scowl had left the warehouse, than a man, young in years, buttoned to the throat, both his hands imbedded in his pockets, entered the warehouse. He went at once to the vacant desk in the partitioned-off room, known as the "counting-house," and tore open the letter on which there was "tuppence to pay."

Tom stood in amazement so great at this act of the silent stranger that, for the moment, he was speechless. But though he could not speak, his eye was strong in its vigilance, and he well watched every movement of the intruder, while he wondered who or what he could be. He concluded it must be either Bonthron or Son.

He was tall and very thin, dark-skinned, with whiskers that just covered his prominent cheek-bones. From top to toe he was dressed in black, including gloves and stockings, but there was an unmistakeable hue of rust about it all.

"DON'T TELL A LIE, BOY! HERE IS THE NOTE."

"Now, then," he said, pulling off his coat, cold as the weather was, "now, then, I will set to work, and address a few remarks to mankind, showing them how they might and ought to live for ever. That by the laws of Eternal Justice——"

Here he caught up the ruler, and dipped it in the inkstand, but finding it would not do the office of a pen, he madly flung it to his feet, exclaiming—

"Everything in the world is against me! But great minds are not to be thwarted by little things! Oh! that I could bring my father to believe in the imperishability of matter! But, no, he believes in nothing but rags. Oh! the cursed, wasted hours, that I have sacrificed to this desk!"

Here he struck it so forcibly with the mahogany ruler that the latter snapped in two. The mad act, and the noise produced by it, startled

4

Tom; and he came from behind the sacks, and stood trembling before the mysterious visitor, wanting to speak, but afraid to do so.

No sooner had Mr. Bonthron, Junior, set his wild, uneasy eyes, upon the boy, than, with three long strides, he reached the shop-door, and, to Tom's great terror, locked it.

"Come here, boy!" he exclaimed. "I'll make a sacrifice of you to the Eternal Justice for the regeneration of mankind!"

He stretched forth his hands to catch Tom, and the terrified boy, shouting "Mur—der!" dodged in and out between the sacks. But madmen are quick in all their actions, as well as determined, and mad Bonthron scampered over the tops of the sacks as nimble as a monkey; and when he came between the two where Tom had taken refuge, he laid hold of him by the collar of his coat, and strongly dragged him to the top, and then exclaimed—

"Oh! you unwilling sacrifice! What do you care about mankind?—you think too much of your life! Oh, how unlike Isaac! Come hither, I say, and let me bind you with cords for the sacrifice!"

"Oh, pray don't kill me, Sir!" pleaded Tom. But he pleaded in vain, for the madman, deaf to his cries and importunities, took some strong cord that lay on the sacks, and while Tom lustily sung out "Murder! Mur—der!" he bound first his hands together, then lifted him like a feather on the sacks, laid him down, and bound his feet.

"Now for a knife," said Bonthron, looking about him.

"Oh, pray don't kill me! Mur—der!"

"A knife, I say!" exclaimed the ferocious man. "How all my plans are thwarted! A knife, I say!" He stamped about the place, and tore his hair.

"Mur—der!" cried Tom as lustily as he could.

"A knife, I say!" raved the madman.

"Oh, pray don't kill me!

"Ha! a hammer!" he cried, seizing one that lay in a corner and quite big enough to do deadly execution on poor Tom, who turned his eyes upon the uplifted weapon with the greatest terror. Mad Bonthron held down the boy's head by his hair, but fortunately for Tom his assailant remembered that Abraham slew Isaac with a knife, and as he was anxious to deal death in the same manner as the Patriarch, he threw away the hammer, and again shouted for a knife.

Once more Tom cried "Mur—der!" His cry at length was heard. Miss Bonthron, the madman's sister, came to the warehouse door in search of her brother at the very moment Tom last called out.

To her horror she found the door locked, and while she heard the boy's cries she did not fail to hear her brother's voice shouting for a knife. Poor lady! What a mockery the gay feather in her hat looked, shading such a face of grief and sorrow. Her velvet mantle, too, seemed as if it had been roughly handled, while her hair was out of curl, and hung in disorder above her cheeks. She had evidently been on a chase, for cold and wintry as the weather was, drops of perspiration sparkled on her terror-stricken countenance.

"George! do let me in!" she cried to her brother.

"Ha! she's after me again!" he exclaimed, startled by his sister's voice, and indeed his madness seemed for the moment subdued by it.

"George! George! open the door!"

"Torment!" he exclaimed, "why disturb me in my religious sacrifices?"

"Do, George, let me in!" again pleaded the sister, shaking the door by the handle.

"Call a policeman," shouted Tom, "or I shall be mur—dered!"

The young lady acted on Tom's suggestion, and, opportunely enough, a policeman passed as Miss Bonthron stood on the stone steps of the house on her way to search for one.

Miss Bonthron hastily explained the case, and the policeman at once became a man of action.

"Hi, here! open the door!" he demanded, well shaking it.

"He wont!" cried Tom, "and I can't, for he has tied my hands and feet, and is seeking a knife to kill me! Burst open the door!"

"How dare you lend mine enemies a hand!" exclaimed the enraged maniac. "I will kill you now without a knife." And he was about to strangle poor Tom, when—crash!—the strong policeman burst in panel after panel with his heavy boot, and to the boy's inexpressible delight, effected an entrance, and soon held the madman tightly by the wrist.

CHAPTER VI.

THE MADMAN'S ARREST—BROTHER AND SISTER —THE PRIVATE "RETREAT"—DEATH OF THE MANIAC.

As we have seen in our last chapter, never was a policeman so welcome to any one as to Tom Brown. When he entered, with the sad and suffering Miss Bonthron on his heels, the poor boy looked nearly exhausted. His mad assailant stood over him grinding his teeth, and literally foaming at the mouth, his hands bent into fists, swinging his long arms rapidly to and fro, with his fiery eyes bent heavenward, exclaiming—

"Let the death of this boy propitiate Thy vengeance—"

He had not got farther in his prayer when the policeman clutched his wrist, and the fair sorrowful face of his sister caught his eyes, and she gently said—

"Don't you know me, George?"

The maniac in solemn reverential tones continued—

"Let the blood I am about to offer—"

"Speak to sister Ellen, George," said Miss Bonthron, with a flood of tears.

Whether it was his sister's name, the tones of his sister's voice that caught his attention it matters not, but he suddenly stopped and groaned heavily.

"Oh, please, Sir, unbind these cords," pleaded Tom to the policeman.

"There, there, don't you holler—you might have been dead by this time had I not come by," said the officer, who really just then had as much as he could do to hold Mr. Bonthron, who made great resistance to the policeman's interference with his "sacrifice."

"Speak to me, George!" said Miss Bonthron, endeavouring if possible to dissipate the black cloud that obscured the poor man's reason. "You know me, George, don't you?—I am Ellen, your sister."

"Sister! sister!" exclaimed the wandering man. "What is that? All titles are but shams and deceptions."

"No, you do not consider Ellen to be a deception, I know that, George. You did not say so when we met at the cottage this morning. You kissed me then, and I promised I would assist you to regenerate mankind."

"Ah! that's what I want!" he delightedly exclaimed. "But it can't be done without a sacrifice, I'm sure of that, Ellen. You know I have well thought the matter out. Now you get a knife—"

"Very well, but we cannot get one here; the people are so ill-natured and ignorant——"

"That's it, Ellen. Now, indeed, you are my sister," and he leant forth and kissed her. "Why does this devil hold me, Ellen?"

"They are all bad people, and very ignorant," said Ellen.

"Ignorance! ah! that's it. Oh! when mankind become regenerated——"

"Yes, and I'll help you, George," said Miss Bonthron, putting his hat on his head.

Like most madmen, he was very cunning, and suddenly pulled his wrists from the policeman's grasp, and made for the door, and but for the officer's alacrity, the madman would have got abroad again. The policeman caught him by the collar of his coat, and his devoted sister gently took his hand. But he now became furious, and raved for a knife. "Grandfather" Grimes happily came down the stairs; and the old man, his white hair flying back, with uplifted hands, exclaimed—

"Oh! that poor young gentleman again! For God's sake, don't hurt him, policeman! Your servant, Miss Bonthron."

"Oh, for a knife!" raved the maniac, violently struggling.

"Go and get help," said the policeman to the little old man, who stood with uplifted hands. "You'll see one of my mates in Fleet Street."

"I'll go—I'll go—but, pray don't hurt him," implored "Grandfather," hastily moving off, buttoned up in a little brown coat, a cloth cap tied down over his ears, and a good firm walking-stick in his yellow, veiny-looking hands.

Grandfather Grimes was not long in pouncing upon a member of the "force,"—a thing not always easily accomplished, for often policemen are as difficult to find as a needle in a bundle of hay.

The two officers had not an easy task, but they managed to handcuff Mr. Bonthron, and carry him down the court to a cab, which conveyed him to the adjacent station-house in Fleet Street.

Miss Bonthron was almost broken-hearted to see her poor demented brother thus bound; and when the madman looked back upon her, and recognised her, and touchingly cried—"Ellen, why do you allow this?" she sobbed piteously, and asked the policeman to let her take her brother home. But they could not—the case must be taken to the inspector at the station-house.

The cab moved slowly along the crowded thoroughfare, with the two officers and the maniac within, while Miss Bonthron walked along by the side of the cab, or as near as the other vehicles would allow her, her gay clothes so sadly disarranged that people set her down for a member of the fallen sisterhood recovering from a night's debauch in the Haymarket. The feather in her grey hat had escaped its fastening, and drooped any way and anyhow but the right, her black velvet mantle was torn, and the velvet trimmings hung like rags about her. But her mind had now a different occupation from dress and appearances—her brother's rolling eye absorbed her whole thoughts and feelings, —monopolised her whole attention.

Young Bonthron in his youth was given to over-study, and after leaving college, and much against his inclinations, but in obedience to his father's wishes, joined the merchant in his rag dealings. But merchandise and trade generally was always repugnant to the young gentleman.

Pity, but his father, always devoted to the trade he had made so much money from, did not discover how strong the bent of his son's mind was towards the learned professions! He would have made a shrewd lawyer or a wise lord chancellor, a powerful member of parliament, or a far-sighted statesman, an eloquent divine, a learned bishop, even a great actor—his attainments were so diversified. But in all he was thwarted by his father—who meant for the best, but who did not judge wisely; so ultimately he joined his father, and the business was conducted under the firm of "Bonthron and Son." Although the latter became partner, he never took an active part in the business.

But genius, like water, will always find an outlet. Young Bonthron spent the day in vainly attempting book-keeping, and the night, when he should have been resting his susceptible brain in sleep, was devoted to political study. Once launched in this atmosphere no one could say to what port he would sail—either a harbour of refuge or destruction. He dreamed long over the delicious fancies of Louis Blanc and Lamartine, until they became realities to him. Young Bonthron had a good heart, and it was no wonder he would like to see mankind in every respect happy, and, like himself, intellectual. He made it his duty to solve the problem. Alas! many another mind has been wrecked in its solution. Young Bonthron's soon gave way under it, and he became a terror to society rather than its saviour.

His madness was long noticed by his father before it became notorious, and was a source to him of many troubles. But the disease grew, until all eyes were acquainted with its seriousness and its dimensions. He would "uphold" in business, in home, and in the streets, about the "regeneration of mankind," and "the eternal justice."

He went mad about it. He had been the inmate of a private asylum, but the good feeling of his family directly they discovered a ray of sanity gladly received him home again.

No one had more kindness shown him from father, mother, and sister than young Bonthron. He was much indulged, and everything done to divert him from his mania. Physicians were privately consulted, and travel was recommended. At great expense and inconvenience he and his father made a continental tour, and for a time it seemed to work a cure, for on their return he regularly went backwards and forwards with his father to the business in the court in Fleet-street.

At the time when this, his second paroxysm, broke out, to the great satisfaction of his family he had formed the acquaintance of a wealthy young lady, whom he met at his father's house. But fortunately for her the acquaintance was of young growth, and had not ripened into love, before the old and dangerous enemy once more made its appearance.

The evening before the morning that Tom Brown found himself at Messrs. Bonthron and Son's warehouse his young master seemed quiet, intelligent, and happy. While his father nursed his gouty leg as cheerful as the pain would allow him before the drawing-room fire, the son played whist with his mother, sister, and the lady that all hoped at not a distant day to see young Bonthron united to.

His spirits, while partaking of an elegantly-served supper in the parlour, were particularly good, although his watchful father noticed with anxiety that once or twice he gnashed his teeth, and that three times he spilt his wine, and laughed somewhat wildly over it.

The party, however, had not long adjourned to the handsomely-furnished drawing-room, where everything was as bright as a good fire, a dazzling chandelier, and the delightful presence of elegantly-dressed ladies could make it, before unmistakable signs of madness once more showed themselves.

The young lady, Miss Goldsmith, was the madman's partner in the rubber.

"Now, partner," said Miss Goldsmith, after waiting some time while he seemed to arrange and disarrange his cards, "we wait for your play, sir."

He paid no attention, but went on shuffling his cards backwards and forwards.

"Come, George," said Miss Bonthron, "trumps are demanded."

"Trumps—trumps—I haven't got any—yes, I have—no—no—but I say I have—what are trumps?" He spoke this quietly, and in the most composed manner. "Why don't you tell me, Ellen, what are trumps?"

"Hearts, George."

"I have none."

"No heart!—what a pity for the ladies!" said the witty Miss Goldsmith.

"George means that his heart has been already disposed of," said his sister.

While the others laughed, young Bonthron drew forth his watch, and suddenly said—

"Excuse me, but at twelve to-night I have to keep an appointment with Oliver Cromwell. See! there is his vision, that beckons me away." Here he violently threw his hand of cards to the floor, and further exclaimed: "That he must and would have a knife to cut his way through the world!"

While he exclaimed, the others trembled. A white froth oozed from his mouth, and his crisp, black hair almost stood on end. Before the ladies had recovered their terror, the young maniac rushed down stairs, caught up his hat in the hall, and had vanished into the dark wintry night before any alarm could be given.

Miss Bonthron and Miss Goldsmith hastily arranged themselves to follow him. They had not gone many yards from the threshold of the front door before they were beaten back by the inclement night. The snow fell fast, the wind blew loud, and nothing but a black, starless sky above. How could young ladies, in drawing-room evening costume, face a night like this?

Miss Bonthron would have gone forward—her love for her brother was strong—but Miss Goldsmith besought her to return. Eventually she yielded, and with a tearful countenance entered the drawing-room.

"What can we do, pa?" she passionately cried.

"Send a servant for a policeman, and let me communicate the facts to him."

This was quickly done; and notice of the fact of a raving madman abroad was given from beat to beat, and station to station. But the dreadful night passed, and no tidings came—no

tidings to soothe or allay the feelings of those who sorrowed within the precincts of that warm and comfortable room.

Only a little time since the apartment, where now nothing was heard but sounds of lamentation, was gay with light, music, and hilarity. Miss Goldsmith made delicious music from the rich-toned piano, while Miss Bonthron's sweet voice sweetly echoed in accord with it. But now, as by magic touch, the place of light was turned to darkness, and the sounds of music were turned into sighs and sobs. One thought reigned throughout—"What has become of him? Oh, will he destroy himself, or others? God send him back to us!"

Miss Bonthron's grief became quite agonising, and serious results were entertained. All tried to comfort her, and forget themselves. Mr. Bonthron implored her to be calm, but his words fell far short of her heart. Every now and then she might be seen looking over the blind, hoping to find her brother; then would she return to her chair in despair.

Mr. Bonthron, though racked with pain in his outstretched leg, was deeply affected at his daughter's grief.

"Come to pa!" he said, tenderly; "he cannot come to you."

Miss Bonthron sorrowfully moved her chair nearer her father, and soon his arm was around her waist, while she rested her head on his shoulder. The daughter's grief prevented any outward demonstration of sorrow on the part of the mother; but nevertheless, Mrs. Bonthron felt deeply the condition of her only son, and was as anxious about him as any of them.

Each present kept their fears to themselves, and kindly encouraged the others to hope for the best and prepare for the worst. Mr. Bonthron was full of regret that he was disabled from going in pursuit of his son.

Every moment of that dismal night was spent by the family in the greatest suspense, and every sound that broke the stillness of the night was eagerly listened to, in the hope that it might prove the return of the mad wanderer.

But no; the long night slowly went, and the morning came, but it brought no tidings of the madman. We say the morning, but it was of that foggy character that it bore the dark likeness of night. The street-lamps were still allowed to burn, and the snow continued to fall.

Poor Miss Bonthron, full of a sister's love, would not be weather-bound any longer. After a small repast of coffee, she took her hat and muff and mantle, and as the clock struck seven the brave young lady was alone on the road, defying fog and snow and cold, in the pursuit of her brother.

Slowly, at first, she walked, methodising in her mind the best way to attain her object. She remembered to have heard that insane people loved the persons, places, and things which, in their lucid moments, they hated. Upon this idiosyncracy of the mad she acted, and took her first steps towards the warehouse of Bonthron and Son in the court in Fleet Street. She knew full well how her brother always detested going thither, and for that reason, when she got into the main road to London, she hailed a cab, and drove to the City.

To her inexpressible delight as much as her surprise there she found her brother, with folded arms, and wet through with the snow, pacing the little court.

Directly he caught sight of his sister he

bounded like a deer through the many courts and intricacies of the neighbourhood, and quickly as his sister pursued he was soon lost to her. She wandered about for some time and then returned to the warehouse, and saw Tom and Messrs. Yapp and Swift. As well as she was able she concealed her errand from them, and they were under the impression that she merely called to say that Mr. Bonthron being ill with the gout would not be at his business that day. After dropping in on a city friend or two, to see if her brother had been there, she returned once more to the warehouse, and there, as we have already seen, found him with locked doors, about to "offer up little Tom Brown as a sacrifice!"

Her opportune arrival undoubtedly saved Tom's life, and her brother from becoming a murderer!

When they arrived at the station-house, the divisional surgeon was sent for, and after much consultation he advised that Miss Bonthron should return to her friends at Clapham, and state it as his opinion that the case was one of dangerous lunacy, and that immediate steps should be taken to place young Bonthron under restraint in a private lunatic asylum.

The young lady was quick in performing her dreary commission, and Mr. Bonthron, her father, at once sent for the family doctor, and the whole matter was confided to his care.

The same day the poor young gentleman was placed in a beautiful "retreat," a complete garden surrounded by hills, where every possible care, both medical and domestic, was bestowed upon him. Some friend or member of his family visited him daily. But he recognised no one.

Sometimes he was calm, but more often violent, raving about eternal justice and the regeneration of mankind. During those paroxysms he was confined in the well-padded strong room. He had not long been an inmate of the "retreat" before, in one of those violent attacks of madness, to the happy release of himself and family, he died, a victim to over-study and a mind too much concentrated on the most abstruse subjects.

CHAPTER VII.

TOM BROWN BOUND HAND AND FOOT — HIS RELEASE AND SUFFERINGS—THE THIEVES' QUARREL—THE INNOCENT SEEM GUILTY— TOM BROWN'S ARREST.

MESSRS. Yapp and Swift, when they returned from the "Lion," were inexpressibly surprised at the scene that met their eyes—Tom Brown bound hand and foot with cords, lying on his back across the rag sacks! Tom's explanation to the astonished men was more alarming still to them ; for nothing of this would have happened if they had been at their business, as they ought to have been, instead of boozing and planning robberies at the Lion.

"It must come out, Swift, that we were both absent," said the nervous Mr. Yapp.

"Yes, but it needn't come out that we were at the Lion," said the deeper Swift. "You won't tell, will yer, young un? I won't let you free of these ere cords before you promise me that."

"I won't say anything if I'm not asked," said Tom.

"And if you're asked—what then?" demanded Swift.

"Why, then I shall tell the truth," said Tom.

"Then lie there and be d——d!" exclaimed Swift, throwing aside the large paper-knife that he was about to cut Tom's bonds with. "That 'ere boy won't suit us, Mr. Yapp," he added aside to the clerk, who was engaged at the desk with the letter that the madman had opened, and which lay there surrounded with three five-pound notes and a cheque. "My eyes! what a lot of money!"

"Who opened this lettah, boy?" inquired Mr. Yapp.

"The man who bound me," said Tom. "Pray, sir, will you cut these cords?—they hurt me very much."

"Bettah release him, Swift."

"You may if you like, Mr. Yapp, but I won't," said the brutish porter.

The clerk was about to do so, when Swift drew him back to the counting-house, and said whisperingly—

"I have a thought. Let us swag the lot of that 'ere money?"

"Impossible!" replied Mr. Yapp.

"Not at all impossible. I have a thought, I tell yer. You hear that mad Bonthron opened the letter——"

"Yes—well?" said the clerk.

"Then, who is to know but that he took all that was in it?" said the knowing Swift.

"Why, the boy," said the clerk.

"D——n that 'ere boy! He only came here to ruin us. To be sure, he's seen the money."

"That's the point," said the clerk. "Otherwise I think with you, Swift, that when the money is missed young Bonthron might safely bear the blame of it."

"Lord! nothink easier. Let us try the case in our own minds like. We were both on us out on business——"

"Yes, on business; go on, Swift," said the clerk. "That is lie number one."

"Out on business, and when we comes home you find the letter on the desk without the money——"

"Good—lie number two," said the clerk.

"Well," said Swift, "you immediately asks the boy who opened the letter, and he says, says he, that the man who bound him opened it."

"That's *true*," said the clerk. "And now I see that the fair inference would be that he bound the boy to take the money."

"No sich thing," said the porter. "One circumstaunce don't foller because of the other. For don't you see, Mad Bonthron could have got the money without binding the boy. He was a kind of master here, don't you see? Look at the letter, it is addressed to 'Bonthron and Son,'—so it belonged to the young man like."

"Yes, I see, Swift. Then why did he bind the boy?"

"Why, don't you know he is mad? And didn't you hear the boy say he was going to murder him for a sacrifice, or some such blasted stuff? And didn't you hear the boy say that he would have been murdered if Mr. Bonthron could have found a knife?"

"Very true, Swift. Then the fair inference would be that, the money being gone, the madman who opened the letter made away with it in some inexplicable manner?"

"To be sure—swallowed it, for what any one

can deny! Ran away with it, and lost it, or gave it away. Lord! what won't a madman do! They are cunning devils, some on 'em are."

"Indeed they are, Swift," said the clerk, who was fast becoming an apt pupil of Mr. Swift's. "I heard once of a madman getting the friend who was to have conveyed him to the madhouse incarcerated instead of himself."

"Well, that's a good 'un, and no mistake! Too great a gooseberry for my swaller!"

"A fact, I assure you," said the clerk.

"It won't do, Mr. Yapp. How could sich a thing have happened?"

"It did happen, for I read it," said the clerk.

"But you are not so green as to believe all you read? Why, I read the other day that there was once a new-born hinfant so fat that it killed its nuss with a slap in the face. Ugh! ugh! Would yer believe that, Mr. Yapp?"

"Well, never mind the great gooseberries," said the clerk. "What about the money? Do you know, I rathah like the feel of these things, flimsy as they are."

"I should rayther think so," said Swift.

"And between me and you and the desk, just now they would be very useful to me."

"They are werry useful to me at all times," said Swift. "But we shall have plenty on 'em by-and-bye, I hope."

"Pray take these cords off, gentlemen! you don't know how they cut me!" exclaimed Tom.

"Let him wait a minute or two," said Swift to Mr. Yapp, "for I have a thought about him."

"In a minute, boy!" sang out the clerk.

"How much is the cheque for?" inquired Swift.

"Fifteen pounds. But it won't be safe to touch that, for we must get it cashed."

"Oh, we must have all! In for a penny, in for a pound, you know, Yapp. It'll be safe enough. All's fish that comes to my net, and I want to make a good haul while I've the hopportoonity."

"What large ideas you have, Swift!"

"Yes, there's nothink small about me, I don't think—hic-cup. Thirty pounds—let's see—that'll be fifteen pounds a-piece, or I can't reckon."

"Yes; but look here, Swift," said Mr. Yapp; "let me have the whole of this, and you shall have fifteen pounds more out of the—the—"

"Go on—there needn't be any more delicacy between us. Out of the what?"

"Lady Blaze's jewels," said the clerk.

"Oh dear no!" said Swift "—hic-cup—I learnt at school—hic-cup—that a bird in the hand is worth two in the tree. So I shan't do no sich a thing. Honour amongst thieves."

Mr. Yapp sighed at the word, and for the moment bent his head on his hand on the desk.

"Oh, you don't like things called by their right names! Ugh! ugh! Well, then—honour among gentlemen!—hic-cup."

"Then you won't oblige me in this matter?" said the clerk.

"Can't, nor shan't," said Swift.

"I'll tell you something that you never knew before," said the clerk.

"Something to the good, I hope," cried Swift.

"I don't know that you would care to know it—for there is no robbery in it, past, present, or future—it is a little affair of a marriage."

"They are not little affairs, Mr. Yapp. I deny it in to-to—hic-cup—in total. A woman will spend your money like a brick, and throw a chainey plate at your head when it's all gone—hic-cup."

"They are rare spendthrifts, I must allow, Mr. Swift. And when once they find out a fellah's love for them, what tyrants they are, eh?"

"Orful!" exclaimed Swift, holding up one of the bank notes to the light. "I call that the prettiest sight in natur', Mr. Yapp. I think they might be easily himitated, though."

"Why your mind is full of robbery, Swift, while mine is full of perplexity!"

"I want to do something great, and live in 'ist'ry, like Turpin and Jack Sheppard, or Robson and Redpath; and had I got half your edication I would do it, too, for I've plenty of pluck and invention. If I could but write and figure like you, and had your gentlemanly appearance, I would get into a bank."

"We have quite difficulties enough to get through in those we have already undertaken. I have a presentiment—"

"What's that?" said Swift, frowningly.

"This—something tells me we shall be found out, even before we have reaped the fruits of our villainy."

"Draw it mild, old feller! A heart like yours had no right to go into the wholesale trade. Petty cash is your style. Why, yer fool! you could as well have been transported—"

The wretched Yapp shrugged his shoulders, and sighed.

"Lord! you want so much incouragement, you do! But there, I can't be always tryin' to make a man of yer. Be a baby, if yer likes, but I decline to be yer nuss! A reg'lar cat, you are—you likes the fish, but you won't wet yer paws for it. You can't keep women—"

"Women!" exclaimed the clerk. "I'm married, Swift. I'm married to a woman that I love. Got children, too, that I love."

"Lord! married, eh?" exclaimed Swift. "And some little Yapplings, did yer say?"

"Yes, two children, Swift—a pretty boy and girl."

"Lord! I should unkimmingly like to see 'em."

"Innocent of all this!" exclaimed the clerk, waving his white hands over the five-pound notes and cheque. "God! what will they do when I'm disgraced and manacled? Let us be honest, Swift! and direct our talents to fairer fields!"

"Ugh! the fairer fields are too green for me. I've no ingenooity to work in 'em. The jewels for me, and then I step it. You should do the same, and take the little Yapplings with yer, if yer loves 'em so much. I shall be glad to get rid of my lot."

"Mine are too much here," said the clerk, touching his heaving heart.

"Lord! if you are nabbed, Mr. Yapp, you'll soon get a ticket of leave, you will, for the chaplain will like your feelings about the heart and all that stuff!"

While the villain spoke a streak of hell seemed, to Mr. Yapp, to pass over his countenance.

The down-hearted clerk had worked with this man Swift for several years, and he always found him quiet, civil, regular in business habits, and as for his honesty, Mr. Yapp, who had every now and then some misgiving as to the righteousness of his own conduct, often wished he had Mr. Swift's integrity. While now he stood before the clerk the greatest villain of the two—nay, the greatest villain in existence—ripe for any rascality, and pooh-poohing at remorse.

"Do, gentlemen, unbind the cords!" exclaimed Tom. "I shall die if you don't!"

"Die and be d——d!" exclaimed the morose, merciless warehouseman.

"Ha! the boy—what are your designs with him, Swift? He shall be bound no longer. I had forgotten him," said the more humane clerk.

"Don't be so fast, Mr. Yapp," said Swift, restraining him.

"Hands off, Swift!" exclaimed the clerk. "I *will* release the boy."

"Hear what I have to say first." Then he whispered in the ear of the clerk—and then the clerk looked at him, and said—

"No, don't drag the poor boy in the mire."

"Anythink to save ourselves, I say. I must take the lead in this matter, or too many cooks will spile the broth. While we undo the cords I will slip a fiver in the boy's pocket—it will damn him and save us. Don't be a fool and show it, as you once said to me. You chop and change about too much, Mr. Yapp. You are a thief, and you're wincing because I want to make a respectable thief of yer. Now come," he said, taking a five-pound note in his hand, and folding it up in the smallest compass. "You can cut the cords of the boy while I plant this in his pocket."

"How will that implicate or injure the boy?"

"Why lookee here! When he goes home to-night, we will send a peeler arter him, and he will find the note upon him. What can be nicer planned?"

"For us or the boy?" inquired the clerk ironically.

"Pish! what is the boy to us? Besides, I owe him a grudge for taking my boy's place. Another thing, he's what you call a moral boy—and moral boys are tell-tale boys—and tell-tale boys wont do in this place."

"And so you would sacrifice him?"

"Him or *you*, whichever you like, Mister Straightlaced," returned Swift, gruffly. "You heerd the boy imperently say that he should tell the truth if he was asked—and the truth would be in his hevidence that he found us—I and you, Mr. Yapp—boozing at the Lion. That fact, if there was any suspicion agin us, would damn us. Don't you see? Do be reasonable, Mr. Yapp! It is all for you that I'm thinking on."

"Then your object is to destroy the boy's character, and so destroy the weight of his evidence?"

"Aye, to be sure, somethink of that sort. I want this thing to rest between the man and the boy—don't care which."

Messrs. Yapp and Swift approached the boy, and while the former commenced cutting the cords which bound the boy's legs, the latter got fumbling about Tom's hands, and while he appeared to be industriously undoing the knots he, unobserved, slipped the five-pound note in Tom's waistcoat pocket. Had the boy put his hand into his pocket he would not have felt it, so small had Swift done up the flimsy paper,—yet important enough to make the innocent boy, to appearances, a thief!

When Tom Brown was released of the cords the madman had bound him with he could not move hand or foot, so benumbed were they, and he continued on his back and burst into a flood of tears.

So tightly had he been tied that the flesh in several places was cut through and through, and the blood could not circulate to his hands or feet. There he remained, his hands outstretched and pressed close together, as if in prayer, and his feet also pressed close together. After the impediment to the circulation of his blood to his extremities was removed, the flesh swelled up about his wrists and ankles, and as the blood returned to the places it had been so long excluded from the pain was most excruciating, and the poor boy piteously writhed under it; it was that pricking sensation commonly known as "pins and needles."

At length Tom could move himself, and in a little time he had power to get off the sacks, but when he got to the ground he was so weak that he could not stand, and held to the sacks for support.

"What can we do for you, boy?" inquired the clerk; but while he did so he felt himself a Judas. Judas! at that moment the double-dealing clerk felt that, compared to himself, Judas was an honest man.

"If I could but walk," said Tom, "I should like to go home. I feel so faint and ill."

"I told yer when you came that this ere place would be the death of yer," said Swift.

"Rest awhile," said the clerk; "you will be bettah presently. Have you had any dinner?"

"No, sir; but I don't care about that. I want to go home."

"And so you shall when you are able," said Mr. Yapp. "Sit down by the fire, and recover. Will you have anything to eat or drink?"

"No, sir, thank you," said Tom. "I feel lost and frightened, and in such dreadful pain in my wrists and ankles."

"But considah, boy, you might have been murdered. Sit down—there," placing Tom in an old wooden chair by the fire, which had been so long unattended to that it had nearly burnt out.

While Mr. Yapp was engaged with the boy, Swift went to the desk, and took possession of the remaining two bank notes and the cheque.

"I wish I had never come to the place," said Tom.

"You will wish so still more yet," thought the clerk, ashamed of the villainy he had participated in.

"I have been very cruelly served," said Tom, "and I don't know what for."

"It is all accidental," said Mr. Yapp. "A thing that wouldn't occur again in a thousand years."

"It wasn't accidental that Mr. Swift struck me over the head; nor was it accidental for all of you to leave me so long bound with the cords when I cried out that they were hurting me."

"The truth is, that in the confusion of affairs you were forgotten," said Mr. Yapp.

"I shall be glad to get home," said Tom, "and I'll take care I don't come back again. My mother will go to a magistrate."

"A magistrate!" thought the clerk. "That will be *my* doom before long."

"One word with yer, if you please, Mr. Yapp," bellowed Swift from the counting-house.

The clerk attended the summons, though hating the voice that called him.

"Better ask the boy about the money," said Swift, in low tones. "How you stare! You don't like, I suppose? Haven't nerve enough, eh?"

"You are demned insolent, Swift!" exclaimed the clerk.

"Hinsolent!" reiterated Swift, stamping his

foot, "that kind of thing would have done yesterday, but it won't do now. You're not my master now. We are equals. Nolledge is power—hic-cup. You have often made sport of me, gentleman Yapp—laughed at my ugly hands—made mock of my yellow-glandered face—hic-cup—told me that the length of my feet proved I was a hidiot—and the length of my ears a hass! Ugh! ugh!—hic-cup—you're a thief, and so am I. Where's the difference?"

"I'll throw the game up!" exclaimed the clerk, in great passion. "Do your worst, you ugly snake! Return that money belonging to this letter!"

"I'll see you d——d first, and then I won't do it," said Swift, coolly. "You're too great a coward to betray me. Your guilt is in your books, which you can't rub out—mine is in this ring, which I can return; and snap my fingers at yer!" suiting the action to the word, and loudly smacking his finger and thumb.

"I'll blow the whole thing, and fix you on the spot—you devil! I'll go to Lady Blaze—"

He was about to go towards the door, but Swift held him tightly by the wrist.

"Would yer?" he cried, with staring eyes of fire. "Remember your young 'uns, and the woman you loves!"

This stern appeal to the clerk's affections melted his determination, and he again became as wax in the hands of the hardened criminal.

"You hit me there, Swift!" he exclaimed. "They must not know my disgrace."

"Nor shall they if you don't be a cur," returned Swift. "Now let me ask the boy a few questions."

"Get the little fellah something to eat—he can have had nothing to-day. And when he gets to prison—"

"He'll have more to eat than he gets outside," interrupted Swift, with hiccups and laughter.

"But he shall have some grub if he will tell us who took the money from the letter."

"I told you before," said Tom, in great pain, "that the ferocious man, who tied me down with cords, opened the letter."

"I know that," said Swift; "but who took the money?"

"No one that I know of," replied the boy, evidently deeply offended with the man who questioned him. "I saw the money on the desk at one time."

"Do you know what money there was?" inquired Mr. Yapp.

"No, sir, I do not. I saw one or two bank notes; but I could not say for what amounts they were."

"And you are quite sure that you did not see Mr. Bonthron, the madman who bound you, take the money?" asked the clerk.

"Quite, sir," said Tom, moving to and fro the chair in pain.

"Get him a glass of wine, Swift, and a biscuit," said Mr. Yapp to the porter, who stood by with folded arms, his ugly eyes full set on the boy, but not in pity.

"Do not get anything for me, sir," said Tom; "I shall be better directly, and then I must go home."

It was just four o'clock, and the postman brought in another letter, saying there was "tuppence to pay" on the letter he had left in the morning, and seeing Tom writhing in the chair, exclaimed—

"Holloa! what's up?"

"Lord," replied Swift, standing like a master

before the fire; "haven't you heerd the noose? And you a postman, too! Ugh!"

"It's funny that I, who bring and carry news, don't know the news," said the man of letters. 'The cobbler's wife always goes worst shod,' you know, Swift. Tuppence to pay, Mr. Yapp. Got a pinch of snuff handy, Swift?"

"Ah, snuff; that's a thing you're always up to," said Swift, grinning at his own joke. But Joe Miller himself would have failed just now to raise the vestige of a smile upon the melancholy face of the clerk.

"What's the matter with you, my little man?" said the postman.

"I'm in pain, sir," said Tom; and Swift satisfied the curiosity of the postman by telling him all the tale of Tom's woes, making very light of them, and ending with the consolation—

"That I told him this ere place would be the death of him."

"It is you, and not the place," said Tom, with passion and indignation.

"Oh, you little willain! I've released you for somethink," said Swift.

"Mr. Yapp released me," said Tom; "I might have died for what you cared."

"No hinsolence, I tell yer," said Swift; "you are only a herrand boy, and shouldn't be himperent to your sooperiors."

"Don't lose your temper, Swift," said the postman. "The boy is in pain, and his wrists are bleeding."

"So are my ankles, too," said Tom; "I can feel it trickling down inside my stockings."

"He's a fayning half—hic-cup."

"No, he's not," said the postman. "There's no mistake about it."

"The boy has been hurt, no doubt," said Mr. Yapp. "A glass of wine would do him immense good, if you will fetch it, Swift."

The porter, glad of another opportunity to visit the "Lion," and after having a little drop at the bar for himself, returned with half a quartern of port, saying to himself, with delight—

"Ha! when the peeler nabs him by St. Pride's Church, and draws forth that little dokiment from his vestcut, he'll want more port."

When Swift tendered the wine to the boy, he declined to take it, and offendedly said—

"I want nothing from you."

The postman and Mr. Yapp pressed him, and at length from the hands of the latter he took a little of it.

"Let him go to the chemist's below and have his wounds dressed," said the postman.

"He shall go home directly he has recovered a little," said Mr. Yapp. "By-the-bye, there will be a terrible row about that letter you brought."

"Ah, how so?" said the postman.

"Why, it contained a remittance of thirty pounds; and when I came in I found the letter opened and the money gone."

"It rests between the madman and the boy," said Swift.

"Who opened the letter?" inquired the postman.

"Why, Mr. Bonthron—at least, the boy says so," said Swift, equivocally.

"And so he did," said Tom.

"It's no joke," said the postman; "somebody's got the money."

"There's no mistake about that," said Swift.

"The worst of it is," said the postman, "that until the thief is found, suspicion rests upon all of you."

TOM BROWN DREAMS THAT HE SEES THE SPIRIT OF HIS FATHER.

"That's what I feel," said Swift. "A feller's character may be gone in no time; and a poor man has nothing but his character to look to."

"I shall lose mine, if I stop any longer," said the postman.

"You've a rare swag to deliver," said Swift.

"Yes; the Australian mail came in this afternoon." And the postman here made his exit.

"Well, I ought to take them ere rags to the wharf; but I shan't," said Swift. "I'm getting cold and hungry, and I'm rather glad its got to tea-time — and I likes tea-time, because its near shutting-up time. As soon as that ere kittle biles I shall make our tea, Mr. Yapp."

"As you like, Swift; but I don't care much about it," said the disconsolate clerk, who sat apart on his office stool, leaning his head against his fur great-coat, which hung against the wall.

Tom Brown rose to go home, and he limped towards Mr. Yapp and told him he thought now that he could manage to walk. At once Swift made preparations to follow him.

"The place wont suit me, sir," said Tom, "and I don't think my mother will allow me to come again. Good-bye, sir."

"Good-bye, boy," responded Mr. Yapp. "Sorry you haven't had a bettah time of it. You may always refer here for a charactah."

"Thank you, sir."

Tom's ill-fate was fast now being sealed. As the boy left the warehouse, limping and slowly, Swift, ready and alive to every kind of villainy, just whispered a word in Yapp's ear, and then the coward was in the court keeping his poor little victim well in sight.

The night was still cold and slushy, and the poor boy limped onwards towards his home and his mother as well as the crowded streets and his painful limbs would let him. We know not why, for it was certainly out of his way to do so, when he got half way down Fleet Street he crossed to the right.

He was downhearted and wretched; he had had enough to make him so. He had been insulted and buffeted with blows; he had been bound hand and foot for two hours by a madman, and the cords had cut his tender flesh; he was cold, hungry, and penniless; he could hardly walk, and yet he was nearly two miles from his mother and his home.

Worse than all, there was a devil at his heels to accuse him of embezzlement, and to give him over to the law.

Before St. Bride's Church in Fleet Street there is a wide, open, well-paved passage, with the redoubtable "Punch" office at one corner. The clock in the church steeple was illuminated, and the poor boy paused in the passage to gaze upwards to the time.

At this moment the hand of Mr. Pouncewell, the detective, took Tom by the arm and asked him if his name was Brown.

The boy, of course, was much startled and surprised to be accosted thus abruptly by a stranger; but he promptly acknowledged to the name of Brown.

"And arn't you an errand boy at Messrs. Bonthron and Son's?" inquired the detective.

"Yes, sir," said Tom; "but I have been so badly treated there that I don't intend to go any more."

Here, to Tom's horror, Swift stepped up before the boy, and said to the detective—

"That ere boy's the boy that had charge of the letter containing the money—hic-cup!"

Tom had a glimmer that he was about to be accused of theft, and he could have fainted. A crowd was just now gathered around the three —the accused and the accusers—and a policeman, as was his duty, stopped and watched the proceedings.

"Now, my little man," said Pouncewell, "what about the letter and the money?"

"I know nothing of either," said the bewildered boy.

"Sure you haven't got not none of the money about yer?" asked the coward Swift.

"Search me, if you like," said Tom, gazing up in the roguish-looking face of the drunken warehouseman.

"He *must* have the money," said Swift. "Search him, hofficer."

"Feel in your pockets, boy," said the detective. "I daresay you will find something."

"I have nothing in my pockets but a knife and a handkerchief," said Tom. "I'm not a thief. Let go my arm, sir," he added, heroically, feeling his innocence.

The crowd inconveniently increased, and Tom's heart beat quickly, and he began to feel faint and oppressed with shame that such an unwarrantable suspicion should rest upon him.

Swift shuffled round to the detective's ear, and then, nudging him with his elbow, softly said—"Search him."

"You have nothing but a knife and handkerchief in your pockets, eh?" said the well-dressed city officer.

"I have nothing else," said Tom, confidently.

"Turn out your pockets," said the officer, "and convince this gentleman"—(pointing to Mr. Swift, who was very proud at the title Mr. Pouncewell had given him)—"that you have not got your master's money."

"It is far more likely that he has it than me!" said Tom, passionately.

"You little thief, what d'yer mean by that?" said Swift, all rage and affected indignation, "Hofficer, do yer dooty!"

"Now, my little man, out with your pockets, and save me the trouble of doing it for you," said the detective.

"You had better take him across the road to the station-house," said Littlewood, the policeman on duty.

"I wont go to the station, for I'm not a thief," said the poor oppressed boy.

A stranger in the crowd advised Tom to turn out his pockets and prove his honesty.

Tom commenced with the side-pocket of his trousers, from which nothing appeared but the handkerchief and knife that he mentioned. The jacket pocket was next attacked, but nothing was found there.

Swift looked eagerly now for the ransacking of the two little waistcoat pockets. Tom placed his finger and thumb in each, and turned them inside out. The small but fatal paper fell to the ground—so small that no one but the guilty Swift noticed it.

"Holloa!" he exclaimed, "what's this?" stooping and picking up the well-folded banknote, which he handed to the detective.

The officer unfolded the paper, and with a self-sufficient smile, which seemed to express the language of the young man from the country, "you can't get over me," said—

"How innocent we are, to be sure! Now, boy, what do you say to this?" holding up the bank-note before his eyes.

Tom's surprise was very great, and the evidence was so strong against him that for a moment he believed himself guilty, and faintly ejaculated—"I know nothing of it."

"Don't tell a lie, boy," said the officer, admonishingly, and the prisoner said nothing more.

A stupor seized Tom, and he was almost carried along between the detective and policeman to the adjacent station, which could be seen from the passage where the foregone scene took place.

"You must come with us, Mr. Swift, and make the charge," said the detective.

"That I shall—hic-cup—do with pleasure," said the half-drunken man, following behind the little prisoner with his hands thrust in his pockets. A great crowd also followed to the narrow entrance to the station-house, exclaiming to each other—

"What a little dodger!"

"What an artful boy!"

"What a little liar!"

"Highly respectable-looking, too!"

"And don't he pretend well!"

"Don't he faint well!"

"Didn't he stare when the note was shown him!"

"How small the young beggar had folded it!"

"How artful, too, to let it fall on the ground!"

These and similar exclamations were made amongst the crowd through which the poor victim passed to his gaol; but Tom's senses were in that apathetic state that they passed by him as the "idle wind," and he was led as a "lamb to the slaughter."

CHAPTER IX.

TOM BROWN AT THE STATION-HOUSE—THE FACETIOUS INSPECTOR.

WHO shall describe the poor youth's sensations, when he found himself within the sombre walls of a station-house, surrounded by policemen, detectives, and a devil in human form, ready to accuse him of stealing a five-pound note?

Never did so much innocence stand at the rail before the inspector as when Tom Brown stood there charged with being a thief.

Tom was a delicate-looking but handsome boy, with all the characteristics, except his clothes, of being a young gentleman. He had a remarkably fine head, with beautiful light, silky hair, dark-blue eyes, the whitest of well-shaped teeth, and a highly intelligent countenance; a lithe, tall, and genteel figure, with hands fair, and faultless shape. The moral attributes as exhibited in the formation of the head were very large; while the intellectual would have attracted the attention of any phrenologist.

"Holloa! holloa! what's the matter here?" exclaimed the tall, sallow-faced inspector as Pouncewell, the detective, and Littlewood, the policeman, with the light-haired prisoner between them, and the villain Swift in the rear entered the large charge-room of the Fleet Street station-house.

"Now, Mr. Swift, step forward, and state to our inspector what you charge the prisoner with," said the detective.

Swift pulled off his hat and shambled to the rail, which in his present state of "beer" was very convenient for him to hold on by, and then he unblushingly said—

"I charge this ere boy with robbing our gov'ner."

"Please to say who is your governor, and what amount the prisoner has robbed him off," said the inspector.

"Our gov'ner is Messrs. Bonthron and Son," replied Swift.

"What are they?" said the inspector, writing down Swift's replies.

"Rag merchants."

"Where do they live?"

"In a court just yonder," said Swift.

"But the court has a name?"

"Oh yes, Bolt Court."

"From which the boy bolted, eh?" said the facetious inspector, and all but the poor little prisoner, who looked from one to the other with wistful eye, laughed outright.

"How much has he robbed Bonthron and Son of?" inquired the supreme official.

"I should say thirty pounds," said Swift.

"But don't you know?"

"Well, sir, we miss three five-pound notes, and a cheque of fifteen pounds," was the reply.

"And how do you know the prisoner is the person who has got it?"

"'Cause you see, sir, we have found a fiver on him," said Swift.

"A fiver! what's that?"

"A five-pound note," said Littlewood.

"I know that, so you needn't interrupt me," said the inspector; "but we cannot take charges given in slang language. The Lord Mayor wouldn't, and why should I?"

"I should have said, sir, a five-pound note," said Swift.

"Then you can only charge him with stealing what you found on him," said the inspector; "the other is presumptive, and that is a thing we cannot deal with, except you can swear and prove to us that he stole it."

"Then I should say he should be charged with stealing the five-pound note," said Pouncewell.

"You have no right to dictate to the accuser what the prisoner should be charged with. It is an illegal proceeding," said the inspector. "The case would entirely fall through, and I should be called over the coals—"

"Pray, sir, what is that? hic-cup!" said Swift.

"What is what, Sir?" inquired the inspector, staring at Swift.

"Called over the coals," said Swift.

"You don't know, I suppose," said the inspector.

"Oh, I know well enough," said Swift, "just as well as you did what a fiver was. Only you said I wasn't to use slang."

Pouncewell and Littlewood took a sly glance at each other, glad that their pompous inspector had "one on his tibby," as they said when they had the opportunity.

"I did say you wasn't to use slang," said the inspector, offendedly. "What would the worthy magistrate say to me if I had entered upon this charge-book"—slapping the large open book before him—"what would he say to me if this boy had been charged with stealing a fiver? I should be expelled the force."

"Hic-cup!" said the ironical Swift, "now I see the difference; you may speak slang to me, but I mustn't to you."

"Exactly," said the inspector, "and for this reason—"

"That what the accuser says is entered in the charge-book," said Pouncewell.

"That's just what I was going to say—so you needn't interrupt me," said the inspector. "You must please to know, Sir," he continued to Swift, "that you are here on a very serious errand; that boy's character rests upon your charge."

"I hope, Sir," said Tom dreamily, "that it does not rest upon what this man says."

"No, boy, not upon what he says but what he proves," said the inspector. "A jury must decide guilty or not guilty."

"I am not guilty, Sir!" said Tom, his spirit rising to the demands of the cruel occasion.

"I am not your judge, nor your accuser," said the inspector; "but I must say that it looks like guilt, or there must have been unheard of villainy at work to make the innocence you assert so deceptive. Can you account in any way for the other money, Mr. Swift?"

"Not in the least, Sir," was the man's reply, "unless the madman—"

"Which is young Bonthron," said Littlewood, the policeman.

"And who was brought to the station this day," said the inspector.

"Yes," said Swift, "unless he has got it, of course I can't say who has; but I has my suspicions, and I daresay they are a good deal like your own."

"You would say that the prisoner had the whole?" said the inspector.

"I should, Sir—hic-cup!" said Swift.

"Then what has he done with it? for he was not off the premises after you came in," said the inspector.

"Oh, he's a cunning, artful boy," said Swift. "It's my opinion that he has planted it somewhere on the premises, and that he was going to take this note home first, and the other the next hopportunity."

"Were you the first to discover that the money was gone?" demanded the inspector.

"No, Sir, our Mr. Yapp was," said Swift.

"And why isn't our Mr. Yapp here?" inquired the precise official.

"We didn't see any occasion for more than one on us—hic-cup—and it was more conwenient for me to come—hic-cup."

"Not convenient! In a case like this we cannot consult the convenience of people. What is Mr. Yapp?"

"Mr. Yapp is our clerk and cashier," said Swift.

"Then he is your superior?" said the inspector.

"Sooperior—hic-cup—well, I don't know that any man is *my* sooperior," said Swift.

"I mean that he holds a superior office at Messrs. Bonthron and Son's?"

"That is another thing—you are quite right there; but I know which has had to do the most work," said Swift.

"That is not to the point," said the inspector. "You have been drinking, my man, haven't you?"

"I don't deny to a little—hic-cup—" said Swift; "but it is the hexcitement of this 'ere case that confooses me more than the beer."

"Is Mr. Yapp at Bolt-court?"

"No, he is not," said the lying Swift.

"He was when I came out," said Tom, "for he said he would give me a character."

"That was before he found you was a thief," said Swift.

Poor Tom was so overborne that he only said—

"I wish, Sir, that you would send for Mr. Yapp; he might speak the truth, which is more than this man is doing."

"I think, Mr. Inspector," said Swift, "that you ought not to allow me to be bullied by the prisoner."

"You commenced first by calling him a thief," said the inspector.

"And ain't he a thief?" demanded Swift.

"Only on suspicion—not proven."

"Why, you seem to be taking part with the prisoner," said Swift.

"Fair play—"

"Is a jewel," said Pouncewell, completing the inspector's sentence.

"That's just what I was going to say—so you needn't interrupt me," said the indignant inspector, using his favourite pompous phrase.

Pouncewell and Littlewood, who knew their superior's weakness for this sentence, again smiled at each other.

"All this is not business," said the inspector; and then to Swift, the accuser, he said—

"I yet cannot understand why Mr. Yapp, the superior person in Bonthron and Son's establishment, should depute you to make the charge, especially as he was the first to discover that the money had been stolen from the letter."

"I don't see, Mr. Inspector, why you should want to see our Mr. Yapp. I should have thought one person was quite enough to make a charge of robbery."

"Don't you dictate to me, Sir," said the inspector. "One person is *not* enough if two would be better. It appears to me you have nothing at all to do with it—"

"Nothing at all—not in the least—hic-cup!" said Swift.

"And, pray, where is Bonthron and Son?"

"The son is in a madhouse, as you know, and the father is laid up with the gout," replied Swift.

"I remember—to be sure—the son was brought here this afternoon. And, pray, is the prisoner the boy that he tied down with the ropes?"

"Yes, Sir," said Tom. "Look at the marks," extending his two wrists; "and my ankles are cut worse."

"A very mysterious piece of business," said the inspector.

"I don't see no mystery about it. The note is found on him," said Swift.

"Good; but who put the note in his pocket?"

This pertinent interrogation of Mister Inspector's made Swift stare, but he had the art to hide his guilt.

"Where is the doubt?" said Swift.

"In law there is a doubt upon all charges, civil and criminal, until they are proved," replied the inspector.

"Why, I'd hang a man on sich proof as there is agin this 'ere boy," said Swift. "What do you say, Pouncewell?"

"It is well for society that you are powerless to hang or to convict, if those are your sentiments. I say, although the note is found on the prisoner, it is only circumstantial evidence, and it is no proof that he put the money in his pocket."

"Who did, then?" said Swift, in the most insolent manner.

"There is the point," said the inspector. "The madman may have placed it there for what I or you know."

"Ugh! ugh!—hic-cup!—not likely, I should think," said Swift, folding his arms, and looking round for applause.

"That may be," said the inspector, "but it is my duty to sift the evidence, and see that the preliminaries of the charge are made as complete as possible."

"May I sit down, Sir?" said Tom. "I feel so weak and ill, and my legs do hurt me so."

"Let him sit there, Littlewood," said the inspector, pointing to a rough seat in the recess of the window.

Tom availed himself of the permission, and, in order that there might be no running away, Littlewood, the policeman, sat by his side.

Tom was still within the view of the inspector, who from his little open window made in the panels of a large partition he could see all over the room.

Tom Brown, when he had seated himself, threw back his head and went off in a stupor or trance. To those around he seemed only asleep or dozing, but, to use the technicalities of the mesmeriser, he was in a state of coma, and became invested with the gift of second sight or prescience.

Strange to say, while in this condition he thought his father had committed suicide, and that while he was in bed, and his mother kneeling beside him, the spirit of his father appeared to him, and warned him against the snares of gambling, intemperance, and dishonesty; and he dreamed that his father's spirit, clothed in white, spoke to him in those cloudy and mystic words:—

"I sought the waters—they opened themselves to receive me—they closed around me, and I was in another world. I am now a wandering, unhappy spirit. Beware, my child!—beware of the snares that led your father to his untimely end! Be honest, faithful, just."

Then Tom thought the spirit was about to touch him, which so alarmed him that he awoke only to find himself in a police station-house, surrounded by policemen. It took Mr. Littlewood by great surprise to see Tom suddenly spring to his feet and cry—

"Father!"

When he was asked for an explanation the boy related his dreadful dream, which, while it made a dismal impression upon him, made more upon those to whom he related it, and Mr. Swift exclaimed—

"He is a feigning, artful covey! That 'ere boy would deceive the devil! and he seems to have all the luck in the world! Now hactually that the money is found on him, Mr. Inspector believes him hinnocent!"

"Who told you so, Sir? Not me. Do you think I'm going to take a charge that any drunken fool might bring before me without investigation? You must please to behave yourself while you are before me, Sir, or I shall lock you up as well as the boy!"

These few words of Mister Inspector rather took the steam out of Mister Swift, and he ceased to be so garrulous and impertinent.

"Perhaps you don't want me any more?" said Swift.

"Yes we do. Look here, Pouncewell. This man tells me that Mr. Yapp first discovered the money to be wanting, and that Mr. Yapp stands as Bonthron and Son's representative; therefore, it is Mr. Yapp that should make the charge, and I will thank you to run up and fetch Mr. Yapp here."

"It's my opinion that you won't find him—it's long past his time for going home," said Swift.

"Go," said the inspector; "he must be found—or I cannot take the charge. Should he not be at the office, where does he live?"

"Don't know," said the surly Swift, not at all liking that the nervous Mr. Yapp should be sent for, as it was the warehouseman's impression he would make a mess of it, and "spile" all.

"Well, we won't anticipate difficulties," said the inspector; "if he is not at the office, return, Pouncewell, and we will then see what we can do with the case as it now stands with the evidence before me. I have not yet interrogated the boy at all—the note may be his own for what we know."

"No, sir, it is not mine," said Tom, frankly, just escaping from the clutches of his dreadful dream.

"Nor you don't know how it came in your pocket?"

"I do not, sir; but I suspect this man put it there, to make a thief of me."

"Mister Inspector, will you please to ask the young willain what hinterest I have got to make a thief of him?" said the exasperated Swift.

"Answer, boy," said the inspector.

"To damage my character, because I told him I would not tell a lie to screen him and Mr. Yapp from drinking at the Lion all the morning," said Tom.

"You are inwenting, now, and no mistake," said Swift. "I wonder you ain't struck dead, or the floor of this 'ere ground don't open and swaller yer!"

"Didn't you say that I might lie and be d——d, and that you wouldn't cut the cords that bound my hands and feet, because I would not promise to say you and Mr. Yapp were not at the Lion?"

"Go it—you can inwent, you can!" said Swift.

"Who released you, boy?" demanded the inspector.

"Both of them," said Tom.

"Who do you mean by both?"

"Mr. Yapp and Mr. Swift," replied Tom Brown. "But they kept me tied for more than an hour after they came in, while they were planning something, and quarrelling, and talking in the counting-house, where the letter was."

"You heard nothing what they said?"

"No, Sir."

"Which of the two undid your hands?"

"Mr. Swift, Sir. My hands were crossed just over my waistcoat pocket, and he could then as easily have slipped the note—"

"Ha! be careful, young 'un, what you say!" exclaimed Swift. "Don't you attempt to hinjure my character!"

"Let the boy speak," said the inspector.

"Are you his counsel?" demanded Swift.

"Don't you be so insolent, Sir," said the inspector. "Now, boy!"

"It is my opinion when Mr. Swift undid the cords he slipped the bank-note in my pocket," said Tom.

"Liar!" exclaimed Swift.

"But for what purpose, boy, do you think he did it?"

"That he and Mr. Yapp might have the other money, and I be made the thief," said Tom, with much shrewdness.

Mr. Swift looked unutterable things, then he exclaimed, with bent fist.

"I would strike you, if I wasn't in a court of justice!"

"The case now assumes a great importance and intricacy, and it is now necessary that Mr. Yapp should be present. Fetch him, Pouncewell."

CHAPTER X.

YAPP'S ATTEMPT AT INCENDIARISM — HIS INTERVIEW WITH THE DETECTIVE.

POUNCEWELL, the detective, was not long in making his way to Bonthron and Son's warehouse in Bolt-court. Fleet Street, amongst other things, is celebrated for its number of courts and narrow outlets, many of which are full of historic interest. The great Dr. Johnson and the intellectual wits and boozers he drew around him has invested the whole of the region of Fleet Street, especially its courts and taverns, with an imperishable fame. Before the very warehouse of the rag merchant in Bolt-court had Johnson and Oliver Goldsmith often promenaded.

Messrs. Bonthron and Son had a large and extensive business as rag merchants, which they exported and imported all over the globe, and fed most of the paper-mills throughout England. Mr. Bonthron was a most indefatigable tradesman, and one deeply respected by all who knew him. No one but the fierce, morose, and grumbling Swift ever spoke a word against him, and *he* was a man who had not a good word to say for any one.

Mr. Bonthron, although a shrewd man, was most unfortunate in the servants he had about him. Messrs. Yapp and Swift had had his confidence for several years, and in many secret ways they had abused it. The rag merchant was an attached man, and would almost pardon any fault rather than dismiss a servant, and surround himself with new faces. This amiable weakness was well known to those about him, and every mean advantage was taken of it.

For Mr. Yapp he had a sincere regard; he was clever at book-keeping—active in business—gentlemanly in appearance—regular in his hours—temperate—intelligent—and, as Mr. Bonthron believed, scrupulously honest. As a return for these characteristics which Mr. Bonthron invested his clerk with, the merchant paid liberally, and always showed towards him the best disposition.

All times the merchant left his warehouse with the most implicit belief in the strict integrity of his clerk; and whether it was business, illness, or pleasure that caused his absence from Bolt-court, he had no uneasiness in his mind as to Mr. Yapp's management or his honour.

Every now and then Mr. Yapp was his guest at Clapham, and at Christmas he always received a handsome present, and a good round holiday in summer. Mr. Bonthron knew nothing of his gay life, nor did he ever suspect that he was leading one.

At one time, indeed, and when his son's reason was overthrown, he had serious thoughts of giving Mr. Yapp a share in his business; and he would have done so had not Mrs. Bonthron been opposed to it.

The rag merchant thought his clever clerk to be as open as the day, and as upright as a quaker. Occasionally he thought Mr. Yapp over-dressed himself; but he soon dismissed this thought, accusing himself of impertinence for thinking anything about Mr. Yapp's private affairs. He knew also that his clerk indulged in cricket, rowing, and other manly exercises, and he thought better of him for it, for Mr. Bonthron was by no means a narrow-minded man, and was the first to encourage young men in the pursuit of healthy recreations.

What a blow it would have been to Mr. Bonthron had he known that he was egregiously deceived in every virtue that he had ascribed to his clerk! Had he known that he was secretly married! that he had been robbing him and falsifying his books! that he had become a liar to cover his embezzlements, and an embezzler to give truth to his lies!

Worse than all, if possible, what would the good old gentleman have said could he have found him, as Pouncewell now did, with candle and lucifers lighting rags and paper in order to fire the premises!

Never did criminal start as Mr. Yapp started when Mr. Pouncewell tapped at the warehouse door, which the clerk had taken the precaution

to lock while he carried on his devilry within. With the lighted candle in his trembling hand, and a kindling fire at his feet, he stared at the door.

"Is that you, Swift?" he asked, after he had recovered his alarm, and to the best of his ability clearing out of the way the damning evidences of his guilty doings, and trampling on the fire he had just kindled on the ground by the sacks.

"I want Mr. Yapp," said Pouncewell.

"What for?—he's gone!—who are you?" he confusedly said.

"I have called from the police-station—"

The clerk's breath for the moment forsook him, and he reeled against the sacks he had been trying to inflame. There was such a terror to the nervous man in the words "Police-station," that he scarcely heard the remainder of Pouncewell's sentence, which was to the effect that he was wanted there by the inspector in the case of Tom Brown the Errand Boy.

"In one instant I am dressing—dressing myself," said the bewildered clerk.

The last spark on the floor extinguished by his boot, Mr. Yapp, fully dressed in his fur coat, with his silver-headed cane in his well-gloved hand, and his hat on his head, turned back the lock and admitted the soft-speaking Mr. Pouncewell, who was also well arrayed in a tight-fitting brown top-coat.

"Sorry, Sir, to have kept you waiting," said Mr. Yapp. "I am now quite at your service."

"Pray who am I speaking to?"

"Mr. Yapp," said the clerk with a slight bow.

"Oh, I'm glad of that; I thought I understood you to say that Mr. Yapp had left," said the officer.

The clerk, in truth, had forgotten what he did say, and he exclaimed with all the ease and nonchalance he was then capable of—

"How curious! The fact is I was dressing, and I was terribly confused when you knocked, and don't know what I said, for I was afraid it might be a call from a lady, and the state of my toilette would not permit me to see her."

The officer slightly bowed his head in assent to what the clerk stated, although it must be said he was not altogether satisfied with Mr. Yapp's manner or explanation. He found him too completely dressed for him to believe that he had been engaged in the manner he said.

Shrewd man was Pouncewell; but shrewdness and suspicion is the detective's stock-in-trade, and he would be but a poor police official who did not keenly cultivate sharpness of eye and intellect.

Pouncewell was quick to notice, as we have before said, the *complete* manner in which the clerk was attired; every button buttoned; each hand had on its glove; the hat too was on the head. To the detective's mind these things would not have been had the clerk *only* been dressing himself. He would not have waited for such scrupulous arrangement of his clothes had he been merely dressing. Such the detective thought, and such was the fact.

The rags and paper ignited by the clerk still smouldered; at all events, to the detective's olfactory nerves there was a smell of burning permeating through the warehouse, and he casually remarked upon it—

"What a smell of burning," he said.

"Do you think so?" rejoined the clerk, sniffing through his nose. "Don't perceive it."

"Very strong, I think," said the officer, testing his observation also by a sniff or two. "Why, there's smoke now by that sack."

"Demn the things!" exclaimed Yapp, stamping his foot on a small heap of rags. "It is lucky you came in, or it might have been serious. I just pitched an end of a cigar there amongst the rags. Demned stupid of me."

"Dangerous at least," said Pouncewell.

"I always light up my cigar when I leave, and never did such a thing occur before. I think it is all safe now."

Pouncewell moved to the smouldering heap, and stamped upon it, saying—

"Rags smoulder and smother, but they wont burn. But that paper close by would soon cause a flare."

"By Jove!" exclaimed Yapp, "you are right old fellah! Never mind," he added with a pleasant smile, "we are well insured."

"But the neighbours may not be so fortunate," said the detective with a corresponding smile," "and we must consider lives as well as rags."

"Devilish good," said Yapp. "Although some lives are not so valuable as rags. What d'ye think that sack is worth?" he asked, endeavouring to divert the conversation from the fire.

"Well—let's see—sure I don't know. Not much I should say."

"Ah, but what is much?" said Yapp, most pleasantly.

"Well, the boys say much is much as again and a half," said Pouncewell, playing into the hands of the humorous clerk.

"Ha! ha! verah good," exclaimed Yapp. "I and you could make a very agreeable evening over a glass of grog."

"That would depend upon who paid for it," said the officer.

"Good again," said the clerk. "What oceans of life you must see to make you so ready-witted. Ha! ha!"

"The life I see is not of a laughing kind," said the detective.

"Criminal—eh?—all criminal life?—eh?" remarked the clerk, unbuttoning and buttoning his fur coat.

"Mostly. Sometimes there is a little comedy with it; but it is generally amongst crime and criminals. Robbery—robbery—few people are honest."

"Demn it—you surprise me. The country is now in a healthy commercial condition, too—not much poverty abroad."

"Oh—yes—but crimes are not so much the offspring of want as extravagance," said the detective.

Extravagance! this one word comprehended the whole of the clerk's mistaken career. He knew it, and felt it—and he thought with bitterness of the wife he loved so passionately. She was extravagant—and he was foolish enough to embezzle for her folly. The remark of the detective wss unintentional—but it was a hit, and a hard hit for all that.

"And extravagance, or in other words living beyond the means—or to be more homely, not cutting the garment according to the cloth—you considah to be the mainspring of all crime?"

"Not all, certainly not," said the detective.

"No, no, no—not all," quickly rejoined the clerk—"I don't mean all. Jealousy, for example, may lead to murder—which is crime you know."

"Rather," said the detective.

"And the shame of a seduced woman may lead to infanticide—"

"Which is also murder," said the detective.

"Aye, to be sure, so it is. Yes—exactly—I see what you mean—just so—that crime—that—"

"What I mean is this," said Pouncewell, "that crime in middle life generally springs from apeing our betters in society."

"I perfectly agree with you, old fellah," said Yapp.

"I have now to trace out two young men, on whom suspicion falls, who have been cutting it fat—"

"Indeed!" exclaimed the clerk, in tones of pity.

"Yes, living on the sly in good style on poor incomes. Furniture, wine, women, horses; and one poor aristocrat, or who wanted to be an aristocrat, positively had half a share in a yacht, and what d'ye think his salary was?"

"Five hundred a year," said the clerk.

"One third of it," exclaimed Pouncewell.

"The devil! you quite turn me round," said the clerk.

"No more," said Pouncewell. "A handsome young man, too, well educated and well connected. But he got spooney on a woman, and she led him into all kinds of gaiety and expense, and his governor for many years—"

"Paid the pipah," said Yapp, finishing Pouncewell's sentence.

"Very much like it," said the detective. "However, I was set on his heels, and my scent being pretty good, soon tracked him; and how do you think I took him?"

"Can't imagine."

"In the midst of making a speech at a champagne dinner with some of his old particulars."

"Gad! what a sell!" exclaimed the sympathising clerk.

"I was the unwelcome guest at that party."

"Yes, indeed! so I should think. How did you manage it? It's rathah interesting."

"Not to Winslow though."

"Was that his name? How long had he been carrying the game on?" asked the clerk.

"A very long time. He was cash-collector to a country brewer. I managed my errand as delicately as possible. First of all the servant denied him—"

"Of course," said the clerk.

"But I said that I must see him; that I came from Messrs. Netherby and Longstreet, his employers. The servant then showed me into a small but magnificently furnished parlour, and while I was surveying the apartment my gentleman came into the room. Such a swell! yet such a gentleman! Dinner costume from top to toe."

"Ha! I suppose so. Dear me," said Yapp.

"Handsome white waistcoat—dress coat and pantaloons of the most faultless fit. Hair well curled and dressed; and he held in his hand a white silk handkerchief; with a face radiant with wine and pleasure."

"Well, Sir," he said, "you are from Messrs. Netherly and Longstreet. What can I have the pleasure of doing for you?"

"What a scene!" exclaimed Yapp, most fully entering into the spirit of it.

"Really—for there is some feeling in a detective's heart—I knew not how to break my errand to him; and upon my soul, had it been consistent with my duty I would have retired, and allowed him to have had his day's pleasure out—he seemed so full of happiness."

"Poor devil!" exclaimed Yapp. "Take a cigah, officer," he added, offering Pouncewell his case, and jumping on a bench to hear the remainder of his story.

Detectives are not backward to a little smoking, and Pouncewell accepted the fragrant gift; but he did not light it, and held it in his hand for the delectation of a more favourable opportunity. But Mr. Yapp availed himself of the present moment, and lit up and puffed away seemingly in the most unconcerned manner.

"You have no objection, Sir," said the detective, "for me to light up by-and-bye? Our inspector would think none the better of me if I returned to our station smoking."

"Demn the inspectah!" exclaimed Yapp. "But do as you like old fellah! Every man knows his own business best." "We'll have a little drop on our way to the station, in spite of the inspectah?—eh, old fellah?" he merrily added, slapping Pouncewell jollily on the shoulder.

"As you please about that, Sir. But as I was going to say, this young sprig of a cash-collector was taken aback as they say in Yorkshire, when he began to understand the real purport of my errand."

"Poor devil!" again exclaimed Yapp, sincerely; for a "fellow-feeling makes us wondrous kind."

"Ah, indeed it did, sir," said the officer. "To a man with a heart, ours is rather a disagreeable duty. People think we are hardened, and hard-hearted."

"Bosh!" exclaimed the clerk. "There are some capital fellahs amongst detectives. Do you know Barrow in the B division?"

"Well; and a capital man he is."

"And a humorous one, too," said Yapp; "he and I have had many a glass together; I hope we may have many more yet, in company with yourself."

"I shall be most happy. Barrow sings a good comic song."

"And he can make a clever speech, and tell a capital story," said the clerk.

"That he can. Those rags smoulder now," added the detective.

"There—there—" said Yapp, jumping from the bench and stamping on them. "I say old fellah, how soon a place might take fiah without care. There has been a narrow escape here, certainly. Now finish your story and I must be off."

"Well," said Pouncewell, continuing his story of Messrs. Netherby and Longstreet's clerk, "he fenced a good deal with me at first, and when he just got an inkling of my visit, he made an excuse to leave the room. But that I couldn't allow, for I saw that he had the street-door and a bolt in view."

"How did you stop him?"

"Oh, I just said that my business was of such an important nature, that I regretted I could not excuse his absence a moment."

"'How.' Explain!'" he cried.

"I could keep him in suspense no longer, but drawing from my pocket a warrant for his apprehension, I said, there, sir, that will explain all!"

"By Jupitah!" exclaimed Yapp. "What a document for a fellah to read."

"He placed his glass to his eye," continued Pouncewell, "read a word or two, and in the coolest manner possible, said—"

"'Enough. I see. I am your prisoner. Call a cab, and take me where you please. I should like to say a word to a lady first!'"

"But I regret to remind you," I said, "that it must be in my presence, for you see you are my prisoner."

"'That I anticipated,'" he rejoined. 'Officer you will find me a sufficient gentleman not to give you the least trouble, or to infringe upon your duties.'

"Here he rang a bell, and a maid-servant entering, with a gold pencil he wrote a few words on a slip of paper, and bade the girl go to the drawing-room and slip it unperceived into the hands of her mistress.'

"Ha! what a missive for her!" exclaimed Mr. Yapp.

"Not a minute passed before a lovely creature, elegantly dressed, entered, and threw her braceleted arms around his neck. But one farewell passed between them—but oh! the looks of anguish and moistened eyes that I then saw haunted me for a long time after. I just heard him say to her in the passage as we made to the door—"

"'Convert all you have, clothes, jewellery, and furniture into money, and return to your mother. Lead a good life, and forget me!'"

"Touching, wasn't it officah?" exclaimed Yapp.

"I assure you it was a very touching scene, Sir; and you would have thought so more had you seen it. But stories, when they have to be told second-hand lose half their interest."

"Very true," said Yapp. "And what, after all, was the young fellah's fate?"

"Transported for fourteen years," said Pouncewell.

"Devilish hard," said the sympathising clerk.

At this moment a neatly-dressed servant-girl entered, and presented a letter and small parcel to the winter-wrapped clerk.

"Pardon me one moment, officah, while I just run over this."

The elegant scented note was from his wife, and ran thus:—

"DEAREST,—

"I have been admiring the darling lace shawl, you kindly gave me last night, all the day. But Mrs. Howard lunched here, and she thought it was hardly large enough for me. I know you won't think it too much trouble—will-you?—to take it back and change it. And should you, honey-bird, see a very nice blue dress, or any colour you would like best, to match the shawl, why you may buy it for me. I really *do* want one very much. Mrs. Howard had on such a rich thing, and looked, as you would say, quite charming. What a good fellow Howard must be.

"I send this by the girl, and hope she will be in time before you leave the office.

"Yours for ever and ever,
                    "MARIA YAPP."

"You can go, Emily," said the clerk to his domestic, "and just say that I got her note and parcel, and will attend to it. Now, then, officah, we had bettah go. It is very inconvenient to me, though. Demn the boy! And what an ass that Swift must be not to be able to do without me. The fellah talks too much, and to little purpose."

"It isn't Swift's fault; it is our cantankerous inspector. The case is complete enough. I took the note from the boy, and one of your people is there to give him in charge for stealing it. But our inspector goes into the case as if he were judge, jury, and counsel rolled into one. Hadn't Swift mentioned your name—"

"Which he needn't have done," said Yapp.

"Of course not; and if he hadn't, you would

TOM BROWN'S ASTONISHMENT AT RECOGNISING HIS FATHER IN THE HALF-DROWNED MAN.

not have been required at this stage of the proceedings."

"No way out of it, eh?" said Yapp, slipping a half-crown into the detective's not unwilling hand.

"You know you've no right to be here—it is after business hours," suggested the bribed detective.

"Good—I see; and it is true, too. I'm so much obliged to you!" exclaimed the clerk,

shaking the officer warmly by the hand. "How will the case be managed, then?"

"Why, the inspector must detain the boy on Swift's evidence; and proper and conclusive evidence, too. Lord! he's guilty enough."

"No doubt," said Yapp, yet not without some hesitation. "At all events, the money is gone; but then the madman might have taken it, or destroyed it."

"That would have been all very well; hadn't

the note been found on the boy, and, of course, the natural inference is that he has planted the other notes and cheque somewhere."

"There is the lettah that contained the money."

"Ha, just so; but there is one thing about the affair that is not clear to me."

"What is that?" inquired the clerk, with a changed countenance.

"How came you and Mr. Swift to suspect the boy after he had left the office?"

"Ha!" said Yapp to himself, "never thought of that; perhaps Swift has, though." Then he replied to the officer—

"Why, you see, some one must have the money, and it just occurred to us that possibly the boy might be the thief."

"Well, so it has turned out. You'll have to be at Guildhall to-morrow. No half-crowns will get you out of that."

"I suppose not, the devil take it!" said the clerk. "I wish now it had all been clapped on to the shoulders of Mr. Bonthron's mad son."

"Well, it would have been better for the boy," said Pouncewell, with a smile.

"And less trouble for all of us," said the clerk. "I hate the job. I shall have to see Mr. Bonthron, too, who, unfortunately, is laid up with the gout. I must take his instructions in the matter."

They walked through the courts, and at a public in Gough-square partook of a glass of "bittah beeah," as the fastidious clerk was pleased to call it, and then parted—the detective towards Fleet Street Station, while the unhappy Mr. Yapp sloped back to the warehouse, to wait for Swift, and other "urgent private affairs."

CHAPTER VIII.

THE RUINED HOME—A QUARREL BETWEEN TOM'S FATHER AND MOTHER—A FLIGHT.

"NINE o'clock, and Tom not come home!" exclaimed Mrs. Brown, as the little cuckoo-clock, which hung in a recess of the room, and whose long weights hung threateningly over the cups and saucers below, struck the hour. "What can detain him? Poor boy! he had no money, and but little to eat. It must be a hard place to keep him such hours as these."

"You had no business to send him out as an errand boy," said the still proud, but ruined, Mr. Brown, who had somewhat recovered his calmness since the morning that Tom left, and now sat over the fire with his wife, his head bent down, and his grizzly beard hanging raggedly over an old great coat, the remnant of happier days.

"Would you see us starve?" replied the wife, who might well be pardoned for speaking in such ill-natured tones to a husband who had been the cause of her misery.

"Answer that question yourself," said Mr. Brown; "do not be so quick to forget the time when I kept you and Tom in luxury—when nothing was too good for you—when you went where you liked, and bought what you liked."

"You cared for gambling more than your wife, your son, or your business," said Mrs. Brown.

"Had my gambling been successful, I should have heard nothing of it; but now I'm ruined you take every opportunity to insult me. Be-

ware, wife! My own losses are hard enough to bear without your upbraidings. I claim comfort from you, and I'll not be put off with reproach."

"Indeed! and who is to comfort me?" haughtily demanded Mrs. Brown. "You had a fortune with me, and now look round this wretched room, and see what you have brought me to!"

"Fortune! I married you because I loved you. You were the wealth I married—the wealth I cling to. The best of us may lose fortunes, but when we lose our hearts we are poor indeed."

"A man who loves a woman would never show it by making a beggar of her," said Mrs. Brown, shaking her head sorrowfully.

"Do not brave me, Jane!" exclaimed the enraged man, holding his beard in a handful. "I'm not far removed from madness, and your reproaches, however much I may deserve them, are just more than I can bear. Your sufferings are poor compared to mine!"

"How can you say so? You seem to suffer nothing but the deprivation of your turf companions."

"My sufferings are within!—here!—locked up!" he exclaimed, beating his heart; "yours find vent in upbraiding the man you have sworn to love and cherish. Swarmed with friends who have robbed me, and married to a wife who thinks more of luxuries than her husband—mine is a deplorable fate!"

"You deceived me," said Mrs. Brown.

"In what?" he sharply returned.

"I never knew you gambled."

"I never knew it myself. It commenced in a friendly way amongst my customers, and grew so imperceptibly that I was almost unaware what I had been doing until I found myself a ruined man! Then——"

"Then you did worse than all," said Mrs. Brown.

"What did I do?" exclaimed the ruined merchant.

Mrs. Brown sighed and shook her head, while a tear glistened in her eye.

"That is no answer. What did I do?"

"Don't force me to say. You know well enough; I promised I would never mention it again."

The ruined merchant glared at her, and she trembled. She rose from her chair, and put on her bonnet, which hung beside the clock.

"Where are you going?" her husband demanded.

"Where you ought to go," returned Mrs. Brown.

"I will be answered in a straightforward manner. You evade my questions by asking others. What did I do?"

He sprang up and locked the door.

"Oh, pray have some feeling for me, Brown," pleaded the wife; "I am more wretched than you think."

"You like to be wretched. When we were well off you were always gloomy and cheerless about something. I never had a home that was worth keeping."

"I never had a husband," retaliated Mrs. Brown.

"'Tis false!" he exclaimed; "you have had the best of husbands. The worst thing you can say about him is that he made mistakes, and that his greatest was when he married you. I might have married a lady of beauty, with ten times your fortune, had I been a money-hunter."

"A fortunate escape for her," said Mrs.

Brown, who knew well the lady her husband alluded to, and of whom in their prosperous days she had been somewhat jealous.

"Yes," said Mr. Brown sternly, standing close by his half-alarmed wife, who crouched towards the bed, his hands thrust in his pockets, "Yes, I gave up beauty and fortune for *you*—you who brave me because adversity has overtaken us."

"Not adversity, but disgrace," said Mrs. Brown, stung by her husband's second allusion to the beauty of the lady he might have married, and laying strong emphasis on the word "disgrace."

Her husband caught her by the wrist, bent his hand, and uplifted his arm—

"Oh, do not strike me, Brown!" almost screamed the terrified woman. Indeed, there was such power in that uplifted arm, such fiery passion in the eye that fell upon her, that it would have terrified a more courageous person than Mrs. Brown. "Do not, I implore you!"

"No—I wont!" he exclaimed, throwing her from him. "I never struck you yet—did I?"

"Never, Brown."

"And while my reason lasts I never will," said the goaded man, resuming his chair. "But I do not feel your unwifely conduct the less. And how much must you have enraged me for me even to threaten you. Take a lesson from your son—he never upbraids his father, but goes forth uncomplainingly and braves the dread circumstances which my fate has introduced him to."

"He is yet too young to upbraid or understand why he has been robbed of a good school and a good home, to be launched as an errand boy."

"You brought that disgrace upon him," said Mr. Brown.

"Shame on you for saying so," said Mrs. Brown, much exasperated. "But a man who would——"

He again rushed at her.

"Oh no, no, no—I won't say it! I have promised not to say it!" she appealingly said. "This passion will lead us both to crime. Let me go out awhile and seek my boy, and recover my senses."

"Oh! Jane, what a poor heart you've got!"

"A broken one, I know," sighed the woman, sitting on the edge of the bed. "O God! where will this misery end?"

Mrs. Brown was born to a good inheritance, nursed in tenderness, and brought up in luxury. She was a well-educated Devonshire farmer's daughter when her husband made her acquaintance.

Mr. Brown, also, was a man of great respectability, and worth several thousand pounds when he married. His father was a wine-merchant of "Merrie" Islington, and when he died Mr. Brown succeeded to his business and his fortune. But he was one of those open-hearted, weak, goodnatured men, and he was soon "picked-up" by the turfite, gambler, and men about town, and became their victim.

Mrs. Brown could have faced adversity that had been the sad product of fair and open enterprise in trade, which, it must be allowed, the ruin now about her was not; but she could not forget that the misery she was now launched in was caused by the secret recklessness of her husband's conduct, and it almost made her mad. The difference between the present and the past was of the most extreme character; great affluence and wretched poverty—luxury and starva-

tion. Her poor boy, too, his fate cut her to the quick, wounded her pride, and deepened her humiliation. Her husband, moreover, was little short of a lost man, without a friend or character.

Unfortunately, too, for Mrs. Brown, her husband, before he was utterly wrecked, borrowed a thousand pounds from her uncle, from whom she had great expectations; but this transaction on the part of her husband, which was quite unknown to her, had alienated her uncle and other relatives from her.

Such is life! Friends buzz about us as thick as flies in summer when we have no need of them. But alas! when we are wrecked and cry for help, there is no one on the coast to hear, no one to man the life-boat and save—but you are left to perish, cursed with the thought that you should have committed the folly of putting so much trust in mankind and so little in God and yourself.

Look now at this ruined wretched pair, calling themselves husband and wife, which God meant to be the dearest connection in His creation; look at them—threatening and hating each other! Their trust for happiness has been in wealth and friends, and not in each other. But wealth and friends having made unto themselves wings and flown away—they are the victims of mad despair. Their marriage oath to each other "for better for worse," "until death us do part," is all forgotten. They little knew it, perhaps, but they loved each other for each other's wealth and position; those alluring things gone, when they should have been thrown deeper and deeper into each other's hearts, they find they have no heart to refuge in.

"I wish I had never seen you," sobbed Mrs. Brown, shaking herself to and fro, in unmistakeable sorrow.

"I may wish the same thing," said Mr. Brown, who with folded arms paced the dismal room.

"You have no right to do so," said Mrs. Brown. "As a wife I have done my best for you and my child. But *you*," she added, with the deepest scorn—

Her husband's scowling eye fell on her, and for a moment stopped her, but then she continued with fearless rage—

"You shall daunt me no longer. You have squandered my money and your own! You have reduced those whom you have sworn to protect to rags, beggary, and disgrace! This"—pointing to the stout wedding-ring on her finger—"I wear only as a memento of my folly—a badge of my slavery!"

"Off with it! That which was presented with my whole heart I will not have scoffed at to my face! Off with it, I say!"

He went rapidly towards her, seized her hand, tore the ring from her finger, and flung it in the fire. The marriage symbol—as if with a voice saying "What God has joined together let no man put asunder"—would not be destroyed, but, unperceived by the passionate eyes either of husband or wife, escaped the fire through the bottom bars of the grate, and lay shining on the hearth.

"Have you any other mementoes of mine to scoff at?" he savagely cried. "If so, let them follow the ring," pointing to the fire.

"I have none," said the wife. "But my father has; one that reflects disgrace upon you, and which, but for *me*, would transport you!"

"I told you before that if ever you mentioned that to me again I would leave you for ever!"

"It was for that I mentioned it; were you to leave me my friends would do something for me and my boy, and raise me from the misery you have plunged us in."

While his wife spoke Mr. Brown dressed himself as warmly as his poor wardrobe would permit. He cried—"Kiss my poor boy for me!" closed the door upon himself, rapidly descended the stairs, plunged into the dark streets, and became a wanderer.

CHAPTER IX.

A CROSS-EXAMINATION AND A COMMITMENT—INSOLENCE AND INNOCENCE.

"WHATEVER has detained you, Pouncewell?" demanded the inspector, after the detective returned from his interview with Bonthron and Son's confidential clerk.

"Easily explained, Sir," was the half-offended reply of the officer, who secretly objected to the inspector's continued assumption of superiority. "I went to find Mr. Yapp, but failed," he added, doing his dirty work for the half-crown bribe.

"How so?"

"Because he was not there," said the detective, falsely and chuffily. "The place was all locked up. It is late."

"Late! seven o'clock!" exclaimed the inspector.

"Late, I mean, for respectable offices," said Pouncewell.

"Then I suppose police-offices are not respectable because they are open," remarked the inspector. "But I presume you mean—"

"Mercantile offices."

"I know that—so you needn't interrupt me," said the testy inspector.

"I told yer our Mr. Yapp would be gone; but you wouldn't take my word for it," said Swift, who sat on a form, while poor Tom was stretched out at length in the recess of the window.

"We don't take anybody's word here, Sir, for things we can prove," said the inspector.

"Hic-cup!" said Swift, in derision.

"Did you find out where this Mr. Yapp lives?" inquired the inspector.

"I tried, but failed," was the detective's false reply.

"Failed! why you have failed in everything, except in getting a glass of ale."

"I won't deny to a glass of ale," said the detective, wondering at his inspector's shrewd guess, "and that happened by my calling at the Lion in the court, to see if Mr. Yapp was there."

"What right had you to suppose that Mr. Yapp was at the Lion?"

"Just because the prisoner said that he and Mr. Swift had been there during the day."

"Aye, yes; oh, so he did; I had forgotten that," said the inspector. "And you didn't find Mr. Yapp there?"

"No, or I should have brought him here," said the detective.

"Had he been there?"

"Oh, yes," said the detective.

"Then, so far, what the boy said is true," said the inspector; "they had been drinking at the Lion. But it doesn't require further evidence to show that Mr. Swift has been drinking somewhere or other."

"That is an insinuation, Sir, against my character as a sober man—hic-cup!" said Swift. "How can yer so forget yerself, Mister Hinspector? It seems to me that it is thieves get all the perliteness here, and honest men all the hinsults."

"Silence, Sir!" exclaimed the inspector, "and allow me to proceed with the commitment of the prisoner."

The word "commitment" thrilled through the little boy that lay outstretched in mental and bodily anguish upon the bench. He looked around for help, but there was none for him; he inwardly prayed for the presence of his mother, but she came not. He turned tearful looks upon the inspector, but they pleaded in vain; he besought them to send for his mother, but he was told to be silent; and then to God he turned his thoughts and prayers, and a voice as from heaven gave him assurance that the truth should be made light, and bade him be of good cheer and fear not.

Tom's villainous accuser, Swift, lolled insolently about all over the place—now he would sit down and fold his long arms, now he would walk about hic-cuping—then he would lean over the rail, and watch the inspector writing. After a while he placed his old hat on his ill-looking head, covered with a lot of piled-up, uncombed, yellowish-looking hair: the rusty hat was evidently too large for the head—a defect he remedied by thrusting his blue-speckled handkerchief between it and his deeply-lined, freckled brow.

"Now, Mister Hinspector," he said, leaning over the rail, and looking impudently in the officer's face, "are you going to take this charge agin that ere boy, or are you not? I can't stop here all night."

"You must wait my pleasure, Sir," returned the inspector. "I tell you one thing, had the charge rested on your evidence alone, I would not have taken it. You are an ill-behaved fellow."

"Holloa! I say, draw it mild, Mister Hinspector," said Swift. "I shall report your conduct to your sooperiors. You are not—"

"Hush! hush!" interposed Littlewood, the policeman.

"Why should I?" saucily retorted Swift. "I'm not to be bullied by no man. D—n the boy! let him go if yer likes, and give him a chance to rob somebody else!"

"Our inspector knows what he is about, and you musn't be impatient," said Pouncewell, anxious to make his peace with his starchy superior.

"That's right, you're all agin me," said Swift. "What! d'yer think that ere thief of a boy—"

"Liar!" vehemently exclaimed Tom, and, regardless of his pain, he sprang to his feet, and there can be little doubt that his passion and indignation would have urged him to attack his brutal villifier, had not Littlewood caught him by the arms, and said—

"Don't you be so fast, young gentleman."

"I'm not a thief!" cried Tom, "and I won't be called a thief. I'd rather die than steal."

Pouncewell and Littlewood derisively smiled at what they considered to be Tom's mock or pretended indignation at being called a thief.

"You can give me no other account of the note, boy, than what you have given?" said the inspector.

"None, Sir," said Tom.

"Then I'm afraid I must take the charge, and the magistrate must decide the case."

Tom burst into a flood of tears.

"You are quite sure, Pouncewell, continued the inspector, "that the note dropped from the boy's pocket?"

"No doubt about that, Sir," was the detective's reply.

"Well, I suppose I must take the charge," said the inspector; "but, let me tell you, Mr. Swift, it is my opinion that no one will find the boy guilty on the evidence before me."

"That don't matter one brass button to me, Sir," said Swift, insolent to the last.

"Perhaps not, and perhaps it may—time will show that. There is more in this case than meets the eye. I'll pledge my twenty years' reputation as City police-inspector upon that; and I say again that if this boy can give a good character from his last place—"

"I was never in a place before," said Tom. "My father was a gentleman, and my mother a lady, and I was taken from boarding-school and placed as an errand boy because they lost all their money, and could not help themselves. Send for my mother, Sir, and she will tell you more than I can."

"What about yer father, eh?" said Swift.

"Do you know anything about his father?" demanded the inspector.

"I know he was a bankrupt," said Swift.

"Yes, Sir, he was," said the honest boy.

"Well, that says nothing; there's many an honest man been bankrupt; that's a misfortune that the best and wealthiest of us are liable to," remarked the inspector.

"Ah!" said Swift, "and, if I remember right, he was nigh upon being committed to Noogate for fraud."

"Oh, he tells a lie, Sir!" exclaimed the boy, knowing little of his father's life or history. "Do send for mother!"

"This conversation will not help us in the matter. I have my suspicions."

"You suspect me, don't yer?" exclaimed Swift.

"Honestly, I don't suspect the boy, although he must go for trial; but on that trial, although you and Mr. Yapp will be witnesses, you won't get off without a few questions from counsel."

"I shan't be asked any questions but what I shall be able to answer," said Swift.

"So much the better for you. You can go now," said the inspector.

"With very much pleasure," said Swift. "I wish yer all good night. And as for you, young 'un, I wishes you pleasant dreams in yer cell."

With his hands in his pockets, he leisurely lolled up Fleet Street until he came to the first public-house, and, too cold or too lazy, he did not take out his hands, but threw back the door with his shoulder, and called for "a pint of stout with the chill off." Then he rambled on to Bolt-court, where he met Mr. Yapp, his brother in crime.

CHAPTER X.

TOM'S DREAM REALISED—FATHER AND SON— A DREADFUL MEETING.

AFTER the cruel-hearted Swift had sufficiently established Tom's guilt before the tall authoritative inspector of Fleet Street station-house— one who gave himself more airs, and assumed a greater pomposity than the Lord Mayor, and

evidently of the two imagined himself to be the superior being—he departed to meet Mr. Yapp at the warehouse, and hence to arrange matters with an old Jew, whom he had known, for good and evil, for several years.

Broken-hearted Tom, faint, weary, and speechless, was for the night taken to the dark cells, preparatory to his morning visit before the sitting Alderman at Guildhall.

What could the poor boy say against such unparalleled villany, and so clear a proof of his guilt? His tears and protestations fell upon all who heard and saw them as weak as water, and all believed him to be the "werriest little willain in the world," as Mr. Swift described him.

"Take him away, Littlewood," said the tall inspector, who, if he had been measured by his own conceit, would have knocked a hole in the sky; "let him make his denials to the Alderman —we know nothing about them here. The five-pound note was found upon him, that is all we have to do with."

The inspector, after the departure of Swift, turned all his authority and legal learning against the boy. To Tom's great surprise and disappointment (for from the past scene he had a right to believe that he had found a friend in the inspector) the officer cross-questioned him, and turned against him, and seemed to make him out guilty.

The little boy—the innocent Tom Brown— stood at the rail of the inspector's office between a policeman (Littlewood) and the detective, who by Swift's orders arrested him by the office of the immortal "Punch."

"Send for my mother, Sir," said Tom.

"The magistrate may do that; we have nothing to do with mothers. Mothers! they would swear black was white to save their children. Mrs. Brown—if there is such a person—would say that we were all deceived ——"

"Or blind," said Littlewood, the policeman.

"Well, or blind—we mean the same thing, so you needn't have interrupted me; and that the boy upon whom the five-pound note was found——"

"And which it was," said Mr. Pouncewell, the detective, puffing out his cheeks, and elevating his knowing eyebrows.

"We know it was, so you needn't interrupt me," said the inspector, who looked upon his harangues with more pleasure and importance than did Demosthenes, and for the reason that he considered them every way greater than ever the Greek orator delivered; then he went on to say—not Demosthenes, but the City Inspector— and while he said it, he leant his long arms upon the open charge-book, and looked through the little door made in one of the panels of the long barricade that divided the rail that poor prisoners were brought up to from the room in which the City magnate held forth to those who were confided to his custody for examination, as well as those in the happier position of making the charge—

"Mind, that boy is young in crime," said the inspector, bending his head to the limits of his iron neck-tie; "those tears are real—so is that fainty look all over him — and if he had been here before——"

"Oh, no; he has never been here before since I've been on the beat," said Littlewood.

"I know that—so you needn't interrupt me," said the inspector, and which he had said a thousand times on other occasions.

"Oh dear no, Sir," said the subordinate

officer. "Come, boy, rouse up!" he said to Tom, who was just tall enough to bend his head upon the rail.

Tom with difficulty partially raised his head from the rail, and except that tears had swollen his eyes, and imparted a redness to them, he seemed like one in a wandering dream, or awakened from a trance.

Pain and pleasure have each their limits; passing those they change their character—pleasure becomes pain, and pain, physical and mental, merges into unconsciousness. Happily for Tom Brown, the sudden charge against him of being a thief—the mystery of the five-pound note being found on him—the terrible presence of the policemen—the pain in his wrists and ancles—and, worst of all, to his loving mind, the thought of what his mother would suffer when she heard of his position, overwhelmed him; and after awhile he became almost unconscious of his existence and of the serious circumstances which surrounded him.

"Take him away to his cell, Littlewood," said the inspector, in a magisterial voice.

The policeman opened a stout door and whistled, and a tall, muscular man made his appearance, with a bunch of bright ponderous keys in one hand and a lantern in the other.

"Another lodger for you, gaoler," said the inspector, putting his head further out of the hole in the partition which divided his office from the outer room, where the other officers stood with their little innocent prisoner.

"My lodgings are almost full, Sir," said the gaoler. "But he won't take much room. He's a respectable-looking boy, too, for a station-house. What has he been after?"

"By his own account, nothing," said the detective.

"Ho! hi! yes! of course!" said the gaoler. "Everybody is brought here for nothing. We never catch thieves—we are after the thieves, but we always catch the innocent."

This irony provoked a good deal of laughter amongst the officials, and of so loud and uproarious a character that it awakened Tom from his dreamy lethargy, and he began to feel the tortures in his wrists and ankles, and the greater one of his dire position.

He stared round from one to another, and the whole circumstance of his being there, which, for awhile, he had been oblivious to, flashed across his mind, and he abruptly exclaimed—

"I never stole the note!"

"Ha! so you said when I took it from your pocket, young gentleman," observed Mr. Pouncewell, the detective.

"And what I said then I say now, because it was the truth," replied Tom, with energy. "I know better than to do a thing like that. What would my mother and father say?—and I wouldn't for all the world do anything that would give them pain."

"I'll tell you one thing, Pouncewell," said the inspector; "the boy don't look like a thief."

"I'm not a thief, Sir," reiterated Tom. "I would rather die than be a thief, or tell a lie! Who says I'm a thief?"

"Why, you heard the charge, didn't you?" said the inspector.

"Oh, yes!" said Tom, "I remember. Mr. Yapp and Mr. Swift accuse me."

"Yes, they accuse you on behalf of your master, Mr. Bonthron," said the inspector.

"How can I see my mother?" inquired Tom.

"Your mother! oh, you cannot see your mother to-night," replied the inspector.

"Don't say so, Sir! Pray do send for her. She won't know where I am, and she'll go distracted."

"I should think she will go distracted when she *does* know where you are," said the inspector.

"Oh, not she, Sir!" said Tom, proudly. "She knows me too well for that. But not to know what has become of me all through the night will be the death of her. Do let some one call and tell her where I am—and tell that I say I am innocent, and that she need not fear, but be patient, as I mean to be, until the truth comes out."

"He speaks well, don't he?" said Littlewood, the policeman, to Pouncewell, the detective.

"Where does your mother live?" inquired the inspector.

"Vine Court, Finsbury," said Tom.

"A very nice place, is it not, Littlewood?" said the inspector.

"About as bad as any in London," replied the policeman. "Not a great way from Cherry-stone Alley—you know, Pouncewell—that runs into Glasshouse-yard, Shoreditch."

"A very salubrious neighbourhood," said the inspector. "Why, what is your father, that he lives there?"

"Father and mother are very poor, Sir, and were glad to live anywhere for a time," said Tom. "He has been well-off. He was a wine-merchant once, and then I was at boarding-school."

"And how long ago was all this?" inquired the inspector; "and how came you in such a state of poverty?"

"I cannot tell you, Sir; I have not been long from school, and know but little of my father's affairs. He was a bankrupt."

"Well, all this has nothing to do with the charge against you," said the inspector. "Let me tell you, young gentleman, that you will have difficulty to persuade the magistrate that you did not steal the note—"

"Seeing that the note was found upon him," said Littlewood.

"That is just what I was going to say—so you needn't have interrupted me," said the inspector, who was waking himself up for another harangue.

"I never saw the note until this gentleman," said the boy, looking at the detective, "took it from my waistcoat pocket and showed it to me."

"I did not take it from your waistcoat—you drew it out yourself," said the detective.

"But you will find it difficult to make the magistrate believe what you say," said the inspector. "The note could not have got in your pocket without hands."

"It was not *these* hands that put it there," said Tom, dramatically, extending his arms.

"Whose then? Mind, you need not answer if you do not like," said the inspector.

"The hands that took the other notes and the cheque," said Tom; "and that was not these, Sir!" he exclaimed again, and with the same action as before.

The officers looked dubiously at each other, then the inspector said—

"It is rather a strange thing, certainly, who has the other money. But the clear inference would be, that the boy had it all—"

"Seeing that one note was found on him," said Pouncewell.

"That's just what I was going to observe—so you needn't have interrupted me," said the inspector, drawing himself up to his utmost height. "But it is not for us to try the case," he added, "although, mind, I have my suspicions that the boy is innocent"—this last sentence he whispered in the ear of Littlewood.

"Who, then, do you think is the guilty party?" asked the policeman, in the same confidential tones.

"Swift and Yapp—the men who gave the boy in charge!"

This communication was made to the detective, and he stared in the face of the wise inspector, as if to say—"That never occurred to me, now!"

But after a pause he said to the inspector aloud—

"I am not at all of your opinion. Both the men you name have been at Bonthron and Son's for a many years, while this young fellow has only been there a day. You see, too, he had the temptation, for the madman broke open the letter, and by the boy's own account it lay on the desk sometime before Yapp and Swift came in from their business."

"Business! Psha! Why the man Swift was half intoxicated when he made the charge; and the other, Yapp, is keeping out of the way. The idea of sending the porter to make the charge, when the superior person, and the person who first missed the money, was at home. But take him away."

Mr. Pouncewell, the detective, was rather surprised to hear the sentiments of the inspector upon the merits of the case, and the half-crown he had received from Yapp rather favoured them, and he well wished now that he had never taken it, for it might possibly get him into a "scrape," and he be dismissed the force with disgrace. Had he told his inspector that little circumstance, the boy would have been released. The more he thought of it the more he began to see the seriousness of his position. He well remembered Mr. Yapp's mysterious conduct when he called—the locked door—the smouldering rags—the confusion of the clerk—and the lying excuse he made about his dressing himself. Altogether Master Detective felt himself in a nice pickle, and the half-crown in his pocket, that he had received as bribe-money from Mr. Yapp, and which was one of the two that Mr. Yapp had borrowed from Joe Bowers, the landlord of the Lion—that same half-crown which he had intended to regale himself with in the evening, hung now like a millstone round his neck, and he heartily wished it and all its associations at the bottom of the sea.

At the moment that little Tom was about to make his exit with his gaoler to his cell for the night, a policeman entered with a man in his custody of the wildest expression of countenance, on which was pictured everything woe-begone, wretched, and desperate. He had no hat on his head, and his poor clothes clung tightly round him as they were heavy with water. Drop—drop, too, as he stood looking around, fell the water from his grizzled beard. His coat and waistcoat were as much open from the want of buttons as from his severe struggles with the policeman who now stood by his side. His dripping wet shirt was open at the throat, and a ragged black neck-tie hung wet and loose about his swarthy throat; his shoes were like suckers on the floor, and at every step

he moved water oozed from the sides and toes.

With all his wretchedness, he had the appearance of a gentleman, as well as an intellectual physiognomy; and could be compared to nothing better than a goodly vessel untimely wrecked.

Everyone looked astonished when Tom sprang from the gentle hold of the man who was guiding him to his incarceration and sprang towards the half-drowned man, and exclaimed—

"Oh! my father!"

"Tom!" cried the man in tones that awakened echoes throughout the office. It was a deep scream, and the man caught the boy tightly round the waist and hugged him close. His listlessness on the instant fled, and all the highest and best feelings of a father took possession of him.

The gaoler was about to remove the boy from the father's tight embrace, but he might as well have attempted to take the young lion from its mother.

"Spare us a minute, Sir!" exclaimed the father with dignity. "It is a wretched place for father and son to meet, and needs an explanation. Is my son a prisoner?"

"Yes, father; they say I am a thief!" said the boy, in choking accents, looking with tearful eyes in the wild face of his father.

"A thief!" reiterated the parent. "What have you stolen? Who says so? You are not a thief, are you? I might have been one—but you, Tom!—oh no, no, no! No one who looks in that honest face of yours will say so!"

"Father, I am not a thief!"

"I know it, dear boy. Ah! my God! my God! All the world is against us, Tom. Oh, I feel faint—very faint."

"Father! father!" exclaimed Tom, as he looked into his face and saw it beaded over with the sweat of agony.

"Come, I say," said the inspector; "there has been quite enough of this."

"What d'ye say now about the boy's guilt?" said Pouncewell to the inspector.

"Well," was the reply, "it looks more like it now, I must confess."

Mr. Brown let go his embrace, and took his son by the hand, looked in his face, and said tenderly and affectionately—

"Some children, Tom, would have been ashamed to own their father in such a plight as this! But you love me, don't you, boy?"

"That I do, father; far too much to disgrace you by becoming a thief," muttered the boy. "They have nearly killed me, father—look at my wrist, and my ankles are worse."

"Ha!" exclaimed Mr. Brown, looking with surprise at the rope marks, "they had no right to do that though you were a thief."

"They have nearly killed me, father."

"And I have nearly killed myself, Tom," said the father. "I could bear the pangs of life no longer, boy. But this cruel man"—(looking towards the policeman)—"and he was cruel to save a life burdened with such sufferings as mine—was too quick for the operations of the tardy river."

Tom painfully thought of the vision in his trance, wherein he saw the spirit of his father.

"I feel faint. Make your charge against me, policeman, and lead us to our cell," said Mr. Brown.

"You won't go together, so I can tell you that before the charge is made," said the inspector, who had been worked into an unusual bad temper by the question of Pouncewell, which was too triumphantly asked.

"It must be as you please, Sir," said the intended suicide.

"Now, Jarvis," said the inspector to the policeman who saved the life of Mr. Brown, "what has this man been doing?"

"Drowning himself," said Jarvis.

"Drowning himself! Why didn't you allow him to follow his inclinations?" said the inspector.

"I wonder, Sir, that you ask a policeman *that*? Isn't it a violation of the law, and am not I on duty to protect the laws against violation?"

"It's a bad law, in my opinion, that forbids a man from drowning himself—quite an interference with the liberty of the subject," said the inspector. "The life of a man belongs to himself, and if God has given him the will and power to take it, and he is fool enough to exercise that will and power and to take it, why what under heaven have any of her Majesty's subjects to do with it?"

"Why, it's a felony!" said Jarvis; "our lives is held in common law not to belong to ourselves but to society—"

"I know that—so you needn't interrupt me," said the inspector. "Look at this man, now—whatever good can he be to society? I look upon suicide this way, and I have thought a good deal upon the subject: a man is at war with society, and society gets the best of him, and the man hangs or drowns himself—don't matter which. It is a fair stand-up fight, and what has the law to do with it? We have too much law, and too little common sense in this country. That's my opinion—now make your charge."

Tom and his wretched father were so much absorbed in their own melancholy feelings that they scarcely noticed or cared about the conversation going on, and which they were so peculiarly the subjects of. They spoke in low melancholy tones about the wife and mother.

"While on duty," began Jarvis, "and just at the foot of Blackfriars-bridge, City side—"

"You had no right on the Surrey side, so it *must* have been on the City side," said the cantankerous inspector. "You didn't go beyond your beat, did you?" he added, staring in Jarvis's face with grey-green eyes.

"I knows my duty, Sir; d'ye think I don't?" said Jarvis; "and my beat is quite large enough and troublesome enough, without extending it into Surrey."

"Well, go on," said the inspector. "You talk a great deal about nothing, it appears to me. Hadn't you said City side, we should have saved all these words."

"When I give a charge I like to be particular," said Jarvis.

"You may be *too* particular," said the inspector; "but go on."

"I hardly now know where I left off," said Jarvis.

"You must have a bad memory, then," rejoined the inspector. "Let me refer," he added, half to himself, looking in his book, and reading therefrom Jarvis's brief commencement to his charge.

"All right," said Jarvis, "well, on the City side—"

"D—n it! there you go again," cried the inspector. "You are a City policeman, ain't you?"

"Yes."

"Then what the devil have you to do with the Surrey side? You make me swear, which you know is not my custom."

"Good. Well, the man—"

"The man? What man, Sir? There are several men present. Prisoner, I suppose you mean."

"I shall never get through the charge, if I am to be taken up and put down in this way," said Jarvis. "I wish now I had let the prisoner drown."

"And so do I—so do I!" groaned Mr. Brown.

"Don't say so, father!" exclaimed Tom. "What should I and mother do without you?"

"Better—much better, my son. I have brought ruin on you both, and my life has been a worthless one. Pray, gentlemen, let us pass to our cell. I feel wretched, faint, and sick. May I make the charge against myself?"

"You look an intelligent man, but you don't speak like one. Who ever heard of a prisoner charging himself? Did you, Pouncewell?—did you, Littlewood or Jarvis?" inquired the inspector.

All the officers appealed to reverently made bows of assent to the Solomon behind the partition.

"You seem in a great hurry for the dark room," said the inspector to the elder prisoner.

"Nothing but life is dreadful to me, Sir," was his melancholy reply.

"He'll soon make another hole in the water," said Littlewood aside to Pouncewell.

"The sooner the better," said Pouncewell to Littlewood.

"I am charged with suicide," said Mr. Brown. "You can make nothing more of it."

"Who says you are? or who says you can? No one but yourself," said the inspector, drawing up his long neck.

"Do not speak, father," said Tom. "We shall be at rest soon. Oh, poor mother! whatever will she think has become of us?"

"Not worse than what has," replied the father. "Your mother, Tom—but there, I will say nothing to pain your affections."

Then he bowed his head to the boy's ear, and whispered—

"You did not steal—tell your father? On your soul, did you?"

"On my soul, no," said the boy, in the most fervent manner.

Mr. Brown stroked his son's head, and brought him close to him, and threw his arm over him, and then sighed—

"Would that I were half as innocent as my child!"

"How shall we see mother?" inquired Tom.

"I should shrink from seeing her," replied his father.

"Oh, father! this ill-feeling between you and mother is the greatest trouble of all to me. I cannot bear it. I would rather die, too, now," and the greatly distressed little fellow put his hands before his eyes and audibly wept.

"Blondell!" cried the inspector to the cellman, "take that boy away! His case is disposed of, and he must not be allowed to make that noise here."

"Hush! Tom, hush! or they will part us," said the father. "Spare him, pray, until I go with him!"

"Take him away, Blondell!" cried the inspector.

Tom clung pertinaciously with both hands to

TOM BROWN IS VISITED IN HIS PRISON CELL BY HIS MOTHER.

his father's arm; but when Mr. Brown saw that the officer was about to roughly handle his son, he entreated the boy to go peaceably.

"But mother, father—we must see her!" cried Tom.

"My boy, we are both of us in the hands of these gentlemen. If they would kindly send a messenger to the boy's mother, I should be grateful."

The only reply was—

"Take him away, Blondell!"

7

To any heart but a police-inspector's the parting between father and son was of a most agonising kind—not so much in words as in looks and sobs. Blondell pushed the boy through the door, and Mr. Brown's ears were pierced by the thrilling cry of—

"Father, don't forget mother!"

"Go on with you!" growled the cell-man, as he drove broken-hearted Tom before him. "Boys should think of their fathers and mother before they commit crime. It is too late after. Go on with you !" he again exclaimed, as Tom once more was about to assert his innocence.

They came to a narrow black door in a long stone passage, where Blondell and his prisoner paused ; then the great bright key was applied to the lock, the door opened, and Tom was more pushed in than invited. The cell-man's lantern was the only light in that gloomy place, in which was nothing but a stone bench for the poor prisoner to recline on.

"There's an end of *you* for the night," said Blondell.

"And my father—do, Sir, bring him here," pleaded Tom.

"Anything else, boy ?"

"Yes, if you would be good enough, send some one for my mother," replied Tom to the gaoler's irony.

"Well, I'm blest if you don't want the whole of your family here. No, no ; one of a sort is enough for a place like this."

And for that night the door was closed upon Tom, and he was left to darkness and his own thoughts.

But this boy was a high-souled boy, and he had been trained in the way he should go by his mother and schoolmaster, and he had been taught his prayers and to love God. The precepts that had been instilled into him were now called into practice, and by that cold stone bench, and on that cold stone floor, and in the winter night's darkness of that lightless room, the boy threw himself on his knees, and audibly prayed—

"Oh, my God! save my father and my mother, and save me ! Keep us from all harm, and deliver us from our great troubles ! Thou knowest, O God, I am not a thief, and that I am in this dreadful place by the falsehood of others. O God! bring the truth to light, and bring my mother to me. Strengthen her until Thou pleasest to send us better days and happier times. Keep Thou the life of my father, and banish all wicked thoughts from his distressed mind !"

Here he commenced repeating the Lord's Prayer, and he had just got so far as "forgive us our trespasses," when his tired nature gave way, and he gradually sank on the stone floor, and that little over-wrought brain was mercifully locked in sleep and forgetfulness.

CHAPTER XI.

THE WANDERER—SAVED FROM SUICIDE— DEATH IN A CELL.

TOM BROWN, well worn out with the harassing and agonising day's proceedings, had scarcely fallen asleep on his cold prison floor, than his wretched father, full of self-destruction, was also committed to his dismal refuge for the night.

His cup of bitterness was full with remorse of his own weak doings, and when his wife upbraided him he could bear life no longer, and he made the rash endeavour to fly from it.

No one can say, however much they might have felt for Mrs. Brown, that her conduct towards her husband was either feeling or judicious. She withheld all sympathy, and whenever she condescended to speak to him it was in tones of offence and words of bitterness.

There was that in Mr. Brown, that, had his wife (which clearly was her duty) bestowed upon him an affectionate care, spoken to him sympathetically, rallied him with kindness out of the remorse that was goading him to madness, he would assuredly have been saved, and made a man of. He would have shunned the grievous errors of his past life, and come out anew in the world, wiser and better.

"A house divided against itself cannot stand." Husband and wife had a dark journey before them ; and had they endeavoured to be a light to each other, they would have soon found their way into brighter paths.

But they cursed each other, while they cursed themselves. They rebelled against the lot that was meted out to them ; then, what could follow but destruction of the direst kind ?

Their noble little boy bore the change of life his misguided father had heaped on him in the most courageous and exemplary manner ; but he was overborne with grief when he learnt from his suicidal father in the station-house that there was great unhappiness between his parents.

He loved them both most affectionately, and his little hands would have done anything to make them comfortable. They should have controlled their tempers and conduct, if only for his sake.

But selfishness is a weed of fast growing, and where it takes root, farewell to flowers—farewell to peace !

When Mr. Brown left his wife in the mad, passionate manner that we have seen, and wandered forth in the dark streets, he had no thoughts of suicide—no thoughts about anything. He fled his wife, and he was regardless whither. With wretched, wild, downcast eyes, and penniless pockets, he walked up one street and down another, unnoticed and unobserved, like a good many other persons, of all grades and all feelings — the fallen woman, the thief, the murderer, even — pass through this crowded world of London.

"What shall I do ?—where shall I go ? God knows—God knows !" were the absorbing ideas of his mind. "She—my wife—*she* can transport me, eh ? Oh, how fallen !—how fallen ! Poor little Tom ! how glad I'd be to meet him ! Bad wife has Jane been ; "—here he deeply groaned, and with his hands in his pockets moved swiftly through the streets, until he came to the cattle-pens in Smithfield, where the heroic martyrs, strong and true in their religious faith, had sealed it with fire.

Without knowing it, he stood upon the very spot where the faithful Anne Askew, one of the earliest martyrs of the Reformation suffered. After being turned out of doors by her husband, a gentleman of Lincolnshire, and a devout Roman Catholic, she was tortured by the rack, and burned at the stake in Smithfield in 1546.

But the man whom we are now following thought not of these things—thought not of the spot he was resting on, even had he known the hallowed ground—he thought only of his wrongs, sufferings, and lamentable shortcomings.

He looked upwards to the sky ; it was cloudy and starless. The small street-lamps that glimmered here and there through the darkness and wintry aspect of the night only mocked him, while the darkness of the outcast's mind only mocked the darkness of the night.

He grasped his head, half denuded of hair, in his hands, and any passer-by might have heard him exclaim—

"I'm mad—mad—mad ! Oh, what is man without money ? Wife !—where is my wife ? Gone with my money ! Transport me, would she ! What would my boy say had he heard that ? He shall never hear that from my lips !

Tom shall never have to say, nor never live to hear, that his father was transported! Oh, how my grief buzzes in my ears!"—here he tightened both hands on the sides of his head.

Cabs whirled to and fro—boys whistled in relief from their day's work — the graceless policeman passed onwards; and a man with an illuminated can of hot potatoes took up his position at the heels of the wretched Mr. Brown.

The ruined merchant moved on—his grief was intruded upon. The first turning that met his wild eye he availed himself of—it was St. John-street. He went along this street, which led to the far-famed "Angel," in Islington, until he came to one of narrower dimensions, that brought him to the ancient gate of St. John of Jerusalem, which spanned the street with its strong and stony arches—a place famed in history for its magnates in chivalry, as it is at this day famed for a meeting-place of the magnates in literature.

But the architecture of this old gate, nor its past or present associations, was nothing to the man with this fiend of wrath and trouble in his breast. Often in his better days and happier moments he called in at the tavern (with which one side of the gate is now occupied), had admired its relics of armoury, and stained windows, and oak-panellings — had hob-nobbed with the intelligent landlord over a cigar and glass of grog in the banquetting-room—had stood with reverence over the portraits and statues of the best nobility of mankind that figure there—but now—now, when he passed under the old gate he was without means, without wife, and a wanderer!

On he went through the little Square, until he came before Clerkenwell Church—where stood a yard well choked with graves. He clutched the rails, and looked upon the homes of the dead. Just now the moon, full of wintriness, broke forth, in the dark sky, but she had enough light for him to read "to the Memory of Isabella Wise, who met an untimely death."

"Untimely!" he mused. "Perhaps like me, she was wretched, and destroyed herself!"

Suicide for the first time had occupied his mind. Suicide! oh! it is a passion of quick growth, and buds and blooms together. It is a fascination—a lure—a thought—an embrace—and we are gone!—gone to God's mercy.

On again he went—streets and churchyard bathed in moonlight, while no light entered his darkened mind—and without guiding his steps, fate governed them, he stood at the foot of Blackfriars Bridge. To his mind, the lamps that burned upon its top, and the moon that struggled for existence in the sky, only pointed to the waters that now shone beneath.

He looked about him,—no one went, and no one came. Stealthily down the steps he went, in the middle of which he again looked round. He saw no one—nothing but a black barge at its moorings met his view. He saw the sleeping water before him—and he hailed it as the balm of Gilead.

A policeman—the guardian of the night—unobserved, saw him, and tricked him, and stealthily stole behind him, suspicious of his intentions.

Splash! Mr. Brown audibly crying, "Farewell to Life!" plunges into the river that had received so many wounded spirits—dastardly, some call them—and would have drowned, but for the aid of the policeman and a man on board the barge, who brought him to the station.

He was taken to the neighbouring station, and there unexpectedly was confronted with his son.

The charge was taken, and he was committed to a cell adjoining his son's. When the dull morning broke, and his cell-door was opened, there lay the body of Mr. Brown stretched on the floor—dead! dead!

The mother knew nothing of this tragedy until she met her son once more in a prison cell!

CHAPTER XI.

MR. YAPP'S INTRODUCTION TO HIS WIFE—THE LOVE-SICK STATIONER—A GREEDY BOY.

By the time the black-hearted Swift had found his way back to the warehouse in Bolt Court, Mr. Yapp, overcome by the narcotic influence of the dog's nose that he had imbibed during the day, combined with the perplexity of his new position, had fallen into a sound sleep.

He sat on a chair, which he had tilted back to the sacks, against which he rested. He had on his hat and his fur-coat as when he went out with Pouncewell, the detective, and his well-fitting boots were crossed over each other.

The remnant of a cigar was between his fingers, and the white ashes had fallen upon the coat. His arms were folded, and his head was low bent on his breast. In the breast-pocket of his frock-coat he had concealed a loaded pistol.

His "dear" wife's lace shawl, which had been sent by her to be exchanged, as if thrown there in passion, lay on the floor by the leg of the sleeper's chair; and the deliciously-scented little note signed by "Maria Yapp," lay by the shawl. Poor Mrs Yapp!—petted little darling!—indulged creature!—luxurious lady!—what would she have said had she seen this indignity offered to her note and shawl! Oh! fie, Mr. Yapp, to treat a wife's fond wishes so disrespectfully.

But she didn't know—did she Mr. Yapp?—by what unholy means her fond wishes had been hitherto gratified. Do you think she cared, Mr. Yapp? Honestly, Mr. Yapp, don't you think if she saw all and knew all, that she would weep more about that shawl lying there in the dirt, than for your agonised mind?

But it is vain putting questions to a sleeping man—that is if answers are required. Indeed, it were cruel to disturb the man from so profound a slumber, to ask him about his guilt. Ever since he had known his charming Maria, those questions had been asked him—not by us, 'tis true—but by the more potent, more alarming voice of conscience!

Often in the dead of night, in the busy pursuits of the day, in his repose or gaiety, he would cry in his soul "conscience avaunt!" But there never was such a tyrant as this indefinable thing which "makes cowards of us all." Yet he means kindly by us—this guard of our purity—and oh! if we could but listen to his dictates, we should be as innocent and happy as the blue-eyed babe.

He looked a handsome young fellow though, did the clerk, as he slept quietly in his chair.

"The pink of fashion, and the mould of form."

Nature's chisel had wrought out for Mr. Yapp a pleasing, intellectual face, with truly a fine nose and brow. We dare not examine the bumps of his head, lest we awake him; but we affirm that any phrenologist at first sight would exclaim—

"That's an honest man! that's an intellectual man! that's a good man in all the relations of life! that's a gentleman!"

Oh, dear, no; there was nothing about Mr. Yapp, either in face, speech, or manners that would have conveyed to the most searching eye that he would have robbed his employers rather than not be well up in the changing fashion of the day. Both he and his wife had princely wardrobes. From head to foot, everything must be tip-top.

"Dear Maria" was of all ladies the most bewitching and most expensive. Any man with an eye for beauty would have forgiven Mr. Yapp for falling deeply in love with her, but we are happy to think that but few men would have forgotten—

"Not that I love beauty less, but that I love honour more!"

But to poor Mr. Yapp—weak Mr. Yapp—Maria's wicked but bewitching eye was beyond all price, and Bonthron and Son during their clerk's courtship and infatuation were made to contribute largely for presents of every kind to Maria.

Before the clerk had the misfortune to make her acquaintance he was expensive enough in his own clothes and general habits; but after that fatal time to stand well with her he did, indeed, array himself in fine linen and purple.

But then it must be said for Mr. Yapp, that before he knew his dear Maria—she that had haunted him in his business and his dreams—he was honest. He would, it is true, "beg and borrow," but after he knew her he found it necessary to "beg, borrow, and steal."

Also it must be said for Maria that she knew it not. Her husband had deceived her—told her he had good means independent of his situation, and that his situation was worth four times more than it was. Had it not been so "dear" Maria would not have had him, for she did not love the exquisite Mr. Yapp sufficiently well, to share a poor salary with him.

Not she. She had been trained to put a price upon her resplendent beauty, and for all that Mr. Yapp could do for her—and all the display and luxury he surrounded her with—still Maria's foolish parents were not altogether satisfied with the match, and often told her that she had married beneath her. That she should have married a carriage and pair—a title—and not a man in a situation.

Whoever could Maria's parents have been to talk like this? to inflate their daughter with such silly notions? to puff her up with pride of beauty? Highborn people of course.

Oh, no; they were only a Mr. and Mrs. Perkins, who lived out of Holborn, where they kept a respectable chandler's shop. But then the silly old pair had been great novel readers, which they borrowed at a penny a volume from a library round the corner; they read that it was a very common thing for beautiful peasant girls to become the wives of lords, and barons, and squires—then why not their Maria? which there never was such a beautiful girl, and all the neighbours said so.

Poor old fools! Poor old Mr. and Mrs. Perkins! they spent a little fortune in accomplishments and clothes for their Maria, and as a poetical punishment for their folly, their Maria has the hapless fate to become the wife of Mr. Yapp, a man with a poor income, and no higher morality than a thief.

It was a very bad job for the Perkinses when Mr. Yapp stepped into their well-stocked little shop for a penny box of fusees—for that was the fatal accident that led to his introduction to the charming Maria; she happened to be in the shop. Not that she ever served in the shop, that was too low, too paltry a thing for the pretty Miss Perkins (not of Paddington Green) to do.

She, God bless her! a benediction that we are prone to offer up for every handsome girl—was trained to be a duchess, like the heroines of some of the penny romances that the old folks revelled in, and unfortunately believed in. "Their" Maria was as good as any of them, and a good deal better—the customers and neighbours said so—especially the customers who ran long scores, and wanted to increase them.

Mr. Perkins's shop was one of very poor attractions for the exquisitely-dressed clerk, and had any one told him when he accidentally dropped in for cigar-lights, and before he had seen the beauty of the chandler's shop, that from that soil a wife would be raised for him, we fancy he would have indignantly exclaimed—

"Demn it, no! Bettah fate for a fellah than that, I hope! I flattah myself that I was born for connection with a highah family than the membahs of a chandlah's shop! Faugh!"

But when Maria, who was not often in the shop, and who, if not at some concert or ball, was usually upstairs with her music-master, or reading novels, handed him the fusees, and her father, apron-bound, took the money, and when his eyes met those of the chandler's daughter, his heart opened and filled with her extraordinary beauty.

He politely begged permission to light his cigar—he was loath to go—he lingered, asking Perkins common questions of the day; he was confused, and knew not what excuse to make that he might remain in the lovely presence of that lovely girl.

Fortune favours the brave, and oh! welcome accident, a shower of rain came on, and Miss Perkins—she herself—kindly asked him to take a seat until the shower passed over.

So many thanks he gave her—so many graceful bows—and then he eagerly seated himself on a little, low shop-stool, and puffed his fragrant cigar—and then—then he began to puff himself, and make the Perkinses believe that he was far other than a lowly clerk at a rag merchants.

"He had been educated at college, that there was a great mystery about his birth, and that an unknown hand supplied him with unlimited wealth."

"Ha!" exclaimed Perkins, a faithful believer in the novels that he read, "you are a child of mystery, sir, are you?"

"Well, there is just this mystery about my birth, that I am either the son of a foreign king or an English earl, I cannot learn which."

"Ha! indeed," exclaimed Perkins, "shouldn't at all wonder, from all I have read. And what confirms it is that you are supplied with unlimited wealth from an unknown hand."

"It is unknown to me from which of the two quarters my income comes; nor can I get the solicitahs, first-class men at the West-end, to tell me, even if they know."

"You'll be owned one of these days, sir," said Perkins, "and I have no doubt find yourself what you believe, the son of a king or an earl."

"Exactly," said Yapp, watching with infinite pleasure the effect his imagination and falsehoods had upon Miss Maria Perkins, as she lingered by the side of an immense Cheshire cheese.

"Bless my soul! I've read of far more wonderful things than that, Sir. What book was that in, Maria, where we were reading about the disowned son, who was brought from the workhouse in a carriage and four, with footmen in scarlet and gold, to take possession of thousands and thousands, and tens of thousands, of cultivated acres; and he had been starving for forty years, as the book said?"

"Thank God, my parents, whoever they may be, have bettah hearts than that. If they kill me at all it is with kindness," said Yapp. "I get game—grouse, pheasants, hares, partridges from all quartahs. By the bye, Sir, I should like to send you a brace of partridges, if you would allow me, as a slight return for your indulgence in protecting me from the showah."

"Pray don't name it, sir," said Perkins, hardly knowing how to comport himself in the presence of so much nobility.

"Look out for a brace tomorrow. I will send my servant with them," said Yapp. "And as for you, young lady, I shall find something for you amongst my jewellery."

The beautiful Maria blushed, and was going to say something, but had not courage to speak to the son of a king or an earl. The gallant Yapp saw her difficulty and diffidence, and at once relieved her by saying—

"Pray no thanks, madam. It's not worth it. You have been very kind to me, and it is the best thing I can do to mark it by a trifling gem."

"Trifling gem!" thought Perkins. "What heaps the gentleman must have to talk like that of gems. Why it beats anything I ever read!"

Then said Perkins aloud—

"I think you ought to thank the gentleman, Maria."

"Not at all, Sir," said Yapp.

"But I say yes, Sir," said Mr. Perkins. "My daughter has cost me a great deal to educate her, and I should like to see a little manners—something for the money."

"Tut! tut!" said the clerk, toying with his lavender gloves.

"I am sure, Papa, I am very much obliged to the gentleman; but—but—!"

"No more I pray you, Madam, about such small mattahs. I should give away more jewellery were there a possibility to do it with less ceremony. I hate—despise—detest ceremony!"

"You see, Sir, your position rather confuses us, Sir," said Perkins.

"Position! ah! Your are a readah, Mr. Perkins, therefore you remembah what the poet Burns says—"

"I only read novels, Sir," said Perkins.

"Indeed! well, then, Burns says—

'The rank is but the guinea's stamp.
A man's a man for a' that!'

"Aftah all, my position may be no bettah than your own. Can't toll, you know—it is all a lottery and a mystery."

"Mysteries, Sir, always come out right, Sir, or all that I have read have, Sir," said Perkins, who now began to ply very humbly before the son of a king, and "Sirred" him to the top of his bent.

"Fine prospects, and all that sort of thing, are very well," said the clerk, trying what effect a little sentiment would have on Miss Perkins, "but I find it no agreeable thing to be without the knowledge who one's fathah or mothah is. There is a cruelty about the thing that frequently troubles me and pains me. You wouldn't like to be in my position, would you, Miss Perkins? you wouldn't like to be a child of mystery—eh?"

"Oh, I would delight in it!" said the young lady, putting back a stray ringlet of her chesnut-brown hair, which was adorned on one side with a pretty red rosette.

"Dear me! should you really?" exclaimed the clerk.

"I mean, of course," said Miss Perkins, explaining herself, "if my parents, like yours, kept me like a lady while the mystery lasted, and when it was revealed that I turned out to be a princess!"

Old Perkins laughed, and so did the clerk, but he did not exactly know at what.

"You see, Sir," said the chandler, "my daughter would like mystery, but she would not like to suffer for it."

"Nor should I either," said the clerk. "But there are a good many children of mystery who are brought up in charity schools, boarded in workhouses, and die unnoticed and unacknowledged."

"Oh, no, Sir, I have no desire to be one of them," said Maria. "As I said before, I should like to have solid evidences—such as a plentiful supply of money, presents of jewellery, a mansion to live in—"

"Etcetera, etcetera, etcetera," said the clerk, laughing.

"Yes, Sir, I should require all those evidences that I was nobly born, or I would rather be Maria Perkins than a child of mystery."

"Believe me, Miss Perkins—and I speak as a child of mystery, and have all the evidences you particularise that I am nobly born—you would be haunted with the desiah to know your parents."

"No doubt, Sir," said Perkins, putting some long sixes in a drawer behind him.

"I can assure you, that amidst all my brilliant life, I have sometimes been wretched with the suspense to know my parents."

Miss Perkins smilingly replied, still toying with her lovely long ringlets—

"If ever those feelings came across me I should order the carriage and go to the opera, or a ball, or somewhere to destroy them."

"Not so easily done, young lady," said Mr. Yapp.

"Certainly not, Sir," said her father, pleasantly. "The fact is, Maria, you know nothing about mystery, and this gentleman does, and what he says, I have no doubt is the truth; and I say it does great credit to his heart to have such good feelings towards his parents."

"Indeed," said the clerk, "my feelings have been so racked, and I have felt so lonely even in the midst of gaiety, that I have often and often wished that I had been born of poor parents that I knew, than live surrounded with the affluence I possess, and not know where it comes from. What is a fellah without a fathah's care and a mothah's smile—eh, Mr. Perkins?"

"Well, Sir," said the chandler, "I must say, that, take the rough with the smooth, I like mystery—it is so interesting. To sit down day after day and not know who you are, or what you will be, I think it must be delightful. Every knock I heard at my door would thrill me with the thought that it was a summons to a throne or a coronet."

"Or to the County Court," said the clerk to himself; and which was the true exposition of his feelings when knocks came to his door. Then he said aloud—

"You have indeed a partiality for mysteries."

"I always had, Sir," said Perkins. "Ghosts, apparations, haunted houses, pixies, gipsys, dreams, fortune-telling, lucky and unlucky days, astrology, warnings, witchcraft, nativities—I believe in all these things, for I know them to be true."

"Ah, indeed," said Mr. Yapp. "Have you seen ghosts?"

"I have, Sir, and more than once," was the chandler's serious reply. "But I daresay, Sir, you wont believe it."

"You must grant, Mr. Perkins, that it is rathah hard to credit," said Mr. Yapp. "It is one of those things that must be seen to be believed."

"Some people, then, Sir, wont believe it, Sir. They explain it away somehow or other, rather than come to the point, and swallow their pride and say they have seen a spirit. I can't bear such unbelief. It is my opinion, Sir, that every man jack of us have seen apparitions, but won't acknowledge them—afraid of being laughed at. Fortune-telling again—why, Sir, I know that there are people that can see into the future."

"You have had your fortune told, Mr. Perkins?" said Yapp, half inquiringly, half quizzingly.

"I have, Sir. And everything the gipsy told me, good and bad, before that girl of mine was born," pointing to Maria, "has come to pass. After that, Sir, don't you think I am justified in believing in the occult sciences?"

"Oh, no doubt," said Yapp, glancing ever and anon at the young lady by the Cheshire cheese, and who every now and then glanced at him, and every now and then their glances, to the confusion of Miss Maria Perkins, met.

"I was told, Sir, when I should marry, who I should marry, how many children I was to be plagued with—"

"Oh, Papa! plagued with!" exclaimed the petted daughter.

"Yes, and I do assure you, Sir, described that child, that daughter of mine, who stands there, to a T," continued the chandler, folding his arms and leaning on the counter.

"She must have described her as being very beautiful," said Mr. Yapp, to the young lady's great discomfort, which was shown by her deep blushes, and the hanging down of her head.

"Well, Sir, she did," said Perkins, with a proper amount of hesitation.

"Oh, Papa!" exclaimed Miss Perkins, with well-sustained modesty. "Then I am quite sure her prophecy is false."

"No it is not, and you know it is not, and I have told you so a hundred times," said Perkins, "and don't all the neighbours and customers say so?"

"And I, a stranger, say so," rejoined the clerk; "for I must tell you, Mr. Perkins, and I do not flattah, that your daughtah—"

Miss Maria, as if anticipating that the clerk was about to say something very complimentary to her well-known beauty, was going to make her exit; and Mr. Yapp in vain begged her to remain, for she knew that her father, when he got on his favourite theme of the mystic arts, frequently lost himself in his enthusiasm, and there was really no saying where he would stop. Accordingly she bade Mr. Yapp—the stranger—the child of mystery—the son of a foreign king or an English earl—a graceful good night!

"To-morrow expect to receive the trifling gem I promised," said the clerk, approaching her and taking her milk-white hand in his; and here such a glance and such a smile passed between them, which gave Mr. Yapp a slight assurance that he was not altogether disregarded by Miss Perkins,

and the young lady the flattering idea that she had found in the clerk another lover.

We say another, for it may well be supposed that the beautiful Miss Perkins had not reached nineteen without many respectable young men making overtures for her hand. Besides, it was generally considered that Perkins was moderately well off, and that, therefore, to marry Maria would be a prize to any enterprising aspirant for her hand.

But, fortunately for Mr. Yapp, who was so suddenly smitten with her charms, she was disengaged; nothing eligible, in her foolish father's eyes, had turned up. The gipsy woman who had told him a handsome daughter should be born unto him, had also told him that she should marry a nobleman; and Perkins, who had certainly seen one part of the prophecy unmistakably fulfilled, was bent in his credulity to await for the other, and see his daughter wedded to a title.

Maria had several excellent offers, but her father, in which he was supported by an equally foolish mother, also a novel reader and believer in the mystic arts, kept them all at bay—opened her letters—and narrowly watched her. One or two well-to-do tradesmen in Perkins's immediate neighbourhood had been among the father's discarded.

One of these, a highly respectable and intelligent young bachelor, who kept a stationer's shop not a hundred yards from the Perkinses, was driven to distraction and death by Maria's charms and her father's refusal.

His name was Townley, and before he made acquaintance with Miss Perkins he was devoted to his business, his dog, and his violin; but afterwards away went dog, violin, and business; he had no heart, no care for anything but Maria.

And for many months he tried everything that the ingenuity of a lover could devise to win her affections. But Maria was not a very susceptible young lady, at least to the tender passion, and her father, foolishly haunted by the gipsy's prophecy that his daughter should marry a nobleman, one day gave Mr. Townley notice to quit and give up the pursuit of his daughter.

From that time Townley became a changed and wretched man—negligent in his business, his appearance, and of life itself. Glad was he when the night came, that he might sit down and weep, and console his broken heart with the society of a faithful Newfoundland dog and his violin.

When Mumford, his errand boy, had closed his shop he would descend into the dreary kitchen, and play the most despairing, piteous airs all in strict harmony with his depressed soul and feelings. The following ballad he was constantly playing, and sometimes a little crowd of passers-by would pause to listen to the plaintive strains from Mr. Townley's violin:—

"In the true horizon's beaming,
     Thee, sweet maid, alone I see,
In the silver wavelets' streaming,
     Thee, sweet maiden, only thee,

"Thee, in day's resplendent sunlight,
     Glancing from the sun afar,
Thee in midnight's softer moonlight,
     Thee in every trembling star,

"Wheresoe'er I go I meet thee,
     Wheresoe'er I stay I greet thee,
Following always, everywhere
     Cruel maiden! O forbear!"

Then pride for a moment would seize him and possess him, then would he play in a most cavalier spirit, and wildly sing—

"If she be not fair for me,
What care I how fair she be?"

Thus would he continue to play and sing away the hours of night, until gentle sleep did overtake him in the old arm-chair; then, stretching his legs out on the broad, warm sides of his faithful dog, and resting his languid hand on his melancholy brow, he would fall into dreams of Maria, and only awake to find himself her wretched discarded.

Many a night has he thus passed, and he only knew when the morning came by the thumping of the boy Mumford on the shutters with his fists for admittance. Sometimes it was a long time before the errand boy could make himself heard, and he frequently had to accompany his thumping with a kick or two from his thickly-nailed highlows.

Mr. Townley could not resist this appeal for admittance, or if he could his shutters could not, and his dreaminess at once gave way before it, and George Mumford was admitted, looking as cold as a keen north wind and frosty weather could make him. The ends of the boy's ears, the tip of his nose, the extremities of his fingers, tingled again with the sharp air.

"It's such a cold morning, master!" cried the boy. "There's a regular jolly slide in the fish-market, and another at the corner of Jupiter-street!"

Mr. Townley made no reply to the boy, and of course the boy thought him a melancholy guy, as he went and sat down behind the little shop desk, without attempting to dust or arrange the stock. However, down came the shutters; and Mumford, the errand-boy, as was his accustomed duty, went into the kitchen to prepare Mr. Townley's breakfast—first paying his devotions, of course, to the bread and butter, although he was not on board wages. But the boy Mumford could always manage two breakfasts; and as for the matter of that, he could duplicate his meals throughout the day, and only regretted that he had not the chance.

George Mumford considered stolen fruit to be the sweetest, and thought *Iago* was quite right when he said—

"He that is robbed, not wanting what is stolen,
Let him not know it, and he's not robbed
at all."

"Tea, or coffee this morning, Sir?" George called up the kitchen stairs to his love-sick master in the shop. After a pause—

"Neither," was the reply.

"Bacon, or eggs?" was the boy's next inquiry; and, to his complete astonishment was answered—

"Neither."

"More fool you," muttered George, as well as his crammed mouth with bread and butter would let him. "If I was master, I should have *both*," he added, putting a lump of white sugar into his mouth.

After the delicious morsel had dissolved itself, and he had qualified it with some fresh milk, leaving his master but little out of the morning's ha'porth—(and of course George was quite prepared to put it on the shoulders of the cat should the milk be missed, which it wasn't; and such was Mr. Townley's state of mind, that had the boy drank it all, it would not have been missed)—

he apprised his desolate master that the breakfast was quite ready, to take his place in the shop while Mr. Townley went below to his solitary meal.

George was a sharp, handy boy, and especially took care of Number One. Still he made his bachelor master as comfortable as he could; blacked his boots, got his meals, opened and shut up his shop, and went his errands—and all for six shillings a week. See, now, what a roaring fire he had made up for Mr. Townley; and how nicely and cleanly he had laid out the meal; and it was his master's fault if he did not come and make a good breakfast.

But his master didn't; and, to the boy's surprise, when he was called to clear away, he found things pretty much as he had left them. But George was a capital trencher-boy, and he never allowed the bread and butter or cold meat to grow stale.

"Oh, dear, what can the matter be!" he exclaimed, when he saw the untasted breakfast before his eyes; and he called to "clear away;" and he at once set to work to "clear away;" and piece after piece of bread and butter was quickly demolished, and he regaled himself with a nice cup of tea, and spread out his corduroy-covered legs on the fender before the bright fire he had kindled, and called his master no end of fools for leaving him such a fine chance of having a second breakfast.

While George turned his back to stir the fire, Mr. Townley's fine tall dog made free to take from the table a well-buttered crust—one after the boy's own heart—which Mumford intended to conceal in his corduroys for his lunch. When he discovered that the crust had been taken away, and saw Neptune licking his lips, and looking with extreme satisfaction out of his intelligent eyes, he exclaimed, holding up his finger—

"Now mind, old fellow, I'll be one with you for that crust. No paunch for you to-day, so mark me; the penny I get for your dinner will buy me a saveloy! Tit for tat, you black-looking thief! Mind ye, if master asks anything about the butter," added George, spreading it thickly on another large slice, "I shall lay it on to you, so I don't deceive you!"

The noble dog watched George in his bread-and-butter operations, and cared for little what he said. He wagged his tail, threw his head on one side, and whined in his impatience, thinking that the boy was preparing the slice for him.

"He, he, he!—ah, ha, ha!—wouldn't you like it, eh? Then see me eat it," said the boy, biting off an enormous mouthful, that filled out both his ruddy cheeks; and while he masticated it he beat a rat-tat-too on the iron fender with his feet, drew forth a penny warbler, and blazed away at a song or two. Then he would again address the dog, who lay comfortably at length before the fire.

"Me and you wouldn't do to live together, because our happetites are too good, and I like to do all the eating myself. You or I ought to get into some gentleman's family; our master ain't rich enough to keep two wolfers. Mind ye, at eleven o'clock I saveloy's your paunch penny; and there goes a piece of bread and butter to eat with it," he added, stowing away the edibles in the side pocket of his jacket.

George Mumford then rose to put away his master's few breakfast things; and he smiled roguishly when he took up the plate with the smallest bit of fresh butter on, and which, when he sat down, might have been estimated to contain a quarter of a pound.

"Look here," he said to the dog, while he pointed to the plate—"who stole the butter? Ah, you thief!—you rogue!—you cunning dog! There'll be a nice row in the house about that. Oh, if master did but guess what a thief you are, d'ye know I think he'd hang you."

The dog moved his head from one side to the other, and pricked his ears, as if anxious to catch the meaning of George's address. He believed the boy to be in sport, and sent forth a loud but playful bow-wow-wow! and then placed his paws on the boy's shoulders, which brought his head on a level with George's.

"Paws off!" exclaimed Mumford, withdrawing himself from the dog's embrace. "D'ye think I'll lark with a dirty dog like you, who would steal a chap's bread and butter? Back, and catch this sugar!"

George took a large lump from the basin, and then he said—

"One, two, three—catch!" while the eager dog sat back on his haunches ready to catch what the boy might throw to him; but George, after disappointing the dog, eventually confided the sugar to his own greedy lips, saying afterwards, looking in the dog's face—

"Wouldn't you like it? Boys before dogs. One for me, and two for myself,"—taking two other lumps from the basin. "Well, I've had my breakfast, and master's none out of pocket by it, for he's had none, and he's only paid for one after all."

When George commenced to put away the crockery in the passage cupboard by the coal-cellar, the dog Neptune stole, unperceived by the boy, up to his master, in the shop. When the boy, with his mouth full and his hands full, reached the cupboard, and not being quite tall enough for the shelf, he stood on a stool, but the stool overbalanced, and away went George and the breakfast things—oh, such a crash!

"What's all that about?" inquired a stern voice from the top of the kitchen stairs. It was not his despairing master who asked; he was too much occupied with the recent refusal of Miss Perkins to inquire about anything that might happen; but it was Mr. Chown, a warm friend and distant relative of Mr. Townley's, and who had just dropped into the shop to see the stationer.

"What's up, I say?" he again demanded.

"It's the dog, Sir," said the ready-witted George. "He's been and broke two breakfast-cups, a saucer, and the glass sugar-basin."

"Why, you lying rascal, the dog is up here!" said Mr. Chown.

Oh, what a "sell" for George. But he was sharp at a lie.

"I said the cat, Sir."

"You said the dog, Sir!" cried Mr. Chown.

"Did I, Sir?—then I meant the cat," said the boy; "she saw a mouse, Sir, and went slap across the things after it."

"There, there, that'll do!" said Mr. Chown. "You're a nice lad, you are; but you wouldn't do for me!"

"D'ye think I'd tell a lie?" cried the indignant boy. "I say the cat jumped up to the milk—"

"That's a good 'un. Just before you said the cat was after a mouse," said Mr. Chown. "Now you say she was after the milk."

"Well, when I said milk I meant a mouse, Sir."

"If you don't leave off lying you'll come to the gallows."

"That's all gallows fine," muttered the boy, but not loud enough for Mr. Chown to hear. "Whew! whew! You're not my master."

Mr. Chown was so corpulent that he had a dread of stairs, or he would have gone into the kitchen; he found it easy enough to descend, but the ascent made him puff and blow and roar; and through this circumstance the boy George escaped his ears pulling, or a kick out of the place.

Mr. Chown now returned to the shop to talk over Mr. Townley's love affairs, and recommending him to go more about and keep a shopman.

George Mumford, besides being a greedy boy, was a curious boy, and he crept to the top of the stairs and listened to the whole of the conversation, and there for some time he remained with his cold hands in his pockets, and his red frosty ears turned down towards the shop door, until he had possessed himself with the "full, true, and particular account" of his master's love for Miss Perkins, which he never before knew that they were more than intimate.

His curiosity satisfied, he blew upon his fingers, returned to the kitchen, danced a jig in his high-lows, and then sat down before the fire, and soliloquised on all he had heard.

"What's the good of a shopman here, I should like to know? I'm big enough to do master's business—taint so much! If master goes travelling it'll be a bad job for me, for there'll be no breakfasts, no dinners. The place will be ruined for me. I hope the new shopman will board here, then master can travel as long as he likes! Why don't he advertise for a new errand boy, and make me shopman on board-wages, eh, old Neptune?" he exclaimed as the dog re-entered. "What I couldn't eat—you should have; that would be jolly, old chap, wouldn't it?" and with this interrogation he mounted Neptune's back, and the patient dog rode him across the kitchen.

Mr. Chown here called the boy up, and to his surprise began to be playful with him. George expected nothing less than a sound thrashing, but he was agreeably disappointed. The fat old gentleman looked quite good-tempered, and said—

"Well, young frosty-face—snow-balling coming on; that will be the time, eh?"

"I never throws any, Sir," said George, with a Topsy-like meekness. "I don't like larks, I don't. I thinks 'em wicked; might knock people's eye's out."

George was well known throughout the parish as a troublesome customer, and Mr. Chown knew him as such, and he could not help laughing at his pretensions to goodness. Whenever he was seen he was always eating, and the other boys called him "Bread-and-butter Bumford."

"I suppose you wouldn't know the way to spend this if I were fool enough to give it to you?" said Mr. Chown, holding up a sixpence. "You'd put it in the missionary box, wouldn't you?"

With a demure sigh (at the same time laughing internally) George said he would give it to his mother for shoes.

"Shoes!" exclaimed Chown. "Oh, your wages will buy them. Couldn't you eat a tart or two?"

"Tart, Sir!" exclaimed George, as if he had never heard of such things; his mouth all the

MR. YAPP SUDDENLY ATTEMPTS THE LIFE OF SWIFT.—*See No.* 9.

time watering at the very name of the delicious morsels, while in imagination he devoured them by wholesale.

"You will pretend next that you never heard of bread and butter," said Mr. Chown. "Don't be sly, boy; it will not advantage you in your career of life. You can buy six tarts for sixpence, can't you?"

"Seven, Sir?" said George, eagerly; "Mr. Honey always gives seven for sixpence!"

George was outwitted.

"Oh, I've caught you, have I?" cried Mr. Chown, pleased to find that he had won an opportunity of giving the boy a practical lecture, and returning the coin to his pocket. "I don't like humbug, George, and I punish it whenever I meet with it. This may not be the first sixpence that your hypocrisy has lost you; let it be the last."

When the money was lost to George's delighted vision, he racked his fertile brain for an excuse to regain it.

"Please, Sir, I didn't know what you meant hardly by tarts; we boys calls 'em windy puffs and jammers!"

"It won't do, boy," said Mr. Chown. "Tell the truth and shame the devil; and if it doesn't make you successful in this world, it will take you to heaven, lad, which is better than all! Now get about your master's work, you little scoundrel, and think of old Chown and the lost sixpence as long as you live!"

The lecture made no impression on the hardened boy, for he went off to the kitchen, muttering—

"Shouldn't I like to meet the old codger in the dark!—wouldn't I snow-ball him!" and then drew forth his crust of bread and butter and devoured it amidst the best of blessings for Mr. Chown, and many regrets that he had been "sold" with the sixpence.

"People will pay for their larks with me, so I don't deceive them! He's master's friend, and if I can't spite him, I will master. It'll be a little difference to them, but it'll be all the same to me. Roo-too-too-o-o!" he exclaimed, giving a screaming imitation of old Punch; and then he commenced—

> "I should like to marry,
>   If that I could find,
> Some very nice young woman,
>   Suited to my mind!"

"And so would master, too—ha, ha! But he's found a nice young woman, and she won't have him. I'm so glad! because he's old Chown's friend. Mariar Perkins—ain't she a stunner, though! What an ass my master, Townley, must be, to think she would have had him. So glad—he won't be able to eat—more for me! What a lark! Thought there was summut up—know it all now! Wish old Chown would fall in love with a gal that wouldn't have him. Would like to go in mourning for him, the fat old buffer! 'Twas a bowl out about the tarts, and no mistake! I'll be one with him—he shan't have his morning paper quite so early; not if I know it! Now for master's boots; and then for master's dinner!—which I hope I shall have the pleasure of eating for him. He feeds on Mariar Perkins—he does. I hope he'll grow fat upon it—it wouldn't suit me, I know!"

Mumford now commenced cleaning his master's boots, singing many a merry tune over them; while he brushed one, he placed the other far under the grate to dry! Turning his back, a red-hot coal fell on the boot and burnt a hole in it. George saw it too late; and, snatching the boot from the fire, he said to the dog, who sat by—

"Mind'ye, that's you!"

The smell of the burning boot ascended strongly to the shop.

"What's that burning, boy?" called down Mr. Chown.

"Only the fire, Sir," was the ready reply.

"That's another tale, George!" said Mr. Chown.

"I've found out now, Sir," said George; "Neptune went too near the fire, and burnt the tip of his tail. Oh, crikey! don't it make a smell! It's all right now, Sir."

"Poor dog!" said Mr. Chown; "send him up, George."

"That's awkward," said George to himself. "If you go up your tail will be examined, and no burning found. I'm not to be made a liar of for you."

Here he rolled up a large piece of a newspaper, set fire to it, and then set fire to Neptune's large bushy tail; and the dog flew up the stairs yelling in alarm, denuded of his flowing hairs.

George chuckled as he heard his master and Mr. Chown sympathising with the dog's misfortune. He was delighted with his own cleverness—he never once thought of the cruelty his deception led him into.

Mr. Townley could not recover from the shock of Miss Perkins's refusal; and on her wedding-day he was taken seriously ill.

His friend Chown was not slow to discover that Townley must sojourn to new scenes; and advised him to sell off, and try what virtue there would be in a foreign land to "raze from his memory the rooted sorrow."

Mr. Townley was passive in his friend's hands; and one day the stationer's little shop was closed, and the unfortunate lover sailed for New Zealand.

George Mumford, after being out of a situation for some time, and in consequence had no opportunity of duplicating his meals, was fortunate enough to learn from Mr. Perkins that his daughter, Mrs. Yapp, wanted a page; and George was installed in the place, and his stout figure well set off his suit of green adorned with rows of gilt buttons.

CHAPTER XII.

THE GIPSY'S PROPHECY—MOTHER AND DAUGHTER—DIFFERENCE OF OPINION ABOUT A SHAWL.

As we have seen, it was a trifling circumstance which first introduced Mr. Yapp to his wife. A box of fusees—which led to a *match* between him and Miss Perkins. Alas! a most unfortunate one for both of them. It was the biter bit. She thought,—or her foolish parents did for her—that when she married the child of mystery, she had mated herself to the son of a king or an earl; while he fondly imagined that after the wedding she would love him for himself, and not for his absurd and lying expectations.

But Mr. Yapp was as greatly deceived in his wife—but with far less reason—as she was in him. She was told by the clerk, and she believed the statement, that he had unlimited wealth to start with, that he kept his situation more as a relaxation than for anything else (as he had a great partiality for mercantile pursuits), and that they must wait for their titles until the mystery of his birth had been cleared away.

He was a handsome young gentleman, withal, and Miss Perkins thought, and so did her mystery-loving father and mother, that he was a great catch; and the old folks, moreover, believed that the marriage would be the fulfilment of the gipsy's prophecy that their daughter should marry a nobleman!

After Mr. Yapp's first visit at the chandler's shop, and when he became deeply enamoured of the charming Maria, like Othello's *Desdemona*, "he came again"—always bringing with him some "trifling gem," or a new piece of music for his inamorata, or some game, or other delicacy of the season, for the delighted Mr. and Mrs. Perkins.

The game, which the Perkinses were led to believe was supplied to Mr. Yapp by unknown hands, was bought by the "child of mystery" in

Leadenhall Market; while the "trifling gems," which they were told were taken from his own inexhaustible stores, were purchased from Benson, the far-famed jeweller of Ludgate-hill; while all was paid for by Messrs. Bonthron and Son.

He had represented himself to the Perkinses as a man of "unlimited wealth," and he was now bound to give the best evidences he could to confirm his statement.

Sometimes, it is true, it was not convenient, or opportunity was not afforded him to attack the coffers of his employers; then, as he grew on more friendly terms with the chandler, he had only to say to him that his remittances were unaccountably behind, and that he was inconvenienced, Mr. Perkins was only too proud,—too happy—too much honoured—by supplying his daughter's prospective husband, the "child of mystery" with what money he required.

In this way Mr. Yapp conferred a great deal of pride, happiness, and honour on the respectable chandler. The money was never repaid, and Mr. Perkins would not for the world risk offending the clerk by asking for it, and was good-natured enough to ascribe it to forgetfulness, and was quite content to wait until Mr. Yapp came into his lawful inheritance of a foreign kingdom, or an English earldom.

From this time forward Mr. Yapp studied fashion and adorned his body. Being a good figure, tall, and of fair proportions, he as much set off the clothes as the clothes did him. He was, indeed, an "exquisite." Gloves, boots, and neckties, there was no end to; while his tailor's bill was always something formidable, for if he paid a pound or two off it, he generally managed to increase it ten.

In cabs and cigars, too,—and for which he had to pay ready-money—the clerk spent something of importance weekly. He could not possibly walk backwards and forwards to his courting, so he always came and went in a Hansom; it would be *infra dig.* for a man of unlimited wealth to walk; and when he could persuade Miss Perkins to accompany him to a public ball, he invariably hired a brougham, taking care to let Perkins know that it belonged to a friend of his, a gentleman of vast wealth.

And it must be confessed, that it was a proud and pretty sight for the old Perkinses to see Mr. Yapp hand their elegant daughter into the carriage—she in complete ball costume, her hair beautifully dressed by an artiste, and bound with a wreath of roses, a fringed and perfumed fan—a gift from the clerk—coquettishly carried in her kid-covered hand, and eyes sparkling like diamonds; while he, in black dress coat and pantaloons of faultless shape and fit, set off by a rich white waistcoat, and hat and boots of first-class make and quality,—a fragrant white lawn handkerchief just peeping from a pocket behind, and a small eye-glass suspended in an imperceptible manner from his neck, and which his ball-gloved hand would ever and anon be affectedly lifted to his bright and penetrating eye, with some sprig or flower of the season in his coat.

In the same expensive and exquisite style would he lead Miss Perkins forth to the opera or theatre.

Sometimes, too, he would be gallant enough to insist upon Mrs. Perkins accompanying them, but not often, for he did not quite agree with the old lady's make-up; not but that it was good, but that it was vulgar, as were her person and manners.

Maria, too, was not over-partial to the society of "mamma" on state occasions with Mr. Yapp—mamma did not altogether accord with her boarding-school notions, where dress and manners were everything, and fathers and mothers nothing.

"Now really, mamma," she exclaimed on one occasion, a little piqued and out of temper, because her marriage was to be observed with privacy; "I cannot think of going with you if you wear that shawl. What would Mr. Yapp think of you!"

"Well I'm sure, miss!" also exclaimed Mrs. Perkins. "You're a fine lady betimes! That shawl, indeed! What's the matter with that shawl, I should like to know?"—holding out at length a large yellow shawl with a broad red border, surrounded with fringe of a variety of colours. "That shawl cost me five guineas! They don't make such shawls now!"

"Indeed they do not, mamma," said Miss Perkins, laughing. "Why, it is quite a fright!"

"It is like your impudence to say so, miss," rejoined Mrs. Perkins, a little roundabout woman, in a brown bombazine dress, a lace bordered cap tied under a double-chin with plaid riband, whiteish eyebrows surmounted by a black front or wig, with half-a-dozen curls on either side. "The truth is, that you don't *want* me to go. But I *will* go, for Mr. Yapp has asked me."

"He only asked you out of a compliment," said the charming Miss Perkins; "I am sure he doesn't mean it."

"Doesn't he, indeed, madam!" exclaimed the outraged mother, sitting down on a bedroom chair, and locking her sausage-looking fingers across her ample stomach. "You're a nice specimen of a daughter, I don't think. Whatever Mr. Yapp turns out to be—a lord, an earl, or a king—he'll rue the day that he ever married *you.* But there, he hasn't married you yet."

"And I am sure I am quite indifferent whether he does or not," said the piqued young lady, fastening a cameo, Mr. Yapp had given her, in her dress before the looking-glass, and adjusting her gold watch and chain round her neck.

"You'd cry your eyes out, you know you would, if such a thing were to happen," said Mrs. Perkins.

"How *can* you say so, mamma?" exclaimed Miss Perkins, now ready-equipped, parasol in hand, for a summer evening stroll with Mr. Yapp, who sat in the shop with old Perkins while she prepared herself for a *tête-à-tête* round the neighbouring square of Lincoln's Inn Fields.

"I *do* say so, madam," said Mrs. Perkins. "Who are you, I should like to know, to despise my shawl! The truth is, that it is *me;* your own *mother*, that you despise!"

"You know better, mamma," said Maria. "The shawl is quite a dowdy. Why you had it before I was born."

"Don't tell lies, miss," said the old lady. "I had it when your uncle John was married, and that's not five years ago, for I went to his wedding in it, and bought it for the wedding."

"I should like to see you at *my* wedding in it," said Miss Perkins, amiably and smilingly.

"It would be far too good for *that;* your wedding is to be a poor affair," retorted Mrs. Perkins. "You have too much pride now, let me tell you, and I'm sure I don't know what you'll be when you become 'my lady.'"

"Nay, mamma, do not be angry," said Miss Perkins, throwing her arms round the old lady's apoplectic-looking neck, in the most coaxing manner. "The shawl, I have no doubt, when you bought it was highly fashionable, but it is quite out of date now."

"Your uncle John would not say so if he were here."

"Uncle John was a sailor, mamma, and had no taste in dress," said Miss Perkins.

"No taste, indeed! He ought then. Why he had been in every part of the globe, and had danced, as you heard him say, with the Queen of Otaheite. And that shawl, he said, was the most beautifullest thing he ever saw; and so it is, and I don't care what you say. And I shall go, and shall wear it."

"I am sure I am much obliged to you," said the piqued daughter.

"I want to talk to Mr. Yapp about house affairs ——"

"Mamma!" exclaimed Miss Perkins, in tones of horror. "Why, you must be out of your mind. To talk to a gentleman of unlimited wealth about housekeeping!"

"And why not, I should like to know? Bad housekeeping will soon bring to beggary the largest fortune. If you don't care for the welfare of your future husband, I do for my future son-in-law; and I know he will thank me for it; and, perhaps, you will, too, when you get more wisdom and less finery in your head."

"Fancy, mamma, you talking to Mr. Yapp about how much flour it takes to make a pie, and what to do with the cold mutton! It is really laughable!"

"Very well, miss," said Mrs. Perkins, smoothing back her wig, and putting on a bonnet just as about outrageous and vulgar as the shawl; "you may be born, as the gipsy woman said, to be a fine lady, I don't at all doubt that, as it was a prophecy, but it is no credit to you to set yourself up above your mother. Your are told to 'honour your father and mother, that thy days may be long in the land.' Fine ladies come to grief sometimes, as I have read. There was Lady Georgiana Revalenta Lillybell, that was in the last novel I read—she was, like yourself, a poor but handsome girl, who married a baron, and after she married she was too proud to speak to her parents and her brothers and sisters. And what was her fate? Ah! you know, for I read it to you. She was put down a deep well by her husband—"

"Which was not well done," said Miss Perkins.

"You may laugh and joke at such matters, madam; but it was no joke for Lady Georgiana Revalenta Lillybell. Beware! there may be a fate like it in store for you. But—but—I'm sure—I—I hope not," she added, sitting down and sobbing.

"Oh, don't cry, mamma," said Miss Perkins, melted by the tears of her emotional mother. "You may come, if you like."

"No—I won't go now."

"Pray do," said the daughter, hoping all the while that she would not.

"I won't," was the reply. "Go! I want nothing from you, and I only hope—I only hope you may want nothing from me. But I certainly shall expect all the money repaid that your father has advanced from time to time to Mr. Yapp."

"No fear of that, dear mamma, and as much more as you may require," said Miss Perkins.

"Oh dear, no! we shall only want our own," said Mrs. Perkins, proudly. "We want nothing from anybody but civility."

"Come Maria!" Mr. Perkins called up the stairs. "Mr. Yapp is impatient for his walk."

The summons was quickly obeyed, and Miss Perkins, after kissing "dear mamma," tripped down the stairs in her flowing summer muslin, and arm in arm she and the delighted loving clerk were soon in Lincoln's Inn Fields, and thence to the Temple Gardens.

CHAPTER XIII.

THE WEDDING-DAY ARRANGED—IN A FIX FOR MONEY—PERKINS SUGGESTS A VISIT TO A FORTUNE-TELLER.

DURING the foregone scene between Mrs. Perkins and her daughter, a confidential conversation took place between the credulous chandler and the "child of mystery," interrupted, ever and anon, by a customer for some of the ten thousand domestic articles sold by the former.

They sat in a little comfortably-furnished parlour behind the shop, with a glass door, through which Mr. Perkins could keep an eye on his business, and at the same time attend to his friends. Mr. Yapp had that day honoured them with his company to tea, and a very nice tea had been provided, far better than any the clerk was accustomed to get. Cake, eggs, ham, muffins, and shrimps, with tea and coffee, were set before him; and, better than all, he was invited in the heartiest manner by his host, hostess, and his dear Maria, to do the viands justice.

At this meal the marriage-day was arranged—memorable in its tragic consequences to all present. The clerk, amidst blushes and laughter, took the measure of Maria's finger—for the plain gold ring, and during the pleasant manipulation he did not fail to squeeze her hand.

The clerk imposed the strictest secrecy upon all present, and Maria was somewhat disappointed to find that he wished the wedding to be conducted in the most private manner—no cards—no bridesmaids—no honeymoon tour—no display of any kind. He had acquainted his "solicitahs" of his intentions, and they, as his best friends, had advised him to make it for the present a private marriage.

Maria, always fond of display, had pictured to herself a grand wedding at least. Twelve beautiful bridesmaids—carriages and four—white satin dress, train, veil, and orange-blossoms—plenty of friends to meet her and greet her, and support her through the trying occasion—the bells to ring—a champagne breakfast—a cake the size of a coach-wheel, covered with sugar and Cupids—and a banquet and ball in the evening to all her acquaintances, after she had left with her husband on a marriage tour.

This was her dream, and it was for this that she partly consented to be married at all. Then judge her disappointment when she heard the clerk's wishes on the matter! She said nothing, frowned a little, and inwardly she felt deeply hurt, and it quite took the charm out of her "child of mystery!"

In truth, Mr. and Mrs. Perkins would rather it had been otherwise—would rather that a little jollification should take place on the occasion; but they also said nothing before the clerk, although they said a good deal, and insinuated more, when they got by themselves.

The marriage preliminaries settled, the clerk expressed himself in the most extravagant language on the happiness he felt, shook hands with his "fathah" and "mothah," as for the first time he addressed them, and lovingly kissed his intended beauteous bride.

"I am very proud to call you my son-in-law," rejoined old Perkins. "I am sure you will find in Maria a good and an affectionate wife; and if you rise to that state to which you are evidently entitled, you will not find her disgrace you."

"What is impossible cannot be!" exclaimed Mr. Yapp, taking the hand of Miss Perkins, "and *that* would be impossible! Having your daughter for my bride, Mr. Pahkins, I care not for state or riches."

"But I do though," thought the chandler. "What would become of the gipsy's prophecy if Maria did not marry a nobleman? And what is to become of the money you owe me if you don't get rich?"

"Happiness, aftah all, Mrs. Pahkins, is bettah than wealth," continued the sentimental clerk, running over with the most delightful feelings at the thought of his approaching wedding with a young lady he really loved.

"No doubt, Sir," said Mrs. Perkins," who sat as president of the bright plated teapot; "but I don't deny that wealth has a good deal to do with happiness. What do you say, Perkins?"

"Most assuredly," returned the chandler; "oblige me with a few shrimps, Maria. In my opinion there can be no happiness without wealth. Hand me some bread and butter, Maria. In all the novels I have read the happiest people have been those who could go about everywhere, and drive round to the homes of the poor and scatter blessings and five-pound notes. I have been poor, you know, Mr. Yapp—you never have. I know what poverty is from experience—you look at it from the height of unlimited wealth. What do you say, Maria?"

"I would rather die than be poor," was her decided answer.

"Demn it!" exclaimed the clerk, of course quite to himself. "They are all a lot of money hunters! Poor devils! I'm sorry for them. They've found no wealth in me—except wealth of intellect and personal appearance — things they don't care a demn about, that's evident. Nevah mind, I dearly love the gal, and aftah I am married it will be quite indifferent to me whose son the "child of mystery" turns out to be."

Then said Mr. Yapp, pleasantly to Maria, who sat by his side at the tea-table—

"So you don't believe in love in a cottage—eh?"

"It would depend greatly who was my husband," replied Maria, leading up to something very pretty in sound.

"Me, for instance," said the clerk, looking lovingly in her bright face.

"*Then*, of course, I could be happy in a cottage," was the triumphant reply, which crowned the clerk's joy for the whole of the evening. Then the rogue soliloquised to himself,

"That sentiment will soon be tested—not in a cottage, but in a first-floor back, perhaps, and then in arrears for rent. My career, my mystery, must soon be blown, and I fear all the Perkinses will be blown up with it. I'm sorry, very sorry,—but it is all the doings of fate. The fusees, her beauty, the mystery-loving father, are to blame—not me. True, I have told a lie or two—but they should have had more sense than to believe me. Unlimited wealth! unlimited impudence, unlimited dishonesty,—had I told them *those* were my possessions, why, then, Miss Perkins would never have been Mrs. Yapp.

That wouldn't suit the state of my feelings. Had I never seen her I should never have loved her. But from the first moment my eye rested on her, her image nestled in my heart—and I vowed to let nothing stand in my way to make her mine. I could not live without her. Selfish, no doubt—but there, there are none of us pahfect."

"Take some cake, Mr. Yapp," said Maria, handing up the plate, and wondering what his thoughts had been engaged in, especially when his face assumed a seriousness unusual to him.

"I will take a few shrimps in preference, Maria, if you will permit me."

"Oh, with pleasure," she said, with a plated spoon handing him some of the cockney's favourite relish.

"Did you ever read a book, Mr. Yapp," said the chandler, "called ' A Snake in the Grass ?'"

"Nevah," said Yapp; "A very interesting, title, though."

"And a very interesting book, too," said Perkins, and he was well supported in this assertion by his wife and daughter. "I sat up one whole night to read it, and I could do it again."

"Let us hear the plot of it," said the clerk, busily denuding his shrimps of their legs and shells.

"It can't be told, but I will borrow the book for you to read at your leisure."

"Is it comic?"

"Oh, no, tragic—well, romance and tragedy combined," said Perkins. "That part, Maria, where the gipsy woman comes out from a cavern on the heath, and lays hold of the bridle of the horse in full gallop, and saves the heir that the cruel uncle was riding off with to bury alive—"

"I remember, papa," said Maria. "But I like that part best where the villain of the novel turns out to be different to what he represented himself, and where the marriage was stopped in time to save her from becoming the wife of a highwayman, instead of the lord he passed himself off as."

Yapp winced—changed colour—felt uneasy—but repressed his feelings as well as he was able, and asked Mrs. Pahkins to be good enough to give him another cup of her excellent tea.

"By-the-bye," said Perkins, "did you ever have your fortune told?"

"Nevah, Sir," said the clerk. "I have no faith."

"I am very sorry to hear that, after what I have told you," said Perkins. "St. Paul says, 'Prove all things.' Will you try now, just to oblige me?"

"Anything, my dear Sir, for that," said the clerk.

"I thank you—I thank you very much," said the stupid old chandler. "It is very kind of you—very kind, indeed!"

"Where shall we go—and when shall it be?"

"There is a very old woman that lives by the Tower—I will give you her address before you go—and, my life for it, she tells you whose son you are, and when, and by what means, you come into your lawful inheritance."

Mr. Yapp set up a laugh and essayed to speak while he laughed, but Mr. Perkins waved his hand and said—

"Not another word about it. You have promised me to go—"

"Yes—and you shall go with me, or meet me there. Give me the address."

The old chandler was in ecstacies. Hurrah

for another convert to the mystic arts ! He called for pen, ink, and paper, and wrote—

"Dolly Spittleberg,
"Crib Street,
"Near the Tower."

"Good, Mr. Pahkins," said the clerk. "I will meet you there at six next Wednesday."

"I shall be delighted !" exclaimed the chandler, putting in his cup for more tea, and begging Maria for a few more shrimps.

"I should like to go, too," said Maria.

"Stuff !" said her father. "You have had your fortune told. Your husband is to be a nobleman—and isn't he one ? What more do you want to know ?"

"A good many things. I should like to know whether I shall be happy—"

"Let me tell you that," said Yapp. "If careful watching night and day—"

"I shouldn't like to be watched," playfully interrupted Maria.

"I mean," resumed the clerk, "that I will tend upon you night and day, and every wish of yours shall be made my law. Nothing shall be spared by me to make you the happiest of wives !"

"I'm sure you can do no more," said Mrs. Perkins, overjoyed at her Maria's prospect of a happy union with a rich nobleman.

"I intend to be your slave," said Yapp.

"Don't be that, Sir—I don't like to hear of any man being a woman's slave," said Perkins.

"Nor I either," said his wife. "I like to see a man in his place, and a woman in hers."

"Mr. and Mrs. Pahkins—you know what I mean ? I mean that I intend in every way to show your daughtah that I love her as nevah was woman loved before. That whatevah may be my fate she shall share it and enjoy it to its fullest."

"Excellent !" cried Mr. and Mrs. Perkins. "I say, my dear Sir, see how mysteriously things work together."

"Oh, wondahful !" exclaimed Yapp, humouring his proposed father-in-law—for the fact was he was rather in want of money.

"But mindy'e, I knew what the fortune-teller told our Maria would come true, although I was puzzled to see how. Noblemen, I thought, would never find us out, and I could not tell how she could find them out. But I never lost faith—not I. And it has been my faith that has kept a wife for you, Sir ; for, Sir, Maria would have been the wife of a poor stationer handy by had I not insisted upon her waiting for the fulfilment of her destiny and the gipsy's prophesy."

"Your faith in mystery has wondahfully contributed to my happiness. I shall evah be grateful for your confidence, and hold in esteem the trifling accident that introduced me to your daughtah !"

"I am very proud of having such a son-in-law," said Perkins, "and so is my missus, too."

"And so I am," said Mrs. Perkins. "I only hope that Mr. Yapp won't forget the old folks after he has got our Maria."

"To do that, Mrs. Pahkins, would be paying a poor respect to my wife," said Yapp.

"She's a proud little minx," said the mother. "When she gets riding about in her carriage with footmen—"

"When," thought the clerk, "that when will be when pigs fly and maggots come to men."

"And dressed like the Queen by her maids—she'll never find her way to the chandler's shop in Cross Street. I know her better than you Sir—she's very proud."

"Of her beauty you mean ; and she has good reason to be," said the gallant clerk, a little to Maria's confusion, as her bewitching blushes indicated. "I'll answah for your daughtah and myself, that you shall have nothing to complain of. You will find us as a united, and, I hope, a happy family."

"I hope so, too, Sir," said the chandler. "I'll answer for me and my wife, that nothing shall be wanting on our part to make everything comfortable and pleasant. Take another cup of tea, Mr. Yapp."

"Thank you, I have had more than enough already," said the clerk.

"I'll put in some more tea in a minute, if you will take another cup," said Mrs. Perkins.

"I would rathah not, thank you, ma'am. And now, Maria, shall we take an evening stroll ? And, perhaps, Mrs. Pahkins will accompany us ?"

"That I will with pleasure, Sir, if I should not be intruding," said the old lady, bustling up from the table, proud, indeed, to cling to the arm of her noble son-in-law.

The clerk rose and politely opened the parlour door for the ladies to retire and prepare themselves for a walk.

CHAPTER XIV.

AWKWARD DISCLOSURES—THE CLERK IN A FIX.
—PERKINS DOUBTS.

MR. YAPP had a great deal on his mind to communicate to his father-in-law—but he hardly knew how to break the ice. Of course it had to do with money—demn it ! his remittances were again behind.

"On Wednesday next, Mr. Pahkins, I shall expect you at Dolly Spittleberg's," he commenced, attacking the stupid old chandler's weakest point.

"No fear in the least of that, Sir," said Mr. Perkins, wiping his mouth and clean-shaved chin with a corner of the table cloth. "Then, Sir, you will see and know a deal more about yourself than you do now."

"I confess, I am half a believer already in the mystic art. It would be impertinent to doubt after what you have told me—and what I myself have experienced. But, curse the thing ! I wish my remittances would come more regularly. I have only had a hundred and fifty pounds for the last month—and the solicitahs, confound them, are out of town. And you see, Pahkins, there is such mystery in the business that they cannot confide it to their managing clerk."

"I see, I see, Sir," said the chandler.

"Worst of all, the solicitahs won't be in town for a month. Gone on the Rhine, and the devil knows where besides."

"'Tis awkward, certainly, Sir," said the chandler.

"Demmed awkward !" reiterated the clerk. "I wouldn't have cared, you see, but for the—the—the mahriage. I must furnish, and get everything arranged for Maria's comfort. Time presses."

"Why, yes, a fortnight is not much time to prepare for a wedding. There is one thing, and under the circumstances, rather a fortunate one, that it is to be private."

"Ha ! what should I have done had it been otherwise ?" exclaimed the clerk. "But as it is

—to do the thing in the humblest mannah—I cannot pull through without three hundred! I could get the money directly from any of my friends, but I am afraid they would be inquisitive, and it would spoil all. For if my intention of mahriage were to be spread it might get to ears that would object to my lowly alliance with your daughtah, and cut me off from my expected inheritance."

"Whatever is done, the advice of your solicitors must be carried out, and the marriage kept a profound secret."

"Oh, yes,—oh yes," said the clerk. "It would nevah do to make it known. Now let me see. I cannot furnish well, can I, Mr. Pahkins, under three hundred?"

"Not well—although *I* commenced housekeeping with twenty pounds."

"Ye-e-s—but—but of course that style of thing would not suit me," said Yapp.

"Oh, dear no, of course not—a gentleman with your expectations must have something near the mark."

"Can't possibly be done for less than three hundred—can't conceive the barest necessaries can be obtained for less. Demn it! what ever is to be done, Pahkins?"

"Really don't know," said Perkins, after thinking awhile.

"Impossible to put the wedding off," said the clerk, pacing the room with his thumbs thrust into the arm holes of his light waistcoat, across which was a chain that *looked* of value, as well as a great variety of pendants which *looked* real. "Wouldn't dream of such a thing!—wouldn't for the world! Demn it, no!"

"Oh, dear no," said Perkins. "But I tell you what, Mr. Yapp—let's see what the fortune teller says on Wednesday. Light may be let in on the whole affair—she may tell us what to do —who to see—and who to avoid. My dear son—"

"He'll find me *dear*, I'm sure of that," thought Yapp, twirling round and round the long hairs of his dark moustache, until they gracefully curled.

"My dear son,—look here, you see—my dear son—"

"Well, Pahkins, you have said so three times, what would you say?"

"Well, I wish I had the money—but I haven't."

"I did not suppose you had," said Yapp. "But it must be raised. I have too much respect—esteem—regard—love for your daughtah, than to allow a paltry three hundred to stand in the way of our union. I care not for myself—but then she shall not suffah. Pahkins—" here he abruptly took the chubbed-faced chandler by the hand, and laid another on his shoulder—"Mine is not an ephemeral love—in me you will find a steadfast son-in-law—not one blown about by the winds of passion—here to-day and gone to-morrow, as they say on the cemetery tomb-stones. And God knows that I love her for herself, and think my dowah as nothing compared to her charms and her goodness. Well, furniture we must have."

"Yes—well?" said Perkins.

"We are both agreed that furniture must be had?"

"Decidedly."

"And we are both agreed that we don't know where to get it from?"

"At present," said Perkins.

"And we are both agreed that it cannot be done under three hundred," interrogated the clerk, still clasping one hand of the chandler's while he kept the other on his shoulder.

"Yes, to make things comfortable, I should say three hundred," said Perkins, looking up with pressed lips in the clerk's scheming face.

"And now, under the circumstances—what—what—are we both agreed to do?"

"I say wait 'till we have seen the fortune teller."

"My mind is in too great a state of excitement to wait. I must answer about the villa to night —Oh! an exquisite,—a delightful,—and yet an economical home! *I won't wait*. I'll go to the solicitah's—speak of my wedding—run all risks of great expectations——"

"No, no, no, don't be rash," said Perkins, a little alarmed, "don't do that, that would be spoiling the ship for a ha'perth of tar. Something must be done."

"We are both agreed on that. But what— what?"

"Well—let me see—upon my word I don't know," said Perkins."

"Dost know a discounter?" inquired Yapp, coming to the point that he had meditated from the first.

"Never did a bill in my life," said Perkins.

"Demm it! nor I. But that's no reason why we shouldn't. Draw on me, or I on you, don't mattah which. Yet it will be bettah for you to draw on me and get it discounted. I will meet it when it becomes due."

Old Perkins hesitated—indeed he very much hesitated—and was silent for a longer time than the designing clerk appreciated.

"You are very dubious, Mr. Pahkins," said the clerk, "You seem to lose your faith in mystery."

"Oh dear, no, Sir, plenty of faith in mystery, but none in bills," said the chandler.

"Then shall the whole affair be off?" demanded the clerk, knowing full well that Perkins would object to have his daughter's affections trifled with.

"That need not be. Wait, I say, until after we have seen the fortune-teller. A day or two is of no consequence."

"A waste of time. But there, I'll wait. Still I don't know why I should; for if the hag says that I am to be king of England, I don't see how that will facilitate me in getting the three hundred."

"Oh, I will do it *then!* do it if I sell all my small properties. Do it, if I sell everything I have in the world!"

"Come, come, fathah Pahkins, that's practical!" exclaimed the clerk, knowing well how to work the oracle, and caring nothing for the future reckoning. He loved the girl, he wooed the girl, and he was determined to allow nothing, however dishonourable, to stand in his way of marrying the girl. Oh, she was such a lovely creature was Miss Perkins. The clerk flattered her well to her father, and then—then he borrowed a couple of sovereigns, for he had—when had he? —no loose money for the evening.

The clerk slept well that night, secure of a wife and secure of the three hundred. He saw a way to outwit Mr. Perkins, chandler and oilman, with the fortune-teller, whose address he had cleverly possessed himself of, and whom he was not quite such a fool as the chandler to believe in.

"Some infernal old beldame!" said the clerk, preparing for a visit to her some time before the chandler would arrive, "whose word and prophesies I will buy for half-a-crown—at least that is all I have to offer her. The rogues live on the fools, and serve the fools right. I'll have the girl—oh how I love her!—and neither fathahs nor employahs shall balk my fancy."

At four o'clock he was on his way to Dolly Spittleberg's, whose wretched residence he had some difficulty in finding. But the game was up if he did not get an interview with the crone, and prompt the crone, before Mr. Perkins arrived.

CHAPTER XV.

MR. YAPP VISITS THE FORTUNE-TELLER AND BRIBES HER.—DOLLY SPITTLEBERG'S HOME. —MR. PERKINS TAKEN IN.

CRIB Street, near the Tower, was celebrated for two things—its extreme loneliness, and for being the residence of an old crone, Dolly Spittleberg. Many of the romantic maidens and silly men round and about the vicinity of the Tower had crossed Dolly's hand with silver in return for revelations of their good and bad fates. But Dolly's fame as a fortune-teller had spread more or less over London, and the credulous and superstitious of both sexes had come from far and near to consult her.

None of her craft excelled Dolly, and but few came up to her in the cleverness of her imposition. Her personal appearance much favoured her in her cabalistic profession. She was little and old—crooked and stern—short and bold— while her sharp chin served as a resting-place for her sharp nose, and her lips fell back in the place where once her teeth had been. A few hairs had grown on her upper lip, and a large wen had settled in close proximity to her left eye.

Dolly was very miserly, and reported to be rich. Her make-up was characteristic of her tribe—a faded red cloak on her piled-up shoulders, and a snake-like twisted stick, with a carved cat's-head for the handle, was rarely out of the grasp of her hand. She generally wore a gown of large-pattern, her red short cloak, and a black silk bonnet of the memorable coal-scuttle shape.

Like a queen, Dolly never rose to receive her visitors, but sat in an old wooden arm-chair, with rails around the back, and whoever consulted her was requested to bring a chair and sit by her side.

Her home consisted of three dull dark rooms, and in the one in which she saw her dupes was an oil portrait of herself, dressed in the same costume we have just described her, in a large black oak frame.

Two graceful maidens made their exit from the room tittering directly Mr. Yapp knocked at the latched door and was told in a squeaking voice to come in.

Mr. Yapp in many respects was a man of the world, and he had now to play as clever a part as Dolly. He did not come there, like most of the fortune-teller's disciples, to be duped by Dolly, but he came to dupe her—at all events to see how far she was accessible to the charms of money.

He had been some time longer than he expected in finding her hovel, and therefore he was obliged to be as brief as possible with his business with her, or Mr. Perkins would be there before he had laid the trap for him.

"My visit to you to-day," said the clerk, after taking a chair as requested, "is fraught with importance to me."

"I know that, young gentleman," said Dolly.

"How should you know?" inquired Mr. Yapp in surprise.

"It is my art to know everything," said Dolly, with a strange laugh. "Do you doubt?"

"Oh no,—certainly not—or I should not have been here," said the clerk, impressed with Dolly's appearance and her assurance.

"I know who you are—what you are—and what you will be," said the impostor.

The clerk stood amazed, and looked at Dolly penetratingly, with an expression on his countenance as if he had been calling her everything but an honest woman.

"What am I?" cried the clerk, at once putting the crone's boasted knowledge to the test.

The old woman said nothing, but significantly held out her aged hand bursting all over with blue-black veins.

"Hem!—yes—I see—money," said the clerk, giving her half-a-crown.

She took the coin and put it in her pocket, and again held out her hand.

"Demn it!—more?" cried the clerk in a bit of dilemma, for he had no more.

"Your visit here is of importance to you—and can you buy things of importance for half-a-crown?"

"I have a friend coming here presently—"

"I know that," said Dolly, impetuously. "You can tell me nothing."

"Stuff, woman! I am not a fool!" exclaimed the clerk, rather annoyed. "When my friend comes you shall have money. Give me faith— who am I?"

Dolly opened a black-letter book with a large brass clasp, and after glancing a minute or two over its pages, and covering one entirely with the court cards from a pack that lay on the table, answered to the great amazement of the clerk—

"A child of mystery. Have you faith now?"

The woman's answer was given in his own language, and was irresistible to the clerk's incredulity, and he almost yielded himself up as another dupe to the crone's witcheries.

"Solve the mystery!—whose son am I?" demanded the clerk.

"A foreign king's! or an English earl's!" was the astounding reply.

"Demn it!"

"Don't swear, young gentleman, in my presence," said the hag, with dignity.

"I cannot express my surprise differently," said Mr. Yapp.

"Why are you surprised?"

"That you should know so much."

The witch laughed—then frowned—then said—

"Go straight to your business—you have a friend that will be here at six o'clock."

"How know you that?"

"By the same manner of means that I know all things else," replied the woman. "Your fortune, William Yapp—"

The clerk started back in wonder and amazement when she pronounced his name.

"Your fortune, William Yapp, is a bad one, and will have a tragic ending."

The clerk turned pale at these words, for there was no room now left for him to doubt Dolly's insight into the future.

"Your life has been one of dishonour and deception. You are here now only to deceive."

LADY BLAZE THWARTED IN HER INTENTION TO MURDER MR. YAPP.

Mr. Yapp's head swam round with surprise at the truth contained in Dolly's terrible words. All his gaiety fled, and he feared the woman who, not five minutes ago he despised, and came to laugh at.

"You are a child of mystery, it is true—but you are not the son of a foreign king or an English earl. Say—shall I tell you whose son you are? You would tremble to know."

"Oh no, no, no!" cried the clerk. "Let me be kept in ignorance."

9

"Better for your peace that you should." said the crone. "You love a maiden, beautiful to behold—that I know. And you come to me to help you to deceive her father, that he might give you money to marry her. Is that true?"

"Oh! wonderful woman!" exclaimed the clerk, appalled with the witch's knowledge.

"It *is* wonderful to be able to tell the fate of mankind. I often wish I could avert fate—but that is a power given to no one," mused Dolly.

"When your friend—your future father-in-law—comes, don't you forget to pay me."

"Will you help me?"

"Leave all to me. The maiden shall be yours."

"Eternal thanks to you!" said the clerk.

"Thanks!—I must have money," said the woman.

"You shall, you shall, Dolly!" cried the enraptured clerk.

"And whenever you have the courage to know whose child you are, come to me. But be advised—'Where ignorance is bliss 'tis folly to be wise.'"

Mr. Perkins arrived, and we need scarcely say that before he left he was terribly imposed upon by the crone and his future son-in-law. Dolly told the young man that an earldom would fall to him by the time (here she took an horoscope) three children were borne to him.

Mr. Perkins was delighted—who would not be?—at the assurance of having an earl for a son-in-law; and Mr. Yapp was soon master of the three hundred. The chandler at once mortgaged for it, and gave him the money.

The villa was elegantly furnished, and soon after poor Maria Perkins became Mrs. Yapp, but never a countess.

No doubt the reader would like to know by what means the fortune-teller was so well informed about Mr. Yapp's affairs of mystery? The fact was old Mrs. Perkins, learning from her husband that her daughter's marriage rested upon the verification of Mr. Yapp's statements, hastened off to Dolly and bribed her to say what she told her. She would not have her Maria's affections trifled with for all the money in the world.

CHAPTER XVI.

THE MURDER PREVENTED. — THE THIEVES' QUARREL.—MR. YAPP THREATENS THE LIFE OF SWIFT.—TOM'S RELEASE FROM PRISON ARRANGED.

WE have made a long, but necessary, digression, in order that the reader should be in full possession of the means Mr. Yapp used to win a wife that he loved, to her ruin and his own.

We will now return to the warehouse in Bolt-court, where we find the elegantly-attired Mr. Yapp still asleep, with his wife's shawl on the floor, waiting for Mr. Swift's return from the police-station.

While he was in this somnolescent state, a woman came quickly down the stairs. Lady Blaze, as we have said before, was always rapid in her movements. She was dressed for going out—that is, she had her bonnet on, and a leather bag on her arm. When she came near the warehouse-door, a smell, as of something burning, attracted her attention, and she paused and looked about. Seeing a light burning in the warehouse, she pushed the door which, not being fastened, gave way, and she entered. At first she saw no one, but presently her fiery eye fell upon the sleeping clerk, who slept with folded arms against the sacks which stood about full of rags.

"Ha!" exclaimed Lady Blaze to herself, as she started back as from a reptile when the sleeping clerk met her gaze. "Has my time, then, come at last for sweet revenge?"

She flew stealthily from the wareroom, and went up stairs as swift as the wind. Then she unlocked her garret-door, threw the leather bag on her bed, wrung her hands, and cried—

"I hope he is prepared! for death—instant death is his fate! Oh! how wronged must I have been to contemplate and do a murder!"

She went on her knees and unlocked her box, from the top of which she took the richest of white satin dresses, trimmed as for a marriage garment. She looked with a trembling lip upon it, and kissed it; then the candle she held in her hand displayed indeed a wonderful mass of jewellery, that sent forth the most dazzling rays and sparkles. Here her malignant eye fell upon an ivory miniature (no doubt the one that Swift spoke about to Mr. Yapp) of a gentleman handsomely dressed in the costume of twenty years ago; and he was, indeed, as Swift said, very much like Mr. Yapp, but more in expression than features. She held it in her hand, looked at it, and cursed it! By the side of a bracelet lay a sharp-pointed silver knife; she quickly took it up, concealed it in her pocket, locked the trunk, and again flew down the stairs.

"Why should he live to torture me? Child for child!" she said to herself, as she came upon the threshold of the warehouse door, drawing forth the silver knife from her pocket, and grasping the pearl handle in the most determined manner. "For four-and-twenty years I have borne my cruel wrong, and now—now he is in my power —I will be revenged! To strike him while he sleeps may be cowardly; but I have been stabbed sleeping and waking for years—for years! *He* is innocent!—what of that? So was *my* sweet girl! It shall not weigh a feather with me. The guilty pair who called him son, in him have left a picture to torment me! His birth was my daughter's death!"

With decision she quietly pushed back the door, and to her horror cast her eyes on Swift, who, while she had been upstairs for an instrument of murder, had returned from the station-house, and now stood there with Mrs. Yapp's shawl on his arm, and reading Mrs. Yapp's note, both of which he had picked up from the floor where the over-wrought clerk had flung them.

Swift was as much surprised to see Lady Blaze when he looked up from the note, as was the woman, with murder in her mind, to see him. Lady Blaze, as well as her confusion would allow her, warily returned the knife to her pocket, on which her jingling keys rested, but not before Swift's quick eye caught the shine of the blade.

"How do you do to-night, mum?" in mock politeness, inquired Swift, who had innocently been the cause of saving Mr. Yapp's life.

The woman, hardly knowing how to account for her presence there, and so much hating the warehouseman, that she could not return an answer to his inquiry, for a minute was speechless. Then she said—

"That she had smelt a burning all over the house, and seeing a light in the shop she stepped in to see if all was safe."

"I've smelt the werry same thing," said Swift, looking round and about him, but before he had finished his sentence, brief as it was, Lady Blaze had made her exit, and returned to her garret. Here she threw herself on her bed and gave way to weeping.

"How fate sports with me! But for that wretch this knife should have rid me of a grief —have satisfied my thirst for revenge!—have made good a solemn vow! And after that the law might deal with me as it pleased—or these hands should take what was no value to me!

Oh! how I am thwarted! When—when—oh! when will the time of my relief come? I must be more desperate! I must have less remorse!"

Here she arose and went to her large trunk and buried the knife once more amongst jewels and valuables. In moving aside the handsome, flowing, white satin dress, she again muttered a curse upon the miniature, and passionately kissed the dress.

Then she locked the trunk, clasped her hands, and bowed her head upon it, and seemed lost in deep and anxious thought. She then rose and paced her solitary room, saying to herself—

"Oh! my dear murdered one! I long, long to be with you! But my guilty soul will never be allowed to reign with your pure spirit. A terrible wrong was done me and you, and I only live to requite it! Let the world say what it will—bah! what have I to do with the world? it cannot repair *my* wrongs!" She then closed the trunk, wrung her hands, and rapidly paced the room, in which there was nothing but the barest necessaries—as a couple of chairs, bed and table—but they were of the best kind, and evidently had once adorned a higher habitation than a garret. The bedstead was Arabian in make, and, of carved, mahogany, while the chairs had seats of green velvet, and it was those articles of furniture, when she moved to the garret in Bolt Court, that first drew forth remarks of surprise from the other tenants.

"She's no bad judge," said Swift, after he had read Mrs. Yapp's coaxing note to her husband. "These things," holding up the elegant shawl, "could not have been got out of *petty* cash. Oh no, Mr. Yapp must have had a dip in something that I know nothing about. He's been a hartful card."

Then he sniffed the air, looked up, and down, round and about.

"There certingly has been something burning here or hereabouts. Rags—paper—smells a good deal like it. Don't see nothink, though. Wouldn't care if the whole place was burnt down, Lady Blaze and all, if I had the jewellery that haunts me night and day, and will haunt me, too, until I has it in these 'ere hands"—holding them out.

"I wonder where our Mr. Yapp could get the money to buy the new dress the wife writes so coaxingly about? What dodgers women are! Here's this ere Mrs. Yapp, just like my old woman—a deal handsomer, no doubt—because Mrs. So-and-so has got what they *haven't* got, why, in course they gives their husbands no rest until they have bought 'em what Mrs. So-and-so *has* got. They don't think, not they, whether we have got the hincomes of Mrs. So-and-so's husband—hic-cup!—that's of no consequence—what they wants they must have, or we are the werriest brutes and villains that ever lived, and who didn't ought to live—and away goes the chayney plates—hic-cup!"

Here the half-drunken man placed himself directly opposite the sleeping clerk, leant against the wall, folded his arms, threw one leg over the other, and said—

"A werry good-looking young man is our Mr. Yapp, and werry clever at figures! He's plenty of muscle, too, but no nerve. What is nerve, I wonder? The want of conscience, I should say. And what is conscience? Don't know, never made his acquaintance! Hope I never may—for he and I should never agree. He's troublesome and cantankerous—nothing jolly about him—won't go in the swim for a good thing—

wakes you up o'nights, and pulls you over the coals about the day's doings. At least I've heerd as much. He sticks to you, and in so far he's werry much unlike a friend, and werry much like a bulldog—hic-cup!"

Looking on the floor, just by the leg of Mr. Yapp's chair, Swift saw the remnants of burnt rags and paper.

"Ha! what's he been up to? You're a slippery customer, Mr. Yapp. I must mind yer, or else you'll trip me up. There's more in that 'ere head than meets my hye. I don't at all believe in yer—you'd hang me if yer could. I knows too much. Two of a trade never did agree. I wishes now I'd kept my own secrets. I always was too good-natured. I have a presentiment—as our Mr. Yapp calls it—that he will either split or murder me! But he's caught a Tartar—I'll watch it. He's a hactor, he is, and tries to deceive. But if he deceives me, he'll only have one more to do, and that's Sir Nicholas Brimstone, who lives in the kitchen that stairs never yet reached." Then he stepped quickly to the side of Mr. Yapp, placed his mouth close to his ear, and loudly cried—

"Halloo, Mr. Yapp, I'm come to arrest you!"

The bewildered clerk sprung in affright from his chair, quickly drew forth his loaded pistol and replied—

"I'll blow out any one's brains who attempts to touch me!"

Swift was not at all prepared for this, and as he hastily got from the level of the aimed pistol, he looked terrified and cowed; for once the bully was taken out of him.

"Why what's the matter with yer, Mr. Yapp?" he inquired in very subdued tones.

"How dare you, sir, alarm me!" exclaimed Yapp, approaching the crouching Swift with the loaded pistol still levelled.

"Lord! only a bit of a lark, Mr. Yapp," said Swift, keeping his eye fixed on the clerk's movements. "I didn't mean to hurt your feelings."

"I have feelings and failings, Swift, and I will thank you not to trifle with them! You've dragged me into an ugly business, one not at all suited to my mind. You're a coward, Swift, to arrest the innocent boy for our robbery—a devil to think of such a thing!"

"But it's done, now, Mr. Yapp, and I have had a great deal of trouble with it, I do assure you, at the station-house."

"*I* will have no trouble with it," said Yapp, "whatever may be the consequences! It is *your* lie and you may get through it as you can!"

"Oh, its all right, Mr. Yapp," said Swift, crouching, cat-like, ready for a spring.

"All *right*!" exclaimed the clerk.

"Yes, Mr. Yapp, the charge has been taken, and the boy locked up."

"And you call it all *right*, do you? You thorough devil! Oh how my finger itches to pull the trigger, and—extinguish such a life as yours!"

"Don't, Mr. Yapp; don't be a highwayman. You'd be hung, you know, if you killed me, then what would your wife and pretty children do? Think of them, if you care nothing for me!"

The clerk, who was thus ruthlessly roused from his deep sleep, was in a fearful state of disturbance. Torn by the extravagance of her he loved—bewildered by the crimes he was surrounding himself with—hating his coarse-minded ally who now crouched for mercy, and in whose power he felt himself to be—deep in debt, and deep in crime, and regardless of life—it was miraculous that he had not shot the villain, and chanced the consequences.

He had designed in his mind the death of Swift, and it was for this purpose he had equipped himself with the pistol, after he had left Pounce-well, the detective.

But Swift's touching, artful appeal, about the pretty children, paralysed his pistol-hand, and he let it drop by his side. The warehouseman watched his opportunity, and here suddenly sprung upon the clerk, and seized the wrist of the hand which held the pistol.

"And now, Mr. Petty-cash Yapp, I'm as good as you! You would murder as well as steal, would yer?"

"Take the pistol for God's sake, and blow *my* brains out! I'm tired of life!" exclaimed the clerk, releasing his hold of the formidable instrument.

"I thank yer, for the hinvitation, but I'm not tired of *my* life if your are of *yourn*," Swift replied, holding the pistol, and looking at it. "Primed and cocked, eh? You meant hinstant hexecution on somebody—was it me?"

The clerk knew not how to reply to the pertinent question. He felt that it *was* for his interrogator, but had not courage to confess it, and after a pause, and after the question had been put again, he replied—

"He was so unhappy that he intended to take his own life."

"Pray don't let me perwent you," said the cold-hearted man, offering him the pistol.

The clerk waved it back with his hand,— saying—

"The time has passed, and so has my courage."

"Very well," said Swift, "then we will lock it away for the present;" unlocking a drawer over which he had control, and placing it there. "Pistols are dangerous companions to men of hot temperaments. You can always have it, Mr. Yapp, when you want it, always and perwided, as the lawyers say, that you use it upon yourself and not upon me: it may be all the same to you, and more agreeable to your humble servant."

The late post here brought another letter for Mr. Yapp. It was from Mr. Bonthron; he wrote to say that he still continued unwell, and that as he must remain at home, he would thank his clerk to send him all the account books, and he would endeavour to look through them, and post up all arrears and balance them.

This was truly unpleasant news for Mr. Yapp. He now saw nothing but discovery before him. He turned sick and faint with anxiety.

"What's the matter, Mr. Yapp?" inquired Swift.

"I'm ruined! utterly ruined!" exclaimed the clerk.

"Don't meet troubles half way," condolingly said Swift. "Fear will be your ruin. Light your cigar, and give me another, and let us talk our affairs over."

"The ring—"

"Well, what about that?" said Swift, when Yapp hesitated.

"It must be sold at once! I must have money immediately!"

"To buy the missus a new dress?" said Swift, plunging his hands into his pockets.

"What mean you, Swift?" exclaimed Yapp, somewhat in surprise where the warehouseman should have got his information from.

"Hasn't she written to you to bring her home one?"

"But how do you know that?" demanded the clerk.

"You shouldn't leave notes about if yer don't want them to be read," said Swift.

"Enough—that's like your coarse nature," said the chagrined clerk. "What right had you to read my letters?"

"Well, I'm sure! I didn't take it out of your desk, your hand, or pocket. I found it on the floor, and thought it was an order for rags," explained Swift.

"All right—no mattah; you are always ready with an excuse. Your mind is ready-furnished lodgings, and the devil has taken them."

"That's devilish good!" exclaimed Swift. "Hic-cup! I'll take a cigar after that."

"Where is the note?" inquired Yapp.

"The note? Let's see, what did I do with it? Shouldn't wonder if Lady Blaze didn't take it," said Swift, pretending to look for the note, which he knew well he had in his pocket.

"Lady Blaze!" exclaimed the clerk. "How could she have it?"

"She called in here while you were asleep," said Swift.

"Ha! has she missed the ring?" asked the clerk in terror.

"Oh dear no!" was Swift's reply. "She thought the house was on fire. She smelt burning, and so did I."

The clerk stared. He had been asleep, and had almost forgotten that small design of his to fire the premises.

"La! what a smothah a bit of burnt papah makes, Swift."

"Oh, werry great," said Swift, significantly, especially when it is mixed with rags."

"With rags!"

"Did you never hear of such a mixture, Mr. Yapp? Look round by that 'ere sack, and you will see it."

"Oh—ah—yes."

"Oh—ah—yes," reiterated Swift, mocking the clerk's confusion; "'spose you've seen it before, eh?"

"You mean where I dropped my cigah?"

"Ah! Mr. Yapp, I think the devil has taken the whole of your house," said Swift.

"I begin to feah that we are too much alike," said the clerk.

"Well, I never yet tried my hand at murder," said Swift. "You would have murdered me."

"You irritated me."

"Ah! but how came you to have the pistol?"

"I told you before—to kill myself."

"That's a lie, Mr. Yapp!" exclaimed Swift.

"Believe me," said the clerk, "but I am very unhappy."

"And you thought if you got me out of the way that you would be happier? There, I know all about it. I wasn't born to-day, Mr. Yapp. You meant murder, and I must beware of yer."

"You've got the pistol, Swift?"

"Yes, and mean to keep it; I shan't give yer a chance to take my life. I shall keep my weather eye up."

"My opinion is, Swift, that you will die in a less pleasant manner than by *my* hands," said the clerk, covering his murderous intentions as well as he could without denying them.

"I shall be hung, you think, eh?" said Swift, "Well, of the two, I prefer the public exit from this world. I should have my name in print, and it would give employment to some of our littery chaps to write my 'last dying speech,' and a 'full, true, and particular account' of my hexecution."

"Well, there's something in that, Swift, to men of ambitious minds."

"And there *might* be another pleasure in the hanging—"

"What's that, Swift?"

"Why I *might* be hung for killing you," was the cutting reply.

"I hope you have no such intention of giving yourself so much pleasure," said Yapp, rather startled at the hint, for he knew Swift was a desperately determined man, and did not vacillate like himself.

"Why just now you hinvited me to blow out your brains!" exclaimed the porter. "What a weathercock you are, Mr. Yapp."

"Surely a man may be excused for changing his mind upon a subject that involves life or death," said the clerk.

"I begin to think, Mr. Yapp, that yer bark is worse than yer bite. I must be stronger minded and not allow myself to be hirritated by your little snarls; treat you more as a spoilt child."

"Cease this bantah!" exclaimed Mr. Yapp. "Read that lettah from the gov'nah, and there you'll find that my ruin is accomplished except money can be raised to make good three or four heavy misappropriations."

After Swift had spelt out the letter, and discovered its meaning, he exclaimed—

"That's jolly!"

"Not for me," said Yapp.

"Oh, ain't it though!" retorted Swift. "You don't like master being away, do yer?"

"I don't like his writing for the account books, for he must discover that they are all wrong—wrong, Swift."

"In the first place he must not have them, to-morrow, which will give you further opportoonity to tinker with them, and I'll help yer with my adwice after you have stated to me fully and clearly the whole case. I've plenty of hingenooity in me."

"I've no way out of it but a restoration of the money, for if I leave the accounts uncredited Mr. Bonthron may choose to write off to the customers demanding payment, whereas they have already paid; on the other hand if I credit the accounts I shall be a hundred or two short in my balance."

Swift stared when the clerk named the amount, and then exclaimed—

"A hundred or two! You have been doing it in a more wholesale way than I imagined, Mr. Yapp. It's a long pull. Lord! the ring will be no use to such an amount as that, even if we could raise the tin on it to-night. Certingly I shall see the Jew, but I would rather have settled with him for the swag."

"But we haven't got the jewellery yet," said Yapp.

"Lord! we haven't done nothing yet. We have only just commenced business," said Swift. "Hush! Hush! Here comes Lady Blaze again. I know her step, its just as fast as if she was running away from a mad-bull. There she goes, and she's gone towards the Lion," here he went to the doorway. "Now there's nothing but one thing to hinder our doing the little affair at once, and making ourselves rich."

"There's no knowing how long she will be out," said Yapp.

"There's the difficulty," replied Swift. "Although, mind yer, I shouldn't be long about

it. Them 'ere keys," holding them up, "would soon be the open sesame. When she came in here just now she was on her way out, but when she saw me she went hastily away and ran up stairs—at least I call it running, she may call it walking. But she's always in a hurry. She's now out again. And what say you, Mr. Yapp, have yer courage, have yer nerve, have yer devil enough to attack the jewellery at once?"

"Oh! dear, no," said the clerk, his breath half taken away by the ruffianly proposition. "I want the money demned badly, too, but I have not nerve, Swift."

"Why you have nothing to do but keep watch," said Swift, "I will go up the stairs, unlock the door, attack the trunk, and bring down the jewellery!"

"But what if you should meet the old lady on the stairs? or what if she should get into the room while you were there?"

"Why I'd kill her! that's what!" exclaimed Swift. "I don't mind blood to serve myself more than you do, Mr. Yapp."

The clerk shuddered and shrugged his shoulders He liked crime done in a more delicate manner. Practically there was very little difference between the two men; one would murder to cover his shame, the other, who had no shame, would murder for revenge or robbery. Yapp, as we have seen, designed to kill Swift on the first opportunity, and had actually planted the pistol to do it with, and although balked now was still determined to take his life because he knew too much, and was fearful lest he should betray him. But both men acted from extreme selfishness, although from very opposite modes.

"Time presses, Mr. Yapp," said Swift, pulling off his shoes in readiness to ascend the stairs with as little noise as possible. "You keep watch at the door, and should Lady Blaze return keep her in conversation with some of your bootiful blarney."

"Ah, but suppose she won't wait and rushes by me," said Yapp, full of fears.

"Look here, Mr. Yapp, I can't be up stairs and down too," said Swift, angrily. "Will you do the up-stair work, and I will do the watchman?"

"Hush!" said the clerk, "some one comes up the court! It may be her."

"It might, and it mightn't," said Swift. "That's easily seen by looking out. What's the good of frightening yourself about nothing? Lookee yer, I've another plan. Let us close the front door and bolt her out, eh?"

"Then she would knock," said Yapp.

"And we should hear," replied Swift.

"And so would the other inmates," was Yapp's reply.

"What of that?"

"Why that some of them would at once let her in," said Yapp.

"Still we should gain time," Swift replied. "And when we heerd the knock it would serve as a warning, and we could hook it from the garret."

"And meet her on the stairs?" suggested Yapp.

"Oh,—there,—if you go on that way why it can't be done at all. You don't 'spose that when men make up their minds to a robbery, that they stop talking it over like a couple of gals, as we do?"

"It's as well to be safe," said Yapp.

"Safety be d——d! Let us be 'bloody, bold, and wigorous!' as Richard says. You've too much chatter and too little pluck, Mr. Yapp. Look here," he added, going to the drawer, and bringing forth the pistol, "that would be my way of doing it!"

"Mind, its loaded!" exclaimed the clerk. "Put it away. There's no occasion for that, Mr. Swift, none in the least. We will have the jewellery, but will do no murdah!"

"Oh, won't we though! But we will if its necessary," replied the brute, handling the pistol in a careless manner that was by no means pleasant to the clerk, who said—

"I tell you, Swift, it is loaded, and you are handling it as if there were no danger. Put it away, that's a good fellah."

Swift laughed at the clerk's fears, and jocularly replied—

"This little thing gives a man a great advantage over another, who hasn't got one—don't it? It's an ugly customer as you made me feel just now. How do yer like it?" he added, levelling his pistol as well as his unsteady hand would permit at Yapp's heart.

"Don't be a fool, Swift!" exclaimed the clerk, shrinking from the aim. "Hist!"—extending his finger—"there goes Lady Blaze!"

"I'm arter her!" exclaimed Swift, making a quick step or two towards the door, pistol in hand, but the clerk stopped him, saying—

"It is too late—she is half way up the stairs."

"Let me go, Mr. Yapp! I'm jist now in the humour for anything! and you will let me do nothing."

"Our plans are not yet formed for the attack on Lady Blaze. It would be rank folly our taking the jewellery from her, just that a policeman should take it from us."

"You're a cur, Mr. Yapp," said Swift, "that's what you are."

"Why, but for me, Swift, you would have blown the woman's brains out on the stairs."

"Don't you believe it. I meant to have seized her, and fastened her in our cellar below, while we went to the garret."

"She would have screamed and alarmed the inmates," said Yapp.

"Mind'ye, I don't care how it's done," said Swift, "but I don't leave this 'ere place to night until the jewellery is safe in these 'ere hands. Fair or foul, I means to have it this 'ere night, so no more palaver, Mr. Yapp. You've got money, go and buy your wife a new dress, I don't want yer."

"Don't let us quarrel, Swift. We are necessary to each other. What shall I do about the books?"

"Burn 'em—as you meant to do," was Swift's snappish answer.

"Who told you so?" asked Yapp, in surprise.

"Look there, Mr. Yapp, look at the hevidences," said Swift, pointing to the half-burnt rags.

"What of that? I told you how it happened.

"You told me, but I didn't believe yer," said Swift. "I can see through a brick wall. Nor did I believe yer when you told me that you got this 'ere pistol for yerself. These were the brains you wanted," pointing to his heavy brow. "And I shan't forgive yer in a hurry."

"I am sorry my word is in such bad odour with you, Mr. Swift," said the clerk, who always "Mistered" the warehouseman, when he wanted to conciliate him. "Give me your

hand, and let us be friends once more, Mr. Swift. You were right about the burning of the books—"

"I knew that!" exclaimed Swift.

"But not about the pistol, by ——." The clerk took an oath to a lie, but it answered its purpose, and satisfied the angry warehouseman.

"Well, I'll believe yer now you've sworn to it," said Swift, "and there's my hand. It was no bad plan either to burn the books—but I've got a better."

"No! have you, Mr. Swift? It would be everything to us, if you could arrange to get those demned books out of the way. They are full of false entries, I don't mind telling you. What are your plans, Mr. Swift?" he eagerly asked.

"Mr. Bonthron wants the books brought to him, as I understand?"

"He does, yes he does, Mr. Swift," replied the clerk.

"And you're afraid that when he gets hold of 'em and hauls them over a bit, he will discover many a thing in 'em that is not right and proper as my Sunday-school teacher used to say?"

"He cannot fail, Mr. Swift!" exclaimed the clerk. "In two cases he cannot possibly avoid it."

"You ought to have managed better than that," Mr. Yapp.

"Ah! Mr. Swift, did you but know how much I have had to manage, you would excuse me for a little blundering. There are now no secrets between us—we stand as confessor to each other—I commenced the little game from the time the books first came into my possession."

"And that's a good many years!" exclaimed Swift. "And I should say amounts to a good many hundreds."

"That it does, Swift. But most of it is now out of date, and can hardly be discovered, unless attention be directed to it. Of course, if Bonthron found anything wrong, the books would be scrutinised from the beginning, when some nice little villiany would be disclosed!"

"Shouldn't wonder," said Swift. "What a fine chance you've had!"

"I was a demned fool, Swift, for touching a penny of money that didn't belong to me!" exclaimed the clerk, with something like sincerity.

"I don't see that. Why?"

"Because it has cost me everything that was worth living for—peace of mind. I've been the most unhappy wretch living, ever since I took the first twelve and sixpence—for it was that small amount I began with, and oh! how the crime grew upon me. I never allowed an opportunity to pass that at all safely admitted of robbery."

"Well, you'd have been a fool if yer had," said Swift. "I never had an opportoonity till now with the jewels, and I don't mean to let that slip."

"I'm only telling you, Mr. Swift. I found one robbery necessary to cover another. But a thief—and I speak after a large experience—is the veriest fool alive. He barters peace and happiness for money, that he might revel in extravagance. He fills his soul with fear—until he starts at the sound of his name. In the midst of his highest gaiety he cannot shake his delinquencies from his oppressed mind—they are with him then—they lie down with him—they encumber his dreams—and they stand rigidly before him in the broad daylight. What is my condition now, Swift?"

"Well, judging from appearances, I should say none so dusty," said Swift, laughing.

"Stuff! I mean condition of mind?"

"Oh, mind! bother mind! They're troublesome things when they become your master. I make the little one I have follow my hinclinations!"

"My mind is not of so subservient a character—not so elastic," said Yapp.

"Then throw it overboard; as a rule never be bothered with a thing that does nothink but trouble you," said Swift, with the tones of a man of wisdom.

"Can't be done, Mr. Swift. And as it is, I would rather be a dog than be the wretch I am. That poor imprisoned boy troubles me—"

"You are troubled then about small things," interrupted Swift.

"Bonthron's books again."

"I can manage them," said Swift.

"Now tell me how, and you will have endeared yourself to me for life. Speak, frankly and fairly!—speak, and relieve me of this incubus."

"What bus?"

"Incubus—terrah—horrah,—that I now endure about these demned books!" replied the clerk, who minced his words and pronunciations like a west-end lady.

"First give me a cigar, and then sit down," said Swift. "Let us spend a happy hour or two. I'm devilish tired."

"And so am I," said the clerk, handing Swift his cigar case; then throwing himself into the chair he had slept in, and crossing his legs.

"Those account books that our Mr. Bonthron writes for in regular course of trade I shall have to take to him—"

"Yes, Swift—well?" said Yapp, eagerly drinking in each word the porter spake.

"Now he lives at Clapham; in consequence I shall have to shoulder the parcel over Blackfriars Bridge."

"Well, Mr. Swift?"

"There is a river beneath the Bridge—where many a life has been drowned, and which surely is capable of destroying a few account books. D'ye see?"

"Not exactly."

"Ugh! ugh! I do though, plain enough."

"Tell me, Mr. Swift! I am anxious."

"I've got the thing pat enough. Look'ye heer. I am going over the Bridge with the parcel."

"Well?"

"Don't interrupt me, as the Inspector at the station-house said, and which I shan't forget in a hurry. Well—when I get on the Bridge what so easy as letting the parcel of books tumble over into the Thames and say it was a haccident, or that some one pushed against me and the parcel tilted bang over into the water?"

The clerk looked unutterable pleasure; he seemed like one respited from hanging, or other violent death. Swift's plan of destruction of the books, thus blotting—or washing—out the traces of his many crimes of embezzlement, so much pleased him that he rose in such hurry to grasp the hand of Swift that his chair fell backward.

"I am grateful to you for life, Mr. Swift!" exclaime d the clerk.

"I'm a good friend but a bad enimy," said the flattered Swift. "Now look heer now, I shall take out two parcels with me—one a dummy,

and the other the books. I shall let the dummy tumble over and preserve the books—what d'ye think of that?"

"No, Swift, no—let the demned books go to the bottom of the rivah! I could not breathe freely—I shall nevah feel safe—while they are in existence. Have another cigah?"

"Arter this ere one that I'm a smoking on."

"Give me your hand, Swift. I feel so happy—you have done it—that I begin to prize the life that but a minute ago I would have hugged the man who would have been brave enough to take it from me."

"I shan't go with the books until to-morrow, and for this reason—that I had better let the parcel go over in broad daylight, and in the face of witnessess. I shall slip like—over goes the parcel, and I shall preach a tale to the passers by about the unfortunateness of the haccident, and how that I shall lose my situation, and there is quite sure to be respectable people who will come forward and state what I say to be true."

"Capital! capital! Indeed you are a friend!" exclaimed Mr. Yapp. "I feel a man again! Let us go and have a dozen or two of oystahs."

"What about the dress for Mrs. Yapp? Hadn't you better go and buy that and make things pleasant at home? You've got a fiver you know out of the letter."

"Demn the dress!" exclaimed the clerk. "None is wanted, Swift. It is the insatiable extravagance of my wife, and my overflowing love for her, that has made a thief of me. Yet I deceived her first—told her that I was a man of unlimited wealth, and never found courage enough to tell her that I told her a lie."

"But why should you have told her that?"

"Because I worshipped her beauty, and I saw no way to make her mine but by seeming rich. And by dodging I have kept her so long in affluence, that upon my soul! it would be cruel now to tell her who she has married. Worse than all, I see too, Swift, that she only loves me for the things I surround her with and not for myself."

"I'd see her d—d first——"

"I can't bear that to her, Swift. I am the villain!—I am the deceiver! She should not be made to suffer!"

"But she knows you are only a clerk, don't she?"

"No, she believes me to be—what in my impatience to win her I told her—a man of unlimited wealth, and only held a situation to employ my leisure and as a relaxation."

"And you talk of my ingenooity!" exclaimed Swift; "why, you lick me by chalks! You've been a Gulliver a-many years, Mr. Yapp!" said Swift.

"Ah, Swift, the first lie told, where is the arithmetician capable of muiltiplying those that necessarily follow to give the semblance of truth to it? But a truce to moralising! You have saved me, Swift! A long time since I felt so happy. You have raised me to the seventh heaven. But the poor boy—I feel that his incarceration will turn out a stumbling-block and a blunder."

"Well, I'm not so sure about it myself," said the warehouseman, much to the clerk's satisfaction. "There are many ugly circumstances about it, and the sharp hinspector seemed to go right to the mark. Had you been cross-examined as I was, you'd have broke down altogether."

"What's to be done, Swift? I wish to heaven you had taken my advice before. But I am glad you see with me now. What's to be done, old fellah?"

"What's become of the other money, was the doubt on the hinspector's mind—and then your absence—and then the boy's hinnocent looks, and his going straight to the mark and charging me with placing the note in his pocket. It's all ugly, I admit."

"Oh, very—very," said Yapp, with a deep sigh. "Get us out of this as cleverly as you manage the books, and you will indeed be a trump of a fellah!"

"You see the charge is taken, and the boy must come before the alderman. But I have it. You take a Hansom cab—drive to the station—hurry in out of breath as it were—say you have driven straight from Mr. Bonthron's, and that the charge against the boy is altogether wrong—that the remainder of the money was taken by mad Bonthron, who opened the letter; and that *he* placed the five-pound note in the boy's pocket."

"Very good, Swift!—capital, Swift! Then how about to morrow?"

"See a solicitor, and get him to attend on behalf of Mr. Bonthron, and explain to the magistrate the whole affair; and take my word for it the boy will be dismissed without a stain on his character. Pouncewell—see him—and he will put you in the way of it over a glass of ale. You may be able to get the boy off tonight."

"How glad I should be if I could!" exclaimed the clerk; "you are indeed a friend. Well, now everything is arranged——"

"Oh, no!—what about Lady Blaze?" said Swift.

"You shall have your own way with her. After we have settled the boy and disposed of the books, we shall be freer to talk of the jewels."

"You thought we had rather too much business on hand—eh, Mr. Yapp?"

"I did, and that's the truth, Swift. Now I'll be off to find Pouncewell; failing that, I shall take your excellent advice about the cab, and a solicitah. I know a capital one for the purpose. I say, Swift, I will go with you and see the destruction of the parcel—and after that, old fellah, we'll have a boat out for an hour or two on the Thames, and a jolly evening!"

"Shall we want this with us?" said Swift, holding up the pistol.

"Psha, no! I hope never again. I like my life bettah than I did!"

"But what about mine—eh, Mr. Yapp? what about mine?"

"Safe for me. When you conceive an idea, there's no beating you from it, Swift. But you are a capital fellah, for all that. Believe me, I never meant to take your life. Why should I?"

"To save your own—d'ye see?"

"Psha! you are wrong, old fellah," said the false clerk.

"Well, none of your tricks, you know," said Swift. "Mind, get up your nerve by to-morrow night, for I swear we'll have the jewels if we have to take the life of Lady Blaze for them."

"All right!" said the happy clerk, turning off the gas and locking up the warehouse door. In the court they grasped each other's hand, and parted for the night.

———

CHAPTER XXVII.

THE LOST RING.—DEATH OF MR. BROWN.—MOTHER AND SON IN THE POLICE-CELL.—TOM DECLARED TO BE INNOCENT.

AFTER Mrs. Brown's encounter with her wretched husband, and after he had left her, the distressed woman, when she had sufficiently recovered, wandered forth in her poor habiliments in the cold dark night, in search of her poor little son Tom Brown.

Half-broken hearted she hastily made her way to Bolt Court, and just after Swift and Yapp had left she stood before the warehouse of Messrs. Bonthron and Son. But there all was dark and closed. What could she do? She knew not, and wandered about the court and Fleet Street, pondering the steps she should take to find out what had become of her incarcerated son.

At length she knocked once at the door, to see if any of the inmates could inform her about her boy. She had but poor hope of it, still it was her only chance. There was no answer to her feeble, timid knock, and then she knocked twice louder.

While she stood at the door, humbly waiting for an answer to her summons, Lady Blaze came rushing down the stairs like a fury. She had just discovered that the ring Swift had stolen was missing from among her jewels.

She rudely knocked at each inmate's door on her rapid way to the street, and in tones that almost said, you are the thief, demanded if they knew anything about a diamond ring? When she got answer, she passionately said—

"Well, some of you have got the ring. I'm on my way to a police-office about it."

When she reached the street-door and saw Mrs. Brown shivering on the step, believing her to be connected with the house or some of the tenants, she abruptly said—

"What about my diamond ring!—have you got it?"

"I don't know what you mean, ma'am," of course, was Mrs. Brown's reply, while she looked at Lady Blaze in considerable surprise. "You have evidently mistaken me."

"Have I, indeed!" exclaimed Lady Blaze; "you live here, don't you?"

"No, ma'am, I do not; was never here in my life before," was Mrs. Brown's reply.

"Then pray what do you want here now?" inquired Lady Blaze in suspicious tones.

"I came to ask after my little boy, who should have been home hours ago."

Lady Blaze cut the woman short, by saying—

"I know nothing about your boy. Where is the ring? Who has the ring? Worth two hundred guineas!" This was as much spoken to herself as Mrs. Brown, then she rushed down the court, even disdaining, bleak as the night was, to pull her shawl around her, and in her speed to the station-house it flew backwards and fluttered as in a gale of wind.

She was soon out of Mrs. Brown's sight, and not long after she stood before the imperious inspector, to whom she gave notice of her loss, its description, and estimated value. When the inspector learnt that it was worth two hundred guineas he stared at the woman, wondering how she came possessed of such a valuable gem.

Indeed he put such questions to her that the sensitive Lady Blaze could hardly fail of understanding that he was suspicious of her, and she testily said—

THE HOUSE ON FIRE.—TOM BROWN'S LIFE IMPERILLED.

"What have all your questions to do with my loss, Sir? Pray don't judge me by my clothes nor my residence—I am a lady!" she added, drawing herself up to her height before the rail. "To those who doubt it, and who have a right to know, I can easily prove it."

The woman's manner and her speech silenced the suspicious inspector, and he made a note of her loss, promised to place it in the police *Hue and Cry*, and advised her to get out some hand-bills offering a reward.

"Reward! I would give anything for the restoration of the ring!" she exclaimed. "The money value of it is its least importance to me."

As she spoke thus her countenance lost its imperiousness and assumed the most abject sorrow. The inspector asked her if there was not a man called Swift on the premises? She answered "Yes." The inspector told her to watch that man. She thanked the officer, then left, and with the same speed that she had sought him, reached her garret home.

10

Mrs. Brown was talking at the door with Grandfather Grimes, when Lady Blaze came up, and she went hurriedly past the sweet-faced old gentleman like a tempest, which extinguished the feeble flame of the candle he held in the dark passage, while he spoke to Mrs. Brown, telling her the sad fate of her son.

Mrs. Brown was weeping violently when the candle was extinguished, and the good old gentleman was consoling her.

"Oh! Sir, this is bad news, indeed!" exclaimed Mrs. Brown.

"Well, so it is, ma'am," said the little old man, smoothing down his long grey thin locks. "But they do say there is a mystery about it. I, myself, saw the poor boy bound with ropes."

"With ropes! Oh! my dear Tom! Do kindly show me, Sir, where the station is," pleaded the distressed mother.

"With pleasure, ma'am, if you will but wait until I get my cap. It is too cold a night to be without one's cap. Sorry that I have nowhere but the passage to ask you in. I won't be one minute," he added, groping his way up the dark stairs to his one room as fast as his aged legs, encased in comfortable hose would let him. Nor was he long before he returned, his cloth cap carefully tied down over his ears, and then he escorted Mrs. Brown to the police-station, where slept her accused son, and where lay the corpse of her husband.

Grandfather Grimes pointed out the station, and the woman shuddered as she went up the narrow passage, and was faced by a number of placards offering all kinds of rewards for all kinds of crime. The old gentleman—his benevolent face downcast at the woman's sorrow and trouble—waited outside for her return.

Tremblingly she entered the office, and falteringly asked the inspector if he had a little boy there by the name of Thomas Brown.

"Yes, we have, and mean to keep him," was the uncouth reply.

"I am his mother, Sir; and have only just learnt that he is here."

"Oh, yes, he is here, and his father, too," was the response.

"His father!" exclaimed the woman, holding for support by the rail.

"And now we have the whole family here."

"What has his father been doing, may I ask?"

"Trying to drown himself," was the inspector's answer.

The first pain that shot through the woman's heart at this news was remorse and self-accusation. She felt that she had been too harsh with her husband, and had said things that had driven him to suicide.

"Do, Sir, let me see my child and husband!"

"Can't do anything of the sort, ma'am; they are locked up for the night," said the inspector.

"Oh do, do! I implore you, Sir. Have some compassion for a mother's feelings!"

"It is impossible. I would if I could—but your feelings must not control my duty."

The woman was on the point of swooning, when Mr. Yapp, in his fur coat, drove up in a Hansom, and entered the office in breathless haste, asking hurriedly—

"Which is the inspectah? I want to see the inspectah!"

"I am the gentleman you are inquiring for."

"The boy is innocent! The boy Brown that you have here for stealing a five-pound note, the property of Mr. Bonthron!"

To Mr. Yapp's extreme astonishment, the woman, Mrs. Brown, who stood by the rail, here fell at the feet of Mr. Yapp, and implored blessings on him for the good intelligence.

"Pray who are you?" he asked of the kneeling woman.

"I am his mother, Sir."

"Whose mothah?"

"Tom Brown's," was her reply.

"I am very glad to meet you, Mrs. Brown,—and glad to find that your little boy is innocent!"

"Who then is guilty, Sir?" inquired the inspector.

"The madman you had here this afternoon. I have just come from Mr. Bonthron's house at Clapham, and the money has been found. In a lucid interval young Bonthron confessed that in his delirium and rage, while he tied the poor boy down, he placed the note in his pocket."

"Well, I never thought the boy was guilty. I have had some experience in truth and falsehood."

Mrs Brown's gratitude knew no bounds—she blessed both the clerk and inspector over and over again; the latter for his good opinion of her son, and the former for bringing news of his innocence.

"Well," said the inspector, "after the news this gentleman brings—by-the-bye, Sir, is your name Yapp?"

"Aw—yes—that is my name; and I much regret that I should have left the office when your detective, Mr. Pouncewell—I think that is his name—called. But I was then on my way to Mr. Bonthron, to learn his views on the mattah."

"Very good, Sir," said the inspector.

"Now I suppose you will release the boy—aw?"

"Indeed I cannot. The charge having been taken, the case must come in due course before the magistrate."

"The devil!" exclaimed the clerk.

"No, not the devil, but the sitting alderman," said the inspector, with a smile.

"H'm — yes — vera good," said the clerk. "Then I had bettah instruct a solicitah to attend and say that there is no case against the boy—ch?"

"You must do exactly as you please, Sir. The boy with the other prisoners—"

Mrs. Brown almost shrieked at the word, which interrupted the officer—who had a horror of interruptions—and he began again—

"The boy, with the other prisoners, will be at Guildhall in the morning by ten. But under the circumstances the woman may see her son."

Mrs. Brown was very grateful; and while tears glistened in her eyes she was led along by the cell-man to the dread abode of her little boy.

In the meantime the clerk bade the inspector a polite good-night, and retired.

"Ha! how do, Grimes?" he said, as he re-occupied his Hansom. "Late for an old man like you to be out?"

Grandfather Grimes made a reverential bow to the great man belonging to Bonthron and Son, and Ha'd and Hem'd, and would have spoken, but the cab drove swiftly off.

CHAPTER XXVIII.

DEATH BY HANGING.—THE MOTHER FINDS HER SON IN PRISON.—THE WEDDING-RING. —MR. BROWN SAVED FROM A PAUPER'S GRAVE.

WHEN Tom Brown's cell door was unlocked the boy was discovered by his mother huddled up in a corner, his face buried in his hands.

The poor mother started back when she saw her son thus—he who had but that morning left her full of hope, and in the best of health and spirits.

"Oh, my poor dear boy!" exclaimed the woman, as the cell-man's lantern illuminated the little dark heap of humanity in the corner. The boy, roused at the well-known voice of his beloved parent, looked up, then settled back in his old position in tears and anguish.

Mrs. Brown fell on her knees and hugged her falsely-accused child to her bosom, and for some minutes their grief was too overpowering to find vent in anything but sighs and sobs and tears. At length Tom said—

"Dear mother, I have such a terrible tale to tell you! I have suffered so much since I left you, and the sight of you is the only relief I have had since I went from home this morning Do you know where I am, mother?"

"Oh, yes, my son," was the mother's answer, while she planted kiss upon kiss upon the boy's cheeks and lips.

"And do you know what I am here for, mother?"

"Yes, my dear boy. And do you know, Tom, that you are innocent?"

"Yes, mother, I and God know it—but no one else," said Tom.

"I know it, dear boy—and the inspector knows it—and everyone knows it now," said Mrs. Brown.

"Then why am I here, mother? Why, mother, if I am innocent, am I confined in this cell?"

"Only until the morning, my child; and I will stop with you. They have found you are innocent!" Here she kissed Tom again and again.

"I am glad of it for your sake and father's," said Tom. "Have you seen father, mother?"

"No, my child, not since he has been brought here."

"Then you know he is here? And do you know what for?"

"Don't mention it, Tom—you'll break my heart," sobbed Mrs. Brown. "I have not courage to see him, even if I could."

"Oh, mother! I have suffered much to-day; but this about father is worse than all. Do be kind to him, mother!"

"I always have been, Tom. But I lost myself to-night; I spoke in haste. He has been a foolish man, and we have been made to suffer desperately for his folly."

"See him, mother, and be friends with him, and cheer him, and tell him I am innocent!" exclaimed the boy, throwing his arms around his mother's neck.

"Can I see my husband, Sir?" inquired the woman.

"Well, I don't mind letting you see him," said the cell-man, "but it is against the rules, and you musn't be long. Follow me! he is in the next cell."

The door was opened, and the light from the lantern fell upon a tall figure stretched out at length upon the stone floor. Each arm was rigidly extended, and his eyes stared up at the ceiling.

"Brown!" said the woman; but there was no answer.

"He is asleep," said the cell-man.

"Oh, no! for his eyes are open," said Mrs. Brown, going to the figure, and at once his distorted countenance showed that his sleep was the sleep of death.

"Oh, he's dead, Sir!—my husband is dead!" exclaimed Mrs. Brown, kneeling by the corpse, and taking its cold hand in hers.

"Surely not," said the cell-man, advancing, while holding the light right over the face of the dead.

"Why, he has tried to hang himself and fell. Look! there is his handkerchief on the ground fastened to the nail, which his weight has dragged from the wall."

The cell-man's solution was the right one. Poor Brown, saved from drowning, had hung himself! His face was black, having a congested appearance about it, and his eyes protruded from their sockets.

Mrs. Brown bent over him, and seemed to mutter a prayer, in which the cell-man plainly heard her ask heaven for forgiveness. The cell-man communicated the tidings of his death to the inspector, and a surgeon was sent for, who could only confirm what was so evident—that he was dead!

Mrs. Brown returned a widow to the cell of her fatherless boy. With reddened eyes she clasped him to her troubled breast, and her hot tears fell fast and thick upon his upturned face.

"Have you seen father, mother?" Tom asked.

The mother knew not how to answer. The boy continued—

"How is he, mother? Did you tell father I was innocent?"

"You have no father, Tom!"

"Mother!" exclaimed the boy.

"I found him dead on the floor, my boy. Ah! Tom, we have lost your father. Don't weep—yet I cannot help it myself. His troubles have been too much for him, and I—I was very unkind to him!"

The orphan boy wept, and the widow wailed, and such a scene of indescribable grief never was enacted in a prison cell before.

"Do take me home, mother, or I shall die, too! Oh, my dear father! I loved him more in his misfortunes than ever. To die a death like this, too!—my father to perish in a prison!"

Tom worked himself up to passionate crying, and he sank on the stone bench and again buried his face in his hands.

The hearts of the widowed mother and orphan boy were at present too big with grief for consolation. Silence as deep as the darkness by which they were enveloped reigned in that cell of sorrow. The mother had no further words for her son, nor the son for his mother. Words were too weak for the occasion, and sighs and sobs and tears were the only vent that each could find for their oppressed feelings.

Mrs. Brown lingered as long with her boy as the good nature of the cell-man would let her; but at length his patience exhausted itself, and he was deaf to her entreaties to be allowed to spend the night with Tom. But it could not be; and with a kiss and an embrace, such as are only known to mother and child in trouble, she quitted the prison, promising to be with Tom in the morning, and accompany him to Guild-hall.

Passing with a step of sorrow through the inspector's office, she inquired, in a voice thick and choked with grief, about the rules regarding her deceased husband.

"Why, there must be an inquest, and then we shall hand the body over to the parish for interment, except you have funds to do it with."

"If I can have but time, I will do my husband's memory more respect than to allow him a parish burial."

"You must be quick about it, then, I do assure you. Directly a few boards can be hammered together the remains of a pauper is soon disposed of."

"My husband was no pauper," said Mrs. Brown, her old pride bristling up. "We were very poor, but we never had parish relief. My father is a man well off—a rich man—"

"Very glad to hear it, ma'am," said the inspector. "It does him no credit, then, to see you all in this state of distress and poverty."

"There are private reasons for that, Sir. My husband did not use him well—"

"Borrowed of him, and forgot to pay, I suppose," interrupted the inspector.

"Yes, he borrowed a great deal of money from him, and squandered it, and this alienated my father from us. But I think and hope he will help us now, and save my poor husband from a pauper's grave. However, I will write and try him."

"I hope you may succeed," said the inspector, which was about the kindest word he had uttered for the day.

Mrs. Brown thanked him for his permission to see her son, and then slowly wended her dismal way home to her dismal habitation, now without husband, without son.

The cat and the puppy belonging to Tom could not understand what had become of the family, and they were truly wretched in their absence. The puppy snapped and snarled at the overgrown cat, and the cat scratched and spat at the dog, and between the two, to use phraseology often applied to matrimonial difficulties, it was literally a cat-and-dog life of it.

But when they heard the footsteps of Mrs. Brown coming up stairs, and when she unlocked her room door and showed herself, it changed their quarrelsome tempers into every possible expression of amiability and joy. The old cat purred, raised her tail, rubbed herself against her, and walked round and about her number-less times; while the more exuberant yellow puppy jumped over the cat's back whenever in her circuit she came in his way, bow-wowed with as much significance as if he said, "I'm so glad to see you," then licked her shoes, and then "cut such fantastic tricks" about the floor that would have made the "gods" shout had he been enacting at a theatre.

But the poor widow's heart was too full of grief to return the warm greetings of the affectionate animals who discovered so much welcome in their actions, and they strove in vain for the smallest notice. At length proud puss ceased all manifestations of joy, and went to her accustomed seat by the fireless hearth, and seemed to meditate on Mrs. Brown's indifference to her caresses, and hoped, at all events, that Mrs. Brown would light the fire, and make things a bit cheerful.

The little dog also grew tired of his Jim Crow performances before his mistress; he didn't ask much reward for them, but he thought they were certainly worth a pat on the head and a stroke on the back; but as they failed to charm and attract attention from the new-made widow, he devoted his services to the cat, for which he got the most shameful treatment over the face and eyes; puss was too old for his unseemly gambols, and she richly chastised him for them, and sent him away crying "pen and ink!" Puss was very spiteful, but no doubt in her present attack she paid off some old debts that she owed the insolent puppy.

Mrs. Brown enlivened the room with the light of a candle, and then she kindled a fire, for she was very, very cold, and then she sat in deep abstraction upon the absent ones, and then she wept, and bitterly accused herself of the part she played in her last scene with her deceased husband. She would have given world's could she recall him to her side again. 'Twas all in vain. He had "gone to that bourne from whence no traveller returns," and all the widow's weeping and wailing could never reach the "dull, cold ear of death."

Like Lady Blaze, she associated with no tenant of the house she lived in, and she was too proud to renew her acquaintance with those she had known in better days; therefore she had the dreary night to pass through unrelieved by a word of sympathy or advice. As the clock struck one she made herself a cup of tea, but when prepared she scarcely tasted it. She sat in her chair, and inwardly prayed for her husband, her son, and strength of mind for herself to brave her troubles. In prayer she found that relief and solace for which the mourner never appeals in vain.

The reflection of a small blaze from the fire fell on her wedding-ring. Her eye fell upon it, and oh! the cruel thoughts that darted through her attenuated frame. Bitterly she repented her words that led to her husband's pulling the ring from her finger and throwing it where it now lay. She prayed—oh! how fervently she prayed—for his forgiveness, while she restored the ring to the finger that he placed it on at her betrothal.

Painfully she contrasted that day with the present. It almost drove her mad. She sought her bed, but no rest, no sleep, was to be found there. She arose, and addressed herself to the difficult task of writing to an offended father. She told him all, and implored his help in her hour of trial, and save her husband from a pauper's grave.

Her letter was written in that truthful yet impassioned style, and was so full of melancholy facts, that it would have moved the coldest heart, and the next post brought her an order on a London banker for twenty pounds, and a moderately-hearty invitation for her and her boy to visit her parents in Devonshire; but she was requested to ask for no more money, as he had not got it to spare.

The act of indiscretion that had so embittered the farmer against Mr. Brown was of a serious character, and might have transported him, as Mrs. Brown, in an unguarded moment, taunted him with. The deceased man knew that at the farmer's death his wife would inherit property from him, she being his only child. Mr. Brown was in extreme need, and well believed that a thousand pounds would save him, and extricate him from his difficulties. He forged the farmer's name for that amount, fondly thinking that, when the bills became due, if he could not meet them, that the farmer would look at it as so much less for his daughter when he died. But the farmer was very wrath, and, glanced at it only from the serious point of forgery, and certainly, but for his daughter's intercession, he would have prosecuted his son-in-law, who, when the bills fell due, was not at all in a position to honour them.

But for his daughter's sake, and in response to her affectionate pleading for her husband, he paid the money, and declined further friendship or intercourse with the Browns. For many months this painful estrangement lasted, during which period Mrs. Brown made many entreaties for reconciliation, but they met with no favourable response from her wronged and grieved father. The one only answer she received was to this terrible effect:—

"Write no more to me. Your husband has defrauded me. Peace is impossible. While he lives, write no more to me."

This cutting reply left Mrs. Brown no opportunity to write again; nor did she. But she now approached her father—who was by no means a jolly farmer, but a stiff, rigid, sanctimonious tiller of the ground, and one who did not love his neighbour as himself, nor did he good for evil—and she only succeeded to the extent of twenty pounds, and a cold request not to ask him for more.

Well, the widow smiled when she received that. It was very grateful to her, for it enabled her to bury her husband in a manner more congenial to her feelings than to see him stowed away in the workhouse churchyard by the cold hands of a parish undertaker, like rubbish in a lumber-room, his only requiem to be—

"Rattle his bones over the stones,
He's only a pauper whom nobody owns."

CHAPTER XXIX.

A WINDFALL. — THE BEGGAR-GIRL. — MRS. BROWN ARRIVES WITH HER SON AT GUILDHALL.—TOM BROWN SET FREE.—THE HOUSE ON FIRE.

THE morning broke without giving the faintest indications of anything but a dull, cold, wintry day, much like the one that had just for ever passed out of existence. Nevertheless it was much welcomed by the Widow Brown, for it brought her nearer to union with her son, whom she always loved, but since the recent death of her husband she had loved, if possible, more than ever.

By eight o'clock she humbly prepared to attend him from the station-house to Guildhall; and by eight o'clock the voice of a little girl who lived on the premises called up the stairs—

"Mrs. Brown, you're wanted! a gentleman wants you."

Of course the widow was astonished.

"A gentleman wants me! Whoever can it be?" she exclaimed to herself. She was so much surprised that she omitted to reply to the child who announced the gentleman, and the little dirt-begrimed girl came to Mrs. Brown's door and repeated the words she had called up-stairs.

"Are you sure, dear, that it is me that is wanted?" said the widow.

"I dun know, ma'am, but he said Brown; I know he did," said the tiny girl, who held in her hand a basin that she was on her way to supply with treacle. Her feet were bare of stockings and shoes, and her long light hair was matted with dirt, and her long green frock was mended here and torn there, and she looked cold and hungry, but yet she smiled, and seemed so obliging and so willing, and so full of service, did that little beggar-girl who lived in Mrs. Brown's house, or the house that Mrs. Brown lived in.

How good the poor are to the poor! Wealth has been denied them; they have been cut down by "man's inhumanity to man" to starvation point; but Providence has given them more than he has denied them—heart and sympathy. Talk of overcrowding tenements — poor creatures! what would they do if they were *not* banded together? Scatter them, and they are, indeed, lost and wretched! Their banding together—their living in community—is a blessing and a power. They help each other. The bread that some of them have is divided with those who have none; the sick are tended by the hale; and the full heart made light by the consolation and comfort of the sympathising of those who feel the pinch as well as they.

This little girl who now stood before Mrs. Brown, ready and willing to do her bidding, had often taken an end of candle or a basin of coals to some in the house to light up and warm a darkened room, and as often borrowed them for the same purpose for her mother.

We say this "little girl," for she had no Christian name, that is, she was never christened except by the residents of Vine Court, and by them she was known as "Zigzag," and for the reason that she was always in and out everywhere, clambering over walls and dust-bins to feed a half-starved goat that was chained in the yard of an adjacent house. And a pretty little girl was Zigzag, as she was seen barefooted on the top of walls, her poor dress and hair floating in the wind.

"Shall I ask the gentleman up, ma'am? or shall I say you are out, ma'am? or shall I say you will come down directly, ma'am?" quickly asked Zigzag, anxious to be serviceable, without any regard to truth or falsehood, the difference between which had never entered her untutored mind. All she cared about was to be obliging, and, seeing Mrs. Brown in some perplexity, she was more desirous than ever to show her attention.

"Some one about my poor boy," said Mrs. Brown to herself. "Say, dear, that I will come down at once."

But almost before the words were spoken a cheery voice cried up the stairs—

"I want to see my old friend Tom Brown!"

The gentleman was impatient of Zigzag's return, and it was he who called; and while he called he ascended the stairs to see what was the cause of the delay. He met Mrs. Brown, but he did not know her, and repeated—

"I want to see my old friend Tom Brown. Can you tell me where I can find him?"

The interrogator was a dapper little man of about forty-five, dressed in the most "horsey" fashion, tight drab trousers and wide-skirted green coat, and a blue bird's-eye cravat bound with a gold, horse-shoe ring, yellow dog-skin gloves, and in his hand he carried a bit of ash stick, while his hat was of the shiniest description, and as round as a hoop. At the top of Vine Court his dog-cart awaited him.

"Come, missus," said the impatient stranger, noticing Mrs. Brown's hesitation, "if you don't know where he is, don't tell me. No harm done

—must try somebody else. I've traced my old friend here, and now no one can tell me anything about him; and 'pon my soul, when I look round this dirty crib, I begin to think I have been hoaxed, for I never can fancy my old friend Tom pulling up in a kennel like this."

"My name is Brown, Sir," said the timid woman.

"You are not his wife, are you?" he inquired, looking at the woman, and perceiving more of the lady in her than he had noticed before.

"I am his widow, Sir," was the melancholy reply.

"Widow! Oh! this is altogether a mistake. I'm on the wrong scent—come to the wrong shop. Sorry you're a widow. Good morning, ma'am. The man I want was a wine merchant at Islington."

"And now he's dead, Sir. You have made no mistake. I am Tom Brown's unhappy widow."

"Well, you do pull me up!" exclaimed the horsey gentleman, after a pause, which he filled up with gesticulations denoting surprise, as opening his eyes wide, pulling off his hat, and placing his hand on the top of his close-cropped head, and puffing out his sunburnt cheeks. "Tom Brown dead! He went the pace very fast, but a better hearted man never lived! I'll take the odds he's gone to heaven! And when did this happen, Mrs. Brown?"

"Only last night, Sir." And then the widow revealed to the stranger the whole of the sad particulars of her husband's death, and her son's incarceration, during which the horsey visitor went through a great deal of his former pantomime, in token of his grief and regret.

"Tom, ma'am, was ever too good-natured, and he got plucked by a set of scoundrels who called themselves friends. I myself owe him a hundred pounds, which he lent me, for many a year, and now I've tumbled into a good thing by way of a fortune, I've come to repay Tom, as is my duty; and if every other fellow that owed Tom money would now do the same, you'd be rich instead of poor, Mrs. Brown. Tom was first favourite with everybody, and I couldn't rest until I repaid him what I borrowed."

Here was sunshine for the widow's heart. Her face sent forth a smile that it had not known for many a long day.

"Look here, missus, here's twenty five-pound notes, new from the bank. I return it in this way because it was just the way my old friend Tom lent me the money. I think I see the dear creature now going to his desk and handing me the tin. I wanted the money deuced bad, too, and I didn't ask twice for it. My heart is in the right place, Mrs. Brown, and I don't forget favours, and when I do may I perish!"

"Never was money so welcome!" exclaimed the widow. "I am without a penny in the world, and I have just written to my father to save my poor husband from a pauper's grave."

"I'm very thankful that the money has come in the nick of time," said the honest stranger.

"Ah, Sir! had this money been here yesterday, I believe my husband would have now been living."

"I wish to God it had, then!" exclaimed the horseman. "But I couldn't bring it before I had it, could I?"

"No, Sir, no; I am grateful to you for bringing it at all."

"Oh! that's all stuff, missus. The gratitude should be on my part, and I do feel grateful to Tom's memory for the loan of the money, and more grateful that I have been enabled to repay it at a time when it was so much needed by his widow. I heard that Tom had been bankrupt, and I thought of my debt to him then; but then I hadn't the money. Now I've got the money, poor Tom's dead! Such is life! Anything I can do for you, Mrs. Brown, I shall always be happy to do. There's my card. I know two or three chaps who owe Tom money, and they were lucky on the last Darby, and I mean to make 'em square it with you. I'd kick any man who forgot to repay borrowed money when they had the wherewithal to do it. I only wish Tom had been here to see that when he lent me the money he lent it to an honest man."

Mrs. Brown thanked the stranger over and over again, then they shook hands and parted. This unexpected windfall of good fortune much lightened the widow's troubles, and oh! how deeply she regretted that her husband had not been there to share it. The stranger's testimony to the generosity of her husband's character was very pleasing to her, and now the poor abused man was dead his virtues seemed to shine resplendently in the gloom.

Mrs. Brown lost not a minute now to reach her suffering boy with the good news of the morning. She was very early at the station, and sat in the inspector's office until the hour arrived for her son's removal to Guildhall. During this interval she explained to the inspector the good fortune that had befallen her, and her desire to give her husband decent interment.

Under the circumstance of her son's innocence Mrs. Brown met with moderately courteous attention from the officer, and he suggested that she should communicate with a respectable undertaker, and get the body removed in a coffin to her house.

But see! here comes Tom, led forth from his cell by the detective Pouncewell, he who had taken the boy into custody. Mother and son—widow and orphan—rushed with delight into each other's embrace. Mrs. Brown interceded for a cab for Tom, who walked very lame, and looked ill and haggard.

A cab was summoned, and the boy and mother and Pouncewell drove off to the court. Just as they were about to start, however, Mr. Yapp's "solicitah" had a few words of conversation with Mrs. Brown and her son, and told them not to be in the least alarmed, for he was instructed to say that the poor boy was quite innocent, and he was also instructed to beg the magistrate to emphatically say in public court that Tom Brown left the bar of justice without the slightest stain on his character, and the solicitor added that compensation would be made the boy for his sufferings and imprisonment.

The cab now hurried on to the court, and the solicitor took another and followed. The poor widow could not refrain from weeping when her innocent, high-minded boy was placed at the bar before the alderman in his fur-trimmed cloak and heavy gold chain. Tom controlled his feelings better than his mother, and while there was no effrontery about him, he stood strong in his innocence before the magistrate, with a very calm face and a dignified demeanour.

The alderman, in dismissing the case, highly complimented the boy for his conduct, and said that it was the most unfortunate affair that had ever come before him, and he thought that Mr. Yapp (who took care not to be present) was much to be censured under the circumstances for not making earlier inquiries regarding the money, and thus have saved an innocent boy from the stigma of a prison. He strongly advised Mrs. Brown to place the case in the hands of a respectable solicitor, for she certainly ought to be heavily indemnified by Mr. Bonthron.

The boy immediately left the court with his mourning mother, who respectfully thanked the alderman for his advice and kindness.

On their way to their wretched home in Vine Court Mrs. Brown endeavoured to cheer Tom's heart by the sight of the money she had had that morning paid her by a debtor to his father. The poor boy slightly smiled, but his father's death outweighed his joy. If he cared for the money at all it was for his mother's sake, and to know that his dear father would now have decent burial.

The sorrowing pair went onwards through the crowded thoroughfares, and they reached home as quickly as Tom's exhausted state would let them.

When they turned into Vine Court little Zigzag was entertaining an audience of small children with her antics and unsophisticated drolleries. She had mounted a large waggon, in the centre whereof she was playing a tragedy queen, after the manner that she had seen at some of the penny theatres, and for this purpose, and to give effect to her regal state, she had bound about her brow a piece of gold paper, which she had purchased for a penny out of the shilling that the horsey gentleman had given her for her trouble in finding Mrs. Brown for him; and Zigzag had, moreover, to make her notions of a queen more complete, bound her feet, which never yet had been trammelled by a corn-producing shoe, with red sandals, and held aloft an old dinner knife, as if about to destroy all and sundry of her subjects.

The little inhabitants of Vine Court stood with much awe before Queen Zigzag, and looked upon her with a deal of admiration as she moved proudly about in her waggon throne, stamping her sandalled feet, and shouting imperiously—

"I am a queen! Obey me, and shout hurrah!"

Her Majesty's dress was deficient of hooks and eyes behind, and the lappet of her shift hung out, which became a mark for one of her mischievous subjects, Water-cress Bill, who, when Zigzag turned round, gave the aforesaid garment a pull, much to Her Majesty's displeasure, and to the amusement of the audience, who sent up a shout of laughter.

It was at this joyous point that the Widow Brown and her son came upon the scene, but they were too much engrossed with their own thoughts of sadness to take any interest in it, and were only too glad to escape unnoticed to the wretched room in the house nearly opposite the waggon that contained Queen Zigzag surrounded by her courtiers.

The following day the dirty inhabitants of Vine Court, little Zigzag and all, were crowded around the house that Mrs. Brown lived in to see the coffin, containing the remains of the ruined wine merchant, carried up stairs. All were deeply affected to see the grief of the widow and her son, and when the coffin was with difficulty landed in the one room, preparatory to its last resting place, the door was closed, and mother and son gazed on it in sorrow and silence.

That night little Zigzag held another performance in the cellar of the house now tenanted with the dead, and in the cellar was a truss or two of hay and straw. Three or four candles were purchased, and, after the performance was over, the children hurriedly departed, leaving behind them one candle burning. During the night the candle and the straw met, and, as the clock struck three, the whole house was in flames.

Shrieks and screams filled the court. Men, women, and children rushed hither and thither in their night habiliments, with alarm broadly pictured on their faces. Little Zigzag rushed forth in flames, and the merry soul perished by fire at the wheels of the waggon which had so recently been her mimic throne.

The Widow Brown here threw open her window in despair, imploring with her hands and cries for help! Tom, in his shirt, sprang forth from another window, crying to his mother—

"The flames are at our heels! There is no escape by the stairs!—they are all on fire! Throw yourself from the window as I shall do!"

Here the boy came forth, hanging from the window with one hand, and besought the crowd below to save his mother, who would not follow him. The height was a fearful one, and although the fire raged and roared behind, the boy paused when he looked down, for certain death was in the terrible leap.

The crowd below begged him to hold on until they could pile up things to break his fall. The waggon was dragged under the window, and was soon filled with hay and straw.

Here came a dreadful scream from the Widow Brown, and her head was suddenly lost to view, and a fearful cry of "Mother!" from poor Tom, who saw her rushing about the burning room entirely enveloped in flames, and, sad to add, she was eagerly consumed by them.

Had she followed her son's advice and entreaties, and hung from the window until help could be brought from below, she might have been saved; but, as it was, she perished.

Chairs, tables, with layers of hay and straw between, were flung one on the other to meet Tom as near as possible. When they had reached the first-floor window, the fire behind would allow the boy no further waiting. It imperatively said "leap or burn!" He made the leap, and saved himself.

CHAPTER XXX.

LOVE IN THE KITCHEN.—AN EXTRAVAGANT HOME.

MR. YAPP's home was a very different affair to the Widow Brown's. The clerk was, as we have long ago seen, a young man of expensive and exquisite taste, and his home and house showed it. It was a handsome villa in Camden Road, which contained a mile of charming residences on each side. In summer the lilac and laburnum waved their graceful plumes before the doors, while tall trees of sturdy growth gave a picturesqueness to the spot all the year round. Wide white stone steps led to the door, on each side of which was a large stone vase for flowers, and beautifully laid-out gardens of evergreens, and the flowers of the season fronted each house. Two large bells, with white enamel handles, were attached each side the gate; over one bell-pull was cut in brass letters, "Visitors," and over the other "Servants." Sun-blinds were fixed to the drawing-room windows, while within all kinds of curtains and blinds of the best description reigned throughout each room.

We shall not stop to catalogue the elegant furniture, but content ourselves with saying that the house was equipped in a first-rate style. Everything was of the best, and everything adapted to its place; and besides being rich, handsome, elaborate, and expensive, there was a considerable air of comfort over the place.

Mrs. Yapp—there she sits now, in the easiest of easy chairs, her foot resting on a carpet stool, leaning back in complete repose, indulging herself with the reading of a new novel, which her stupid old mystery-monger of a father had this day brought her, and enjoined her by all means to read before she went to bed.

The last time we made the acquaintance of this lady she was Miss Maria Perkins, at the little oil shop in Cross Street. But now and for four years she has been Mrs. Yapp, fondly looking forward one day to be the Countess of Somebody. But at present she was enjoying the comfort of "unlimited wealth," and therefore could afford to wait patiently for her title.

Poor old Perkins had nearly been stripped of everything by his son-in-law but his business, which happened to be a very good one. All his little properties had been sold long ago, or mortgaged, for the benefit of Mr. Yapp, and a good deal of it was in the Turkey carpets at Mrs. Yapp's feet, in the black satin dress now on her back, and in the gold watch and chain hung by her side, and the hat and feather on the table. Messrs. Bonthron and Perkins were made to pay the piper—and it certainly showed the clerk's consummate ingenuity to keep the ball moving so long.

Mr. Yapp dearly loved his wife; and if woman is to be loved for her beauty, Mrs. Yapp was a woman to be beloved, and she had the most perfect control over him; and taking him at his word, and believing him to be a man of unlimited wealth, she was determined to deny herself nothing; therefore what she wanted she had, with the exception of a brougham, and somehow or other she could not get Yapp to buy one. He always had some excuse, his chief one being, and which partially satisfied her, that horses and carriages would descend to him with the title and estates.

Mrs. Yapp looked very beautiful this evening as she sat alone with her book, the fire cheerfully burning in a handsome bright steel grate, and the rich scarlet curtains diffusing a radiance over the large room, while the chandelier that hung over the centre table emitted the most beautiful colours from the hanging lustres.

The two pretty children had retired for the night, and there was an agreeable silence about the place, broken only by the musical ticking of the large beautiful timepiece, surmounted with a fine figure of Old Time cast in bronze, and which stood before a noble pier-glass on the black marble mantel, while the small mirrors round and about the room in their rich gilt frames lent a delightful brightness to the room. The little toy-terrier that played with the pile of the hearthrug at the lady's feet also added to the comfort of the apartment.

Mrs. Yapp was waiting with pleasant expectancy the return of her husband with a new dress, which she made sure her "honeybird note" could not fail of coaxing from him.

We have endeavoured to show the luxury and comfort that reigned above stairs at Camden Villas; we will now go below and look deeper into the domestic arrangements. In the kitchen we found our old friend, George Mumford, fat as good living could make him, attired in a suit of green, with rows of buttons broke out all over his chest like the measles on a child's face.

George had pleasanter quarters at Mr. Yapp's than at poor Townley's, the stationer, where we first met with him. Over a roaring fire he sat, and a plump young woman kept him company. They were having a comfortable supper of cold roast beef, pickles, the remains of a rice pudding, cheese, and a full mug of beer.

"I'm vexed about one thing," said George, foaming up a glass of beer.

"Whatever is that?" inquired the ruddy-faced girl.

"There's no cold batter," was the reply. "I should have made a good supper but for that. Missus likes pudding and so do I, therefore you should mix more batter than you do, and I've told you so afore."

"You told me—a bit of a boy like you," said the young woman.

"Keep your temper, Sarah, and pass me the pickles; meat is nothing without pickles, and both together aint much without batter."

"There was some pudding put away in the pantry, that I remember."

"Then the cat must have had it, Sarah; and I'll twist her neck if she comes any of them tricks with me. I never touch her meat; don't let her touch mine. Pass me the cheese—or stop, I think I'll have another piece of meat first—that nice piece of brown, that master is so fond of."

"I won't cut it—there's sure to be a row about it if it's gone," said the girl.

"Lord! there's sure to be a row about something, so it had better be about that, for that piece of brown is worth a row."

"You're the most howdacious boy I ever lived with."

"How you keep on calling me a boy," said George. "I'm seventeen, and weigh more than master. Don't look so pretty, Sarah, or I shall certainly come and kiss you."

"I'd scream if you did," said Sarah, her black eyes all a glow, and her cheeks redder than ever.

"I haven't quite courage enough; I'll just go and get a glass of 'bittah beah,' as Master calls it, and then look out for squalls. I say, Sarah, I would'nt give a dump for this place if it wasn't for you."

"Well, you are a-talking, George," said Sarah.

"I wouldn't, 'pon my soul!" exclaimed the fat boy, with his short crop of reddish hair; and with a great piece of bread and cheese in his hand he tilted back his chair on its hind legs.

"You are a-going it," said Sarah. "What do you see in me, I should like to know?"

"Three things that I much admire. A round-aboutedness—a straightforrardness—a scrumptiousness—and you make capital batter."

"Don't be a fool, George," said Sarah.

"Oh, I'm no fool, Sarah; you may take my word for that. I wish to heaven that you would invest your savings in a cook's shop and marry me. Isn't that straightforrard, Sarah?"

"I think it is, indeed. Marry you! Why, I'm old enough to be your mother."

"Not so, Sarah; just old enough and handsome enough to be the mother of my children," said George, getting hilarious.

"THIS IS THE BLADE TO TALK TO YOU!" CRIED GEORGE MUMFORD, FLOURISHING THE KNIFE.

"Come, I say, don't get talking like that, or I shall go up stairs," said Sarah, affecting to be deeply offended.

"Now look here, Sarah—and there's my hand upon the bargain—I'll have you if you'll have me!" said George, in complete earnest, leaning forward and holding out his hand to the coy domestic. "You would find me the best young woman's companion out. I'm clever—"

"At telling lies and eating pudding," interrupted Sarah.

11

"Come, I say, now *you're* a-going it," said George. "Pudding! I'm not pertikler, for he eats everything that comes in my way. Let's be serious. It is not often that a man—"

"Call yourself a man?" said Sarah.

"As good a man as that baker feller that's after you!" exclaimed George, springing from his chair, and setting himself out to the best advantage of height.

"It'll be a many years, George, before you've

got a beard like that baker feller, as you dare to call him," said Sarah, with warmth.

"Ha! ha! a carotty beard like that! Why, I *wouldn't* have such a beard," said the jealous youth. "But there, Sarah, have doughy if you like. Lord! I don't care! a person of my appearance can always find a wife. Have that man who turns the bread sour with looking at it if you like. It shows horrid bad taste, though, when you could have had *me*."

"Had *you!*" exclaimed the girl, half in jest, half in earnest. "Why what do you think my mother would say if I married a boy of seventeen?"

"I'm going on for eighteen! Besides, shan't I soon grow older?" demanded George, regaling himself with a draught of ale to keep up his spirit in the attack upon Sarah's heart.

"You are too young, George, to know your own mind," said Sarah. "Besides, if I loved you ever so much, you've nothing to keep a wife upon, and I am not going to be fool enough to marry a man and keep myself."

"Why what's that baker chap got to keep a wife?" George asked in the most contemptuous manner.

"Baker chap, indeed! Please to call him by his proper name, Mister Woodhead," said Sarah, proudly tossing up her head.

"Mister Blockhead!" exclaimed George, much "riled" at Sarah's sticking up for the dignity of her lover. "I wish I had him here," said George, spitting in his hands, then bending them into fists, and standing before Sarah in pugilistic attitude.

Sarah laughed derisively at George's fighting propensities, which only more and more exasperated the page, and he fenced at his shadow on the wall in the most furious manner.

"You've riled me, Sarah! I'm not going to have any young man cracked up before me, or compared to me. Mr. Yapp's page, indeed, to be put a one side for a common journeyman baker! Well, I never! I thought you would have snapped at the offer of my hand, and only too proud to have invested your savings in a cook's shop, and made me master."

"I should have been a fool."

"Mind'ye, Sarah," said George, oracularly, "some people think too much of themselves."

"And you are one of them," rejoined Sarah, "a little upstart like you to think of me, who could have a life-guardsman if I liked."

"Who'd have a common soldier? Bah!" said George, who was determined to underrate all Sarah's lovers; had she said that she might have had the commander-in-chief, or the lord high admiral, George would certainly have though them inferior to Mr. Yapp's page in buttons.

"And I could have a serjeant in the police," said Sarah.

"Could you indeed!" exclaimed the exasperated youth. "For heaven's sake, Sarah, look above these men. Have *some* regard for your respectability—have *some* haspiration above a bobby or a baker! Watch it, Sarah. Here am I trained to the habits of a gentleman, six meals a day and a lunch between each—"

"I shouldn't like to have to support you," interrupted Sarah.

"But you would if you had any love for me," said George Mumford. "Love wouldn't begrudge twelve meals a day if a chap could eat 'em."

"And you'd be the chap that could, if you had

the chance," said Sarah, quite fearless of wounding the feelings of the over-fed page.

"Trust me for that," said George, breaking off a lump of cheese with his finger from the half of a fine Cheshire that was placed on the servant's table.

"What, haven't you done supper yet, George?" exclaimed the girl.

"Done supper!" retorted George, in surprise. "You may ask that question when it is all gone. I've done with the meat; but if you think I'm going to leave a morsel of that rice pudding, you must think me a duffer—which I am not."

"Eating and drinking, that's what you're in love with," observed Sarah. "I b'lieve you'd marry your grandmother, if she offered you plenty of batter."

"I shall have batter if I like it," said the indignant page, brushing off the crumbs of his supper that were thickly strewed over his green and buttons. "I'm not to be stinted in my appetite for you, who don't have to pay for it."

Here George's attention was arrested by a little significant whistling at the kitchen entrance.

"I s'pose you don't know who that is making that horrid row at the gate, Sarah?"

"I'll go and see." returned the young woman.

"No, you don't," said George; "It'll be more proper for me." And the jealous page left the kitchen in a fury of wrath. He knew it was the baker.

"Is Miss Bunsen in?" said Woodhead, "dressed all in his best to walk abroad with Sally."

"There's no such person lives here," said George, in most uncivil terms, his fingers tingling to pitch into the baker.

"I mean Sarah, George."

"Who are you a-Georgeing on?"

"*Mister* Mumford, then, is Sarah in?"

"She's gone to bed," was the tart answer.

"Why, I saw her shadow through the blind of the kitchen window, not a minute ago."

"Then you saw what you oughtn't to saw," said George; "she's ill, and can't come out."

"Why, I heard her laughing, and I hear her now," said the baker, quietly teasing the page, and puffing the smoke from his briar-root pipe into George's eye, unintentionally of course, and he begged the page's pardon for it; but there was a wicked smile playing, Puck-like, about his face.

"Don't do it again, that's all," said George. "None of your larks with me. Make no mistake. When I smoke, I smoke a cigar."

"One of your master's, I daresay," said the baker; "the ends, probably, that you find in his pockets when you brush his clothes."

This was gall and wormwood to the page's pride, which was materially increased by the appearance of Sarah, and he turned upon the impassive girl with a look of thunder.

"What do *you* want?" he demanded, holding the garden-door as if about to slam it in the detested face of the baker.

"I thought you would catch a cold, George, and I've brought your hat,"—she fixed her eyes while she spoke on her lover the baker, and George was quick to perceive that they were making sport of him,—"you know I wouldn't like you to catch cold."

"There, that'll do for a tale," said George, making a rude face at Sarah. "You came to see this vulgar man, and I'll tell missus."

"What's the matter with George——"

"Mind'ye, if you call me George again, I'll punch your head! So I give you warning."

"Well, then, Mister Mumford, what's the matter with you?" repeated the baker, ironically giving a handle to the youth's name.

"He had no batter for supper," said Sarah, laughing; and of course the baker laughed too.

George was fairly jockied out of his wits, and he resorted to his old habit of lying when he was in emergency, or wished to conceal the truth. He was a capital liar; and if vice was ever to be rewarded, George should have a medal—ay, large as a coach-wheel—with this inscription:—

"Presented to George Mumford by a large circle of his admiring friends, for never having told the truth in his life; for being the most mischievous and ingenious liar of the age; and for his exemplary assiduity in cultivating this noble propensity from his infancy to mature life."

Directly the laughter had ceased, he turned upon Sarah, and said—

"Who did I catch kissing master? Ha!"

"Perhaps yourself, George," said Sarah.

"No, you—and you know I did. Ha!"

The baker darted a suspicious look at Sarah, who was as innocent of such an impropriety as Tom Brown of stealing the five-pound note, or George of ever telling the truth.

"Now, George, you are a-going it," was all the girl could say to such a charge before the worthy young man she was plighted to.

"Oh, I s'pose I didn't, did I?"

"I should think not, indeed!"

"Oh, there's a lie!—and didn't you ask me not to tell?—and didn't I say, 'Oh, Sarah, I've caught you, have I?'"

The girl laid hold of George's button-ornamented jacket, and gave him a good shaking.

"Come—I say—now you're a-g-g-going it!" exclaimed the pale page, as well as Sarah's shaking to and fro would let him speak.

"I'll shake your life out, if you tell lies of me!" cried the indignant girl; and no doubt she would have given the mischievous page further chastisement had not the baker interfered, and released her hold from George's jacket, she having, as he thought, given him jacketting enough.

"You don't believe him, do you, Mr. Woodhead?" she asked, in tones that evidently showed she would not like her character injured with him, or fall in his esteem. "Because if you do, say so, and upon my life I'll have the thing all cleared up directly master comes home."

"Well, Sarah," said the hesitating baker, "you must allow that it is a very unpleasant thing for me to hear! I certainly should not like to marry any young woman whose lips so overflowed with kisses that she was obliged to give them to those they didn't belong to."

"That's all stuff," said the honest girl, "and it won't do for me! Now, you please to come into the kitchen and wait till my master comes home; I'll have the matter out."

"'Taint likely master will acknowledge it, is it, Mr. Woodhead?" cried George, stirring up the girl's ire.

"And do you really mean to say that you saw me kissing Mr. Yapp?" asked Sarah, with a face of fire and an eye of fury.

"I didn't say you was a-kissing master; I said master was a-kissing you!" said young hopeful.

"And where's the difference to my character!" exclaimed the girl, fixing her strong hands once more on George's livery; "tell the truth, or I'll shake it out of you!"

"D-d-don't be v-v-violent, Sarah!" cried the boy.

"Tell the truth, then! Did you see what you say?"

"N-n-no; I d-d-dreamt it!" replied George; and the girl, much relieved that she had sustained her character of faithfulness with the baker, who now had no further doubt in his perplexed mind but that the assertion was a lying, spiteful invention of the boy's.

The clean and honest baker now took the page in hand, and commenced by sternly asking him—

"Now, what do you think you ought to be done to?"

"Done to! What for, I should like to know?" said the sneaking George, looking most contemptible and sheepish as he stood in his confusion before Sarah and her lover.

"For telling a bare-faced lie," was the baker's answer.

"That's as good as calling me a liar!" exclaimed George, bristling up to the baker, taking care, though, to put his hands in his pockets, believing that Mr. Woodhead would not be cowardly enough to strike him if he kept his "fives" out of sight. "That's a hinsult! and a hinsult is what one gentleman should not take from another without resenting it."

"Gentleman!" derisively said the baker; "u little, coat-brushing, boot-blacking, door-opening, batter-eating boy like you to call yourself a gentleman!"

While the baker reckoned up the proud page in this severe manner, the boy shuffled about, puffed out his cheeks, threatened with his big round head barely covered with hair, made faces at his hated opponent, and then said what he was much in the habit of saying when he had nothing else to reply—

"Well, you are a-going it! It's a very good job for you, young man, that I'm in no fighting humour!"

"No, Sarah has taken that out of you."

"It would take a man to do that, so I don't deceive you. You must be a coward to expect me to strike a woman."

"A liar is the worst of cowards," said the straightforward baker. "The harm your lie would have done this young woman would have been more serious than striking her."

"What do you mean by a lie? I've told no lie! Didn't I say that I dreamt Sarah was a-kissing Mr. Yapp; and ain't dreams true?"

"Don't talk any more with a scaramouch like that, Mr. Woodhead," said Sarah, applying an epithet to George with which she associated great contempt.

"Now you're a-going it!" said George; "what do you mean by a scaramouch?"

If Sarah could define what "scaramouch" meant, she didn't; but, for George's edification, we will—it means, a buffoon in motley dress.

To the boy's terror, the baker, stern in his quietness, said, in response to Sarah's beseeching him to say no more to the buffoon in motley, "That he had not half done with him yet, and that he meant to give him a good shaking. You shook the truth out of him, Sarah; and I'm going to shake him for telling a lie."

"Why, you wouldn't be coward enough to hit a fellow with his hands in his pockets, would you?"

"Take 'em out, then," said the baker, sparring up to the boy, as much to frighten him as anything else.

"Now, mind'ye," said George, solemnly, and turning pale, "if you strike me, or touch me, I shan't retagliate, but I shall call a 'bobby' and give you in charge, Mister Blockhead——"

The baker laid hold of him by each arm, when George exclaimed—

"Woodhead, I mean!—I beg your pardon!"

"Aye, aye," said the baker; "and you must beg Sarah's pardon, too, or I'll give you such a rap on the head!—such a twister of twists!—such a roley-poley——"

"Well, when you've quite done with me——"

"Which I haven't," said the baker, "nor shall I until I have given you something to remember never to tell a lie again."

"Let me go, or I'll take the law of you, Mr. Blockhead — Woodhead, I mean," said George, correcting himself, when the baker began to shake him again. "This is as-s-ault and b-b-battery — a p-p-punish-able of-f-f-fence!" he screamed and stuttered with the shaking.

"Beg Sarah's pardon!" said the determined baker.

"Well, I do. Will that satisfy you? I only did it for a lark, Sarah knows that. It would have been nothing to me had she kissed Mr. Yapp."

"It would have been something to me, though," said the baker; "and to her, too, for she would never have been my wife, and she's there to hear me."

"Nor should I have deserved to be had I done so base a thing as that little wretch has charged me with."

"Well, you're a-going it again!" said the sheepish George, wishing himself a thousand miles away.

"Let him go, dear Richard," said Sarah.

"Dear Richard!" exclaimed George; "you're a-going it more than ever."

"Let the boy go into his supper, he is hungry every ten minutes," said Sarah, laughing, now that she had established her virtuous fame with the baker, who still tightly held the be-buttoned boy by the sleeve of his jacket.

"He shall have supper with me to-night," said Woodhead, about to cut a stout branch from a garden tree near where they stood.

"Mind'ye, you'd better not," said George, in the shakiest manner.

"No, Richard, don't cut the tree; Master would be angry about it," said Sarah.

"But he would be more so if he knew what this young varlet had said about he and you," retorted Woodhead.

"And he shall know it, too, take my word for that," said Sarah. "And now, Richard, I will tell you before his comical face——"

"Well, I'm sure!" exclaimed George; "its as good a face as yours any day or Mister——"

The baker lifted his hand, and the bounceable page, all the pluck taken out of him, was silenced before he finished his sentence.

"Now let us hear all about it, Sarah," said Woodhead.

"I don't want to hear her tale," said George; "and, as two is company and three's none, I shall return to the kitchen."

"You won't go until I like," said the baker.

"Won't I, though! How dare——"

The baker again raised his hand, and the troublesome boy was again silent.

"You must stop and hear what I have got to say," said Sarah.

"Stick to the truth, and I don't mind; but I have a horror of lies," said George.

"You hate lying about as much as you do batter," said Sarah, which raised another laugh against George, who looked as black as thunder, and who would have been off like lightning had he the chance of escape from the tormentors he had fairly brought upon himself.

"Well, Richard," continued the young woman, "as we were sitting at supper to-night, he actually had the impudence to make love to me."

The baker was a little jealous of that sort of thing, and really did rap George on the head; at which the boy bent his fists, looked defiantly at his opponent, and cried—

"Well, you are a-going it! Mind'ye, I shan't stand much more of this game. Look out for squalls to-morrow. I'll summons you. Fighting is against my principles—none but blackguards fight—or I should just knock you down! And as for you, Sarah——"

The baker upraised his hand again, and the boy stopped his anathema on Sarah.

"Yes," continued the damsel, "he actually asked me to marry him and forget you!"

George saw the terrible effect this revealment of his passion for Sarah had upon the baker, and to appease his wrath, exclaimed—

"Why, I wonder you are not ashamed at telling such lies, Sarah. You must have some spite agin me, I think. Now, I'll tell the whole truth, so I don't deceive you. Didn't you say that you didn't like the baker because he had a carrotty beard?"

This was a dig for the baker, and he looked rather astonished at Sarah, for he thought his beard was the chief point of his attraction with young women, and especially of her whom he almost regarded as the wife of his bosom.

"You only say that again before me, and I'll break every bone in your body!" exclaimed Sarah.

"He don't seem to have any; he appears to be all fat," said the baker.

"My fat ain't at your expense, so you needn't hollor," said George; "you are both of you a-going it agin me. When I tell the truth——"

"Which was never in your life," interrupted Sarah.

"You're another—that's what," said George, taking from his pocket a knife, which he quickly opened and revealed a long blade. "I won't stand any more of this bullying. You are telling a parcel of lies about me, Sarah, and you do it to aggravate me, because you know I hate lying—except in bed sometimes. Ha! stand off!" he cried to the baker, who was planning to spring upon him and wrest the weapon from him. "It won't do. This is the blade to talk to you if you don't step it."

"I won't budge an inch for you or your knife," said the baker.

"You may stop there all night if you like; but hands off me. And as for you, Sarah, I shall tell missus about your letting men into the garden at this hour of the night."

"Tell what you like about me, if you will only tell the truth. I don't fear then about what you can tell."

"You didn't nudge my foot under the table? I 'spose that's a lie, too?"

"A downright lie," said Sarah.

"And I 'spose you didn't ask me to buy a

cook's shop with my savings and make you my wife? That's another lie—eh?"

"Worse than any you have yet told, you young scoundrel," said Sarah. "That's what you asked me to do—he did indeed, Richard. His savings!—why, he hasn't got sixpence! He borrowed a shilling of me to pay for the mending of his shoes."

"Aw—because I had no small change—aw," said George, putting on the graces and affectations of Mr. Yapp, his criminal master. "Aw—you can have what silvah you like to-morrow—aw—or now—only I haven't any about me—aw!"

"You puppy!" exclaimed the baker, upraising his hand, but not daring to approach the boy, who held aloft the blade, which shone in the moonlight.

"Your mastah, you mean, bakah—aw," retorted George, cleverly enacting Mr. Yapp.

"Put the knife down, and I'd crumple you up with one hand."

"Aw—don't you wish you may get it?—aw, have no desiah to be crumpled up—aw—therefore mean to keep it, you very common man. And as for you, young woman—aw—you may take warning, for admitting low men on the premises at unreasonable houahs—a burglah for what I know undah the disguise of a lovah—aw—"

"And pray what is the meaning of all this, Sarah?" demanded Mrs. Yapp, who came suddenly upon the scene. "Pretty conduct, I declah! I have rang the bell at least a dozen times, and could get no answer. What is your business here, Sir?"—this to the baker, who leant against the tree smoking his pipe, and who at that moment certainly wished himself in the oven with one of his batches of bread.

While Mrs. Yapp was interrogating the baker her back was turned on George, and he availed himself of the opportunity with long strides to slope off to the kitchen, and regale himself with a pickled onion and a mouthful of beef which happened to be cut in the dish.

Poor Richard was in a dreadful fix, and his faithful Sarah, with all her pretensions to truth, had a *leetle* of the inventive genius of Mumford when occasion, as now, required it, helped him over the stile, by putting on a sort of whimpering countenance, and saying—

"This young man, mem, has come with a message from my poor mother, mem, to say that she was very unwell indeed, mem; and that if it would be no inconvenience to you, mem, she would be glad to see me for a few minutes to-morrow."

"I should be very glad if your mother sent her messages earlier," said Mrs. Yapp, who had protected herself from the cold of the night by a large and handsome Paisley shawl, which she held tightly around her; while Sarah so truthfully explained the baker's errand, at least with the same amount of truth prevalent amongst domestics, her lover sneaked away, very little pleased with his evening's entertainment.

When Mrs. Yapp walked through the back garden and reached the kitchen, of course George was attacked by his mistress.

"And you, Sir, what think you your master would say had he seen your interesting pranks before his house at this hour of the night?" said Mrs. Yapp.

George had properly arranged himself for this meeting with his mistress; the clever page had settled down in the most studious manner to a religious tract that had been left at the house that morning by one of those intrusive mendicants who trade in piety.

On his mistress putting the above question to him, he looked round in the utmost surprise and astonishment, first at the demure Sarah, then at his displeased and stately mistress.

"Did you speak to me, mum?" said the innocent youth, rising and standing by the side of his chair.

"Indeed I *did* speak to you, and I shall not fail to tell Mr. Yapp, when he arrives," said the lady. "Both you and Sarah have very much —much annoyed me to-night."

"As for me, mem," said Sarah, "I couldn't help my poor mother falling ill."

"And for me, mum, I warn't in the garden at all," said George, "I have been reading this tract on the 'Sin of Lying' all the evening."

Mrs. Yapp looked astonished at the boy's audacity, but George withstood her gaze with extraordinary *sang froid*.

"How dare you, Sir!"

"What, read this tract, mum?" said George, failing to understand his mistress in any other way.

"No, sir! and you know I meant nothing of the kind. I saw you in the garden with a knife in your hand."

"*Me*, mum?—*me* in the garden?—*me* with a knife? You have quite frightened me, mum," said George.

"How?" frowningly asked Mrs. Yapp.

"Because, mum, you must have seen my spirit, which is a token of my death. Oh! I'm so nervous. A knife in my hand, too!—that is a token I shall be murdered!"

"And do you mean to tell me that I did *not* see you in the garden?" inquired Mrs. Yapp, really half inclined to doubt her own senses, the boy played his part so well, and looked so astonished and alarmed.

"I'm certing you did'nt mum. I wish you had, for you must have seen my spirit. And my grandmother's spirit was seen before she died, and so was my father's. Oh! I shall go mad! I'm sure to be murdered to-night! I feel ill already. I must go to bed—I must go to the doctor's—I must go—oh, I don't know where!" cried the performing boy making an exit as rapid as his fat would let him, from his mistress's presence.

"I am amazed!" exclaimed Mrs. Yapp, looking after George in his mad flight. "*Could* I be mistaken, Sarah?"

The young woman knew the extent of George's lying, and she was really afraid to support her mistress, and she equivocated by saying, while she stood like a stranger in the place, with a corner of her apron in her mouth—

"I wasn't a looking, mem."

"I cannot believe you. What a curse servants are!" said Mrs. Yapp, with considerable warmth.

"I'm sure," said Sarah, "I don't want to be a curse to anybody. I can leave, mem, when my month is up."

"You can quite do as you please about that," said Mrs. Yapp, hastening out of the kitchen, muttering to herself, "The *idea* of my being forced from the drawing-room to a scene like this! Liars, both of them; I have no doubt of that."

When the lady of leisure returned to her handsome apartment her eyes fell upon the imposing time-piece, which was on the stroke of eleven.

"What!" she exclaimed, "so late as that. And where is Mr. Yapp, I should like to know? How an interesting novel kills time. I wish he would come, for I am most anxious to make acquaintance with my new dress, which I am *sure* he will bring me. If he does not it will be the first time he has neglected to fulfil my wishes, and I shall not have to thank him."

She paced the elegant room almost in a light, dancing step, looking admiringly at herself as she tripped it past the mirrors, holding a lace handkerchief coquettishly in her hand, while every finger was adorned with a ring of price.

What a pity no one was present to render her homage! She seemed in such excellent humour.

Weary of the display of her charming figure wafted about the apartment, and which she was so capable of rendering more so by her graceful deportment, she sat down at the grand piano, and played, with considerable skill, pieces from "La Traviata," an opera (not saying much for her moral taste) she was passionately fond of, and making it her boast that she had seen it six times without the smallest diminution of interest. She might not have been aware of it, but she was revelling in harlotry, made palatable by delicious music, as physic by bon-bons.

Like a person "used up," Mrs. Yapp could not for long devote herself to anything. Excitement she craved for, and when there was not the whirl of gaiety and movement about her, why then the hours were dreary, time was slow, and an unhappy kind of ennui possessed her.

She was a mother, but she would not accept the cares of one, and the pretty children only knew her by her face, never by her caresses. Dress and society were the real occupations of her butterfly life, and when her beauty drew forth admiration from some naughty beau, why then Mrs. Yapp could indulge in a little flirtation, and as the tender passion is composed of such inflammatory and combustible material, one of Mrs. Yapp's coquetting smiles would soon set it ablaze.

There was one of her male admirers—she was too handsome to have any amongst her own sex —who gave Mr. Yapp a little uneasiness. He, too, lived in one of the beautiful villas in Camden-road, and had more means than morals. Mr. Yapp was his debtor, and this fact gave Mr. Cumberland—we will divulge his name at once —more position, and standing, and voice in the house than could be, or ought to be, agreeable to to any man who called himself the master of it.

Mr. Cumberland was a good-looking man of about thirty-five, and derived a high income out of something in the City (there was a little mystery about this) that gave him a great deal of leisure. The only thing Mr. Yapp was his superior in was his dress—in dress no one could approach the criminal clerk. But Mr. Cumberland had a happier art of winning over the ladies to his side. He knew their weakness and susceptibility better than Mr. Yapp, and he knew how to attack it, where he thought it was worth his valuable while to do so. He was a fox—a cunning fox.

A married man Mr. Cumberland put down as a married fool, who was always at a disadvantage with his wife to a visitor. A husband he assumed and knew was not always in the happiest temper—crossed by the trials and troubles of business. Visitors, who have none of the husband's cares to ruffle them, call in their holiday attire and holiday temper, and the unthinking wife exclaims what nice, dear, amiable gentlemen they are! not at all like *her* husband, who is a brute and a bear! With these feelings she becomes an easy prey to the visitor villain; he talks soft, and kind, while her husband talks loud, and looks ill-tempered.

Don't be deceived ladies! the men—the visitors you admire for being "nice, dear, and amiable," are often the veriest brutes and bears at home, if the veil could be lifted. Your husbands have more interest in you than any visitor can have, and you do them a serious injustice, and expose your own ignorance by being led away by the nose. Husbands and wives are found to be "much of a muchness." Pray be content with each other and make the best of your bargain, for you never can better it; and although the "nice, amiable visitors," may be very attentive to you at table, pretend sympathy with all your troubles, listen to your small-talk, nurse your babbies, play with your children, cry "dear, dear me!" at your husband's foibles, which he learns from you who never ought to have revealed them—if you could only know that man as he is known at home, you would only exclaim—

"Why he's as like my husband as two peas! only a great deal worse!"

At home and abroad are two different things. We, all of us, put on and off our tempers as we do our clothes; we adapt one to the seasons, the other to those we associate with. Therefore, seeing that there is such a moral likeness in mankind, better fix on our hearts and memories the text "have patience one with another."

In nine cases out of ten, Mr. So-and-so is no better and no worse than Mr. So-and-so. This to wives. To husbands we would say that your friend's wife is, however she may smile upon you, and however comfortable she may make you, is not as good as the one at home who is now anxiously waiting your arrival.

Mrs. Yapp had a very ill-conditioned mind. It had been fed on novels and romances, which showed the world and mankind in every way but the right and the true. Her very marriage with her husband, was from the most romantic motive that the imagination was capable of. She had no real love for the man, but worshipped the title she was silly enough to believe he would one day inherit. She had taken a leap in the dark and fallen upon ruin.

Mr. Yapp's first intimacy with Mr. Cumberland was made in a billiard-room, and after this they constantly met, and being neighbours, this led to their visiting at each other's home, when Mr. Cumberland soon commenced, step by step, to treat Mrs. Yapp as a child would a pretty toy.

He cultivated a beautiful garden, and he would generally go abroad with some choice fruit of it in his coat, and the first imprudent flirtation between Mrs. Yapp and Mr. Cumberland was about a young rose, which the lady so much admired that the gallant gentleman took it from his button-hole and gave it to her. Mr. Yapp was present at the presentation, and although he did not like it, he said nothing.

How often the purest things, the fairest flowers, have been made instruments of crime! How many tortures to the mind has the passage of a flower from one to another been!

Mr. Yapp was a man of the world as much as Mr. Cumberland. He watched the growth of intimacy between the bachelor and his wife— he watched it and treasured it. It was a scorpion to him, but he kept it stinging in his breast. He was not ordinarily a jealous man, but his wife was so young and so beautiful, and he loved her so much and so deeply, and Mr. Cumberland had so unmistakeably shown his admiration of her, and the lady had so unmistakeably received his attentions with pleasure, that he might well be forgiven for being disturbed.

As we have seen, Mr. Cumberland was a gentleman of leisure, and once or twice he had dared to call at the villas while the poor clerk was busy with Mr. Bonthron's books in Bolt-court, and racking his brains to keep up the wealthy character he had assumed.

This indiscretion he had learnt from his faithful page, George Mumford, and, from this moment, George became the clerk's confidant, and he was requested to report all he saw and heard, and the mischievous imp did so with a vengeance. No half-tales for George; he had a fine imagination, had Mumford, and could make mountains out of molehills, and he stood well with his master, and "fooled him to the top of his bent."

Mrs. Yapp's patience at length became worn out. Twelve o'clock. No husband—no shawl —no dress. She sat herself in the elegantly-carved chair, and pondered over a good many things; even her fond lover, Townley, once came to her unoccupied mind. At length she took from the table her velvet-bound album of photographs, turned over face after face, and while she pondered on that of Mr. Cumberland, she fell into a deep sleep, and unfortunately left the book open at this particular portrait.

Not long—not half-an-hour by the clock—after she had been lost in her repose, before a Hansom cab rattled up to the villa, and Mr. Yapp, as gay as a lark, sprang out, and before he could settle with "cabby" and knock, George, as quickly as his "roundaboutedness" would let him, was at the door to let him in, and take his hat and assist him off with his fur-coat—was ready, and active, and willing. to fetch or carry, run up-stairs or down-stairs, or, indeed, do anything his jolly young master might require at his hands and service.

"Well, boy," said Mr. Yapp, in confidential tones, "any news? anything happened? any one been?"

George looked round and about before he answered, as if he had the profoundest secret to communicate, and then, in the same tones as the questions were put, much to Mr. Yapp's relief, he said—

"No news—nothing happened—no one been."

The page could not very well help noticing that there was a great deal about Mr. Yapp's manners to-night that he had never observed before, and he was a curious observant boy. The clerk was excited, looked care-worn and travel-worn; his hair was disarranged; his hands were gloveless and not over clean; there was a fishiness about his eye which plainly indicated that he had been drinking without being drunk, and his hat and coat were pulled off and given to the page with a haste and violence that made George stare, and say to himself—

"Master's been on the loose. There'll be a row."

As Mr. Yapp ascended the stairs to the drawing-room, George asked if he would like supper, and the answer being in the negative,—

"More fool you," thought George, wending his way to the kitchen, where Sarah, like her mistress above, was sound asleep by the fire, while the cat was on the supper-table regaling her sleek sides off the cold ribs of beef.

"Well I'm sure you're a-going it!" exclaimed George. "Excuse me," giving puss a rap in the head, "that's a thing I can do without your assistance."

The cat vanquished, the page then addressed himself to the sleeping girl.

"Sarah!—Sarah!" he gently said, stooping, placing his hands on his knees, and looking in her face, "lets you and I be friends and have a little supper together."

She did not hear, and he then twisted round a corner of his pocket-handkerchief to a sharp point and tickled her nose with it. She awoke, and looking at her disturber, she indignantly said—

"I will thank you not to take such liberties with me."

"Lord! I only want to be friends with you," said the youth.

But Sarah would not yield to his advances; took a candle, and, without a fond good-night, forsook the kitchen and went to bed, while poor George, who had nothing to eat since supper, once more made his acquaintance with the beef and pickles.

"I wish I'd kissed her now. I'm a fool. I've lost a good chance. Handsome young women shouldn't fall asleep before a handsome young men. "I like the girl very well, but I like my supper better, after all," mused George, carving at the tit-bits from the joint. "When I love a girl better than roast beef, I shall vote myself a hass! And when I marry a woman without tin I shall vote myself a hass! And when I marry a woman who cannot keep me well in batter, I shall vote myself a hass! And if I don't serve out Mr. Blockhead, I shall vote myself a hass! And if I don't have a piece more beef, I shall vote myself a hass! And if I don't hang that cat for a thief, I shall vote myself a hass!"

So George went on eating and moralising until a decided sense of sleepiness came over him, when he rose, put away what eatables he had left, then inquired if his master wanted him any more, and, receiving a favourable answer, went straight to his bed; and it was not long before his dreadful snoring might be heard all over the house in the dead quiet of the night.

When Mr. Yapp entered his drawing-room, he stood in the centre and gazed on his sleeping wife. Should he wake her with a kiss? or should he wake her at all? and if he did wake her, what should he say about the dress and shawl, and what had detained him? These few questions passed in his mind as he paused before her. Then he stole behind her chair, and, as he was about to fling his arms round her neck, his eye fell on the album on her lap, her hand resting on the portrait of Mr. Cumberland.

Here was "confirmation strong" of his suspicions.

"Demn it!" he exclaimed to himself, and stole away, much displeased. "And has all the guilt I have committed for her ended in this! Oh, that I could tear her from my heart! Why should I cherish a thing there that loves not me!"

In his misery and jealousy he walked against the table, and a book fell therefrom to the floor, which awoke Mrs. Yapp. He sprang towards his wife, and excitedly said, placing his arm round her neck—

"Well, love, are you glad to see me?"

"If you have got my new dress and shawl," she coldly replied.

"How shall I excuse myself?"

"I want no excuses—I want the dress," said Mrs. Yapp.

"You shall have a beauty to-morrow."

"To-morrow," reiterated the lady; "but why not to-night?"

"The fact is, darling, your request came late—just as I was coming home, indeed. Then Sir Everard Wildbore called on me, and would insist that I dined with him at his club, and I—I—"

"This is the first time that you have allowed anything to stand between me and my wishes; and I am very much displeased and disappointed, Mr. Yapp."

"Oh, do but forgive me this one little time, and I'll never do so any more," half-sang, half-said Mr. Yapp. "Whose portrait have you been looking at, love?—not mine, for a guinea," he added, taking the album from her lap. "Oh, oh!—I see; yes—Mr. Cumberland. He's a good-looking fellah, is he not, Maria?"

"I think so," was the exasperating reply. "I tell you what he looks like, shall I?"

"Yes, yes," eagerly said Mr. Yapp.

"He looks like one that would not have disappointed his wife in a new dress had she asked for one."

"But he has no wife, poor devil," said Yapp, trotting out his partner's opinion.

"More the pity," said Mrs. Yapp, "for I think Mr. Cumberland a very gentlemanly man, and one that would make a nice husband. Hadn't I been married—" she paused.

"Well?" inquired Mr. Yapp.

"If I hadn't I should have liked him very well."

"What a tyrant marriage is, Maria, that it should stand between us and our likings," said Yapp; but his wife, by her silence, seemed indisposed to continue the conversation. "What a pity you had not met with Cumberland before me."

"What a pity you should not have brought my dress. And pray where is the shawl?"

"I left it at the place where I bought it," said Mr. Yapp, with a ready lie. "You shall have both dress and shawl to-morrow night."

"May I depend? I really very much want them," said Mrs. Yapp.

"Not very much, Maria, eh? Still, as my word has been given, to-morrow you shall have it. Did you ever count how many dresses you had?"

"Number is nothing. I really have not one that is fashionable either in make or colour," she adroitly replied. "But if I had a hundred, and wanted another, surely it would have been your duty, if not your pleasure, to have bought it for me."

The clerk assented by nodding his head; and then heaved a sigh, so sad—sad and sorrowful—that it could not fail to attract the attention of his wife, who never sighed but for pleasure.

"Dear me," she exclaimed, "the first time I have heard you sigh. What can the matter be?"

"I often sigh to myself, Maria," said the clerk, throwing out his long legs on the hearth-rug and folding his arms. "But I have always too much regard for your happiness to intrude my griefs upon you."

"Griefs! I never heard of such a thing. What griefs can you possibly have, I should like to know?—you, a man of unlimited wealth!"

"Come, Maria, suppose, after all, I turn out to be nobody but plain Mr. Yapp?"

"Then I should be extremely disappointed," was the lady's plain answer.

"And you would not love me then as now, eh?" cried Yapp, who wanted balm for his troubled mind.

"Pray do not talk such nonsense," said the lady, averting her head. "Such a supposition as yours is not to be thought of."

"Indeed! I have been thinking of it all day."

"You have no reason, I should hope, for thinking so?"

"Oh, dear, no!" said the clerk, quickly but falteringly.

"Then why torment me with such folly? There can be no doubt you are connected with some great family, else where does all the money come from?"

"Ah, where?" sighed the clerk, knowing too well the solution of that mystery.

"So if there is no title, there is sure to be abundant riches; and if we cannot get one, why, then we must be content with the other."

"I wish you may get either," thought the clerk.

"You know we have a party on to-morrow night,—Mr. Cumberland is coming, and——"

"It cannot be, love," quickly interrupted the clerk; "I have an important engagement with my friend Sir Everard."

"I will not put off that party for any one—there!" said Mrs. Yapp, emphatically. "Bring Sir Everard here."

"I dare not for the world—at least for the present," said the clerk.

"What, more mystery?" exclaimed Mrs. Yapp; "in truth, I am getting rather tired of mystery."

"Then what must I be, love? Living to my years without the knowledge who was my father or mother!"

"Well, I don't care; I shall not put off my party. I am not going to be made ridiculous for anybody."

"Put it off for me—won't you?"

"For no one," said Mrs. Yapp, her pretty face mantled with a considerable amount of ill-temper. "I have foregone a great many pleasures for you, Mr. Yapp. See what a plain and humble bridal I was content with. I decline to discuss it; but I won't put off the party. Mr. Cumberland and others would laugh at us."

The mention of this gentleman's name, coupled with the discovery of his portrait on his wife's lap, plainly showing that she had been engaged with it before she fell asleep, created in magnified shape the green-eyed monster in the clerk's full-troubled breast:—

"Oh, jealousy! thou bane of pleasing friendship,
  Thou worst invader of our tender bosoms,
  How does thy rancour poison all our softness,
  And turn our gentle natures into bitterness!
  See, there she sits! once my heart's dearest
      blessing;
  Now my changed eyes are blasted with her
      beauty,
  Loathe that known face, and sicken to behold
      it!"

"Hold the party for what I care!" exclaimed Mr. Yapp, more wrathfully than he had ever spoken before. "Hold it! Enjoy it! Forget me! I must train myself to indifferentism!

THE CHILD WAS SAVED! MR. YAPP SWOONED AND FELL TO THE FLOOR.

Grow regardless of your charms as of your actions!"

Such a blaze of passion Mrs. Yapp was unprepared for. She opened her bonnie blue eyes as wide as the lids would permit, and said—

"Are you mad, Yapp?"

"Almost—atmost," was the sad reply. "To think that I should have married a woman who would not defer a paltry party for her husband! What wouldn't I do for you. What have I not done for you?"

"What a storm about nothing!" exclaimed Mrs. Yapp, and she made a stately exit from the room, leaving her husband in the deepest despair.

After his wife thus abruptly left him to his own reflections, he gazed on the door which she passed through, and exclaimed—

"What an insensible woman. What won't she do when she knows all! Well, well, the pain will be less to me when she discovers who she has married. Instead of a coronet on my

12

brow, she may yet live to see a halter round my neck. The sooner the better for me, for my life is now a living death." Here he rang the bell violently, and receiving no answer (for his rogue of a page had gone to rest), he shouted wildly through the house for "George! George!"

No one heard his call but Mrs. Yapp, and as this was the first show of excitement and irregularity on the part of her husband she was alarmed at it, and totally failed to understand the cause of it. She sat on the edge of the Arabian bedstead, while her heart beat fast with agitation.

It must be confessed that Mr. Yapp's outburst of passion and opposition to her wishes was abrupt and sudden, and taken in contrast with his past namby-pamby treatment of her, it would have appalled a stouter-hearted woman than Mrs. Yapp.

"George!" again echoed through the house, and was heard without by the passing policeman, who paused and looked up to the windows, but seeing a light shining through the drawing-room blinds he moved on, satisfied that the voice he had heard proceeded from one of the inmates.

Mrs. Yapp's pride would not permit her to see what her husband wanted, and she allowed him to call again upon the boy, and this time the boy heard, but he was too snug and comfortable to turn his "roundaboutedness" out, or to reply.

"Let him call, if he likes, it will do me no harm; but if I get up from this snuggery, I shall vote myself a hass! He wants a little conversation about my interesting pranks in the garden. I 'spose if I was to holler down and say I was asleep, he wouldn't believe me." And George laughed at his own little jokes.

"George! demn it! why don't you attend, sir?" once more exclaimed the now more enraged master.

"I'm paying the strictest attention, but I don't come," said George to himself; and if any one had looked into his room at this moment he would have discovered by the moonlight that bathed his bed with its beams, the fat face of the page puffed out with inward laughter.

"What would I give for so sound a sleep as that poor boy is in!" mused Mr. Yapp, as he leant his elbow on the bannister. "Let him rest, I'll not disturb him."

Then he returned to the apartment, the grandeur of which mocked him, and seemed to cry "Thief!" and out of his wretched mind he replied, "and fool as well as thief!" He looked round upon the place, and shook his head, and extended his arms, and in tones of deep grief and regret he cursed himself for his folly.

"Tit for tat! I've deceived her, and she would now deceive me." he reflected as he flung himself into the arm-chair his wife had vacated. "But I deceived her out of love for her; she would be false to me because she loves another. Cumbahland! would to heaven that I could engulf him in my impending ruin! Oh! that I had the lively brains and dull heart of that fiend Swift. No, no Master Cumbahland, you have not a *fool* of a husband to deal with. I have my eyes open—wide open *now*. Beware!" he said, as he looked upon the *carte-de-visite* of Mr. Cumberland, wearing his most captivating smile. "None of us know what we were born for. It might be my fate to be hung for you. But why shouldn't *she* die! She is the offender! Cumbahland's death would not make her love me more. No, no—'tis *she* that should die. I have tried all man knows to win her heart, and

failed. 'Tis *she* that should die! Poor soul! methinks, too, that she would prefer death than live to know what she must soon know. The children——"

Here he paced the room, meditating plans of the most momentous bearing.

"God bless their little hearts!" he exclaimed, as he took a hand-lamp from a handsome chef-fonier, and with quiet steps traced his way up the carpeted stairs to the room where they slept in innocence and peace.

As Mr. Yapp described them to Swift, they were, indeed, a pretty pair of children. Where could be found a more pleasing picture than this the father, with his mind full of every crime, now looked upon? Each child lay on its back, with their arms inverted under each other's head, showing that they had fallen asleep in the depth of their affections. The room was full of moonlight, and the lamp had lost its power. The rosy colour on the children's cheeks alone denoted that they were living, so still they lay, and so gentle was their breathing.

The pretty little girl—so like mamma!—her long brown tresses carefully curled in papers, ever and anon smiled radiantly in her slumber, as though she had been playing with a new doll; while the little boy seemed in a deeper and sterner kind of repose, as if he had fallen asleep fretfully, because he was not allowed to remain up for his papa.

Mr. Yapp was a merry, entertaining father, and both his children adored him as much as he did them. He usually overflowed with animal spirits, and was therefore always a welcome companion to his children. He would be his little boy's horse, and his little girl's clown. The nursery and garden were strewed with toys that papa had bought them; no end of dolls, dolls' houses, horses, whips, drums, carts, hoops, and skipping-ropes. And as for their dress,—when Mr. or Mrs. Yapp walked abroad with them, every one commented on the beauty and exquisite taste displayed in it.

The father looked for a long time on the sweet sleeping countenances of his little ones. But what a sorrow exhibited itself in that father's face! He felt his villainy more than ever. Every time the smile played on little Bella's face it was a dagger thrust to his wicked heart.

"Would that I had been childless!" escaped his lips. "A felon father to own so much beauty, and so much innocence! What an entanglement! What shall I, can I, do? Something I must and will do to ease me of this load! Better they should perish than live to know their father was a malefactor or transport! Oh! what terrible thoughts possess me! Murder now to me is as familiar as the face of these little ones! Wife—Cumbahland—Swift—Lady Blaze—myself, have risen to my gory mind for destruction! And now *these*! And yet—and yet—"

He said no more, but took the pretty Bella from her warm rest to his arms, and oh! how he kissed and hugged her! Then he stole from the chamber with the child to the drawing-room, where the child awoke and cried. The cries of the disturbed child broke up the mother's pride. She came quickly from her apartment, and went direct to the drawing-room, and passionately expressed her astonishment at Mr. Yapp's conduct.

She failed to see the clouds and sorrows of her husband's mind. Of course she observed something unusual, but treated it only as a fit of ill-temper, which she did not choose to chase or soothe away. Indeed, she thought that *she* had the only reason to be ill-tempered, to receive no shawl, and threatened to have her party put off.

But she was sorely puzzled when she saw her first-born stretched out crying upon the hearth-rug, while Mr. Yapp was turning out the contents of his pockets on the table, as if in search of *something*; keys, money, papers, were turned out, as was also a silver-mounted pocket knife.

He met his wife's piqued face with one of uncommon tragic terror; and when she raised the crying child to her arms, and asked if he was mad, he looked for a moment full of the wildest confusion, put his hand to his burning brow, staggered, fell swooning to the floor, and cried—

"Wine! wine!"

Mrs. Yapp placed the alarmed child on the couch, soothed her fears, and brought forth a decanter of port from the cheffonier, and administered some as well as she was able to her outstretched husband. While she did this kindness her husband raved incoherently—at least it was so to her. She failed to understand the significance of such epithets as " Lady Blaze!" " Let us kill them all, Swift!" "I must have money!" "Cumberland's a villain!"

The last raving of the unconscious man was spoken plainly, and Mrs. Yapp drew back in great perplexity as to what her husband could possibly mean by speaking of his friend in that manner.

"Hush! my darling," she cried to her child. "Papa's ill, do not cry. Whatever is the matter with you, Yapp?" she inquired, releasing his neck-tie and opening his collar. "Have you seen Cumberland to-night? Speak to me! Take more wine."

The clerk groaned, and she put her hand through his long hair to admit the air to his burning brow. He turned, and asked where he was? and where was Swift?

"Who is Swift, dear?" said his wife, without taking much notice of what he said, only anxious to bring him to his senses. "Come, Yapp, get up, and sit by the fire, and I will sit with you."

She held his hand in hers—it was cold as death. But she was very glad to see him open his eyes, and then little Bella's crying attracted his notice, when, to his wife's surprise, he exclaimed—

"Take the child from me! I'm not to be trusted with it! Are you sure she's living?"

"Living!—It is little Bella, Yapp, that you brought just now from her bed? What for, eh?"

"To comfort me," he replied, with a sigh.

"Come, arouse yourself, Yapp; something has excited you. I cannot think what has disturbed you."

"Leave me, Maria. I must grow calmer before I speak to you. How came I here? I am not drunk."

"You fell in a swoon. Get up and sit by the fire."

"Pa! Pa!" cried Bella, getting from the couch and walking to her father, and when she embraced him with her fond arms, a tremble and a chill ran through his agitated frame. He kissed her tenderly, affectionately, and passionately, then said—

"Take her to bed—and you go too."

"Do you know the time, Yapp?"

"What is time to me?" he cried, rising from the carpet. "Do go to bed. I will come presently."

"Have you seen Cumberland to-night?" she asked.

He looked black at her, and replied "No! Have *you?*"

"Whatever do you mean?"

"I suppose I may ask you the same question that you ask me," he replied. "And there is more reason in my question than in yours."

"Why?"

"Because I found you asleep with his portrait on your lap."

"A mere accident, I do assure you," said Mrs. Yapp. "It might have been you, or my father, or my mother, that the album was opened at. I had been looking at all of you, and sleep overtook me, it appears, while I glanced at Cumberland."

"I wish you could assure me that it was accidental. But you have received him in my absence."

"Oh, you jealous man! He called one day, and you surely would not have had me slam the door in his face?"

"It would have been what he deserved for his impertinence," said the clerk.

"He is your friend, is he not?"

"But I do not wish him to be *yours*, understand. You may not know it, Maria, but all your actions plainly show me that you love that man."

"Indeed! 'tis not known to me, then," said Yapp with energy.

"But it is to me, though. I have a pair of penetrating eyes, which is of more importance than ears to unravel love's subtle web. But go to bed. I am weary, worn and wretched!"

"And what about, I should like to know? Does the party disturb you?"

"Oh, a variety of things. I'm tired of this mystery and all its surroundings. I am in debt to your father—"

"And he has written to-day a very urgent note about it."

"Has he? Well, I cannot help him. I am sorry for him, but I cannot help him."

"He says your bill is due to-morrow, and that he shall be ruined if you do not pay it, for it will be impossible to renew it."

"Then he will be ruined. I have no money —can get no money."

"What! Indeed!" cried Mrs. Yapp. "This is amusing! Surely you would not ruin my father?"

"I would ruin no one if I could help it."

"Would not Cumberland lend you the money?"

"Perhaps so—if *you* asked him," said the clerk, in biting tones. "He would do anything for *you*. Demn him!"

"Mr. Yapp!" exclaimed his wife in surprise, "you forget yourself!"

"I wish I could! I should be happy then! You did wrong to marry me on the basis of a mystery, and the cunning of a fortune-teller!"

"You implored me, Sir, or I never should," said Mrs. Yapp with indignation.

"I implored you because I loved you!"

"And why did you love me?"

"For your beauty," said Mr. Yapp. "But you loved me—"

"For your unlimited wealth," interrupted his wife. "If the beauty you discerned in me was to fade, your love for me would fade also."

"But I love you while it lasts. Now my

wealth has failed to awaken in you any true regard for me. Now if I become a beggar or a felon—"

"A felon!" exclaimed Mrs. Yapp. "Whatever are you saying?"

"I mean—aw—you know what I mean," said the confused man. "I mean that if my wealth became limited—"

"I can wait no longer discussing ifs and buts. If you have deceived me you have also deceived your own children, and I hope your conscience will reward and recompense you for your achievement."

With her little girl in her arms she was about to leave the room.

"Stay, Maria," said the clerk, more in his ordinary tones.

"No, I'll wait no longer. I begin to doubt you, Mr. Yapp. But mind, my father shall not be ruined by you, though I am to be. I will sell everything in the place before he shall suffer."

With these words, her beautiful face full of determination to carry them out, she left the apartment, and her husband followed her.

CHAPTER XXXI.

A CURIOUS PAGE. — A WIFE'S SUSPICIONS. — LETTER-WRITING, AND LETTER-OPENING.— A RENEWAL OF LOVE IN THE KITCHEN, AND STRIFE IN THE DRAWING-ROOM.

THE clerk lay down with murder in his mind; he rose with murder in his thoughts. Trembling with agitation as his better nature upbraided him with his guilty designs on his little children, he hastily dressed himself, but not with his usual particularity. Husband and wife spoke not to each other, and both bitterly repented that they should ever have met. Through that tedious night they had lain by each other's side, but not for each other's comfort.

The clerk slept, and terrible dreams haunted him; he waked and groaned; Mrs. Yapp sighed herself to sleep, and when she awoke, she wept. The veil had been partially and rudely torn from her vision, and her eyes were somewhat cleared of the gold-dust that had been flung into them.

Too late!—too late!—but she now reproached her mother and herself for the silly and deceptive part they had played with the fortune-teller. She felt that her father would never forgive them if he discovered the deceit that they had so foolishly assisted in.

By nature she was cold and passionate, characteristics that do not often exist in the same person; and her bosom now swelled with detestation of the man, though her husband and the father of her children, who she believed had deliberately deceived her, and galled the pride her fond and flattering parents had inflated her with.

"Hat, coat and boots, boy!" called Mr. Yapp to his page, as he descended the stairs in carpet slippers and red-flowered dressing-gown, of rather a loud pattern, to the comfortable breakfast parlour. Here awaited him his usual sumptuous fare—tea, coffee, chocolate, cake, toast, eggs and bacon; and better than all, this cold morning, a bright hearth and a good fire, before which his well-blacked Wellingtons were placed for warmth.

George Mumford, with the demurest face in the world, waited on his master, fearing every moment that he should have to defend himself for the scene in the garden with the hated baker, (for he was not aware that his mistress had been too seriously occupied with matters of deeper import to tell him.)

Mr. Yapp ate rapidly, and to George's mind hardly knew what he was about, and the boy referred it all to a scolding that "missus" had given him for stopping out.

"I shall look out for Mr. Cumberland, Sir, and watch it," said the forward youth, proud of his master's confidence, and Mr. Yapp could not have admitted a more tormenting imp to his friendship—"but I think I saw him in the road,—looking up to the drawing-room window, where missus was. I won't be sure, Sir. But if it wasn't him it was a gentleman very much like him. And I think I saw him kissing his hand—but then it might have been to our Sarah, for she was upstairs making the beds."

"What time, boy?" demanded his master, not so much moved as George would like to have seen him.

"Just as I was sitting down to lunch, Sir," was the reply, for the page dated every transaction by the meals.

"I cannot tell the time from that circumstance, for you are always at lunch—at least they tell me so," said Mr. Yapp, pulling on his boots.

"'Tis spite told you that, Sir; people are envious of me and jealous of me, Sir,—and you know, Sir, what jealousy can do."

"What do you mean, boy?" exclaimed Mr. Yapp, enraged.

"I don't mean nothing that I say, Sir," said George, alarmed at his master's displeased countenance; "I have had no edication, Sir, and my grammar is bad; it is always getting me into scrapes. And as for eating, if people would tell the truth, they would say as I was a very little eater."

"Then what you eat seems very well to agree with you," said Mr. Yapp.

"You musn't judge by appearances, Sir; I own I'm fat, but I was born so, and the doctor told my mother that I should not live long, for I was full of disease and precociousness, Sir."

"Mischievousness you mean, George," said his master.

"Oh, dear no, Sir; the most spiteful person I know wouldn't say that of me."

"Help on my coat, boy," said Mr. Yapp, rising from the table of good things without, to George's pleasure, consuming much.

The fur-coat buttoned, and after Mr. Yapp had placed his well-brushed hat on his head, a thought occurred to him, and he bade the page bring him pen and ink, and he reseated himself, and hurriedly wrote two notes.

"Should Mr. Pahkins call, give him that; and should Mr. Cumbahland call, give him this. By-the-bye, I should prefah that you took Mr. Cumbahland's note to him at once."

"After breakfast you mean, Sir?"

"Well — yes — aftah breakfast will do. But make haste, or you will fail to save him the journey here."

"Oh, I'm never long at my meals, Sir," said George. "And if Mr. Cumberland calls while I'm out?"

"Bettah take Cumbahland's note to his house; and take his note immediately aftah breakfast. I wondah that had not occurred to me before. for I certainly don't want him here. Now call me a Hansom."

While the boy was gone for the vehicle, Mr. Yapp heard the laughing voices of his children, who had just awoke from their night's slumbers. He went to their chamber, and they flew into his open arms. Such gladness, such joy, they showed to see papa, that it was with extreme difficulty they would release him from their embrace. How he wished that his wife loved him like this!—yet how much more he wished himself free of his crimes! But he saw no way out of them but by committing greater and graver ones—and then take his chance.

George announced the cab as awaiting at the door, and a fine tall, dashing horse the page had chosen to convey his master to the City, one capable and willing to make short work of it from Camden Villas to Fleet Street. George had to go some distance for the vehicle, and the boy returned in it, and as he rode in it he fancied himself a swell gentleman, and to his great delight the dreadful baker passed with a batch of hot bread on his head, and the boy "hoy! hoyed!" him, and when Sarah's lover turned round, the page placed his finger to his nose, and said—

"This is the way we do it—aw! I'm going to give my Sarah a ride—aw—you common man!"

The baker was about to put his batch down and attack George in the vehicle, when the boy exclaimed, "Drive on, cabby!" and the last the page saw of the baker, he was lifting up his leg, making George unmistakably to understand that if he could have caught him he would have kicked his "roundaboutedness."

"Bolt Court, Fleet Street," said Mr. Yapp, as he jumped into the cab. "Drive fast!"

Before he did this, however, he gazed up to the windows in hopes to catch a glimpse of his wife, that he might wave his hand to her. But the fair face of Mrs. Yapp appeared not.

There was a fine long firm road before the horse and driver, and advantage was taken of it, for the horse flew along so swiftly, yet so easily, that the spokes of the wheels could hardly be seen, and the bright brass harness shone resplendently as ever and anon the rays of the bright sun poured down on it.

The page watched the carriage out of sight, and heartily wished he was master, and devoutly hoped the cab would run over the bakah—aw. Out of sight, out of mind. George forgot his master, and eagerly thought of himself and his breakfast—self and eating and drinking being always associated in the mind of the page. There was a fine repast for George when he returned to the kitchen, for his master had not partaken of much of the good things that had been set before him.

"Half-past nine by the kitchen clock, and my bargain with my stomach was to breakfast by eight. I must make up for lost time," he said, taking two slices of toast and doubling them, and eating them at three mouthfuls; and while he did this he cracked an egg and poured himself out a cup of strong chocolate.

Then his eye fell upon the two notes his master had left him to deliver, and taking another slice of toast from the plate, he went out and returned with a glazed pan full of water, on the top of which, seals downward, he placed the notes, in order that the water might nullify the adhesive matter with which the envelopes were fastened.

"I hate secrets," he said, as the notes floated on the top of the water. "Had master told me what they were about, or had left them open, he might have saved me all this trouble, for I should not have been a bit curious to know. Just the same with the pantry; beef, and bread and butter is locked away, I'm quite ravenous to get at 'em; but if the door is left open, why, Lord! batter-pudding wouldn't tempt me to touch it! Oh! I've an abomination of secresy or mystery—and there's a good deal of both about this place."

Another cup of chocolate and a piece of bacon were now in demand, and George sat in his master's cushioned breakfast-chair, and crossed his legs, and threw his handkerchief over his knees, in his master's fashion, while he held his cup in his hand, and mused and chatted away to himself about all sorts of things—

"When my missus wasn't my missus, but was plain Maria Perkins—no, let me correct myself, she was never *plain*, but always a very good-looking young woman as ever any young man could wish to look upon,—well, when she was Miss Perkins, I was often and often in the humour to brush up to her myself, when I saw her in the shop. It was a very bad job for her that I didn't, for it was always my opinion that she loved me, and there can be no doubt in my mind that is the reason she now keeps me at a distance. But my master, Townley, was in love with her then, and it wouldn't have been right on my part to have endeavoured to have supplanted him. I hope I was too honourable for that."

The page was so lost in his own conceit that he failed to observe that he filled his mouth with a large spoonful of a very rotten egg.

"A bad egg, by jingo!" he exclaimed, with a face that betokened he had anything in his large mouth but that which was palatable or agreeable. "Damn it!—ah—filthy—ah—nasty—faugh!" he cried, rushing to the fireplace to relieve himself of the effete matter, and then washing away the taste with a gulp of chocolate and a lump of sugar.

"I wish now that I'd left that egg for Sarah," he said, resuming his seat. "She's not a young woman of much taste, it might have gone down with her, but it's come up with me. Master shouldn't leave me eggs that he wouldn't eat himself. It is not the thing—not what one gentleman should do unto another. I shall now be obliged to eat two eggs to take away the taste of that one—faugh!"

He went to the pantry and came forth with two more, and set them on the fire to boil.

"If Sarah is too proud to come to her breakfast, I am too proud to call her; and if she's going to sulk with her breakfast, she's a hass! She make's good toast, does Sarah, and I cannot give her better proof of it than by eating it."

He now took the notes from the bowl of water on the top of which they floated.

"I wish master would not seal his notes, it gives a chap so much trouble to open them, and I make it a point to allow of no correspondence to pass through my hands without my being fully informed thereon. That's how I found out Sarah and the baker. See what good comes of knowledge. Had I posted the letter to Mr. Blockhead or Woodhead—they are much of a muchness, especially Woodhead—I should have known nothing of their billing and cooing. Whereas now I know it, I shall prevent it. I took a copy of that letter, and as I want a laugh, I will just look at it:—

"Dear willm

            i ham verey hanggery with you For the hobsrvashon You mad when i met You Last nite at motherses. My Crinnylean hindeed hindesent! Let me tell you that it was no more hindesent than Anybody elses that was at motherses! Nor half so Hindesent has marryan sweetman's that you call bootifull, and witch nobody else does, and witch you calls miss Sweetman, while you calls me Sarah hand not Miss bunsen. Hand you sayd other cutting things witch my bussum will not soon forgit. You may say that you sayd it in Fun, but i don't like sitch Fun, hand if you would have me to Bee you Wife, you will Bee more carefull in Future. i shall ware my Crinnylean has big has i like hand shan't hask no Young Man's leave. i'd give up any Young Man rather than give hup my Crinnylean. if i here nothink from you in Reply i shall considder hour engagement at a hend.

                    "Sarah bunsen."

"Bravo, Sarah!" exclaimed George, laughing heartily over the letter. "She was a going it when she wrote that. I should like to show it to her for a lark. Wouldn't she flare! Now for master's note to Mr. Cumberland, who is a cunning cove, and no mistake. But as he pays me well, I shall stand his friend with missus."

George read—

"DEAR CUMBERLAND,

    "Briefly I have to complain of your calling here in my absence. I am unwilling to believe other than that it was a friendly call, but I can assure you that it places you in a false position with me, and is not agreeable to Mrs. Yapp.—In haste,

                "Faithfully yours,
                    "WILLIAM YAPP.

"P.S. Mrs. Yapp was premature in arranging a party here for to-night without consulting me; and as you were to be one of her guests, I regret to say that, as it does not hit my other numerous engagements it is unavoidably postponed. You know to-night I have a heavy match at pool with Harry Overend, and which I could not possibly put off. No doubt you will be curious enough to look in and see the play. I have every confidence in winning."

"The party off!" exclaimed George. "That's good! All the things ordered, too! That's better! Mr. Puffery's pastry will be here very soon, and I'll answer for it it won't grow stale. There'll be a jolly go in for me and Sarah, 'specially me. Mr. Cumberland won't keep away, not he—he's nuts upon missus, and its my opinion missus is nuts upon him. And as nice a pair they'd make together as anybody would see in a day's walk. As to that, master's a good-looking chap, but of the two Mr. Cumberland is better."

The boy now attacked Mr. Yapp's note to his father-in-law, Mr. Perkins, oilman, Cross-street, High Holborn:—

"MY DEAR SIR,—

    "Maria has told me that you run short of cash. Demn it! so do I. Is it not unfortunate? But you know, my dear Sir, that here we are all of us relying on the solution of the mystery; and, according to the respectable fortune-teller, that cannot be solved until after the birth of a third child, and then coronets and estates will be mine, and I need hardly tell you that what is mine is yours. You know you can always have my acceptance if you can melt it. The payments

from the unknown hand have been very irregular lately, and it has much distressed me, for you see I know not whom to apply to. Maria, I regret to say, has shown a little impatience because I desired that a party she arranged for to-night should be put off. It would not be right, my dear Sir, me owing you so much money as I do, just now to live extravagantly. I was taken very ill last night, and swooned; fortunately Maria was standing by, and with her usual kindness, was very solicitous for my recovery, and succeeded in restoring me.

    "Hoping that I shall soon have it in my power to make you amends for all your kindness,

            "I am,
                "Dear Sir,
                    "Very truly yours,
                        "WILLIAM YAPP.

"P.S.—I would have given you a call, and smoked a cigar with you, but upon my word the wealth I have hitherto had has brought me such a large circle of friends, that it is quite a difficulty with me how to arrange my time."

George thought he heard his mistress's footstep on the stairs, and quickly sealed the notes; and as they were confided to his care, he placed them in his pocket, and then he began his impertinent comments:—

"Mr. Yapp owe Mr. Perkins money! Well, I'm blowed! And can't pay him! I'm downright stunned! There's a pretty little game going on, and I'm afly to it. I see the end of it. Mrs. Yapp will run away with Mr. Cumberland or vicey vercey, which means one and the same thing, and my master will hang himself. I always thought his cravat one day would be tied under his ear—tchick! But master may rely on it that I has my wages afore these dreadful things happens. Well, well, it has almost taken my happetite away,"—putting a lump of cake in his mouth; "Hadn't it a been for this cake, I could eat nothing more, I'm that affected. I couldn't for the life of me eat common food."

George pondered over the state of things his exorbitant curiosity had put him in the possession of.

"There's a nice little swindle going on. I know master owes Mr. Cumberland tin, because I saw a note in his desk that let me into that secret. And I know every tradesman round and about is in for it. And I know the very clothes I've got on isn't paid for, because the tailor told me so, which is very unpleasant to my feelings. It's bad enough to wear livery, but to wear a livery that ain't paid for is galling indeed to a man with the feelings of a gentleman."

With the air of a master he left the breakfast-parlour to seek Sarah, and tell her all the news he had purloined from the notes.

He descended into the kitchen, and there was the young woman at breakfast by herself. George had his slippers on, and went on tiptoe behind Sarah's chair, and patted her rosy cheek with his finger; which so much frightened the girl, that she jumped up and screamed, and then upbraided the boy for his "imperence."

"There's a row about nothink," said George, "Had it been the baker you'd have fainted in his arms;—why don't you faint in mine? I shouldn't be angry—aw! I thought you would take the opportunity to show your affection for me—aw!"

"You imperent morsel, you!" exclaimed the girl.

"Morsel! you must have a nice hidea of size

if you call me a morsel? Come and sit down, Sarah, and let there be no row between us. We are fellow-servants—you are good as me, and I'm as good as you, and a great deal better."

" Indeed !"

"Why, of course; everybody says that a man is superior to a woman. But I don't care about that; you may be a great deal better than me—and that is saying a very great deal—but anything to please you."

"Stuff !—you never will please me; you tell too many lies for me."

"Now, your agoing it agin, Sarah !" exclaimed the boy. " Keep your temper, there's a good young woman. Shall I boil you a hegg or two to relish your breakfast ?"

"None of your heggs for me."

"Not my heggs, but master's," said the facetious youth. "Come, I'm not proud, I'll have a little breakfast with you; I haven't had any yet—at least, only a rotten hegg that master left."

"And do you think I b'lieve you ?"

"That's unkind, Sarah. If you won't have me in marriage, don't hinsult me. I've a tender heart."

" Go on with your rubbidge," said Sarah. "Now I must go and prepare missuss's breakfast."

"Let missus wait. I've secrets to tell you."

"I'll be bound you can't tell me anything I don't know," said the young woman."

"Can't I, though! Do you open letters, Sarah ?"

"Only my own."

"Then you're a hass," said George.

"A what? You young—"

"I mean a donkey—that's all I mean. Don't be angry."

"You're a hinfernal boy, and I shall be very glad when my month is up to leave this place."

"If you leave, I shall leave. So I don't know what will become of master and missus. What a beautiful crinnylean you've got on," said George, attacking Sarah's weakness, and the young woman's temper melted immediately.

"It ought to be," she said, "for it's a new one, and cost a good bit. Do you like crinnylean, George ?"

"I hadmire it above all things! and it does so become you, Sarah. Don't Mr. Woodhead like it, Sarah ?"

"Not much," she said, with a toss of her interesting head.

"He can't have much taste, then," said George, following up his attack.

"I've given him a bit of my mind on that subjik, and he likes crinnylean better now; and he wouldn't have me if he hadn't."

"I should think not, indeed. I say, Sarah, I'm still open to an offer, if you and the baker should tumble out."

"That's not likely, George, for the day is fixed," said Sarah, blushing with pride.

"I hope he'll break his neck—"

"It would break my heart if he did," said Sarah.

"Now you are a-going it," said George. "You only say so to spite me. But never mind, I must do what I can to keep up my happetite."

"What secrets have you got to tell me, George ?"

"Well, the party is put off !"

"Lord! I knew that a hour ago," said Sarah, which sorely puzzled the boy to think that his fellow-servant should have known what he did not an hour ago.

"Who told you, Sarah ?"

"Why missus, to be sure; and she is now writing notes to her friends who were coming. Haven't you got anything else to tell me ?"

"Yes, I have," said George. "Master is jealous of Mr. Cumberland."

"That is news !" exclaimed the girl. "He's a nice man, too, is Mr. Cumberland—so funny and agreeable."

"I think so, too," said George, beckoning her to his side. She reluctantly came.

"I've got another great secret for you, Sarah," he said, with his mouth so full of toast that the butter oozed out on each side. "There's no one here but our two selves, is there, Sarah ?"

The girl looked round, and so did George.

" Because it would be as good as my place was worth for any one but you to hear what I'm going to tell you."

"Well ?" said Sarah, panting with the curiosity the page had excited in her.

"Master's hard up for money! He ain't got none! He owes Mr. Perkins—that's Mrs. Yapp's father—a lot. He says that a fortune-teller told him when he had got three children he should have coronets and estates! What do you think of that for a tale ?"

"But who told you all this nonsense, George ?"

"Nonsense! Do you think I invented it ?" demanded the page.

"But who told you ?"

"Wouldn't you like to know? I ain't going to give you a pull upon me, you may take my word for that. You'd tell the baker, and he would tell master, and I should get the sack without a character."

"I promise you not to tell. I give you my real word of honour."

"Can't you make it a kiss instead, Sarah ?"

"Now, George, I'll tell Mr. Woodhead as sure as I'm alive, if you begin any of that nonsense again."

"Who cares for him? Bosh !" exclaimed the page, his old jealousy returning. "That man will serve you out about the crinnylean after you are his wife, and then you'll wish you had me."

"Now, if you don't drop the subjik, which is not a right and proper one for me and you to be talking about, and, seeing that I've got a young man, and going to be married, I shall just smack your face."

"Well, you just are a-going it! If you were to hit me, mind it would be worse for the baker. I'd knock him down the first time I saw him. You may laugh, but that's my style of settling matters."

And George went through a terrific pugilistic pantomime before Sarah; and if the baker only stood before him, and if the baker's hands and feet had only been tied, or he would have promised not to have opposed George, certainly he would have got the worst of it.

"Sit down, do, and don't make a fool of yourself," said Sarah.

"I'm incapable of that—aw—you're afraid—aw."

"Rubbidge! tell me who told you about the estates and coronets ?"

"Shan't."

"Another pack of lies," said Sarah, "and I was a fool to listen to such rubbidge."

"What do you mean by rubbidge, you ignorant young woman? If you do not speak correctly—aw—I shall have to leave—aw. I cannot beah so much ignorance—aw."

"You little puppy! I wish Mr. Woodhead was here."

"What! the man who don't like crinnylean—aw!"

"What do you know about the crinnylean?"

"Your man, the baker, showed me your ignorant note to him, in which one word was not spelt correctly. And both of us had a nice laugh over it."

"That's another lie!" exclaimed Sarah. "Now you tell me what was in the note?"

"A rare lot of your bad temper, I can assure you. You wanted to be called Miss Bunsen, because your man, the baker, called Mary Ann Sweetman, Miss Sweetman; and didn't you threaten him with turnips if he didn't apologise? Don't I know?"

Sarah was very much astonished; there could be no mistake about it now, the boy must have seen the note.

"I shall see Mr. Woodhead to-night, and if he has been mean enough to show you my note, he and I shall part. I've got a good mind to show you some of his notes to me, just for spite. He must be a very mean man to show anybody his letters from a young woman."

"I would if I were you, Sarah. Do show them to me, just for a lark. Do Sarah, get 'em now."

"Wouldn't you like it? But I won't do anything so shabby. Mr. Woodhead would very much like for you to know all the nice names he had called me, over the left."

Mrs. Yapp's bell here rang, and Sarah left in a hurry; and George moved his fat sides about as if he had been very busy all the morning. He stirred the fire, rattled the breakfast things as if he had been putting them on one side—whistled—and pulled himself together in the most business-like manner.

CHAPTER XXXII.

LOST A DIAMOND RING.—LADY BLAZE DISCLOSES HER NAME.—JOE BOWERS AND HIS DAUGHTER BIDE THEIR TIME.—YAPP AND SWIFT CONFER.

LADY BLAZE was a most indefatigable and determined woman. After she left the police station, where she had been to give information of her lost diamond ring, she went home, and wrote out in a fine bold hand a small placard for the printer:—

"TEN POUNDS REWARD!

LOST OR STOLEN

A DIAMOND RING!

of great value, with the initials C. H. S. engraved inside the hoop of the ring. Whoever will bring it to Mrs. Walpole at Messrs. Bonthron and Son's, Bolt-court, Fleet-street, or give any information that may lead to its restoration, shall receive the above reward."

It was about nine o'clock at night when Mrs. Walpole (for her right name was now avowed in the placard) discovered her loss, and before ten, such was the energy with which she worked and infused into others, that that little bill was posted in a dozen or more places round and about the neighbourhood.

Bonthron and Son's shutters had two or three pasted on them, and Joe Bowers, landlord of the Lion, smiled significantly at his daughter when Lady Blaze presented herself and asked him to be good enough to place a bill in his window and another outside the bar.

Miss Bowers and her father were very civil to Mrs. Walpole; and when they read the placard they expressed as much sympathy with her as their coarse natures would permit—in short, they did everything and promised everything, but tell her (which they well knew) who were the thieves that had her diamond.

Joe took his daughter, who was showily dressed, and her hair beautifully curled, on one side, and said—

"Keep your own council, gal; there'll be a greater reward offered yet, and then I shall split. Ugh! ugh! they shouldn't have talked so loud."

"But I thought your name was Lady Blaze," said Joe Bowers, looking inquiringly into the handsome, but now turbulent-looking face of the woman.

"I know not why you should, Sir; I never told you or any one else that that was my name," she offendedly replied.

"I beg pardon, ma'am," said Joe, making the best bow that he was able. "It must be a valuable ring to offer sich a reward for it. I had no idea that we had sich rich people live in our court."

"Ah! Sir, there are a good many things in this wicked world and in this court, too, that you have no idea of," said Mrs. Walpole, in melancholy tones.

"That I can very well believe, Ma'am. May I ask your opinion whether the ring has been lost or stolen?"

"I have hardly thought about it; my mind has been so much occupied with my loss. Its intrinsic value is very great, that my life almost depends upon its possession."

"When did you miss it, Ma'am?" asked Miss Bowers.

"Not two hours ago."

"Were you in the habit of wearing it?" asked Joe.

"Oh, dear, no; it was locked away with my other jewellery—I mean in a large trunk with other things," added Mrs. Walpole, as if she regretted mentioning "other jewellery."

The publican and his daughter stared at each other when Lady Blaze inadvertently spoke of her concealed treasures, of which she was so anxious that no one should suspect her of possessing.

Both Joe and his daughter had seen a great deal of life in all its phases, but still, much of life as they had seen, they had never before met with a woman living in a garret in a court, who was the owner of a quantity of jewellery, and could offer "Ten Pounds Reward" to the finder of a diamond ring.

"Help me, Sir, as much as you can to bring back the jewel that I prize, and I shall be grateful," exclaimed Mrs. Walpole, who seemed in such haste that while she spoke, she held the ill-painted door of the Lion in her white hand—and it was remarkable, and certainly was an evidence of the respectability and nobility of her birth that her hand should be so fair and of such lovely formation. Her teeth, too, were exquisite in their whiteness and preservation, and with the exception of a wildness of manner and an excitement of speech, her whole deportment was that of a high-born woman.

"YOU SHALL NEVER LIVE TO DO THAT!" EXCLAIMED SWIFT, SEIZING LADY BLAZE
BY THE WRISTS.

Miss Bowers thought herself something of a lady before she witnessed so much of Lady Blaze —but now she sank into utter insignificance —Miss Bowers's notions of a lady were measured in degree entirely by her showiness of dress, the jewellery she displayed, and the demonstrative action she made while speaking.

Miss Bowers for once in her life experienced the truth of a sentence to be found in one of the plays of glorious William Shakespeare, "to the manner born,"—who was just glorious because he could not help being glorious—not that he ever felt himself to be glorious except under the genial, jovial influence of sack. By this remark we mean to say that he never felt himself glorious from a *conceited* point of view. Shakespeare never felt himself to be other than human,— would hob-knob with his friend—chuck his friend's wife under her chin—laugh, and sport, and make grimaces with his friend's children; mourn with his neighbour, help his neighbour, love his neighbour as himself, eat a rump steak,

13

kiss a pretty girl,—talk things with some old crony that the age we live in would denounce as unfit for ears polite—lark with the "watch"—and tumble to bed as "drunk as Chloe."

But after all, the great glory of Shakespeare was that he had no idea of his greatness, and therefore never raised any assumption upon it. He never strutted about as most of our writers now do, as if the great "I am" was stamped on their fronts—especially our great authors, to whom their is too much worship given, and who are far too weak-minded to receive it with a proper grace.

Enough. Mrs. Walpole was a lady by birth and education, and Miss Bowers had just sufficient sense to perceive it.

When she left the bar of the Lion, Joe Bowers's daughter could not help regarding her as a perfect lady. Had Lady Blaze chosen, she had the means to dress like a duchess, but living as she did in a garret, for a purpose hidden from every one but herself, she attired herself in a manner consistent with her very humble abode. She now stood before Joe Bowers's little bar, with her fine bust and shoulders covered with an old black shawl, and her broad-browed head crowned with a rusty, black velvet bonnet, while a well-worn silk gown with a broad, black stripe, completed her lowly attire.

Cold as the night was, she had no gloves on her white and taper fingers, which had no other adornment than her plain gold wedding-ring; but had those soft fingers been closely examined, marks of rings on every finger might have been found.

But nature had indelibly stamped superior birth upon her manners and features, and all her attemps at disguising it, only served to make it more obvious. Joe Bowers and his daughter unmistakably felt that they stood in the presence of no ordinary woman—although if they had been called to define in what the difference consisted they would have failed, as would also anyone of higher intelligence. So subtle, inexplicable, and indefinable are the qualities of a lady. We are made to *feel* them, they cannot be described :—

"Oh fairest of creation ! last and best
Of all God's works ! creatures in whom excell'd
Whatever can to sight or thought be form'd
Holy, divine, good, amiable, or sweet."

Mrs. Walpole was a lady, but she was a lady who had evidently received some deadly wrong, and her soul was in arms with feelings and passions that could neither be justified nor explained.

"Do you happen to know anything about a man Swift, who works at Bonthron and Son's?" inquired Lady Blaze of Joe Bowers.

"Only that he is a pretty good customer of mine, as is Mr. Yapp, who is cashier," said Joe "You don't suspect that he has got the ring, do you, Ma'am?"

"I find it difficult to suspect any one, for I never once left my door unlocked for a minute since I lived there."

"Then if that's the case, Ma'am, my belief is that you will find it about the floor, dragged out with something or other from the trunk," said Joe.

"I hardly hope so," said Mrs. Walpole, "for I have already made a careful search."

"Them old garrets in which you live have very bad floorings, worn out with age, as I may

say; the ring may have got down between the chinks and crevices of the boards."

"That is a very excellent suggestion. Every board shall come up before I sleep," said Lady Blaze. "Can you tell me of a carpenter? I don't mind what I pay him, if you would kindly send me one directly."

"I know lots of carpenters who will be glad of making a little overtime. I don't know if there isn't one in the taproom now. Bill Naylor!" he called, turning to the taproom door.

"Hi ! hi! Master Bowers," was the reply, and there issued forth from the room a very tall, scrubby-looking workman in a flannel jacket, with a short pipe in his mouth, and a two-foot rule obtruding from his trousers' pocket. "Here's Bill Naylor, and what do you want with him?"

"Have you a mind to a bit of a job, Bill?" said Joe.

"What's the nature of it ?" inquired Naylor.

"This lady——"

"You *are* polite, Joe," said Naylor, who was astonished at the landlord designating the woman who stood by his side in clothes as rusty as his own wife's, as a lady.

Lady Blaze breathed hard, and slightly scowled on the mechanic.

"Come, I say, Bill, if you don't want a job, say so. I thought I'd give you the chance."

"And I thank you, Joe, but as my day's work is over, and I'm in for a game of dominoes, I'm not going to take my coat off any more for any one, or for any work, until I go to bed."

Bill Naylor returned to his chums in the taproom—rattled the dominoes—filled his pipe—drank his beer—and said as much to himself as to any one else——

"I'm not so fond of money as to make myself a slave for it. I've earned my family's bread to-day, and that's as much as ought to be expected from any man—at all events, they'll be disappointed who expects more than that from me. Whose lead is it, Jem?" he inquired of his domino opponent, a man of the same grade as himself.

"A queer fellow, that, Ma'am," said Joe Bowers.

"I cannot wait to discuss that," said Mrs. Walpole. "Know you any one else that you can send me? But why should I trouble you? I will find some one myself."

"You can of course please yourself, Ma'am," said Joe. "But I know a man who would be glad of the job, if he's at home."

"Then I will thank you to send him. I have a few more places to call at with these placards, and I shall be at home in half an hour. Mind, if the carpenter is not there by that time I shall not wait but seek one for myself. Your suggestion is too good to admit of delay."

"I hope when the boards are moved the ring may be found, Ma'am," said Miss Bowers.

"If so I shall not forget to make you a very handsome present for your father's suggestion," said Lady Blaze. "You do not happen to know where the man Swift lives ?"

Miss Bowers, who was not quite so good at keeping secrets as her father, was about to give the information, when the landlord, who had now a good chance of making money out of Mrs. Walpole's loss, unmistakably nudged the foot and elbow of his daughter, which stopped her reply, and her father answered—

"I never did know where Swift lived, though

he comes here often enough, too. To be sure it is not my business to know."

"True, true," said Mrs. Walpole. "I wish you both good night."

She planted a few more placards about after she left the Lion, taking the last to the station-house, where it was quickly posted up amongst others of a more startling character, as "Found drowned!" "Murder!" "A child lost!" "Great embezzlement!"

Amongst such announcements as these, Lady Blaze's placard of "Lost or stolen, a Diamond Ring," however great the value to her, appeared as nothing to those who read it in comparison with the other losses.

When Mrs. Walpole reached home, there was the carpenter Joe Bowers had sent, waiting for her, with his basket of tools slung over his shoulder—nor was it long before he was on his knees in the garret tearing up the floor, while Lady Blaze anxiously looked on, holding a candle, and turning over the dust and dirt beneath the dilapidated planks.

After the carpenter had pulled up and restored the flooring round and about the region where the trunk of treasures always stood, and Lady Blaze finding nothing, her hopes began to fail her, and she thought it utterly useless to continue her search further; and by twelve o'clock she paid the carpenter and dismissed him.

"It must have been stolen!" she exclaimed. "But how? By whom?"

She went and examined the lock of her door, and then the lock of her trunk. But she got no clue to it, for the keyholes gave no evidence of having been tampered with.

She sat down and gazed up through the sky-light of her room to the bright winter sky, which was well studded with sparkling frosty-looking stars. She sighed heavily and moaned about her deceased daughter—she that was to have worn the handsome, cherished wedding-dress in her trunk, and exclaimed to herself—

"She *was* a star indeed! So bright! so loving! She stands before me now—oh, how palpable! how real! 'Tis her blessed spirit! and her last words pierce my ears—'Mother, he is false to me! my heart is broken!' And the vow I made over her grave, for four-and-twenty years has not been fulfilled. Yet I've done well! for his son is dead to him—curse him!—as well as my daughter to me! Bless her! though dead she is ever with me. Dear, unhappy girl!"

She sat silent for a long time, and then fell asleep for awhile, and was abruptly awoke by the candle setting fire to the paper bound round it and causing a great flame and spluttering.

She sighed and shivered, undressed, and went to bed.

CHAPTER XXXIII.

SWIFT CONFINES LADY BLAZE IN A CELLAR.— MR. YAPP PLEADS FOR HER LIFE. — SHE ESCAPES. — THE RING FOUND. — YAPP HAS NEWS OF HIS LONG-LOST FATHER.

MR. SWIFT, who did not live far from Bolt Court, after his diabolical accusation of poor Tom Brown at the station-house, and his subsequent interview with Mr. Yapp, went drinking about from one public-house to another, and got at length in such a glorious state of "beer," that he did not reach home for the night. He made himself very jolly with one of the five-pound notes stolen

from Bonthron and Son's letter, and was ready to stand treat with all and sundry that he met with—and being by nature a gossiping, old-womanish sort of a character, he knew a great many people who lived and worked in and about the slums of Fleet-street.

Like himself, all his friends and acquaintances were good customers to the publican, and they met nightly at one or other of the hundred bars or skittle-alleys of the neighbourhood.

Mr. Swift was a noisy, talkative, busy man, and was not to be put down by any one. He laboured under several false flattering impressions of himself. He thought he could sing a good song; and if singing consisted in noise and bellow, why, then, Swift was a vocalist, indeed! He also thought himself a poet! But his gift of poesy extended no further than making "cat" rhyme with "rat," "dog" with "bog," "beer" with "cheer," "he" with "she," "life" with "wife," "shilling" with "willing." But the greatest mistake of Swift's was, that he considered himself a honest man—but he took his cue of honesty from "Every man for himself," and from Rob Roy's law—

"Let him get who's got the power,
And let him keep who can."

No man really knew so little of himself as Swift. Had he known himself, he would have trembled. Naturally he was a swaggering, bullying, overbearing, coarse, cruel, ignorant, lying. low-lived villain! He cared for no one—loved no one—had mercy upon no one—but himself. For self he would have hung his dearest connection. He was a fiend walking the earth in coat and trousers.

Yet, until now, it was never known that he had committed an offence against the law; his offences hitherto had only been against the moral law, which, by too many of mankind, are considered venial. But the temptation of Mrs. Walpole's jewellery at once developed the whole of his wicked propensities to commit daring crimes.

With Mr. Yapp he was utterly disgusted, because the clerk had some slight misgivings left about right and wrong; some conscientious scruples about murder; some small fear about punishment and disgrace; a little tenderness for wife and children.

"Had it not a-been for that d—d Yapp, that woman should never have lived to have printed that 'ere bill!" he muttered to himself, as half drunk, half sober, he pulled up in the morning before his master's shutters in Bolt Court, and read the boldly-printed placard about the missing ring which he had concealed in his pocket.

"Mr. Yapp may be a werry fine gen'lman to look at, but there's no go in him. He'll drawl and sprawl, and aw—aw, and jaw, jaw, when he reads this. There must have been a tile off of my hupper story, when I told our Mr. Yapp anything about that 'ere ring,

No one from me will git that ring
Even if for it I do swing."

After this effort in what he called poetry, he unlocked the warehouse door, and entered the shop; and before he opened the shutters he stole down into the cellar, and by the little light that was admitted from a grating in the court, he examined round and about the brick wall.

The cellar was long and dark, and there were three several brick arches in it. He traversed up and down, but the darkness defeated his purpose. The gas-meter was at his feet, and he turned on the gas, then he took a loose match from his greasy waistcoat-pocket and lit a jet, which served to show him a little loose brick-work near the ground at the bottom of one of the arches.

"That'll do hexcellent well!" he exclaimed, stooping, and with the aid of a piece of an old iron hoop from a cask rotting by the arch, he drew forth a brick; then from the watch-pocket of his trowsers he took the ring, which sent forth the most resplendent sparkles of light in that dark cellar.

"Bide yer there till yer wanted," he said, placing the ring in paper, and then putting it in a cavity left by the brick, and then restoring the brick, and kicking it in its place with his foot.

"Bide yer there till the hubbub has blown over. And if I had my way—and I will have my way yet—with as good a heart, I'd brick up yer rightful owner with yer!"

Lady Blaze had passed a melancholy night, and was early astir; and as Swift emerged from the cellar after the burial of the ring, she stood before him in the middle of the warehouse. He was hardly prepared for the lady's visit, and would have preferred that it had not been made. But the scoundrel was equal to all occasions, and after a moment's pause, he coolly said, as she stood on the top stair that led to the cellar—

"Good morning, Mrs. Walpole."

"What about my ring, Sir?" said the lady.

"If you think I know anything about yer ring more than that you have lost it, why then yer mistaken, that's all. And I don't see why you should set upon me; you don't know me to be a thief, do yer!"

"I know nothing of you," said Mrs. Walpole, shrinking from the glare of the man's sottish-looking eye. "I am making inquiries about a ring."

"Then yer should learn to make yer hinquiries in a proper manner. What about yer ring, indeed! Yer would hinjure me as well as my boy, would yer?"

"Your boy was insolent, and I complained to his master about him, and he very properly discharged him," retorted Mrs. Walpole.

"You'll be served out for it yet, you proud hag!" exclaimed Swift.

"How dare you, Sir! Look to it that you are not also discharged on my complaint."

"You shall never live to do that!" exclaimed the fiend, darting on Mrs. Walpole, seizing her by both wrists and dragging her down the cellar stairs. So quickly this was done, that she had but time to give one scream—which no one heard. The last six stairs reached, he jumped with her from the top to the bottom, and they both fell on the ground.

Swift soon regained his feet, but the ill-fated lady received a blow on her head, which for the minute stunned her, and the reckless man dragged her along the ground to the innermost arch, to which was attached a heavy door. Having got her inside this, he let her fair hands drop, saying—

"Lie there, you werry proud hag! and if it prove yer grave it'll be a better one than you deserve!"

He closed the door upon the lady, who scarcely breathed, and he locked it.

The compartment of the cellar in which Mrs. Walpole lay outstretched on the earth was not bove eight feet wide and ten feet long, and was boarded off from the other part. The cellar itself was a dismal place indeed. It was used for nothing but the most useless lumber, and very seldom was it visited, and seldomer still by any one but Swift. The damp hung on the walls, which were festooned by dark cobwebs and overrun by fat spiders, while every here and there were holes which showed that the rat also held his carnival here.

It was indeed a dismal place! How could that man leave a woman there to live or die? But Swift was a man without a man's feelings.

After he had done his first morning's work, he emerged from the cellar; and although at every pause in his footstep from the cellar to the wareroom, his ear encountered a woman's groan, he took no heed—he tarried not—he repented not—but went to his morning's duties with the feelings of one who had immured a dog rather than a woman.

"She came across me at the right time. I should not always have had nerve—that's what our Mr. Yapp calls it—to do what I have done. She won't be missed, for nobody owns her. More work for the p'lice. Well, they're a hidle lot—and if it warn't for men like me and Mr. Yapp they'd have nothing to do. Her groans ain't pleasant though, and if our Mr. Yapp was to hear them, he'd say—'let her out, that's a good fellah.' Our Master Yapp has a tender heart, he has. But my heart is like the one in the play that I saw the other night—'tis a 'Dead Heart.'"

He was about to unscrew the shutters of the room, when he suddenly stopped, and with open mouth and shrugged-up shoulders, he exclaimed—

"That was a shriek! There's danger in that woman yet. I'll pile up some of these 'ere sacks of rags round and about her prison, and so drown her groans and shrieks."

He opened the door that led to the cellar, then took on his back a sack, and then he suddenly threw it down, and muttered—

"This is baby's work! This is going round, and round, and round, in our Mr. Yapp's fashion, instead of short, and sharp, and straight, in mine."

Full of determination—full of crime—Swift seized a knife—(one of those thin long-bladed knives used by warehousemen and ham and beef shopkeepers), and cried to himself, looking upon the edge, which was at the service of any one, either to cut a slice off the staff of life, or with a little dexterity cut off a head—

"This will rid her of her groans, and me of the annoyance of listening to them."

He reached two stairs towards the spot where he had thrown Mrs. Walpole, or Lady Blaze, and the knife dropped from his hand, striking stair after stair, until it reached the bottom, and lodged with a dull sound upon the earthy cellar floor.

"I won't deny that I don't like the job, more than I wish that I don't like the woman. Arter all I don't hate her enough to destroy her. I wish she'd come up those 'ere stairs and hit me,—or spit at me—or call me a willain—or hinsult my boy—then she would bring that passion in my heart and that blood in my weins as is necessary to take a life! But I never felt so tame, so much like Mr. Yapp afore. I'll let her out—she's sure to do or say something to make me in a passion—and then I should like to see the man who would dare to stand between Lady Blaze and that 'ere knife which fell from my weak hand? D—m these groans! they make a complete baby on me! I wish our Mr. Yapp would come—but Lord! he's no use. Murder must be done in red-hot passion, when reason's napping. Hark to her groans! I wish I was deaf, or she was dead! But it's no good—crikey! there was a shriek! What I can hear, others can hear. I'll let her out. D—d if I ain't afraid to move. I know what nerves are now. Didn't think I had any afore."

The sailor's wife, who had but a few hours since lost her baby, with sorrowful footstep came down the stairs to take in her morning's milk from the man at the door.

"Some one comes!" cried Swift, deeply terrified with the deed he had committed. He was paralysed with fear; at length he decided on adopting his first mode of destroying Lady Blaze by heaping sacks of rags around the hole she was in, and thus deaden or drown her dying cries and groans.

By the time he had descended to the cellar with the first sack and returned to the wareroom for another, Mr. Yapp had arrived, and his steps were arrested at the front door by the placard concerning the ring.

"Oh, Swift, I am so glad to meet you!" he exclaimed, rushing into the shop. "There's no time to be lost now! What I feared, you see, has happened!"

"What's that?"

"The ring!—she's found it wanting! You've read the bill, haven't you?"

"I should think I had, and a many times over. And there's no denying, but its wery hugly, and werry unexpected. How are yer nerves this morning, Mr. Yapp?"

"I've had a most wretched night of grief, Swift, and I feel ashamed to say the dreadful thoughts I have been haunted with."

"You must get rid of shame, Mr. Yapp, for we've a great deal to do to-day."

"I fear we have, Swift."

"And you must get rid of fear likewise," said Swift.

"Ha! what groan was that I heard?" exclaimed Mr. Yapp, with a troubled countenance, "and there, another! Don't you hear, Swift?"

"I've heerd them afore this morning," was the sulky reply.

"Whatever have you been doing, Swift?"

"Not a-firing the primises, Mr. Yapp," was the tantalising reply.

"Don't taunt me!" exclaimed the clerk. "What have you been doing?"

"What ought to have been done yesterday, and then that ere bill about the ring would never have been on our shutters."

"You alarm me, Swift! You have not killed her, eh?"

"I couldn't have done that, or you wouldn't hear her groan," said Swift, morosely, and in mocking tones. "Lock the door, put one of them 'ere sacks on your shoulders, and follow me."

"Oh, Swift! you bring the heart of me to my mouth! And so the day has commenced with murder?"

"Don't preach to me, Mr. Yapp! Don't be a hidiot! There's the key; let her out if you like!" he exclaimed, throwing a rusty key to the ground.

The clerk picked it up, and recognised it, and knew the door it belonged to.

"Is Lady Blaze there?"

"Lady Blaze ain't her name. Read the bill. She's Mrs. Walpole."

"Do not be so curt, so captious with me, Swift," cried Yapp, in tones that might have been deemed pleading ones. "Tell me, there's a good fellah!—what have you done?"

"Take up that 'ere sack and follow me," he said, pointing to a sack, while he went and arranged another for his own broad shoulders.

"That groan again!" exclaimed Mr. Yapp.

"Yes, I heard it," said Swift; "but it was fainter than the others."

"She is dying, perhaps!" suggested the clerk.

"That's what we want, ain't it?" asked the malicious warehouseman.

"We! What have I to do with it? I escaped being a murderer last night; do not make me one now!"

Mr. Yapp trembled from head to foot.

A long, loud, piercing shiek came up the cellar-stairs.

Swift left the sacks by which he was standing and rushed to the drawer where he had put Mr. Yapp's loaded pistol, and drew it forth, saying—

"I had forgotton that I had such a good friend so handy. I'll be master of the primises now," he added with a bravo's swagger.

The clerk fell on his knees to Swift, and cried—

"Let your first act of mastery be to blow my brains out!"

Swift held the pistol aloft in the air, and said, in the coolest, possible manner—

"I've only powder for one. Besides, your life is no good to me. Keep it for yer children's sake. Hush! that groan seemed like dying," said Swift, as a low, prolonged wail was heard.

"Oh! yes, Swift, there's death in that," said the terrified clerk. "Would that I were so near my end! Be a friend and fire, Swift!" he imploringly exclaimed.

"You have no jewels," said the warehouseman, "and I don't choose to be hung just for putting you out of your wretchedness. I don't do something for nothing. It ain't remoonerative. Get up, yer cur!"

"I'm all that, and more," said Yapp. "Rid me of my worthless life! Don't let me live to betray you!"

"She groans loud agin! Get up and follow me to the cellar!"

"Not for the world!" exclaimed Yapp, rising from his knees. "She has done me no harm."

"She has me, though, and my boy too."

"That's not much, Swift. Don't take the woman's life for that."

"I am not a going, and you know it," said Swift. "It ain't through malice that I would kill her, but just because she stands between me and the jewellery."

"But we saw how to get that without committing murder. You have been premature in what you have done. I do assure you you have."

"Stuff! you know nothing about it. She came down here and almost accused me to my face of having stolen her ring."

"She must have read it in your face, Swift; so difficult it is for thieves to wear the visages of honest men."

"Well I'm sure! you're a nice man to say that I carry thief in my face. What must yer own be, then?"

"As bad as yours—worse, if possible," said the clerk.

"Help! help!" were now the cries which issued

from the cellar and which barely reached the shop, they partook of so much feebleness. The men stared at each other for a moment, when Swift said determinedly—

"This must be stopped, and I'm the man to do it! Lend a hand, Mr. Yapp. It's the only way out of it, however much yer may dislike it. You hold her while I shoot her."

"I'd shoot myself much sooner," said Mr. Yapp.

"There's no choice, I tell yer," said Swift, angrily.

"Let her out, I say!" said Mr. Yapp.

"That she might go to a magistrate, and charge me with an assault! I don't seem to see it. My way is the best, and here goes. She has neither husband nor children, and here goes."

"She wears a wedding ring," said Yapp, "so she is either married or has been. And she may have children for aught you know."

"I don't care if she has—don't care if she was suckling a baby—nothing can save her now. She must die, I tell you, and you know it, Mr. Yapp. All you want is to get it on my shoulders."

"It is not so, Swift. All I want is to save the woman's life, and you from murder. Last night I thought we arranged how things should be. First, there was your excellent suggestion about the account-books."

"I throw no books into the Thames until Lady Blaze is settled. She must be half dead now, and you must make up your delicate mind to assist me with the other half."

"I cannot—that's plain," said Mr. Yapp. "I should loathe myself for ever after. I feel sick at the very thought of such a thing."

"What would yer have then?" demanded Swift. "If you let her out what will you say to her, and what d'ye think she will say to me? And, mind ye, what she sez to me she sez to you —for we are both in it, don't yer forget that, Mr. Yapp. And as sure as a gun we shall have the officers here soon about the ring."

"I see, Swift, I see; we are in a dreadful mess!"

"No mess at all. You begin a job, and only half carry it through—'tis that causes all the mess! We ought to have been clear off with the jewellery by this time, and time passes, Mr. Yapp, so I don't deceive yer!"

Yapp, listening to the teachings of his tutor, painfully felt the perplexity of his position. In a moment, as it were, all his troubles crowded in upon his mind. He thought of the wife who didn't love him, of his children born to disgrace by his own actions—of his debts—of his lying life—of his frauds.

Swift saw that Yapp was growing consentient, and he was very anxious that the clerk should have a fair share of the responsibility of the crime.

"What are your plans, Swift!"

"Kill the woman—take all she has—sell it to my friend the Jew—and hook it," he quickly answered. "There, what d'ye think of that?"

"And what if the woman is not killed?"

"Why she would split upon us," said Swift.

"How could she? She doesn't know that you have got her ring, does she?"

"No, she don't; but then the sharp eyes of the police are prying into the matter, and somehow or other they generally scent their game. As you say rogues cannot look like honest men."

"Time, Swift, time. I see now more what you mean. Time presses, I see now."

"Why, for what we know, our guv'nor might be here directly," said Swift, urging on the clerk.

"Ha! he might indeed!" said Mr. Yapp. "Then all would be out, and I shall be ruined."

"And transported without doubt," said the fiend Swift, "and your wife and children disgraced."

"Ha! yes! you see it all, Swift! you see it as I see it. Is it not dreadful? I was honest once."

"There could have been nothing in your way to take, then," was the man's facetious reply to the clerk's moralisings.

"You are mistaken," old fellah! I have been honest among plenty of property."

"Then you had no need for it," said Swift. "There's not much honesty in not taking what yer don't need. Had yer wanted the property you talk about you'd have been as great a thief then as now. The man who has not strength enough to deny himself taking what 'his'n his'n,' is a thief; and the man who does deny himself under pressure is the honest man."

"I accept your definition, Swift; it is very true," said Mr. Yapp.

"And I'm sure we are under pressure now," said Swift.

"And have not strength to deny ourselves?" replied Yapp.

"Therefore, we are —"

"Thieves!" exclaimed Yapp, promptly taking his cue.

"Well, I think we have carried that out very dramatical," said Swift.

"Now, if you kill the woman—what about the body—eh, Swift?"

"One thing at a time—that's my maxim," said Swift.

"No, you're wrong; it must be considered as a whole. The body must be provided for. Then again the woman will very soon be missed—she might have been seen coming in here."

"And she mightn't," retorted Swift. "Time presses, Mr. Yapp!" he cried. "Let this woman be silenced, if she ain't already, for I have heard no groans this past two or three minutes—let her be silenced—then upstairs to the trunk of treasures—then to the bottom of the Thames with the account-books—and then to the Jew— then a division of the money—and then I'm hoff!"

"Your course seems clear. But you forget that wherever you go, you will carry murder about with you."

"And that's a thing I mean to forget," said Swift.

"You'll not have the power. The figure of Lady Blaze will haunt you night and day. Oh! Swift, I have been through the fire."

"You're a rare chap for fire! You don't seem scorched much," said Swift, regaining his old cold dare-devil state of mind.

"I mean I've felt the pangs of villainy so long that—"

"You ought to laugh at it by this time. It should be natural to you. This is my first step in crime, and I seem at home with it already. Holloa! hark! She's not dead yet—she's kicking at the door—wiolently kicking, too! Come, Yapp, there's no time to lose I tell yer! It must be settled now, or my word for it we shall be scented by the hofficers."

"Is there no alternative but murder?"

"None that I knows on. That's plain, ain't it? The shutters ought to be down before this. We shall be suspected—this d—d hesitation of yourn will blab the whole affair. Come—you must, and shall be in it! I don't much like the job myself, and that's truth. But there is no way out on it. Come on! Time presses! People will be in and out presently."

"If you fire the pistol below, won't it be heard over the neighbourhood?"

"There's something in that, by jingo! Didn't think of that, Mr. Yapp," said Swift, considering. "And the powder would smell, too."

"Yes, Swift," said Mr. Yapp.

"Do you know I begin to think that we are a couple of blunderers!"

"Why did you lay hands on her?" cried Yapp.

"'Cause she hinsulted me; that's why. But I'm not to be baffled. There's other things at hand. There's that 'ere hammer that lies there—"

The look of the hammer, as it lay with its large broad head on the floor, in association with Swift's design on an inoffensive woman, thrilled the soul of the sensitive clerk.

"One blow with that 'ere would spoil her beauty, eh, Mr. Yapp?"

He took the hammer, and returned the pistol to the drawer. He would not trust it to the custody of Mr. Yapp, who was very changeable in his ideas, and impulsive in his actions.

"Come, Yapp, you stand by, while I strike the blow. That is not asking much from yer," said Swift.

While the clerk was struck dumb at the blood-thirsty proposition, the two men stood aghast, for Lady Blaze's footsteps were heard coming up the stairs. In a minute, wild, but still commanding, she was about to rush between her would-be murderers to make her exit from the shop. But Swift quickly seized her by one wrist, while Yapp, influenced by the rapid action of his master in crime, seized her by the other.

There was a black bruise on her fair broad brow; her dress was besmeared with damp earth, and her long hair, slightly tinged and grizzled with grey, hung, some over her eyes, some over her shoulders, and some down her back.

She looked terrible with wrath, and her eye beamed with passion as she glanced from one to the other.

At first she made no attempt to free herself; but finding that her looks of anger had no effect upon them, she struggled for release.

She was a strong woman, and her strength was wonderfully augmented by her passions and feelings, and she would soon have overcome the only half-determined clerk; but Swift—ah! he was another specimen of humanity altogether—Swift was as resolute as she was, and being a man, and of greater strength, he held her wrist as in a vice. Lady Blaze felt there was no escape from him.

After Lady Blaze had somewhat recovered from Swift's rough handling and the fall with him to the bottom of the cellar-stairs, and when she found that her groans, and cries, and shrieks, and screams, were unheeded by any but her assailants, then she looked round and about the dismal place she was confined in, and a large stone met her eye.

With this stone she attacked the lock, which time had partially loosened from its fastening to the door. These were the knockings which Swift heard when he exclaimed "She's kicking at the door!"

With the stone referred to she indefatigably worked until she had struck the lock to the floor,

when the door flew open, and Mrs. Walpole, to the confusion of Swift and Yapp, unexpectedly and surprisingly appeared before them.

The touch of Mr. Yapp, although he held her in a far gentler manner than Swift, seemed more obnoxious to her than the strong grip of the latter.

"Would you follow in your father's steps?" she demanded of Mr. Yapp, glaring at him.

"Father! what do *you* know of my father?"

"That he is a murderer!" was the appalling reply.

"Ha!" exclaimed Yapp, letting the wrist of Lady Blaze drop from his hand as if the news of his father had rendered him powerless to hold it.

Mr. Swift seeing the effect Lady Blaze's words had upon the clerk, said—

"Don't b'lieve her, Mr. Yapp. She is deceiving yer."

"Liar!" exclaimed Lady Blaze.

"That ain't werry nice language for a lady," said Swift.

"Who is my father?" inquired the clerk.

"I decline to answer, William Yapp."

"A murderer!" muttered the astonished clerk to himself, and then he asked—

"And, pray, who did my father murder?"

"My daughter," was the stern reply.

"Was he hung for it?" satirically inquired Swift.

"That is not *your* business, you vulgar fellow!" she replied. "Release my arm, Sir!"

"Oh, dear, no," retorted Swift.

"And why, pray? What is your object with me? What is the meaning of this treatment? You shall be answerable for it."

"You don't have the chance if I know it," said the barbarous man. "You have hinjured my son."

"He was a scoundrel!" exclaimed Mrs. Walpole.

"Don't yer say that agin, you hag!"

"Spare her, Swift."

"Don't plead for me with *him*!" she exclaimed. "If you would serve me, fetch hither a police-man."

"He dares not!" said Swift, with a chuckle.

"Is he your master?" said Lady Blaze, looking straight at Mr. Yapp, who hung his head in shame.

This was a question that sorely puzzled Mr. Yapp how to answer. This was a situation he was totally unprepared for, nor could he tell what part to play in this the new drama of his eventful career.

Mr. Yapp looked at Swift, and the latter could not, and did, not fail to understand their meaning, which was to release her.

"Not I," said Swift. "Take her arm, Mr. Yapp, and help me with her to the cellar."

Mrs. Walpole screamed aloud, which took Swift off his guard, and then she suddenly and strongly twisted her arm round, freed herself, and flew towards the door.

"Scoundrels! both of you! and both of you shall suffer."

She was about to make her exit, when Mr. Yapp, terribly fearing what might result out of this assault, started the subject of the ring.

"You have lost a ring, Mrs. Walpole?"

"You *know* I have."

"I know only from reading the bill outside. You don't suppose I have got it, do you?"

"And why not, pray? You that come of a murderer—"

Mr. Yapp's lips quivered at these words, and his face turned white, and to Swift's horror he exclaimed—

"Tell me about my father, and you shall have your—"

"Ha! ha!" exclaimed Swift, stopping the clerk in his sentence. "Beware what yer after, Mr. Yapp."

"Shall I have my ring?" eagerly said Mrs. Walpole. "Shall I have my ring? Oh, do give it me! I'm sure you've got it now! Do give it me, and I'll forgive all but your father's murder!"

Yapp was silent, but his looks were too transparent for the woman not to see that he had the ring, or knew where it was.

"He ain't got yer ring," said Swift.

"Have you?" demanded the woman. "Don't hesitate—my heart and my life is bound up with its possession."

"Look ye heer now," said Swift, "What'll yer stand if I give up the person who has got it?"

"What do you mean by stand? If money, I'll give you anything! Pray restore it,"

"The bargain first. What'll give? Will yer stand a twenty-pound note for it?"

"With pleasure!"

"And will you give me a clue to my father?" asked Mr. Yapp. "Will you unravel the mystery of my being? See what feeling you show about a paltry ring——"

"Oh, no, no, not paltry! Did you but know the association with that ring, you would have compassion on me. Oh! those vows! those broken vows!"

"But what have they to do with my father?"

"All!—everything!"

"You are deepening the mystery! Do you speak truly? Do you know my father?"

"I speak truly, and I knew your father!"

"I think she's mad, 'pon my soul I do."

"Swift, good fellah! this is momentous to me! do not make light of it."

"Ah, but one thing at a time, if yer please, Mr. Yapp. Can yer pay the twenty pounds down on the nail?"

"I'll pay it down," was the reply.

"And my father?" said the clerk.

"You may never know him," was her slow, solemn answer.

"Ah, but I will! I will! if you know him!" passionately exclaimed the clerk. "I won't be juggled with any longer."

"And she is a juggling, Mr. Yapp, take my word for that 'ere," said Swift. "She knows no more about yer father than yer do yerself!"

Mr. Yapp just then thought with Swift. Yet there was something so real, yet so mysterious, about Lady Blaze, combined with her always following him from place to place—her interview with him by the cathedral—her possession of the jewellery that Swift described as enormous—were circumstances that Mr. Yapp could not treat as things "light as air." Yet when she charged his father as the murderer of her daughter—he could not but doubt that she was mad.

"Why did my father kill your daughter?" inquired Mr. Yapp.

She shook her head. This was her only answer.

"Was he tried for it? Was he hung?"

"Oh no; but I have made him suffer twenty deaths! I've made him suffer the pangs and torments he has heaped on me! He has thrown an impassable gulf between me and my child—I have thrown one between you and he!"

"But I won't bear it, Mrs. Walpole," exclaimed the clerk.

"You live—my child is dead—"

"How did my father kill her?"

"He broke her heart, poor soul!"

The woman shed a tear, and the brutal Swift laughed outright.

"Ugh! ugh! its all out now, Mr. Yapp. Nothing more than a little love affair! Ugh! ugh!"

"Nothing more," said Lady Blaze, but there was such a pathos in these words and the expression of them that touched the heart of the more refined and feeling clerk.

"She calls a broken-heart murder! What d'ye think of that, Mr. Yapp? I told yer she was mad. Ugh! ugh!"

Mrs. Walpole condescended no reply to Swift's coarse observations, but returned to the subject of the ring,

"In one hour you shall have the money—shall I have the ring?"

"I must get it first, yer know," said Swift, taking care not to commit himself. "I didn't say I had got it—please yer to understand that."

"Oh, you can get it, if you try," said Lady Blaze.

"That 'ere is another question," said Swift, while Mr. Yapp seemed in profound deliberation on the mysterious woman before him, and the news she had communicated to him. It gave him great surprise to think that at last he should be in the presence of one that knew his father, whom he had never seen—never heard of. What! news of his father? It seemed to change him quite; and, as if by magic, the best feelings of a son engrossed him.

"Do I bear my fathah's name?" asked Mr. Yapp.

"I will stand no further question, until I have the ring when I will confer with you about you father!"

"Pray give it to her," said Yapp.

"Two words to that," said Swift. "First of all, I haven't got it."

"Who has?" sharply retorted Lady Blaze.

"That's not your business," said Swift. "Get the money here in one hour—make it twenty-five, if yer like, for it will give me a deal of trouble to get it—and you shall have the ring."

"I thank you very much!" exclaimed Mrs. Walpole, and the thought of having the ring restored to her brought sunshine to her face.

"Ha! but you've got to make me promises as well as pay me," said Swift. "You must swear to ask no question. You must swear never to tell a soul who found the ring. You must swear to forget and forgive everything that has passed this morning. You must swear—well, I think that's enough—I don't think I've omitted nothing that can harm us, have I, Mr. Yapp?"

The clerk's thoughts had prevented him from paying any attention to what was going on. He was on the threshold of discovering his father and his whereabouts.

"Can't you speak Mr. Yapp?" cried Swift again. "Is there anything else that she ought to swear to afore we give up the ring?—I mean—of course—yes, I mean afore we get the person who has got it?"

"I cannot direct you, Swift. Is my father living? And my mother—who is she?"

"I will not be questioned now," said Mrs. Walpole.

GERTRUDE LAMBERT READS THE BIBLE TO HER FATHER AND TOM BROWN AS THEY LAY ON THEIR HOSPITAL BEDS.

"When? Considah what my feelings must be! Considah how I must burn to meet a fathah that I nevah saw! You must tell me more! Do, I beseech you!"

"All things, and all mysteries shall be cleared up together. My life is bound up with yours. The father that has made me wretched has made you also! Oh! do not detain me longer. One hour from now I will be here again," she said, drawing from a concealed part of her dress a watch that made Swift stare, because of its massive gold cases.

"One question, do answer me!" exclaimed Yapp. "Does my fathah know where I am?"

"Oh, no; your absence is his punishment," was the reply.

"Who keeps me from him?" imperatively demanded the clerk.

"I do. Now I will stop no longer."

The clerk was about to detain her—not rudely —but with more questions.

"Let her go, Mr. Yapp," said Swift. "Lord! we all live in the same house, as it were—you can

14

see her by-and-bye, and have out yer cobble-whobble when I'm behind my pipe. But here, I say, you haven't sworn to my conditions."

"I will do that when you give me the ring, and I give you your reward," said Lady Blaze, glad to make her exit.

"Wery well, mum; that'll suit me if it will suit you," said Swift, with great politeness; but before he had finished, the woman he addressed was half-way to the garret for her bonnet and shawl.

"We shall come well out of it, arter all, Mr. Yapp," said Swift, after she had left. "That is if she don't play us false. I shall git twenty-five pounds of her—that'll be twelve-pun-ten each."

"None of it for me," said the moody clerk, who now scarcely knew what position to assume in the criminal affairs in which he was so deeply involved.

"You are downhearted, Mr. Yapp," said Swift. "You don't like to lose the ring, eh?"

"I don't like to lose my fathah, Swift," retorted the clerk. "Mine is a most unhappy position."

"Aye—oh—yes—no doubt," said the ware-houseman. "But I think a little daylight is being thrown upon it. Lord! who knows yet who yer may turn out to be? If yer chance to be a haristocrat—and by the size of yer hand and yer style of dress, I shouldn't wonder—why then, I say, old feller, you'll make me yer Johnny, won't yer? I've a pertikler good calf—look'ee heer," he said, pulling up the leg of his trousers half over one of his dirty stockings.

"You pester me, Swift," said Mr. Yapp, not at all well pleased with his friend's banter. "Have a little regard for a fellah's feelings! One doesn't find a fathah every day in the week. I've been in search of mine for twenty-five years."

"And p'raps when you find him you don't find much," said the tantalising Swift. "Or he must be werry different from his son if he is."

"You are merry, Swift," said Mr. Yapp.

"Well, twelve-pun-ten—twenty-five-pun, if you are too proud to go halves—is not to be sneezed at this cold morning, when nothing hangs by it. There's no robbery in the matter now you know."

"Ah, yes—but it is no use to me, Swift. My game must now be to make myself a honest man—to blot out the past—turn over a new leaf—"

"Them 'ere account books must be turned over first," interrupted Swift. "And I'm just in the humour to do it in the way I planned last night."

"Well—no—thank you, Swift; but the circumstances of the morning have altered my determination. I shall go straight to Mr. Bonthron—confess all—"

"Then you will be straight transported—that's my opinion," again interrupted Swift, who stood at his ease against the sacks, with his hands in his pockets.

"Well—I think—I don't know though—yes, I'll chance it. Mr. Bonthron is not a bad sort if you hit him right. To rob him as I have done is bad enough. But to destroy his books would almost be the ruin of him."

"How so? Don't see that," said Swift.

"Why he would be at the mercy of every one. Who could say or prove what he owes or what's owing to him? Besides, it would cast a slur

upon his business, and give him no end of trouble. No, let the books remain—I'll take my chance with the guvnah."

"We-l-l," said Swift, stretching forth his arms and yawning. "You're a fool, that's all."

"Oh! a demned fool, I know that old fellah! But I'm not a fool for doing the best I can for those I have so mercilessly injured."

"Now, down with the shutters. We must begin business in earnest, after I've had a drop of gin and beer. Then these ere rags—that ought to have gone yesterday, by-the-bye—shall be carted off to Pickford's. I say, Mr. Yapp, how about the money out of the letter? How much have you got left out of your five-pun-note? And what are yer going to do?"

"Whatever is to be my fate?" mused the clerk, pacing the wareroom, while Swift unscrewed the shutters.

"Why, you'll be a transport—that's what'll be your fate," replied the porter, although the clerk was not addressing his thoughts to him.

Mr. Yapp started at these words from his gloomy reverie. He first scowled on the man who used them, and then he said—

"And that's to be my fate, is it, Swift? Then it will be well for me and fathah, too, if we never meet. If it be true what that woman says—"

"And which I don't think is," interrupted Swift.

"We have no grounds for doubt. True, she is a mystery; but she is not a liah! We have evidence of her wealth, and it is now certain that she has a hand in my fate. The miniature, Swift!"

"Oh! hi! ah! as like yer as anything could be! I'd forgotten that," said Swift.

"Your memory must be dull then. Why, only yesterday morning you would almost make me believe Mrs. Walpole was my mother!"

"And I'm not so sure that it won't turn out so now," Swift replied.

"But she evidently hates me," said the clerk.

"Lord! that's nothink, that ain't. P'raps you ought'nt to have been born."

"Why?"

"'Cause you might be a hillegitimate son of a West-end swell; and after yer birth yer father might have grown tired of yer mother, and left her. There's sich cases as them."

"But why does she divide us?"

"'Cause, p'raps, he might be werry fond on yer—and she does it to spite him."

"And she is certainly a revengeful woman," mused Mr. Yapp, for the moment led astray by Swift's plausible solution of his birth.

"Oh! she's a rewengeful hussy! Look how she served out my boy!" exclaimed Swift. "And see what a spitfire manner she came in about her ring!"

"That was excusable," said the clerk. "The ring appears to be of some peculiar importance to her, independent of its money value. What are the initials on the ring?"

"D—d if I know now!—I'll go and see," said Swift, going out to look at the placard. "C. H. S.," he said, after he returned.

"Where is the ring?"

"Buried," said Swift. Mr. Yapp, by his looks, expressed surprise.

"You don't suppose I was fool enough to carry it about me, after I read that ere bill?" said Swift.

"Where have you planted it?"

"Where it could never be found by anyone but mesilf, as Paddy says. Follow me, and I will show you; and you shall see me bring it from its hiding."

"Throw back the shutters first," said the clerk. "Let us, at all events, put on a seeming of business."

"We ain't been hidle. We've done business—"

"But it won't bear the light," said Yapp.

"Then don't take down the shutters," said Swift, in jest, and laughing at his facetiousness.

"Sport with it if you like, Swift. But it is my belief that there is something at work that will yet make us sorry for what we have done."

"Not me," said Swift. "I'd as soon be transported any day as live with my old woman. So I ain't much to fear."

"You're a hero, Swift! There's no fear in you," said the clerk, while the warehouseman failed to see his satire, but thought the clerk was complimenting him, which much tickled his vanity.

"Bedad! no, I never knew fear in my life! When a boy, I could skin a worm, torture a cat, knock down my brother, kick my sister, and throw a ruler at the head of my schoolmaster—"

"That shows the hero, Swift!" exclaimed the clerk.

"Lord! I've done more walorous deeds than them. Afore I was sixteen, I fought with a man, and beat him, stabbed one schoolfellow in his side, and cut off the finger of another—"

"Enough, enough, Swift! I have a poor, weak heart, and cannot bear the recital of such chivalric deeds. Down with the shutters, and get the ring. Mrs. Walpole will be here presently to redeem it."

Swift obeyed; and before he had let daylight into the shop, he beckoned the clerk to the cellar, where he had embedded the ring, and resuscitated it, and placed it in the hands of Mr. Yapp.

"There's no mistake about it, is there, Mr. Yapp?"

"It is, indeed, a beautiful gem!" exclaimed the clerk, examining it by the jet. "Yes! the initials correspond with the bill—there they are, Swift—d'ye see,—C. H. S., in Old English letters."

"Is that what you call Old English? Lord! I never seed it afore! It is d—d hugly, and werry unreadable. Our forefathers and foremothers must have been werry clever people to have read books printed in such characters as these."

Display, the ruling passion of the clerk's mind, did not even desert him now, troubled as he was. He placed the diamond on his finger, and longingly, lovingly gazed upon it.

"You never had sich a gem on yer finger afore, I should say," said Swift.

"Nevah! and in truth I am loth to part with it. Take it away, it shall tempt me no more."

"I have a thought, Mr. Yapp!" exclaimed Swift.

"What now, Swift?"

"I'd rob her yet, if I had time," said Swift.

"No more of it, there's a good fellah!" said Mr. Yapp.

"Lord! we've had none yet," retorted Swift.

"If I had time, I'd take this ring to a lapidary, get him to take out the diamond, and put in paste! Ain't it a fine hidear?"

"I'll have nothing more to do with your fine ideas!" said the clerk.

"You like yer own better, do yer?" said Swift.

"I do, Swift," was the reply.

"I never heerd yet that you had a hidear! What is it?"

"Honesty, Swift," quietly but emphatically said Mr. Yapp.

"'I'm a young man from the country, and yer don't come over me,'" half said, half sung Swift. "Yer have no honesty from conwiction; 'tis all through fear that makes yer honest. Yer would rob, steal, and murder, if you was sure it wouldn't be found out."

This hit of Swift's was unanswerable. The clerk felt the truth of it, and stammeringly said—

"Nevah mind—aw—Swift—aw—I mean to be honest—the motive is—aw—nothing."

While they were thus engaged dissecting each other's principles, a gentlemanly man, of middle age, came in, and said that he had seen Mr. Bonthron last evening, and he begged him to call and request Mr. Yapp not to fail to send his account-books.

The clerk was dumb, and could not conceal the alarm this request caused him. It changed the current of his views entirely. Swift was right; the clerk felt himself a thief by nature, and a coward by nature.

The warehouseman saw the clerk's commotion, and readily said to the gentleman—

"I'm jist agoing to pack the books up, Sir. Might I hask how our good master is, Sir?"

"Very unwell, indeed," was the answer.

"Werry sorry to hear it," said Swift. "Our Mister Yapp ain't at all well, either."

"I have been—aw—in great pain—aw—all the morning," said Yapp, following up the clever cue Swift had given him.

"The weather is very unfavourable to health," said the gentleman. "There are a great many people ill, indeed. The Registrar-general's return shows an enormous increase in the tables of mortality. But my friend Bonthron is very much changed. His son has been a great trouble and care to him."

"Werry great indeed, Sir," said Swift.

"Ah! I fear his to be a hopeless case," said the clerk, following the line of conversation his master, Swift, had cut out for him.

"I fear so, too," replied the gentleman. "Good morning! Don't forget the books. They may amuse Mr. Bonthron's mind, if nothing else."

"He won't find much amoosement in 'em, I guess, will he, Mr. Yapp?" said Swift, directly the gentleman had taken his departure.

"He must never have the books, Swift!" exclaimed the clerk.

"Holloa! Your hidears never seem to work—they're not fast colours. Better stick to mine."

"I will, Swift, I will! I could not go to Bonthron, and confess myself a thief. Let's play the game out. You're a clevah fellah, Swift! Pack them up, Swift—and—aw—"

The clerk paused, hoping that the wicked Swift would help him with words. But the warehouseman was determined that the clerk should give expression to his meaning, and said most tantalisingly—

"I wait my master's orders!"

"You know what we have been talking about," said Yapp.

"I hardly can," said Swift; "we've talked about sich a many things to-day. The last thing was that them ere books should remain for Mr. Bonthron's hinspection, and that yer would go straight to him, and say that yer had been a-robbin' him."

"'Tis true, Swift; but you need not show me

up quite so cruelly; I'm changeable enough, God knows: and God knows what I suffah! But you need not increase my pain of mind by your taunts. You remembah too much and too little. The books are demanded, and I have not the courage to carry out my previous determination, but am prepared to carry out yours. Take the books—and—"

"Well?"

"You know, don't you?"

"'Pon my soul I don't!"

"The Thames—"

"Oh!—hi—yes—"

"Take them, and sink them."

"That's straight-forrard orders enough," said Swift. "And I'm too hobedient to neglect the orders of my superiors."

The books were well packed by Messrs. Swift and Yapp, and a goodly parcel they made. The ledger and cash-book were a load in themselves.

"Once in, they'll soon find their way to the bottom," said Swift, quoting King Richard's remarks when he directed that the bodies of the young princes should be thrown into the Thames.

The parcel packed, Swift jumped up on the counter beside it, and said—

"Here I stop, until Lady Blaze comes up to the scratch with money for this 'ere ring!"

"What if she returns with a policeman?" suggested Mr. Yapp.

"She's under oath," said Swift. "Besides there's that about the woman, arter all said and done, that would make me take her word. No, no, she'll be here at her time with the money. I wonder where she will get it from?"

"Can't tell," said Yapp. "'Tis a great puzzle altogether."

"It's my opinion she's werry rich."

"And it is mine too," said Yapp.

"And it's my opinion that we ought to make something out of her."

"I must get information of my fathah out of her," said the clerk.

"I should have thought you had had quite information enough about him," rejoined Swift.

"Why, pray?"

"Didn't she say he was a murderer? Didn't she say that he had murdered her daughter?"

"Broke her heart, she said. All that is what I must and will learn about," said the clerk, with a spirit of determination.

"Well, her time is up," said Swift, looking at the shop clock.

"And here she comes," said Yapp, moving back as if half afraid to meet her.

But the cool Swift did not budge an inch, but kept his seat on the counter, playing a rat-tat-too with his heels on its side.

After Lady Blaze had made her bargain with the robber, Swift, for the restoration of her valued ring, she made haste to her garret, went to her trunk, and from a corner that Swift had not penetrated, she took a cheque book on the Bank of England, and while the blood-red sun looked down from the misty wintry sky, she filled up a cheque in her own favour for fifty pounds, which she signed, "Miranda Rachel Walpole."

She wrote quickly, in a bold, black, masculine hand, with a broad black line drawn under her signature, while the whole manner of her performance with the cheque plainly indicated that it was not the first time she had drawn one.

She presented it herself at the Bank, and it was speedily exchanged for ten new crisp five-pound notes, and with those in her hand, she once again stood in the wareroom.

"Now, Sir, I am prepared with the money—where is the ring?" she eagerly asked.

"Well, mum, there is the ring," said Swift, holding it out that the lady might see it, "where is the money?"

She gave him four of the ten five pound notes. The notes rustled in Swift's coarse hands as he counted them over.

"One more, please mum," he said, looking impudently in the face of Lady Blaze. "I must have another."

"There!" she exclaimed, giving him one more. "Now give me the ring!"

"Can't you make it another?" said Swift, coaxingly. "I'm a poor man, with a large family, and I've had a deal of trouble to find it for yer."

"Don't be greedy, Swift, you've been well rewarded," said Mr. Yapp, who could not bear to see the lady further robbed.

"You just shut up, will yer? If the lady likes to be generous, what's that to you?" said Swift.

"If you will tell me where you got it, and who had it—"

"Yer oath!" cried Swift. "You promised not to ask no questions."

"Nor will I. Give me the ring and let me go!"

"There!" said Swift, "take it. Sich finery is no good to me. With these 'ere," holding out the notes, "a feller can get a little bread for his family."

Mrs. Walpole was about to leave, when Mr. Yapp, who had been biding his opportunity, said—

"Might I speak with you alone for a few minutes?"

"You!" she exclaimed. "If you knew me and my purpose you would avoid me."

"My fathah! Tell me where to find him!" he cried, and followed her.

"Never!" she replied.

"Demn it! I will know," he exclaimed, following her to the foot of the stairs.

"Beware, William Seymour—"

"Ha! my name Seymour?" exclaimed the clerk. "The initial on the ring. Was that ring my fathah's?"

Lady Blaze had accidentally revealed too much.

"I'm but a woman!" she cried, "but if you move one step nearer me I'll not answer for your life!"

The clerk was motionless, while she wended her way to her garret, and slammed and locked the door. The clerk gazed on her till her figure was lost in a winding of the wide, rotten, old staircase; and when he looked round, the rascal Swift was grinning on him, and said—

"Yer servant, Mister Seymour! Well, I never did like the name of Yapp, it always put me in mind of pap, and pap put's one in mind of babies. Seymour is a better style of thing altogether, and becomes yer better, and has a haristocratic sound."

"I'm almost mad, Swift!" cried the clerk, in tones that indicated a very perplexed state of mind. "Who can this woman be?"

"Yer mother—that's my opinion," said Swift, bluntly.

"That's nonsense! And if I thought so, I swear I'd crush you to my feet for your treatment of her! But she's no more my mother than she's yours. She has unintentionally let out my name, though—"

"And a good name, too," interrupted Swift.

"'Tis all mystery as yet! Demn it! I'm tired of mystery."

"Git these ere books off yer mind, and then you'll be happier," said Swift. "These 'ere notes—will yer have one or two on 'em? they're good things to troubled minds. They'll comfort yer."

"What if they should be my mother's?"

"In that 'ere case, what's your mother's is yourn," said Swift.

"There's a limit to that way of reasoning," said the clerk. "At present I will have none of them. But mind, the fifteen pounds must be restored."

"What fifteen pounds?" inquired Swift, who very well knew, without further explanation.

"The fifteen pounds taken from the lettah, the robbery of which was to be fixed on Tom Brown, the Errand Boy."

"Oh—ha—I remember. By-the-bye, have yer heerd, Mr. Yapp, that that 'ere boy narrowly escaped with his life from fire last night?"

"No—is it true?"

"Oh, it's werry true! And mind ye, that 'ere boy will yet come to some hawful end. There's a good deal of howdaciousness about him."

"I nevah discovered it, Swift. My opinion of the boy is far more favourable than yours. He certainly was badly treated here by you and mad Bonthron," said Yapp.

"I don't see it. He was imperent, and took my boy's place. And all he got he desarved."

"We'll discuss that point no further. My mind is troubled about other things. Shall the books be destroyed? that is the question."

"As Hamlet says; and I must say you are quite as long a making up yer mind as he was. You'll hesitate too long, it's my belief. I shall cool upon the job soon, and not have nerve to do it. Now then, Mr. Yapp—To be, or not to be?"

"Those books destroyed, Swift, I should be free of every evidence that could criminate me!" mused the clerk.

"In course yer would."

"Away with them, Swift! I'll send a note by you to Mr. Bonthron; it will give a resemblance of its reality. Make a good job of it. Watch well your opportunity that no boats are about to pick up the parcel."

"I'm not a fool!" cried Swift, lifting the parcel to his left shoulder. "What about our bit of boating arter the job is done?"

"You'll soon be back, Swift."

"Yes; it won't take me long to tread on a bit of horange-peel, and slip the parcel into the river. 'Tis cold, though, for a boat, ain't it? I ain't got no fur coat; but I shall line my hinner man with a drop or two of gin arter this 'ere job is got over."

"Aw—I like rowing in cold weather," said Mr. Yapp. "You soon get warm, and the rivah is freer of other craft. Aw—we shall be jolly enough, Swift, take my word for that."

"Why, yes, a man must be a hass if he can't be jolly with these 'fivers' about him."

"But you must pay back the money from the lettah," said Yapp.

"Stuff o' nonsense! I shan't do no sich a thing! Besides, I only had one of them ere notes, and you and the boy had the other two. Besides, agin, you can say they were hentered in the books."

"That will not avail us, Swift; the entry may be made but the money must be produced or accounted for. It will spoil all if we fail to get that money."

"Well, yer had one, the detective has got another, and there is the third," he said, in the most unpleasant manner, taking one of the notes he had received from Lady Blaze, and dashing it on the counter.

"The one I had is spent, or all but a few shillings, so I must ask you for another," said Yapp. "And as you offered me half of Lady Blaze's payment—"

"And which you declined."

"True, true; nor would I have a penny of it did not necessity force me."

"But yer a-forgetting that you are disappointing me. I shall understand you by the rules of contrary in future. I daresay you'll put it all in yer own pocket—ugh, ugh! I know yer, Mr. Yapp."

With this grumbling speech the porter departed with his load; and as Mr. Yapp looked after him, tottering beneath it as he glided out of Bolt Court to the Bridge, he said—

"When those books are buried in the Thames, it is my purpose to make *your* grave there also. You know too much to live! You dead, methinks then I shall have nothing to fear but my own conscience. But conscience and I have been so long at variance, that it cannot trouble me more than it has already done. He is a bad man is Swift, and society will be bettah for his riddance; and *I* shall be safe from his treachery. I have a fathah now, and the crimes of his son must be smothered at every hazard to him. I could not—would not—live to be the slave of Swift! His coarse effrontery would wound me every minute of my life. I cannot beah to think of such a life! Rather a thousand times would I embrace death, or live with the devil! He is clevah in emergencies—so am I! He will not find me when I have him on the Thames the milksop he puts me down for. He shall die! and then I may be able to hold up my head again, and meet my fathah without a pang of feah!"

He returned to the office, and went to his desk; answered the morning's letters; but his mind was in too perturbed a state to sit still, so he would write a line or two—then pace the shop—then resume his writing.

The task was a serious one that the clerk had confided to the trustworthiness of Swift; and, oh! how he longed for his return, and hear him report the deed as done! Then again would he repent him, and twice had placed his hat upon his head to follow Swift and stop him.

While he was in this unenviable state of vacillation, Swift returned, and when asked if it was all right, he exclaimed—

"As right as a trivet!"

CHAPTER XXXIV

TOM BROWN IN HOSPITAL.—MAKES THE ACQUAINTANCE, AND EXCITES THE COMPASSION OF MR. LAMBERT, A RICH LAPIDARY OF CLERKENWELL, AND HIS DAUGHTER, GERTRUDE.

AFTER Tom Brown's memorable escape from the fire in Vine Court, he was taken, in an insensible state, to the hospital, and was there found to have received an injury to his spine in his leap from the second-floor window to the waggon which was placed beneath to break his fall.

In that fire his mother perished, and the poor boy in her lost all that was dearest to him. The dead body of his unhappy father was also consumed, as well as the money which the "horsey" gentleman had honourably paid to Tom's mother in discharge of a debt that he had owed his father.

Father dead—mother dead—Tom now was alone in the world; and the nightshirt in which he lay on that hospital-bed was all the property he could call his own. So wretched and so deplorable at this moment was the youth's hapless state, that it would have been a mercy had he never wakened to a consciousness of it.

But the inscrutable Providence that had saved him from the raging fire, and that had seen fit to remove his father and mother from him, well supported him in his hour of bitter need.

After lying in hospital a day in a state of unconscious delirium, the tender treatment of the nurse, the medicines of the skilful physician, and the supreme quiet of the ward he was in, brought him to his senses, and, unhappily, to a knowledge of his great loss and pitiable position.

The large, clean, airy ward in which Tom was confined was well filled with beds containing the sick and the dying. Doctors and nurses were stealing about from bed to bed, doing their utmost to assuage sufferings that were too often beyond their skill.

There was a quiet in that blessed place, so grateful to the sick and wounded that filled the beds about the ward, and so imposing to the patients' visitors who walked in and out, some with faces of woe and despair, and others with hope. Physicians and surgeons nimbly moved from bed to bed, and the young students followed them with their cases of horrid instruments and splints in their hands, while the nurses were also active in attendance to receive their instructions—what was to be done with this patient, and what with the other?

There were many cases in the ward where Tom laid, melancholy and touching to behold. The quiet of the place was only disturbed by the groans of the suffering and the sighs and sobs of mourning women and children around the bedsides of the poor patients.

"It must come off, my dear!" cried a physician in decided tones to Gertrude Lambert, a fine young girl of about sixteen, and the daughter of a middle-aged, Jewish-looking man, who lay passively with his broken arm in a white sling outside the bed-clothes.

Gertrude was well dressed in mourning for her mother, whom, not many months ago, she closed her eyes and consigned her to the grave. Now her father absorbed her attention and sympathy. He had fallen from the top of an omnibus and broken his arm. He was a very respectable man—a lapidary in Clerkenwell—and reputed to be rich.

Gertrude was his only daughter—his only child, and a dear, affectionate creature she was; and the sweet graces of religion had been early implanted in her mind by her revered mother. Gertrude was not a gloomy religionist, nor a narrow-minded one; although she worshipped at the altars of her national church, and followed out all her forms and doctrines, she fully believed that all who worshipped God in spirit and in truth would find favour in His eyes, regardless of the sect they claimed to belong to, or the roof they assembled under for worship. Her creed was of that enlightened nature, that she felt herself as much in communion with the Creator while wandering abroad amongst His fields and groves—His hills and valleys—or ministering to the comforts of His creatures—as bending the knee to Him under the church's roof.

Religion with Gertrude Lambert was by no means a dead letter, as it too often is with the mere professor of it; it showed itself in all her daily actions, as well as in her dress, manners, speech, and deportment. She blessed the dying bed of her mother, and comforted her widowed father. Besides a sound religious education by an enlightened mother, her father had the means, and liberally used them, in her scholastic education. She was all-accomplished in everything but dancing;—to dancing, both Mr. and Mrs. Lambert, who were usually of one mind, decidedly objected, not in itself, but that it was too often made the precursor of evil; as a cheerful, healthy bodily exercise they valued it, but it too much entrapped the young into a love of dress, late hours, and a society too entirely worldly. Therefore it was an accomplishment forbidden to Gertrude. Ah! but to hear Miss Gertrude play on the harp or piano, if the listener had a soul for music, he could imagine no other than that he was in the region of heaven. She could read and appreciate Shakespeare, Scott, and Milton; and her religious feeling rather attracted her to those divine authors rather than repelled her. She could play chess, draw, paint; and there existed about the little house they lived in at Clerkenwell, many beautiful evidences of her skill in needlework.

Her industry knew no bounds; it was Gertrude here, Gertrude there; now she was by her father's side in his little shop, arranging and polishing some of the precious stones; now in the kitchen or in the bedrooms helping her mother in domestic duties. But never mind what duties she was engaged in, she was always beautifully clean; not only were her hands and face made bright and pure with ablutions, but her teeth and nails—(so often denied a fair share of attention by too many young English ladies)—were remarkable for the care bestowed on them. Her light brown hair—woman's chief ornament—was dressed as plainly as it well could be, parted in the middle and well brushed off from her temples, and firmly bound in a plait behind, while the gloss upon it had been produced by a free exercise of the brush, and not plastered over with pomade, as some of our idle belles avail themselves of to save their labour.

When we first met with her in the accident ward of the hospital in which Tom Brown and her dear father were helpless inmates, she was a fine grown, lady-like girl of rather more than fifteen, dressed in black crape dress and black crape bonnet, with jet bracelets on her wrists and a long string of black beads round her neck. Her face was fair—very fair—and she had a deep blue eye, well set beside a well-formed nose; but, above all else, the holy expression of her face was never overlooked—it seemed to indicate that her mind was engaged in devotional music, there was such bright ethereal happiness pervading it, as well as the sublimity of a psalm. Just now it was slightly tinged with melancholy—she was new to a mother's loss, and her father was suffering in a hospital.

When Mrs. Lambert lived, a Sabbath evening at her house was something to remember and devoutly to admire. In a snug room, all the furniture of old Spanish mahogany, with as many members of the church as the room would conveniently hold, when Gertrude would take her harp and entrance her audience with the most divine singing and music; and then at parting would she pray, and her praying was something sublime in its simplicity and sincerity.

When the hospital surgeon said that her father's arm must be taken off, or he would not answer for his life, she almost swooned in the arms of the nurse who stood by; but she valorously checked herself to sustain her dearest father under the doctor's fiat.

"Do you hear, my father?—do you hear what must be done?"

"I do, Gertrude," said Mr. Lambert, with a smile and a tear.

"And will you be strong, and bear the operation?" she asked him, with a loving kiss.

"But for you, my child, I would rather have died and followed your mother to the abodes of the blest, than have submitted to it. But for *your* sake I will submit to anything to live! For what would my precious Gertrude do without father or mother?"

"Dear father, I pray God to give you strength for this necessity," exclaimed Gertrude.

"No one else can," said Mr. Lambert, calmly. "I hope, too, that He will comfort you during my hour of trial, and before He restores your father to you. And if, Gertrude, it is His pleasure to take me from you—"

"Oh, no, father—no! I feel assured you will be saved through it," said Gertrude, falteringly.

"I was only going to observe, my child, that if it be His will to take me, that I have set my house in order. You will be a wealthy orphan, Gertrude."

"No, father, without *you* I shall be poor indeed!"

"You love God, Gertrude, and have learnt to bend to His will in all things, and to trust in Him. Oh! Gertrude, you cannot measure the happiness that that knowledge gives me! Look on the sufferers around!—look on that poor boy by my side—lost his father and mother in a fire, Gertrude, and now lies there without a friend in the world. See, Gertrude, there are worse troubles to bear than ours."

"I know it, father, and it shall be our care, when you have passed through the danger, to spend our wealth and lives in doing the best we can to ameliorate and lighten the woes of others. What a beautiful face that boy has," she abruptly added, as her eyes fell upon Tom, lying there in a quiet state of unconsciousness.

"I have dwelt upon it ever since the poor lad was laid in the bed. There is a sorrowful tale connected with him, which for the time, Gertrude, made me forget my own."

Mr. Lambert's outspoken interest in Tom Brown could not fail to create one in Gertrude, but just as she was about to speak the head surgeon, attended by two students came to her father's bedside. The instrument in the hands of the young men appalled Miss Lambert's heart. Her more heroic father saw the change in her face, and encouragingly said—

"Do not fear, my darling. I shall get through it."

"Aye, to be sure you will," said the surgeon, and he beckoned the nurse, and requested her to withdraw Gertrude.

"Oh, no; let me remain to support my father," begged Gertrude. "He will bear it better if I am with him."

The father set his eyes on the surgeon with a quivering lip, as if asking that his daughter might be permitted to remain, but the answer was imperatively No.

"She cannot aid us," said the surgeon, "and it can possibly do her no good to be present. Be satisfied, my dear young lady, that your father shall have my best care, and that you need apprehend nothing but that he will soon be restored to you in health. His constitution is excellent, and during the performance of my neccessary duty he will not know so much about it as I do. Nurse, the boy Brown moans, repeat his draught, and slightly raise his pillow."

Miss Lambert flew to her father and affectionately kissed him, and he felt her tears fall on his open brow.

"Dear Gertrude—if—if I should not recover the chloroform——"

"We will not think of it, dear father," faltered Gertrude.

"But *if* it should be so, my child," said Mr. Lambert, rather petulantly, "do not, I entreat you, give any ear to Walter Graham."

"I promise you, father—I have promised you before. Why allow your mind to be occupied with such remote things at a time like this?"

"Because Walter's father, on the morning of my accident sounded me upon my views of betrothing you to his son. I was shocked at the proposition of making a matrimonial engagement between children, as it were, and I told him so."

"You did well, dear father," said Gertrude.

"But I fear, should anything occur to me—for all results are in the hands of God—I am apprehensive that Walter's father would renew his wishes with you, and over-persuade you. The Grahams are a worldly family, and above all things I would have you marry into one where the name of Christ is heard and adored. The Grahams are needy, and seek an alliance with you for your fortune, which is considerable. But it is not for their need that I advise you against them, but for their worldliness."

The stout nurse took Gertrude by her arm, and gently led her into an ante-room of the ward, and she had no sooner entered it, then she fell on her knees by a chair, and devoutly and audibly prayed that strength and recovery be vouchsafed her father.

After this outburst of filial devotion, which smote the heart of the nurse who stood by—she who was so well used to the mourner's tears and agonised suffering—Gertrude arose, and the prayer that she had poured forth to heaven for her father, had much composed her own tender, lacerated feelings.

"Taking off an arm ain't much, my dear," said the nurse, kindly trying to encourage the young lady. "You would never do for a hospital nurse, I can see that," she added, with a cheery smile.

"Tell me, nurse, your opinion of my father—"

"Why that he is a man quite strong enough to undergo a little operation," said the nurse, treating the subject that gave Gertrude so much uneasiness and concern as something of the most insignificant character. And really the woman's mind and eye was so familiarised with the most serious and complicated surgical operations, that what would have chilled the blood of another she could look upon and talk about in the most ordinary manner.

After she had laconically replied to Gertrude, she regaled her dumpty nose with a pinch of snuff, and although she was free from the coarseness of many of the sisterhood, nurse's face betokened that she was in the habit of taking a little "speret," it was a large fat face sprinkled here and there, with "gin blossoms."

"Och! he's dead, mum!" exclaimed a poor Irish woman, wildly rushing from the ward where the surgeon and students were engaged with Mr. Lambert's arm, to the ante-room where were the nurse and Gertrude.

"Who dead! My father?" screamed Miss Lambert. Oh! what a thrill for her; and how could she have thought other than that the Irishwoman brought tidings of Mr. Lambert?

"Your father—no, my dear," said the smiling nurse. "This woman's husband—that's all. No one thought he would live, Mrs. O'Carroll, I was up the whole of the night with him, and both me and the doctor saw plain enough he couldn't recover."

"Oh my poor Mike—you've broke your widdy's heart at last, have ye? Och! and why would ye go up that ladder, when ye knew you were so dhrunk that you couldn't stand on the pavement! Och hone! och hone! I'll never forgive ye!"

The grief exhibited by the Irishwoman made Gertrude forget her own, and by a few kindly words she tried to assuage it. But the grief was too new to be ministered to, and all that Gertrude could say or do was but little heeded by the voluble woman. With a large red handkerchief that did duty for a shawl round her shoulders, and a bit of a cap bound with a broad brown riband across her head and tied under her elongated jaw and chin, with a heavy pair of nailed boots laced with leather on her feet, she sat on the bench, howling, and moaning, and talking, and shaking her body to and fro.

It appeared from the nurse's statement to Gertrude, that "Mike" was brought in on a shutter having, as Mrs. O'Carroll intimated in her first grief, been foolhardy enough to have ascended a ladder while intoxicated, and fallen from the top of a house, fracturing his skull and thrusting his ribs in upon his lungs.

The poor woman's grief exhibited itself in the oddest possible manner; it only found vent in reviling her dead husband. Yet there was the deepest pathos in it, and the truest love.

"Och hone, Mike! och hone! the divil take ye, why were ye such a fool! Ye're gone and left me all alone, alone! and me and the blessed childre' will nivir forgive ye. Och, ye cruel man! to think of the dhrink and forgit us that will nivir forgit you!"

"What sin and suffering intemperance brings into the world, nurse!" exclaimed Gertrude Lambert.

"Ye nivir deserve a prayer for yer sowl, Mike! Och hone! ye knew how we loved ye, and to go and serve us like this! To take away yer blissid life and to leave us all alone, alone! with nothing but the union before us for our bit of bread. I'll nivir be mesilf again! nivir indade!"

"Look here, Mrs. O'Carroll, better that the poor man should have died, than live and be a burden to himself and others," said Gertrude.

"Och hone! Mike would nivir have been a burden to me and his darlings. Wouldn't I have worked the skin off my bones to have supported him? But his swate face I shall never see again! Och! why did ye die, Mike?"

"Nothing could have saved him, Mrs. O'Carroll," said the nurse. "You know everything was done here for him. And really the poor man did suffer so much that if you loved him—"

"And didn't I love him? Och! Mike, didn't I love ye? Was there anything in the wide, wide world that I thought to good for ye? Mightn't ye have eaten gold could I have bought it for ye? And oh! to serve me thus!"

"We are all the subjects of sorrow in this world, Mrs. Carroll," said Gertrude; "and the more we resign ourselves to the will of God the happier we shall be."

"Och! Miss, but it was not the will of God, nor the Blissed Virgin, that my Mike should perish."

"Yes, Mrs. Carroll, God rules all things. He is the Great Governor of the universe, and all creatures here below are in His keeping."

"I belave it, Miss, I belave it; but maybe ye don't know what it is to lose a husband!"

"I have recently lost a dear mother, and only prayer and submission to the Divine will sustained me through the terrible deprivation. You must pray, too, Mrs. Carroll, and pray for your husband."

"Indade I will not, Miss; I will pray for mesilf and childre, but not for poor Mike—he doesn't deserve it at all—at all. He couldn't be contint with gitting a dhrop more dhrink than he could carry, but he must have been foolhardy enough to ascind to the top of a ladder, and make orphans of his swate childre' and a widdy of his poor heart-broke wife, Och, hone!"

The consolation Miss Gertrude ministered to the new-made widow was also consolation to herself, for it subdued for the moment her own intensity of grief for her father.

"How will I tell my childre' that they have no father? How will I brake the news to little Kate?"

Gertrude was much touched by this lamentation of the poor woman, and offered her best services.

"If I hear good news of my father," said Miss Lambert, "I will walk home with you, and comfort your little ones, and—"

Here another portly nurse entered—the one who generally waited on the surgeon with sponge, hot water, splints and lint, during his operations—and asked for Miss Lambert.

Gertrude stepped forward, and oh! how pleased she was to see a smile upon the woman's face, for it at once impressed her that her father was safe.

"Well, we've got it over, Miss," said the second nurse. "Your father bore it very well; indeed, he felt nothing of it, for since you left the surgeon has determined not to take the arm off."

Gertrude embraced the messenger of such good news. A serious weight was lifted from her mind. Her heart leaped up with joy, and pleasure shone in her face.

"And will my father recover without the loss of his arm?" she cried, in tones of pleasurable surprise.

"There can be no doubt of it, Miss Lambert," said the nurse. "The last examination of the arm altogether altered the surgeon's previous opinion. The favourable change that he then discovered had taken place in the limb decided him that he would not remove it."

"Oh! let me go and congratulate my dear father!" exclaimed Gertrude.

"Not now; he is in a quiet sleep, and I hope he will continue to sleep throughout the night."

Whether it was the nurse's words, or her

THE BURGLAR SEIZED TOM BROWN BY THE THROAT.

manner in speaking them, that created a little suspicion in Gertrude's mind, we cannot say; but there was a shock conveyed to her senses, and she had the temerity to appeal to the nurse not to deceive her.

"In what, my dear?" was the interrogation from the surprised matron.

"Indeed, nurse, the news of my father seems too good to be true; and when you said that he was in a quiet sleep, I began to fear—"

"Fear what?" said the nurse, as Gertrude paused.

15

"That he was dead, nurse; and that your womanly tenderness prevented your saying so; and that you told me he slept as an excuse for me not to go to him."

"Oh, dear, no," said the nurse. "We conceal nothing here, either to friend or patient. We have no roundabout method here, Miss. We go straightforward, whether it be to take off a limb or communicate a death. The business of this place is generally too urgent for us to delay it, either for condolence or congratulation. When I told you that your father was as well as a man with a broken arm could be, and that he was in a quiet sleep, I told you the truth, Miss."

"And how shall I reward you?" exclaimed Gertrude Lambert. "When I come to-morrow I shall bring you both a token of my regard for your great kindness to my father."

"Oh, don't name it," said one nurse.

"Pray don't mention such a thing," said the other. "As you walk through the ward you will see that your father sleeps. But do not speak, nor touch him, nor kiss him. It is so important that he should not be disturbed."

Gertrude implicitly obeyed, and as she passed her father's bed, she paused a moment, and then retired to her home in Clerkenwell, grateful to God who had so mercifully saved her father.

The morrow came, and Gertrude was early at the hospital, in affectionate attendance upon her father. He was so much better. She sat and read the Bible to him; and, Tom's bed being next, the boy too could hear her beautiful voice, for he had recovered his senses, and discovered that he was an orphan; and the words that Gertrude read—" I will be a Father to the fatherless"—fell with great comfort upon the boy's almost broken heart.

After this, Gertrude came day after day and read at her father's bedside, and talked to little Tom, and so did her father; who, hearing of his forlorn condition, promised that when they both got released from hospital, he would take him by the hand, and take care of him.

About a fortnight from this period, Tom Brown had at last found a happy home at Mr. Lambert's, lapidary and diamond merchant, Clerkenwell, who was a good man and a rich one.

How wonderfully one thing springs out of another! From that which we deem evil comes good!

From this accidental introduction to Mr. Lambert may be dated the most important epoch in Tom Brown's eventful life.

CHAPTER XXXV.

TOM BROWN'S NEW HOME.—THE BURGLAR DE-TECTED.—GEORGE MUMFORD AND THE STREET BOYS.—MRS. YAPP OFFERS HER JEWELLERY FOR SALE.

THE void that had been made in the happiness of Tom Brown's existence by the loss of his father and mother had been filled, as well as such a loss could be, by the friendship of Mr. and Miss Lambert. They had received the poor orphan boy into their delightful, intellectual home in Rosoman Street, Clerkenwell, and the lapidary very soon made him useful in his interesting and lucrative business.

While his industry was carried on by day in the little shop weighing, polishing, assaying, buying and selling, gold and silver articles of antiquity, and diamonds and rubies, and other precious stones, connected with Mr. Lambert's business, his evenings were permitted him to be passed in the substantially-furnished drawing-room in friendly intercourse with his master and his master's daughter.

These evenings were spent in the most re-fined manner—reading, devotional music, con-versation on the topics of the day, and an occa-sional chess encounter between Tom and Ger-trude—a game the young lady had taught the

lad, who had now almost become her master at it.

Tom had a large aptitude at learning anything that either his duty or his pleasure was engaged in; therefore it was no wonder that he became a proficient at chess, for, after his business duties of the day were over, no pastime afforded him greater delight, and he would play and work out problems with his young mistress (although she never assumed that position, and Tom was never made to feel his dependence) for hours together, while Mr. Lambert would sit over his cigar and wine and newspaper, or engage himself with his accounts.

Mr. Lambert was a Jewish-looking man, and we have little doubt but that Jewish blood was in his veins, for there was a great deal of the Israelitish character in his habits and manners. While he was honest and even liberal in his dealings with all men, he was stern and frigid in his intercourse with them. He had high tastes, but there was nothing cheerful about him, and certainly he never condescended to frivolity. He was unbending and unyielding in what he conceived to be right, and the Conservatives had no better friend amongst the people, and the Church no truer disciple, than Mr. Lambert.

Although his trade was large and lucrative, Mr. Lambert's expenditure was on a very limited scale; hence the wealth he had heaped up had become something considerable. Judging the lapidary by his unused riches, he might be deemed miserly. But this term is comparative, for while Mr. Lambert neither indulged nor allowed profusion in his domestic or personal arrangements, there was always a plentiful supply of necessaries, and Gertrude was denied neither clothes or money.

The heal-all Time had materially subdued Tom's grief for the dreadful loss of his dear father and mother, as it had Gertrude's for her parent; yet occasionally, in the brightness of the day and the stillness of the night, by tears and melancholy he would audibly express his feelings in deep devotion to their memory. Once or twice Gertrude found him alone and weeping in the back parlour.

Her sudden entrance confused him, for the boy was generous enough not to intrude more than he was occasionally invited to do his grief upon his benefactors. She knew why he wept, and with the greatest delicacy, as if by accident, in the evening she read—beautifully read—an appropriate poem, which contained the sub-joined stanza :—

" Weep not for her ! She is an angel now,
    And tends the sapphire floors of Paradise !
All darkness wiped from her refulgent brow.
    Sin, suffering, sorrow, banished from her eyes,
Victorious over death, to her appear
The vista'd joys of Heaven's eternal year.
        Weep not for her !"

Tom was never so happy in his life as now, and oh ! how he wished his father and mother were living that they might see the nice place he had got. Mr. Lambert had fathomed his whole history, and one or two of the lapidary's friends well knew the boy's father when he was in business at Islington.

Mr. Lambert took peculiar compassion on the orphan boy, and made his care of him a kind of thank-offering to Heaven for his safe deliver-ance from the hospital without the loss of an arm. With this feeling strong in his religious mind, he began to look upon Tom almost as his son, certainly as his care, and there was nothing in their intercourse that approached the relations of master and servant.

But quite irrespective of all the surrounding circumstances under which they met, Mr. Lambert and his daughter liked the boy for his own sake. He was a respectable, amiable, well-behaved, intelligent boy; and, dressed in a handsome suit of mourning that Mr. Lambert bought him before he could leave the hospital, he was considered by all a very pretty boy.

Gertrude grew very fond of him, and they both found an exquisite pleasure in each other's society. With Mr. Lambert's entire approval, they would sometimes take their evening walks abroad together, and Tom was always in the family pew at Clerkenwell Church; and on several occasions he accompanied Gertrude and her father to deck her mother's grave in Brompton Cemetery with flowers and *immortelles*.

At these times Tom Brown deeply regretted that, although his mother and father were dead, he had not even the privilege of visiting their graves—they had no graves! The cruel fire had done its work so mercilessly that it had not left a vestige of their dear remains.

While at the grave of Gertrude's mother the young folks would pour out to each other encouraging words of sympathy at their loss, while the father would "improve" the occasion by talking to them of the seriousness of death to those unprepared for eternity, always closing his observations with a tribute to his wife's memory.

Tom's first birthday at the lapidary's was celebrated by Mr. Lambert presenting him with a gold watch, while Gertrude gave him a handsomely-bound church service; and both were richly rewarded by every day finding the orphan boy was worth all their care and kindness.

He took to the lapidary's business, and pursued it with unabated industry, and considerable skill. He was at once honest, willing, obliging, and content, and besides being a favourite with the Lamberts — the people who had rescued him from his forlorn position with the heart to make a man of him—he was esteemed and well spoken of by the lapidary's numerous people who had business at the old-fashioned shop in Rosoman Street.

Mr. Lambert bought old gold and silver out of date, jewellery, and rare coins, as well as carry on his ordinary business of lapidary and diamond merchant. Bowls, drawers, and an iron safe, full of all kinds of these articles, might be found stored away ready for smelting.

Tom Brown had not been many months at Mr. Lambert's when his master, one dark winter's evening, when the snow was falling fast, and picturesquely covering everybody and everything that was exposed to its white, soft-falling flakes, and when few people were abroad, had business out, and left his house and treasures in his and Gertrude's care.

This opportunity had been watched for by a burglarious ticket-of-leave man, who for long had his eye upon the lapidary's shop—at least, the contents of it. He watched Mr. Lambert out of his house and out of the street, and then he returned, did this tall, bulldog-looking man, with a bull-dog's strength, and promenaded the street deliberating on the best way to get inside the unpretending house with a gable roof and an ancient frontage.

The burglar had a terrible physiognomy.

Newgate was stamped on all its lineaments. How could such a man, with such a face, ever have been trusted with a ticket of leave? He looked to have been the offspring of a generation of unadulterated criminals.

At length the burglar decided on his plan of attack, and, desperate as it was, he delayed no longer, but pursued it. No one passing, he knocked at the door, and Tom left the game of chess in which he was engaged with Gertrude, and, nothing suspicious, answered the summons.

No sooner had the boy opened the door than the burglar, as he had planned in his mind, without a word seized him by the throat, with the object of thrusting him back into the passage and closing the door on him.

Fortunately for Tom, and unfortunately for the daring burglar, the inclement night, and the heavy snow-storm, determined Mr. Lambert to return; and almost before the boy could send out a scream of alarm, the lapidary came upon the scene, and loudly called "Police!"

What word so awful to a burglar's ears? The villain quickly released the boy, looked round, and then made off in haste, leaving nothing behind but a blessing of oaths and the footprint of his heavily-nailed boots in the snow that had settled on the ground before Mr. Lambert's door.

Tom's life was once more miraculously saved! and, for all that can be told, in all probability had the burglar forced his entrance, he would have sacrificed Gertrude as well as Tom, had they in any way opposed his burglarious designs upon the rich and portable property of the lapidary.

The return of Mr. Lambert was as lucky a thing for himself as for his boy and daughter, for that desperate burglar would certainly have cleared his shop of its valuable contents. Mr. Lambert gave notice of the occurrence to the police, and took other precautions to keep his precious wares free from the invader's hands.

Tom had not been many days at the lapidary's when, one afternoon, an elegantly-attired lady pulled up in a brougham-cab, while on the box with the driver was seated a remarkably fat boy, a page, well dressed in tight-fitting green adorned with braid and brass bell buttons, while his beaver was looped up with gold strings.

But the clothes of the lady's page were the least consequential things about him; it was the consequence and assurance that he carried in his jolly face and manners that were his most attractive features.

George Mumford rode on the box of the cab with his arms folded, and his body upright, disdaining to exchange one word with the ill-dressed cabman who was bowling him and his mistress from Camden Villas to Rosoman Street.

He received the chaff of the errand-boys who happened to cast their eyes on him with the most ineffable contempt; but when one boy met him who knew him when he lived at Mr. Townley's, and vulgarly sang out the opprobrious epithet, "Bread-and-butter Bumford!" he darted such a scowl upon him that his eyes became obscured by the extreme lowering of his eyebrows, and he bent both his fists at him, and, further to express his contempt for him, he spat upon the ground, and proudly adjusted his liveried hat on one side of his thick head, and cockishly and defiantly brushed up his hair by the side.

The boy ran along by the side of the cab, and laughed at Bread-and-butter Bumford's antics, and while he ran, and laughed, and chaffed the page, why, of course—other vulgar boys did the same, and by the time the cab reached Rosoman-street, it was besieged with a crowd of impudent boys yelling and shouting.

Mrs. Yapp, the lady inside the vehicle, of course was ignorant what cause to assign this disturbance, and would most certainly rather have been without the distinction her page had brought upon her, more especially as she courted privacy more than observation.

When the cab reached Mr. Lambert's shop, the page, as was his duty, and as well as his "roundaboutedness" would allow him, got from the box, opened the door, handed his mistress out, and then followed her into the shop, awkwardly bearing in his arms a brass-bound mahogany case, tied up in brown paper.

George Mumford, in his conceited mind, considered the carrying of a parcel at all times as beneath his dignity, and he puffed and blowed when he placed it on the counter, that his handsome mistress, if she thought anything at all about the matter, could have thought no less than that her page was about to faint. After he had delivered himself of his heavy bundle, he made a bow to his mistress, and asked her if he should detain the cab?

"Certainly," was Mrs. Yapp's reply, "and remain with it till I come out. I shall require to be driven to my father's, in Cross-street, Holborn."

"Very good, mum," said the page, leaving the little shop (which was then presided over by Tom Brown), but not to remain with the cab as he was desired by his mistress, but to find his way to the nearest penny pie-shop, and the shopkeeper rarely had the good luck to have such a rapacious customer as George Mumford. Kidney-pies, apple-pies, beef-pies, and eel-pies, the page tried them all one after the other to the extent of nine, which was pretty well considering that only two hours since he and Sarah had made a breakfast with cold meat and eggs.

But two hours George thought too long for any reasonable being to go without food. To his mind it was a starvation period, and very injurious to any person's health; and moreover he was quite sure that he never should have been the fine, handsome young man he was had he neglected his eating and drinking. He never did, and he never would, let envy say what it liked. Besides, eating and drinking was a part and parcel of his wages, and he wasn't going to starve himself to benefit Mr. and Mrs. Yapp, or any other master or mistress.

These were George's profound meditations in the pie-shop—indeed, these were the tenour of his thoughts, here, there, and everywhere.

"Your pies, master, would be all the better if they were larger," he said to the pieman.

"Can't afford it for the money, Sir," was the tradesman's reply, leaning over his bright tin-can of pies. "There's good meat in my pies, and good meat is dear. And as for their being small, that can be got over by eating more of them."

"That's jolly fine," said George; "but you can't eat more of them without paying, and that ain't always convenient. But really they are nice juicy pies, 'specially the heel ones, and—aw!—the fact is—aw—I should like to take home half-a-dozen—aw—or a dozen, to my fellow—aw—sahvant; but I am short—aw—of change!"

This was a good try-on of the page's, but it was no go; it wouldn't bite with the pieman, and he at once saved the boy any more expenditure of his ingenuity by saying—

"I am sorry for that, Sir, for I never give credit."

"I didn't ask you—aw—did I?"

"I thought you meant me to understand you so."

"Aw—you're demned fast—aw," said George, putting on his tip-top air and graces. "Dahsay you don't know who I am?"

"Daresay not," said the pieman, who began to be much amused by the youth's swagger, and his livery lent an additional comicality to it.

"I am—aw—the head page—aw—with her Grace—aw—the Duchess of Windahmeah—aw!"

George was as attached to his lying as his eating and drinking, and gourmandising.

Some of the boys that followed the cab took up their post at the pieman's window, and grinned in much astonishment at the voraciousness and impudence of the head page of the "Duchess of Windahmeah." Not content with their laughter at the shop-window, they must give audible voice to their chaff.

"What a mouth for pies!" exclaimed one with a bag on his shoulders, and a shadow compared to the over-fed page.

"He can eat, and no mistake," cried another.

"Ain't he a fat 'un!" exclaimed a third.

"He's got fat enough for the lot of us," cried a boy who was considerably more in size than the others.

"And you have impudence—aw—for all the world—aw," said George, in reply. "How different, pieman, City-boys—aw—are, from those of the West-end—aw!"

"I mustn't say a word agin 'em," said the honest pieman, "those boys are my best customers."

"Then your pies don't seem to be very fattening—aw," retorted George. "I can see the ribs of everyone of them; and if they don't hook it—aw—they will feel my fist about them."

The big boy borrowed a penny from one of the other boys, and went into the shop, and stood face to face with the lavishly-dressed page, who soon saw that a little game was intended at his expense. The street-boy was as clever at apeing a snob as was the page, and he began by saying, throwing back his head—

"Ah, my friend, Sir Bobbery Bowlegs, I declah! Shall I have the pleasure of tossing you for a penny pie—aw?"

"Thank you, Sir Dirty-white Blubberhead, but I never toss," said George. "I should lose caste in the Windahmeah family—aw—if it was known that I gambled with a dirty City-boy—aw. Pray what have I to pay, pieman—aw?"

"Altogether is tenpence, Sir," said the shopkeeper.

"I protest—aw—I had only nine pies," said George.

"That's true—but one was a tuppenny one," said the pieman.

"You should have mentioned that," said George, "before I ate it."

"You didn't give me time; 'twas the first pie you took, and was gone before I could say you've tucked in a tuppenny."

The boy who had entered the shop on purpose to get the fat page out for a scot, was quick to discover, by George's blank look, that he was a penny short of his score.

"Can I be of service to Sir Bobbery Bowlegs?" he inquired, with a bow and a saucy laugh.

"I'm obleeged to Sir Dirtywhite Blubberhead—aw—for his kindness—aw, but had not her grace the Duchess of Windahmeah—aw—

been waiting for me, I should do myself the pleasure—aw—of punching his head!"

"I'm quite at Sir Bobbery's command," said the big boy, bending his dirty fists, and sparring up to the terrified page, who receded from his attack as far as the counter would permit him. The boys outside roared with laughter to see the fat boy's terror.

"It is well for you that it is opposed to my principles to fight," said the blustering page, making the same lying excuse to the boy as he did to the baker.

"You're a duffer, Sir Bobbery Bowlegs!" exclaimed the lad. "I'll fight you with one hand for a tuppenny pie;" and he was about to pull off his coat, when, fortunately for George, the cabman looked in to say that his "missus" wanted him.

The page was much confused; and to improve his perplexity, the boy gave him a bonnetter, which sent his hat over his bursting-out-of-head-looking eyes, and then stepped it. When the page recovered his sight, and found that his assailant had gone, he showed considerable indignation, and exclaimed, making himself up pugilistically—

"I'd knock that dirty fellow down if I had him here!"

"Here, you can have me," said the boy, who had not gone further than the window, where he stooped behind the other boys.

George would rather not—he was in a hurry—the Duchess of Windahmeah was waiting; but as these trumpery excuses did not satisfy the boy, he continued sparring, and chaffingly said—

"You're afraid of yer fat, yer cur!"

"Let the boy alone," said Cabby, "his missus is a waiting for him."

"I don't care who waits for him," said the pieman, "he don't leave here till he's paid me for my pies."

"Who's a-going?" said George, "there's your ninepence."

"Tenpence I want," said the shopkeeper, coming from inside his well-stored counter of pies in every variety of make and price.

"I've no more small change," said George.

"Then you must get it. You've been too bounceable and too insulting. I don't mean you to come over me."

"Here's a storm in a teapot," said Mumford. "Cabby, pay the man a penny, and I will give it to you again when we drive over to the Duchess of Windameah's."

A very noisy shout followed this speech, and the cabman could not himself resist a broad grin while he paid the penny, and released the pompous page from the clutches of the pieman. But even now the rabble would not allow him to depart in peace to Mr. Lambert's shop; they hurrah'd, and shouted, and chaffed, and called him "Guy!" and "Cure!" and "Duffer!" and "Johnny," and other names which we care not to perpetuate in print.

The page could do nothing but retaliate by looks; and if looks could kill, there would have been a great slaughter of the "Innocents" in Rosoman-street that day. But the looks of the fat page fell harmless upon the juvenile rabble, and they did nothing more than feed the mischief which his dress, extraordinary "roundaboutedness," and ludicrous and offensive manners had attracted around him.

Before he reached the cab and his mistress, the boy who had hailed him as "Bread-and-butter Bumford," while he rode by the side of the cabman, came upon him again, and rudely said—

"Now you please to pay me that sixpence I lent you when you lived in Cross-street while you were errand-boy at Townley's, the stationer."

"Cross-street! Townley! Errand-boy!" exclaimed the page. "Never heard of such a street—don't know such a stationer! Don't you attempt to humbug me, for I owe you no sixpence, and shan't pay you none. You've made a mistake, my man."

Mumford's lies were of too barefaced a description to deceive any one, much less the lank, low-looking youth who now accosted him.

"You liar!" he exclaimed. "D'ye mean to say that your name ain't Mumford, and that you lived in Cross Street, at Townley, the stationer's?"

"I don't think I'm 'xactly called upon to give you my history," said the page, drawing himself up with as much indignation as one who was evading the truth could assume.

"But you're 'xactly called upon to pay me my sixpence, and if you don't I shall go and ask Mrs. Yapp, your missus, who is now standing in Mr. Lambert's shop. I know Mrs. Yapp very well."

"Why, he said his missus was her Grace the Duchess of Windmill Hill!" shouted one or two of the page's other tormentors.

"I said no such a thing," said George. "I said Windameah! It shows what liars the whole of you are, and I hate a liar! Call a policeman, cabby! I can't abide these insults any longer. No gentleman is safe now-a-days."

"Gentleman! That's cool!" was now the derisive shout.

"Look in my face, George Mumford," said his creditor, staring at the page with all his might, "and tell me if you don't know me! and if you don't remember my lending you sixpence!"

"What's the good you're asking me questions if I'm a liar?" cried George, emphatically.

"It won't do, fat-head!" exclaimed the boy. "You won't get over me, so I don't deceive you! You know Bill Sparrow afore to-day, and you know he's given you a good licking afore to-day."

"Now you are a-going it!" cried George, resorting to his old system of humbug and evasion, and never straightforward, except to the dinner table, and then no line so straight, no arrow so swift, no scent so strong.

"Pay me my sixpence!" again demanded the pertinacious youth, who was taller and certainly thinner than George Mumford. "Pay me my sixpence, or I'll roll you in the running gutter!"

"Lord! sixpence ain't of much consequence to me at most times, but I don't happen to have one now," said George.

"Ask your missus, Maria Perkins that were," said Bill Sparrow, with a leery look.

"Maria Perkins!" this was, indeed, bringing down George's mistress—the Duchess of Windameah—to the very smallest dimensions.

Still further, to the page's horror and confusion, Bill Sparrow went on to say—

"Your missus, and your missus's father, and your missus's mother, has often served me with a ha'penny dip and a pen'orth of pickled ingens. I don't know 'em now, I 'spose?"

"What do I care what you know? But you seem to me to know too much," said George, trying to move on, but Bill Sparrow placed him-self before him.

"And I know your mother—she keeps a mangle, and gets up my Sunday shirts," said Bill Sparrow.

This revelation brought another shout of laughter from the bystanders, and the most dis-dainful looks from the page.

"Come, I say, young feller," said cabby to George; "I ain't a-going to leave my cab any longer; I've no business to have left it at all, and p'raps now I shall be pulled for it. Let the boy go," he added, addressing Bill Sparrow. "If he owes you anything, call at his house for it."

"Hookey! where does he live?"

"Well, I can tell you where I took his missus up. Number fifteen—"

"No, no, cabby," said George. "I can't have such rag-tag at my house. If the fellow—aw—wants a sixpence, lend me one, and I'll pay you when we arrive at the villa—aw."

Cabby at first demurred, but at length, to end the little affair, became the page's banker. Just as the scene was over, Tom Brown came in search of the cabman and page; and when he found them he bade them make haste, for the lady was quite prepared to leave, having settled her business with Mr. Lambert.

Tom hastened back, and George took to his heels and long strides, leaving the yelling, chaffing boys behind him. When they reached Mr. Lambert's, which was only the length of the street from the pie-shop, Mrs. Yapp, with a most dejected face, mingled with considerable passion, was standing at the lapidary's door.

"Wherever have you been, Sir?" she sternly said to her page.

"Me, mum? Oh, yes, mum—please mum, I took the opportunity, being in the neighbour-hood, of calling to see a sick sister, and the sight of me, mum, who she hadn't seen for many a year, so affected her that she died in my arms, mum."

"If I could believe you, George, I should be very sorry for you. But you can lie as fast as a horse can gallop, and why your master has kept you I cannot conceive—only I fear that he is as great a liar as his servant," she added, in under tones to herself.

"Don't be hard upon me, mum, at a time like this, mum. A lot of wicked boys, too, mum, when they saw me a-crying began chaffing me, and calling me names."

"You must have been a coward indeed to have suffered that. Surely you were big enough to have chastised them."

"I could have thrashed them altogether at any other time, mum; but my feelings was so much hurt about my sister, mum."

"Ah, well!" said Mrs. Yapp, "return that case to the cab, and tell the man to drive quickly to Cross Street."

"And stop at Mr. Perkins's, mum?" said George.

"Yes; but let him first drive to St. Paul's Churchyard."

"Where there, mum?"

"I really forget the name, though I well know the shop. Put me down at the north of the Cathedral, and that will do. Come, be quick."

"This case ain't so heavy, mum, as when I took it into the jeweller's," said George, placing the mahogany case on the seat of the cab, oppo-site where Mrs. Yapp seated herself.

"Nor are you quite so active as when we left home," said Mrs. Yapp, drawing down her veil, and requesting her page to order the cab onwards.

While the page regaled himself with penny pies, and while the street boys were chaffing him, Mrs. Yapp conducted her business with the lapidary.

When she first entered the dark shop with a low ceiling, she saw no one there but a genteelly-dressed boy in deep black, and a somewhat sorrowful face. She inquired, of course, for Mr. Lambert, who was recommended to her as a dealer in gold, silver, and jewels, by a very old friend of hers, to whom she had confided many confidences.

Mrs. Yapp—whether the reader has yet disco-vered it or not—was a lady of great deter-mination; and when she told her husband that she would sell everything in her home rather than that her father should be ruined for want of the money Mr. Yapp owed him, she certainly meant it; and this, her first visit to Mr. Lam-bert's, was an earnest of the manner in which she intended to carry out his resolve.

On the morning after the memorable night that Mr. Yapp took his little girl from her warm bed with the darkest of purposes, and when he had left for his office in a Hansom cab, she packed up everything of value and that was portable in a mahogany case, a kind of table-desk—even the very drops from her small, shell-like ears, and the bracelets from her wrists—ordered Mumford to attend her in a cab, and drove, without interruption, to Mr. Lambert's, jeweller and lapidary.

"My father has been good and kind to me," she mused, as the cab drove onwards to Rosoman Street, "and he shall not be ruined by my mis-takes and my mother's folly. But her folly transpired through a fondness—a fatal fondness—for me. My mother has unintentionally duped my father, and my husband has *deliberately* duped us all. Oh! this silly love of mystery and fortune-telling, what has it brought us to? Ruined!—ruined!—all ruined! Oh, poor father and mother, what will become of them? And my dear, dear children!—what will their inhe-ritance be? I care little for myself, but I *do* care for them. Everything that my father's money bought shall be sold to pay him, even if I leave myself and children without a bed to lie on! His presents, indeed!" she exclaimed, shutting up the case; "I should despise myself if I kept one of them while my father remained unpaid."

After George had placed Mrs. Yapp's maho-gany case upon the lapidary's counter, and had left for the pie shop, the lady inquired of Tom Brown if Mr. Lambert was at home.

"He is, Ma'am," said the boy, looking up from a rare old gold coin he was at the moment of her entrance interested in; "what name shall I tell him?"

"That is of no consequence," was the reply. "He does not know me personally; but I wish to see him, if I can do so. You may present my card, if you please," she added, drawing from her sable muff a tortoiseshell card-case.

When Tom read the name of Yapp on the card, he turned as pale as death, and the card trembled in his hand. So palpable was the change in the boy as he continued to gaze on the card, that the lady asked what was the matter with him, and he stammered—

"Nothing, Ma'am—only that I—I—very re-cently lived with a—with a—Mr. Yapp."

"Indeed! And where was that?" inquired the lady.

"At Bonthron and Son's, Bolt Court, Fleet Street," replied Tom.

"How strange!" exclaimed Mrs. Yapp. "My husband is engaged there. And pray what did you leave him for?"

"I was very badly treated, Ma'am," said Tom; "not so much by Mr. Yapp, but by a man called Swift."

"Ha! Swift," exclaimed the lady to herself. "The very name Yapp mysteriously mentioned when he was delirious!"

Then she asked Tom many particulars about Swift and the place generally.

"I was only there one day, Ma'am," said Tom; "but in that day I suffered more than I shall ever live to forget. They tried to make me out a thief, by placing a five-pound note in my pocket that did not belong to me," he added, bursting into tears; "and they locked me up in a station-house all night, and after all they found I was *not* a thief."

"Had Mr. Yapp anything to do with that?" inquired the lady.

"Oh, a good deal. I could hardly make it out, but Swift every now and then seemed to be Mr. Yapp's master. They were drinking and quarrelling the whole of the day that I was there. The alderman advised my mother—but she is dead now," sobbed Tom, abruptly breaking off his narrative; and he was about to leave the shop to seek Mr. Lambert, when Mrs. Yapp asked the boy—

"How did Mr. Bonthron treat Mr. Yapp?"

"I never saw Mr. Bonthron, Ma'am," said Tom. "He was home ill the day I was there. I don't know much about any of them; but I feel positive in my own mind that they placed the note in my pocket only to cover some of their own guilt."

"You say *they*—who do you mean, boy?" asked Mrs. Yapp, in great uneasiness.

Tom paused before he replied, and then he evaded the question by saying—

"That he might be mistaken—it was only his impression—"

"But who were the persons you had that impression of? Not my husband, surely?"

Tom felt himself in a very unpleasant dilemma, but he could not tamper with truth any further, and although he was very reluctant to hurt the feelings of the lady, who breathlessly waited his reply, he said—

"I think both Mr. Yapp and Mr. Swift have been robbing their master. I hope I'm wrong, I'm sure I do; but by what I saw and heard, and their trying to make me out a thief, I don't think I am."

The boy's outspokenness appalled Mrs. Yapp; for it pointed in the direction where her suspicions were tending—that her husband was nothing more nor less than a swindler.

She interrogated the boy still further, and after eliciting everything that he knew concerning her husband, she bade him call his master.

Mr. Lambert now walked slowly into the shop with the card in his hand, and made Mrs. Yapp a bow while he looked steadily in her face, and then went behind the counter while Tom stood by his side.

"My name is Lambert, Ma'am; what may I have the pleasure of doing for you?" and while he spoke he stroked his long beard.

"I have a variety of jewellery that I wish to dispose of—you buy, I believe?"

"I do. Be seated, Ma'am."

"I am hard pressed for money, Mr. Lambert; and as I have brought my mind to part with all the jewellery I have to pay a debt my husband owes my father, I hope you will deal as liberally as you can with me."

"You may rely, Ma'am, that I will do so," said Mr. Lambert, with a quiet dignity.

Mrs. Yapp unlocked the case, and displayed, before the twinkling eyes of the lapidary, a number of rings with all manner of precious stones, bracelets, pins, brooches, earrings, silver cream and milk ewers, table, tea, and dessert spoons, and a gold watch and chain, a silver teapot, two silver hunting watches, two gold pencil cases, a musical snuff-box, a gold back comb with pearls, a child's gold cup, and a variety of other things suitable to a lady's toilette.

"I am told that all these things I now submit for sale," said Mrs. Yapp, surveying them with a regretful eye, "are of the very best make and material."

"They are the reverse of that, Ma'am," said Mr. Lambert, looking critically at each article. "They are inferior in every particular."

"You surprise me!" exclaimed Mrs. Yapp, with a look of disappointment. "They were presents from my husband, and made from time to time on birthdays and other occasions."

"They are not at all what they seem; they are articles got up for the cheap market, and to delude those who are not judges of them. That ring, now—do you know what your husband gave for it?"

"I think he told me twelve pounds ten," was the lady's reply.

"Twelve pounds ten!" exclaimed Mr. Lambert, looking at the lady as if he thought she was trying to defraud him.

"Is it too much?" said Mrs. Yapp.

"Too much, Ma'am? Why the rings altogether are not worth that sum, nor ever cost it, take my word for that. They are counterfeits."

Mrs. Yapp started back, and looked at the lapidary.

"You do, indeed, underrate them," she said. "There is a great difference between buying and selling."

"There should only be a fair and proper one," said Mr. Lambert. "Believe me, I do not condemn what you have brought to dispose of in order that I might buy them cheaply. My trade is not conducted in that manner, I do assure you, Ma'am. Yet I tell you again that all your rings together are not worth twelve pounds ten. Try elsewhere, Ma'am, if you have no faith in my estimate of the trinkets. I am not covetous to buy any of the articles."

"I am amazed, Sir!" exclaimed Mrs. Yapp. "You must be deceived."

"I am not, nor do I wish to deceive you," said Mr. Lambert. "And, perhaps, Ma'am, after what I now tell you, you would like to try elsewhere. I see you are disappointed, and if your husband gave twelve pounds ten for that ring (which I can hardly credit), all I can say is he has been defrauded. Its true value is about thirty shillings."

Mrs. Yapp could now think no other than that she had married a very base fellow—a liar, and a swindler! She could have sunk into the ground with passion and mortification. At length she rallied herself, and quietly said—

"Give me what you please for them, Sir. I am compelled to part with them. Indeed, had I for one moment known that they were the trumperies you state them to be, I would never have received them, much less have cherished them as I have done."

"We should not look at presents from their value, but cherish them for the giver's sake," said Mr. Lambert.

"But I do not like to be deceived," replied Mrs. Yapp. "My husband need not have said that ring cost him more than it did."

"His only motive could be to enhance himself in his wife's estimation. But I must not be a special pleader for falsehood. The teapot and gold cup are the only genuine articles in the lot, Mrs. Yapp. The jewellery—"

"Do the best you can for me, Sir, and I must be satisfied," said the lady interrupting Mr. Lambert, in tones that indicated impatience and anxiety to rid herself of presents from a husband who she was now learning to despise.

The lapidary took pen, ink, and paper, and slowly estimated and catalogued the articles one by one, affixing a price to each as he went on. Mrs. Yapp paid little attention to what he was doing; she sat with her chin poised on her hand, nursing her wrath.

When Mr. Lambert surveyed the child's gold cup, Mrs. Yapp was deeply touched. Her father presented it to her little girl—a christening gift. The mother's blessing quivered on her lips, for her beautiful cherub girl—but it must go—grandfather must not be ruined, while she had one thing to sell.

"Now, Mrs. Yapp," said the lapidary, "I have come to a total, and the most I can give you for the whole is—how much do you think?"

"I have not the remotest idea. Not half what I was led to expect,"

"Pray how much might that be?"

"One hundred and fifty pounds."

"You will be deeply disappointed then, when I tell you that that sum—thirty-eight pounds twelve shillings—" holding out for her inspection the sheet of calculations—"is the utmost I can give you for them."

"Take them, Mr. Lambert—for I am sick of the sight of them!" she passionately exclaimed. And then to herself she thought of her wronged father and the deception practised on her by a man whom she was compelled to call her husband.

Mr. Lambert wrote her a cheque on his bankers for the amount of the purchase, and then she ordered her page to take the empty case to the cab, and drove off to her father's in Cross Street, Holborn.

CHAPTER XXXVI.

MR. SWIFT DESTROYS THE ACCOUNT BOOKS.— THE MURDER ON THE THAMES.

"As right as a trivet, I tell yer!" exclaimed Swift, after his return from Blackfriars Bridge, in reply to the clerk.

"I'm grateful, Swift! very grateful, old fellah!" exclaimed Mr. Yapp. "I'm glad it is done, now it is done. I am saved, Swift—you have generously saved me! Now for the boating!"

"I'm a thinking it is very cold for that," said the warehouseman, shrugging up his broad shoulders, and rubbing his hands. "Such a splash the parcel made in the water, while I

went plump down on the pavement! Ugh! ugh! it was cleverly done, though I say it. A good job that orange-peel was in season, warn't it, Mr. Yapp?"

"Oh, your ingenuity would have found something else," said the clerk.

"Leave me for that," said Swift. "Only there's been a lot of letters, yer know, jist now written to the papers about haccidents that has arose to Her Majesty's subjects through a-treading on horange-peel. Then what so nat'ral that I should be a wictim to the carelessness of other people?"

"I see, Swift—I see; you've managed well," said Mr. Yapp. "Now, what follows?"

"What follers is this 'ere, and it must be done immediately and at once," said Swift, bringing a card from his pocket.

"What's that, Swift, eh?" asked the clerk, showing an inward alarm.

"Why, don't nothing hoccur to yer?" said Swift.

"Nothing," said the clerk.

"Don't yer think it would only be nat'ral that you should see Mr. Bonthron, and commoonicate my haccident to him?"

"See Mr. Bonthron! I couldn't for the world!" exclaimed Mr. Yapp. "Yet he must be seen, or written to, by one of us."

"One of us!" reiterated the warehouseman. "It would be out of place for me to go. This 'ere card is the card of a 'Mr. Dingwall, Heath House, Dulwich.' He saw me fall, and saw the parcel go over the bridge; and a werry nice gentleman he is, and when he saw my grief, and heerd me say that it would be the ruin of me, he hinstantly told me not to fear—that it was a haccident, and that he would only be too happy to give his testimony to my employers to that effect. And then he gave me this 'ere card, which I considers of werry great importance."

"And so it is, Swift!" cried Mr. Yapp. "That card, and that gentleman's testimony, cannot fail to impress Mr. Bonthron with the truth of the business."

"Although the only truth about it is that the books are destroyed."

The clerk heaved a groan, and, as if intensely thinking, bit his lip, but said nothing.

"What are you thinking on, Mr. Yapp? Nothing to no purpose, I'll be bound."

"I was only thinking of my villainy," said Yapp.

"Lord! and what's the good of that? Let others think of that. As the old play says, 'Tan-ta-ra-ra-ra—rogues all!'"

"But you cannot deny, Swift, that Mr. Bonthron has been a good, kind master to both of us?" said Yapp.

"Well—yes—pretty well, as masters go; though, mind ye, he ought to have riz my screw this Christmas."

"The Christmas has hardly passed yet. Still, you are well paid as it is; few warehousemen get as much as you do."

"Oh, I dont mean to say, if I was on my hoath, that Mr. Bonthron is no skinflint. I've grumbled a little about him now and then, and so have you. There's a great deal of pleasure comes from grumbling, 'specially when one has nothing to grumble about. A good grumble does a person good—a fine thing to the feelings to work yourself up to the point of being a hinjured man, and all the world agin yer."

"I cannot see it, Swift. You go deeper into human nature than I can follow," said Mr. Yapp,

"I SHALL FIND MY SON AFTER ALL, YOU YELLOW-SKINNED WITCH!" EXCLAIMED
SQUIRE SEYMOUR — (See No. 17.)

who was evidently occupied with other thoughts than the subject under discussion.

"Human natur'," said Swift, in the most learned manner, "isn't much of a thing to rejoice in. Look at the noosepapers—they'll tell you at a glance what human natur' is."

"They show all sides of it—the good and the abd, the bright and the dark; things to admiah, and things to shun. I would prove, Swift, from the newspaper, that human nature is a great and mighty creation, and in some instanecs as

bright as Heaven itself. 'Tis we—we, Swift—who disfigure and disgrace it!"

"Thank yer for nothink," said the warehouse-man. "Don't judge of other people by yerself, Mr. Yapp. I've done nothink wery wrong, I haven't. If I have, it's all been done for you."

Mr. Yapp could not very well deny this statement, and shrank under it.

"You told me to destroy the books—"

The clerk started.

"Why didn't yer?" said Swift.

16

"I did," said Mr. Yapp. "Oh! I shall tell no lies about it. I am the thief! I am the robbah! Feah nothing you, Swift.

"Well, and you needn't fear nothink either, if you didn't make a d—d fool of yerself."

"And that I've done for these six years past," said the clerk, in tones of deep remorse.

"I should think yer had a long practice at it by yer looks."

"At what?" said the clerk.

"At playing the fool," replied Swift. "That's plain, ain't it?"

"And must I beah this insolence!" exclaimed the clerk, bending his fists, unperceived by his tormentor.

"Ugh! ugh! What a knack you've got of calling things by wrong names. I didn't mean what I said to yer as hinsolence, but as education, as good, sound, wholesome adwice."

"What would I give for your indifference, Swift!" cried the clerk.

"It's all the work of training," said the warehouseman, with a quiet, Satanic smile.

"You'd cut a throat, and laugh at the deed!" said Mr. Yapp, compressing his lips."

"That 'ere would depend whose throat it was," retorted Swift, facetiously.

"That would mattah little to you."

"Oh! but it would, though; for I couldn't laugh if I'd cut my own—ugh! ugh!—could I, Mr. Yapp?"

The clerk disdained to reply, but went to his desk, took a sheet of note-paper, and, with pen in hand, pondered over the style in which he should address his employer, while communicating to him the loss he had sustained in his account-books.

While the clerk was engaged in his difficult and unpleasant task, Swift whistled away in the most honest fashion, cleared up the warehouse a bit, and told the clerk—

"That while he was writing that 'ere note he would run into Joe Bowers', and get half a pint of beer."

"Demn it!" exclaimed the clerk, throwing the pen across the desk; "I know not what to say now I have commenced."

"Take yer time, Mr. Yapp. You used to be werry swift at correspondence; and I have heerd our honoured master—"

"Dishonoured now," said the clerk —"dishonoured by me who should have been his truest friend, because he trusted him. 'Tis a coward's trick to stab a man in the dark!"

"Yer ain't a-stabbed him, have yer?" said Swift, in affected surprise.

"I'm much obliged to you for your good feeling," said Mr. Yapp, offended with the callousness of his helpmate in crime.

"Lord! I only want to rally yer out of yer gloom," said Swift, "Afore yer write that 'ere letter come out with me, and have a drop of Joe Bowers' old pertikler."

"No, Swift, no, I cannot rest, eat, or drink before I have completed the —— business!" he exclaimed with an oath very unusual to him.

"Can I help yer? 'Spose if I give you the hideers and you do the penmanship—eh?"

"I'm almost mad, Swift!" exclaimed the clerk, pacing the shop with his hand to his burning brow. "I fear that I cannot escape detection. And oh! my poor, dear children!"

"Write yer letter to our respected governor — that's the best way to do yer children good. Take your pen, and let us begin, Mr. Yapp."

The door opened, and a carman looked in, his nose red with the cold. Producing an order from his capacious pocket, he said—

"I've got the waggon for two ton a rags for the wharf. They was to have been delivered yesterday."

"A good many things was to have been done yesterday that wasn't," said Swift, stepping forward. "We was too busy yesterday, warn't we, Mr. Yapp? Howsomever, there they are, already packed, and I'll give yer a hand with 'em."

Then he slid over to the desk, and gently said—

"While I do this, finish yer letter. Tell him how much you regret the haccident, and that everything in the power of mortal man has been done to recover the books from Davy Jones's locker.

Swift and the carman now fell to work amongst the sacks, and quickly cleared the shop, and filled the waggon, waiting in Fleet Street, with them. And after the carman was ready to start, Swift proposed a drop of beer; and accordingly a drop of beer was had, and a crust of bread and cheese, and the whole qualified with a drop of gin. When Swift returned to the warehouse, the clerk met him with his letter to Mr. Bonthron. When he placed it in Swift's hands, the warehouseman exclaimed—

"Why, blow me, if you ain't been a-crying over it! It's wet with tears!"

"Is it, Swift?" said the clerk, slightly confused,

"In course it is, and it won't do. Look! there's a tear-blot there, and another there! It ain't respectful to the governor to send him such an unsightly thing as that."

"I cannot write it again, Swift. My feelings overcame me at having to play so hypocritical a part, and I wept. There, now you know! You never wept in your life, did you, Swift? Too much of a man for that, eh?"

"Well, I should say I were. Now let's see what you have wrote. You read it to me, Mr. Yapp, for I should blunder over it all day."

"As you will, Swift," said the clerk, with emotion, taking the paper from the warehouseman, and reading the following with a choked utterance:—

"'Bolt Court, Fleet Street,
"'January 5, 1863.

"'DEAR SIR,—It grieves me to communicate a serious occurrence that has befallen your house. At all times anxious to give my very best attention to your wishes— What villainy, eh, Swift?"

"Read on, and don't interrupt the letter. I werry much like the beginning," said Swift.

"'At all times anxious to give my very best attention to your wishes—'"

"Werry good!" cried Swift.

"'I despatched Swift—'"

"I'd rayther you'd have said Mister Swift. You can alter that, for you must copy it."

"'I despatched Swift,' continued the clerk, 'with your account books. You will bear me out I'm sure when I say that I could not possibly have given them to a more trustworthy, honest, sober fellow.'"

"Than me? Oh! that's werry good indeed, Mr. Yapp. I thank you for that," said Swift, again interrupting the clerk in his reading of the letter.

"Good, but not true," said Mr. Yapp.

"There—there—don't spoil it by any observation. Go on with the letter," said Swift.

"'But,' continued the clerk, 'careful as he was, an accident befell him. As he told me, and which a gentleman, whose card I enclose, is quite prepared to substantiate, when he had reached the middle of Blackfriars Bridge, he trod on a piece of orange-peel, lost his balance and fell, while the parcel on his shoulder containing all the books went over the bridge. I was almost mad when he brought me the sad intelligence, for I know the seriousness of the loss to you. I took upon myself to offer a reward of twenty pounds for the recovery of the parcel, and got half-a-dozen boatmen, with drags, at once to put off from the shore—'"

"You've pictur'd the thing to the life!" cried Swift. "That's werry good about the boatmen. I gives you credit for that. Werry fine hacting hindeed! And do yer know I think that had better be carried out."

"What?"

"Why, we ought to get the boatmen out on the hunt for them. I could direct them to the exact spot—where they *couldn't* find 'em."

"I see, Swift—yes! that must be done—and everything must be done to give our deed—"

"Don't say *our*, Mr. Yapp," said Swift. "I worked for you, and you are my master, you know."

"Well, then, *my* deed," said the clerk. "You are a capital friend, Swift."

"Well, I have been a friend to yer, whether you know it or not."

"A friend so far as this—that you will take all the emoluments of a villainy, but disclaim partnership with the responsibility."

"I've had no hemoluments, except yer call abuse hemoluments," said Swift. "Don't be quite so fast."

The clerk thoroughly understood his customer, and felt and knew that his freedom was not worth a pin's fee while Swift lived.

"Finish the letter—the best you ever wrote," said Swift.

The clerk obeyed, and continued—

"'God grant the boatmen may be successful! It will afford me the greatest pleasure to tell you that they are. Believe me, Sir, that I could not feel more the loss of them if our positions were reversed. The man, Swift—'"

"I don't like the 'man Swift.' It is werry disrespectful. Better say Mr. Swift."

"We can alter that. As I have written so I will read. 'The man, Swift, is also deeply concerned—'"

"So I am—werry deeply indeed. Yerself can't be more consarned than I am."

"The transaction won't bear a joculah treatment," said the clerk. "A few words more, if you care to hear them."

"Don't be cross. Yer know I shall be glad to hear the finish of the hadmirable letter."

The clerk once more resumed—

"'The man, Swift, is deeply concerned, and much feahs the loss of his situation, which having filled so many years, he would regret to lose. I would have come to you, but the business would not permit it. Awaiting your commands, and hoping soon to see you in Bolt Court,

"'I am, dear Sir,

"'Your obedient Servant,

"'WILLIAM YAPP.

"'To Edward Bonthron, Esq.'"

After the clerk had finished, he struck Swift on the shoulder, and exclaimed—

"There! will that do, old fellah?"

"Hadm'sole!" cried Swift. "As pat as truth, a' i will go down as sich. Copy it out hinstantry, and make the few alterations I suggested. And while you do it I will go and have a drop of beer. I'm famished."

The clerk set to work at his task, and just as he had accomplished it, and sealed the letter, a common-looking woman of about fifty years of age, with a grey eye and a white eyebrow, rather a long nose, and execrable teeth, with hands showing their acquaintance with soap lathers, opened the door and fixed a look upon Swift that made him tremble, and certainly took all the bounce and *sang froid* out of him. She continued to gaze on him and on nothing else, and he continued to quail before her as much as a man under sentence of death. Worse than that—she bent her fist at him, and he expected nothing else than that she would fly at him; worse than all, she advanced close to him, and shook her bony fist in his frightened face.

Swift would have been very glad to have receded from her, but there was no chance of that; and he was about to implore her mercy, when she exclaimed, in a very husky, masculine voice—

"You blackguard! and where was you all last night? None of your lies, now! Where was you, I say, last night?" she asked again, more emphatically than before, beating her fist on a bench by her side, like some wild itinerant preacher pouring out his action on the cushion of his pulpit while holding forth before a congregation of ignorant rustics.

"Look here, Mrs. Swift," interposed the clerk; but before he could complete his pacific speech, she interrupted him by saying—

"Ah, Mr. Yapp, no one on the face of this earth knows what I has to put up with from that vile man! There's a nice eye he gave me on Sunday night!"—drawing her brown hair well sprinkled with white off the region of her temple, which concealed a very bad black bruise—"I ask you as a gentlemen, Mr. Yapp, if that was a manly thing to do?"

"And didn't yer throw a chayney plate at my head?" cried Swift.

"And didn't you throw a pint of beer in my face, you viper?" retorted the infuriated wife.

"And didn't you——"

"No, I didn't," replied the wife, before she knew the question her sot of a husband was going to ask her.

"Hear what he has got to say," said Mr. Yapp.

"Say! Oh, you don't know what a liar he is! That man would lie away the soul of any one! Ah, Mr. Yapp, I've had a nice life with him for fifteen years."

"Mr. Yapp knows yer, so you needn't snivel afore him," said Swift, regaining his courage.

"Faults on both sides, I dahsay," said the peace-making clerk. "Sit down, and calm yourself, Mrs. Swift."

"No, Sir, thank you," said the woman, shaking her head at her husband, who stood with his hands in his pockets against the sacks.

"You needn't a-wag yer head agin me," he said.

"Look in my face, Swift, and say where you was last night?"

"I'm not a-goin to look in yer face, it ain't handsome enough for me, and a good bit too sarpenty."

Mrs. Swift caught up the weight that Tom Brown threw at her husband, and she was about to aim it at his head, when Mr. Yapp held her by the arm, and said—

"Had that struck your husband it might have killed him."

"And I wouldn't have cried for that!" she exclaimed. "Many a woman has been hung for killing a better man than he. I should break my heart with joy if he was dead!"

"And so should I," mused Mr. Yapp; "and if I succeed in my plans we shall both soon rejoice."

While this dreadful thought ran through his mind, the clerk averted his head and went to his desk.

"I tell yer what it is, old Mother Chatterbox, if yer don't hook it out of my place of business, I shall take yer by the shoulders and put yer out! I've had quite enough of yer sarce, and I don't have no more on it. You've had your say, and now you heer mine!"

"If you was to touch me, I'd give you something you should never forget," said the woman.

"You've done that already," said Swift; "yer don't chayney plate me for nothink, I can tell yer."

"Then you'd better not show your ugly self in my house again. I'd sarve you out—I'd murder you if you did!"

"Yer heerd her threaten my life?" said Swift to Yapp.

"Oh, how I wish she would carry out her threat!" inwardly exclaimed the clerk.

"Yer heerd her, Mr. Yapp? I'll take the law on her, and I shall want yer hevidence."

"My good fellah," said the clerk, in low strains, "I was paying poor attention. Indeed, the quarrels between husband and wife with me are a bag of moonshine, and they go into one ear and out at the other. After all, I'll be bound that you both love each other, and would weep rather than rejoice if death or other circumstance should part you."

"The devil a bit!" cried Mrs. Swift. "I should like to see myself a-crying for a brute like him!" Here she gave such a chuckle of derision that might have been heard all over the premises. When her chuckle was concluded, Swift said—

"And as for me, if yer were in yer coffin, I'd get jolly drunk; and on yer tombstone I'd write yer hepitaph—

The devil will say, now she's gone home,
What! Lord-a-mercy! Mother Swift
a-come!"

"Pardon me laughing," said Mr. Yapp; "but really the quarrels of husband and wife deserve no more serious attention. And pray, Mrs. Swift, what is the occasion of this tempest?"

"Tell our Mr. Yapp that," said Swift. "You're frightened—and yer better go about yer business, and not come here and hinterrupt me in mine."

"You know I'm not a woman to be frightened, and if you was only out in the court or at home, you'd have these hands or the frying-pan at your head. And you shall have them now, if you stand there and make game of me!"

"She's drunk, Mr. Yapp," said Swift, who would not have dared to say one word to his violent spouse had he been at home. She was the only person he feared; and although he certainly caused the bruise on her temple, and threw the beer in her face, it was not until after she had struck him with the frying-pan, and threw sundry articles of crockery at him.

Mrs. Swift was a gin-drinker, and associated with women of the same tastes as herself. She was always in a semi-intoxicated state; always muddled, fuddled, and quarrelsome, without being absolutely drunk; and it really must be said in extenuation of Swift, that, bad as he was by nature, his unfortunate bosom partner had made him worse. Her character had blighted his home; and Swift's "darling" boy—(as complete a young rascal as any in London town)—the apple of his eye, was indebted to his mother for all his wickedness; but this wickedness the obtuse but fond father failed to see, and only recognised it as pluck and spirit.

"Come, Mrs. Swift, be friends with your husband," said Mr. Yapp, going towards her; but she shrank from him and his proposition, and exclaimed—

"Friends with he, Mr. Yapp! Fiddle-de-dee! Here, that's what I'd do over his grave if I had the chance!"—here she caught up her old merino-dress much higher than her ankle, and commenced a little jig. "And as for his Mrs. Jones that lives in our house, I'll tear her eyes out when I gets home! That's what its all about, Mr. Yapp." Here she emphatically struck the shop floor with her unwieldy family umbrella.

"There's no Tartar about her, is there, Mr. Yapp?" said Swift. "She's a nice young woman for a small party, ain't she?"

"Really, Mrs. Swift," said the clerk, "we cannot have any more of this row here. However bad your husband may be, his house of business is not the right place to come to expose him. Had Mr. Bonthron been here you would have lost him his situation."

"And would I have cared that"—snapping her fingers—"if he had? Not I! No, not that!" —again snapping her finger and thumb.

"Perhaps not until Saturday night came round," said the clerk, "and when no wages were forthcoming."

"What's his wages to me, Mr. Yapp?" she exclaimed. "Look at my hands—they've done a little work in their time, and can do it again. They can earn my bread, and my boy's bread, and a drop o' gin, too, perwided I likes to have it."

"Yer didn't think so last Saturday night when yer waited with yer basket at the bottom of the court, and kicked up a shine 'cause I kept a shilling or two back of my wages."

"And while you lives with me I will have your wages. Next Saturday, mind ye, you don't have a farthing out of 'em! There, what do you think of that?"

"Nothink," said Swift, who became bold enough to laugh at her."

"You may laugh; but not one farthing shall you have. What will your Mother Jones do for her drops of gin then?"

"Oh, I see, Mrs. Swift," said the clerk, "you are jealous, and we are jealous only where we love. I thought before you were an affectionate couple."

"Phew!" exclaimed the woman, adjusting her dirty straw bonnet, which, in her passionate antics had fallen back from her narrow head, and which was trimmed with a garland of flowers with the most glaring colours, large enough, but not fresh enough, to furnish a "Jack-in-the-green" on any first of May. "Phew! love that bundle of filthy ugliness!"— pointing at Swift with her family umbrella— "jealous of he, indeed! You are wrong there, Sir, if ever you was wrong in your life! I never did love him, and he knows that very well, if he would speak the truth; but that he never did since I've unfortunately been acquainted with him."

"Werry well indeed I knows it," said Swift. "And I knows more than that—I never loved yer—never could habide yer."

"That puzzles me," said Mr. Yapp. "I have often heard of people coming together or marrying with only one heart concerned in the mattah; but I nevah before heard of a wedding between a couple that had neither love nor regard for each other. How did such a singular thing happen, Mrs. Swift?"

"I only knows about myself, Sir," said the fury. "I married that man, like a goose, out of spite to a man he wasn't fit to hold a candle to."

"And I married you 'cause you had five pounds, which I was hass enough to think a fortin'. If you hadn't a had that 'ere five pounds I wouldn't have touched yer with a pair of tongs."

Mrs. Swift suddenly turned upon her unsuspecting husband and dealt him a sharp blow with her extensive "gingham" under the ear, and would have repeated the blow had not the warehouseman dexterously got behind the sacks, and Mr. Yapp with difficulty prevented her from following.

"I'll tell you about a pair of tongs!" she exclaimed. "Mind you don't get a taste of the poker when you come home!"

"You're drunk," said Swift, looking up from behind the rag sacks, and then bobbing his head down again before she could make a reply.

"Now, really, Mrs. Swift, I must ask you to leave," said Mr. Yapp. "I and your husband have a great deal of business to transact."

"Ask the wretch where he was the whole of last night," said Mrs. Swift, showing, after all, that she was not so indifferent to her husband's whereabouts as she affected.

"Really I must decline," said the clerk, "for it is no business of mine."

"But it is of mine, Sir," said the woman. "I'm his unhappy wife, Sir; you don't seem to think nothing of that. What would your wife say if you was to stop out all night?"

The clerk answered the—to him not altogether unimportant—question in his own mind by thinking and fearing that his wife would not care much whether she ever saw him again, but he evasively asked Mrs. Swift—

"How do you know I'm happy man enough to have a wife?"

"Of course I don't know that," said Mrs. Swift; "but I'm sure she'd kick up a row if you had."

"Perhaps so, ma'am; but you must excuse me saying that I have not time just now to discuss those delicate questions. I really must again ask you to leave."

"Dear me! who are you, I should like to know?" she asked, turning upon the clerk a look far from delightful to contemplate. "I tell you what I believe, now. I believe you are as bad as my wicked husband."

"She's a-giving you a taste of her tongue now, Mr. Yapp," said Swift, again raising his head into the daylight, which his shrew of a wife observing, made another effort to reach him with her umbrella, and she would certainly have disfigured that head more than nature had already done had not the clerk stopped the way.

"I tell you what it is, Sir," said the woman to the clerk's interposition between her blows and her husband's head, "I shall make it my business to stop here until Mr. Bonthron, your master, comes in."

Swift, when he heard these words, could have fainted, and Mr. Yapp hardly knew how to deal with her now she had taken this position.

"Mr. Bonthron, or my master, if you like that term bettah, Mrs. Swift, won't be here to-day. He is detained from business by illness, and in consequence I have double duties to perform."

"That won't do for me, I do assure you, and I intend to wait here until I see Mr. Bonthron, and speak a bit of my mind about both of you. I'm one of these women, Sir, who don't put up with bullying from any one."

"Turn her slap out!" cried Swift, coming from his hiding.

"I feah I shall really have to do so," said the clerk.

"Well, here I am," said Mrs. Swift, uprearing her umbrella. "Touch me, if you dare! either of you, or both of you. Why, I'd spin the pair of you round my little finger."

Mr. Yapp stood aghast at his formidable antagonist, while Swift was not displeased to see the clerk's astonishment.

"How would yer have liked to have had, fifteen years of connoobial bliss with her, Mr. Yapp?" he inquired.

"Well, here I am," said the virago, shaking her umbrella in a manner that well showed she was very capable of using it in other ways than keeping a shower of rain from her flowery bonnet—"here I am, and neither of you are man enough to turn me out."

"Every man has his duties, Mr. Swift, and the policeman as his. I hope you understand me," said the clerk.

"Oh, we won't stand no nonsence with her," said Swift. We want no policeman for her. I'll put her out myself!"

He was about to seize her, but she fenced so well with her umbrella, using it backwards and forwards as a mower would a scythe, that her husband was unable to seize her.

"I would to heaven that they would kill each other!" exclaimed Yapp to himself, while he looked upon this encounter between man and wife, "That vixen of a wife will soon be a widow—that horrid man will soon be dead—and I soon shall be a murderah! But what of that? My crimes will then be all to myself—locked up in my own brain. He dead, I shall only have myself to fear! And what's the life of such a wretch as that worth? Nothing. Better the world without him, and by these hands the world shall be bettered! The life to come! Oh! I'd rather die with murdah on my mind than that my children should live to be pointed out by the icy finger of their fellows as a felon's children!"

"I'd blow yer brains out if I had a pistol!" cried Swift, who was provokingly kept at bay by the umbrella of his wife.

"You're a duck, Mr. Swift, you are! You'd always do something if you had something. Pistol indeed! You don't love me enough to be hung for me. If you was as valiant as you are ugly—Ha! would you?" she exclaimed, increasing the mowing action with her umbrella as Swift was about to close upon her.

"Really, Mrs. Swift, you had bettah—"

"Dear me, Mr. Mincemeat-man," cried the woman, cutting the clerk very short in what he was about to observe, "if you are a fool don't speak like one."

"On, ain't she drunk!" cried Swift.

"Not with your money, nor your master's—mind that, Mr. Yapp," said Mrs. Swift, addressing one part of her significant remark to her husband, and the latter pointedly to the clerk; staring at him the while, and crowing with evident pleasure when she saw that she had wounded the cashier's feelings. She had smote the dishonest man, and his guilty soul leaped with terror to his face.

" You are a nice specimen of a woman," was all he could retort. " How dare you, ma'am! What do you mean to insinuate ?"

"Ah ! you're too learned for me. I never learnt anything at school but honesty; and when the honest class was called up you was always absent."

Mr. Yapp looked angrily at Swift, for there was no mistaking the words of the wife; and the wife must have learnt the clerk's misdoings from her husband.

"Demn it, Swift!" exclaimed the cashier, " what does your wife mean ?"

"How can I tell yer?" saucily replied Swift. "I've been married to the termagant this 'ere fifteen years, and could never hunderstand her yet. She's the wilest woman on this side Jordan, and I shall be very glad when she gets on the tother."

"See what a liar he is, Mr. Yapp," said Mrs. Swift. "He knows my meaning as well as you do. And you know, don't you ?"

"I? How should I know?" cried Yapp, with an assumed indignation. "You must speak plainer before I can understand you. The excellence of your mannahs no one can fail to understand, but it takes a longer acquaintance than I have had the honour to make with you to interpret your speech."

"I'll be bound to say that I make your master understand me," said Mrs. Swift.

"Mr. Bonthron is not here, ma'am, and I must beg of you if you have any charge to make against me, that you will make it now, and in a mannah that will enable me to reply to it."

" Lord ! she's no charge, so you needn't flurry yerself," said Swift. " Take no notice on her, Mr. Yapp. Her face shows that she would swear any one's life away."

" If I could, you shouldn't live long, nor Mother Jones either."

" She's a werry nice woman is Mrs. Jones, and you are not fit to be her scullery-maid," said Swift.

The uncommonly large bosom of Mrs. Swift rapidly and sensibly heaved at this dreadful remark of her husband. What could be more irritating to a jealous wife than to be underrated by her husband in comparison with another woman? The wife's wrath mastered her, and she struck right and left at Swift with her umbrella, now striking him across his head, now across his shoulders. While he receded from her she followed, until he escaped behind the cellar door, closed it upon himself, and stood firmly against it. The woman made but one attempt to move the door, and finding it a vain task, with her umbrella in her hand, in martial style she marched up to the clerk, who brooded over her insinuations, and said—

"And now, Mr. Yapp, what have you got to say to me ?"

"Nothing. What have you to say to me?"

"That you're a thief!"

" Woman! who is your authority for that accusation ?"

"The man behind the cellar-door," said the woman, with a demoniacal satisfaction in her face that she had made strife between Swift and his master.

"Don't believe her, Mr. Yapp," called Swift, from his place of safety. " She always was a liar and a drunkard!"

"You're a demned traitor, Swift!" exclaimed the clerk. " Your wife I'll forgive; but you—nevah!"

"Lord! won't yer, hindeed?" cried Swift.

"Nevah!" retorted Yapp. "And if I had you here I'd twist your neck!"

The bolt of the cellar-door was instantly pulled back, and Swift came forth, his eyes terrible to look upon.

"Here I am, and here's my neck, Mr. Yapp," he said : "twist it if yer dare. Make no mistake. Though I fly from a woman, I'm good for the best man in England, and I'm sure you can have me at any time."

"But is it pleasant to be called a thief, Swift?" mildly said the clerk, who was quietly biding his time.

The clerk was painfully made aware that Mrs. Swift knew as much as her husband about his criminal doings with his employer's money; and let Swift deny what he would, she could have got her information from no one but the detested warehouseman.

What now to do he knew not. Two persons to know his crimes ! He had carved in his mind a dreadful death for one—but how could he deal with the other? But the books being gone, she could prove nothing even if she were disposed to be malignant.

Swift felt confused at his wife's betrayal of him, and tried to carry it off with vulgar bravado.

Mr. Yapp had the humour strong on him, to have throttled both miscreants—man and wife—had he had the power. But just now it was his interest to play the pacific, and swallow the husband's treachery, and the wife's insults.

"Look here, Swift," he said, " your stopping out last night has made your wife angry, and when women are angry they don't care what they say or what they do. Now don't let us forget ourselves because she does."

"That's all very fine," said Swift, "but had she pummeled you with that 'ere blessed humberella as she has me, yer wouldn't be quite such a lamb, Mr. Yapp."

Mrs. Swift bent her fist at him.

"My dear fellah," said the clerk, " you must considah that you gave the first provocation by stopping out all night."

"And I'll never go home again!" cried Swift.

"You won't if I know it," said the clerk to himself.

"If you value your life you'd better not," said Mrs. Swift, shaking her "gingham" at her lord, if not her master.

"Come, come, Mrs. Swift, don't begin the quarrel again. Leave us now; you can see Mr. Bonthron when he is in business——"

"And I will, too," she interrupted him by saying.

"Very well; but don't stop now. Swift shall come home early and take you to see the new pantomime."

"Go to the play with him!—not if I knows it," said the wife.

"You'll never have the chance, so I don't deceive yer. I shall take Mrs. Jones."

"Let me get at him !" cried the wife, rushing towards her husband, who again took refuge in the cellar. Finding herself checkmated by her husband's flight, to the joy of the clerk, she left the warehouse, vowing vengeance on "Mother Jones," and she trapsed down the court as fast as her clattering clogs would let her.

She had not long turned her back on the warehouse, than the affrighted Swift came forth, and the two men, after passing a few complimentary remarks on Mrs. Swift, then transacted a little necessary business before they made their holiday on the Thames.

Swift got a helper of his, when he was more than usually busy, to take charge of the warehouse in their absence. The porter at first demurred to the boating. It was too cold, and he would prefer having a brisk walk to a certain skittle alley, and spend the afternoon and evening there over a glass and a pipe.

The clerk overruled this, and persisted on the boating, and coaxingly took Swift by the arm, then hailed a Hansom and drove in the direction of a celebrated boat-master's in Lambeth. They lit up cigars as they drove along, and pulled up twice for "nips" on the road. Close to the boat-house there was a small picturesque "public" that looked out on the river; they went into the parlour and again regaled themselves before taking water. From the window they had a good view of the Houses of Parliament, on the other side of the Thames, and Lambeth Palace on their right.

"Now I don't care one fig what yer say, Mr. Yapp, but I maintain the water looks plaguey cold, and I wote that we remain here and enjoy ourselves by that 'ere nice cheerful fire."

"Nothing like a good row to warm yourself, Swift," replied the clerk, looking from the parlour window on the water. "After ten minutes' exercise with the oar, you'll say, I know, that nothing could be niceah."

"Lord! I know what rowing is afore to-day. I've often and often pulled from Eel-pie Island to Battersea. The Thames was once upon a time like my home. From Richmond to Woolwich I know every bit of it except the bottom."

"And I intend you to make an acquaintance with that this night, if I'm not foiled," mused Mr. Yapp. And then to the unsuspecting warehouseman, he said, laughingly—

"Don't talk about the bottom, old fellah! for that is a part of the rivah that I have no desire to visit."

"I don't think either of us are quite *prepared* for that," said Swift, ordering another "go" of gin and hot water.

"No more now, Swift, said the clerk, who, had he been narrowly watched by any one, would have disclosed a restlessness in his looks and manners. "We will row to a capital house this side Battersea Bridge, and will put in there for a swig, and we can smoke as we pull along."

"I shall have another glass here, I tell yer," said Swift. "And you shall have another glass too. It ain't often we come out on the spree, and I want you to taste a little of Lady Blaze's money."

"As you wish, Swift."

"We shall need it I tell yer," said the warehouseman. "There's no mistake about it, I can see the water is werry cold, and if we don't well line our hinsides with grog, which is better than all the great coats ever made by Moses and Son, we shall feel it."

"Don't discuss it, but ordah it," said the clerk, catching up a newspaper, but his attempt to read was a sham, his mind was too intent on murder for that.

The grog was ordered; and while it w being drunk the clerk exhibited great impatience for the boat. Before he had half-finished his glass, he said—

"Come, Swift, come, or we shall be overtaken by the night."

"I shan't hurry for the night or nothink helse. When I gets behind a glass of grog, I don't like to be flurried. You're a d—d sight too fond of rowing to be a companion of mine. Sit down—or 'spose you go and has a pull by yerself, while I remain here and roominate about my old woman—and Lady Blaze—and Tom Brown—and the haccount books."

While he spoke, he thrust the poker in the fire and violently stirred the red fuel until the blazes reflected themselves in his face.

"The thoughts you would cultivate are those I would destroy," said Mr. Yapp. "They are more painful to me than to you, Swift; so come on, old boy! and let us go up the rivah and have a carouse!"

"Oh, if its for a carouse that you are arter, I'm your man!" cried Swift. "Drink up lads, and lets away." Thou he did the "double shuffle" before the fire, and loudly sang a stave of the "Jolly Young Waterman."

"That's it, Swift! that's it!" Let us be jolly. Let us drown dull care!" cried Yapp, tossing off his glass. "I think we've smoothed all the ugly things wery nicely over, and we ought to have a treat for our ingenuity."

"Ingenooity! Ah! Mr. Yapp, where would yer have drifted if it hadn't a-been for my talent?"

"God only knows, Swift," said tho clerk. "Nor would I have cared a curse had I been childless. But the loving countenance of a dear little innocent——"

"Bosh! now yer are snivelling again," said Swift, "if children trouble yer don't talk of 'em. I say, Master Yapp, now I think of it, yer could never had any faith in me, or yer would have told me yer affairs afore."

"How could I, my dear fellah! When one is led into the paths of dishonour, he is not likely to make companionship. Besides, it would have been dragging you into the mire, and really, Swift, I had too much regard for you than that."

"But, I tell yer, two heads are better than one," said Swift. "Then again yer never told me you was married."

"No—I did not—the fact was—was—Swift—"

"There, there, that's enough; don't rack yer brains to tell a lie about it. It wasn't my business to know that yer was married and had a pair of children."

"It was no unfriendly spirit that made me conceal it from you. The fact was that my marriage was so deeply connected with my crimes that I could hardly divulge the one without the other."

"What! is Mrs. Yapp in the robbery?" inquired Swift. "Women have always got a finger in a bad pie."

"In this case you are wrong, Swift. She knew nothing of it, and although she had the produce of my folly, she was as innocent as you are—"

"But I knew all about it," said Swift.

"I mean that she spent the money, but knew nothing how I came by it. And I must say that for her, Swift, that had she known it, or dreamt of such a thing, she would rather have perished than touched one farthing of it!''

"You've a higher opinion of women than I have, then," said Swift. "My belief is that they will do anything for money. Bother 'em, I hate 'em! They've ruined me!''

"And me, too!" responded the clerk. "But then I sought my ruin—''

"By having anythink to do with 'em, you mean?''

"Oh, no—not so," said Yapp, "I led my wife to believe that she had married a rich man, and I was bound to keep up the lie in the best mannah I could.''

"Oh, yes, I begin to see," said Swift, "Mrs. Yapp thought yer were werry rich, and lived haccordingly.''

"That's it, my dear boy," said the clerk. "So I have had to keep a fine house—a fat page and other domestics—supply her and the children with handsome clothes, and make presents of jewellery—give parties—''

"And all without a hincome.''

"Without a honest income," said Yapp.

"I 'spose you owe above a lot," said Swift.

"I don't know how much—nor do I care. Safe out of the criminal courts, I care nothing about insolvency or bankruptcy. I wish I could get to owe twenty thousand! Debt is easily sponged out—but crime, nevah! A man who owes a few thousands for wine, clothes, furniture, &c., &c., is looked upon with respect, Swift—but he who steals the value of a pin is degraded to a thief, and runs the risk of being transported.''

"Yes, ain't that kind of thing werry hinconsistent?" cried the moralising Swift.

"Oh, very! But we won't stop here to discuss the laws we live under," said Yapp. "Our brains have been worked enough, and now that we have freed them—''

"One more glass," said Swift, not caring to be bored with Mr. Yapp's speeches. It will steady our hands with the oars. Not another word," as his murderous companion was about to object —"not another word, I tell yer. I hinsist upon it, and I'll stand it. You know I'm a trump when I've got the tin.''

"One more, then," said the compliant Yapp; "although I'm afraid of the darkness.''

"Then you must be d—d unhappy; for the darkest night is not at all equal in colour to Mr. Yapp's mind.''

"Demn it, Swift, don't insult me while I stop," said Yapp. "But ordah the stuff, and I'll just step below and see the boat prepared.''

"Werry good," said Swift, pulling the little drab-coloured bell-rope, which was responded to by a coarse, buxom girl, one whose face betokened that it must have been something unusually low to have raised a blush upon it. Swift was soon on free-and-easy terms with the serving-wench, and, after a few "how-dye-dos" and sundry squeezes of the hand, she returned for two more smoking glasses of Scotch whiskey-and-water.

"And you really don't mean to say that you are venturesome enough to go on the water in such cold weather as this?" said the girl.

"I don't know about being wenturesome," said Swift, "but it is foolish. But the young gentleman with me will have it, and I'm one of those—here, have a drop with me—I'm one of those good-natured people—you see it in my face, don't yer?—who can't say 'no' to nobody. Lord! you ain't drank enough to drown a fly!''

"But I has to drink fust with one and then with another, that it makes a good drop through the day.''

"Well, well, so it does; and between you and me and the fire, I likes a good drop through the day, and I likes a good drop at night. You're a pretty-patterned thing, Susan——''

"Oh, there, that's all stuff for an old man like you to go on so. There's the bell in the tap-room, now. I really must go.''

"Ha! Swift, caught you with the girls, have I?" cried Mr. Yapp, entering the room. "Don't leave, darling, because I have come. I declah, a very pretty specimen of a woman!''

"Yes, but she says we are a couple of fools to go on the water in such weather as this, and I'm quite of her opinion.''

"Oh, nonsense; the boat is ready, and here is a strong arm and a willing heart to pull her along. Come, arouse ye, Swift!''

"Lord! I'm not asleep—so don't make a noise. There"—drinking from his glass—"and there"—finishing it. "Now let's see—what's to pay?—hic-cup.''

The girl received her due, and the men left the house on the river; and Yapp first, they walked down a rough, stony incline to the rotten old boat-house which bordered the Thames.

The afternoon, far advanced, was bleak and cold, and a slight mist was abroad on the water, which was now undisturbed as far as the eye could reach, with no other craft than an old barge sailing lazily along with the imperceptible tide.

"All right, yer honours!" said a rough Jack of a fellow, in boots to his hips and a tarpaulin hat, pushing off the boat. "A fine night for a row," he added, thrusting his tongue in his cheek, but of course not to be perceived by their "honours.''

Mr. Yapp gave unmistakable evidence of his skill with the oar, but Swift seemed all strength and no skill; while the former tripped lightly about the boat until they were fairly on the deep, the latter sprawled as if he were drunk, while he was nothing more than fuddled.

"Sit there, Swift," said the clerk, "while I get her off. That's it—but don't pull just yet, until I've got her off the shore. There—there—now we are nicely off, and if we pull steadily together we shall have a capital row.''

Onwards they pulled; but it was evident that the management of the boat rested with the clerk, who was very dexterous at his work, while Swift puffed and blowed, and showed that the labour was too intense for his wind.

"I call this werry hard work," he said.

"You have hardly got your hand in yet," replied the clerk. "By the time we reach Vauxhall you'll begin to enjoy it. I call it jolly!''

"Well, every one to his taste, as the girl said when she kissed the cow," said Swift. "But, lord, I knows every hinch of this ground, although it is many a year since I was so far up the river! There's the back of the old Horse and Groom! Ah, many and many a game of skittles have I, and a mate of mine as was then, had there. Do yer know if Mrs. Green keeps that house now?''

"Eh, Swift?" said Yapp, who was deeply thinking over something of importance, and was paying but poor attention to the drivellings of his companion.

"Well, you are interesting! getting me out

GEORGE MUMFORD, IN TERROR, DISCOVERS BLOOD ON HIS HANDS AND ON HIS MASTER'S COAT.

with yer, and then paying no attention to what I say!"

"I didn't exactly catch the name you mentioned. Don't let us begin snarling, Swift; for I mean to have a pleasant day with you, or it won't be my fault."

"Can't we pull ashore at the Horse and Groom and have a nip? I'm gitting unkimminly tired."

"We'll pull a little further on yet. I know a better house than that dirty-looking hole."

"Then I can tell yer it ain't, Mr. Yapp When I used to call at that 'ere house it was beautifully clean. You only see the back view, and all along the Thames is werry dirty."

"So it is, Swift, but picturesque. I like the old Thames; and I've had some delightful nights and days upon it."

"Nights!"

"Oh, yes; 'when the moon is on the water.' I have often been rowing solitarily over its face, singing and smoking. But those happy days are for ever gone! Nothing but trouble before me now, and that is a sad thing for a young man like me to say."

"Well, yer are gloomy now, and no mistake," said Swift, labouring with his might at the oar, and by no means keeping in time with his companion.

"Gloom! I've known nothing else for years, Swift, and for years I've not been what I have seemed to be. Like the lark, outwardly I have been gay and cheerful, but there the resemblance to the heaven-bound bird must end, for while that has soared aloft I've gone down—down to hell, Swift."

"Don't go on that way, Mr. Yapp! That ain't being jolly!"

"No, it is not; I was only talking, Swift—talking for a little sympathy. But you are a philosopher—you don't permit trouble to make a home in your heart, do you, Swift?"

Oh! what a self-sufficient smile came on the face of the man who was appealed to, and then the smile became broader and broader until it culminated in the coarsest laugh. Poor Yapp heard the brute chuckling; he could not see him, for, of course, his back was turned to him.

"Yes to be sure, Swift; you'd laugh in the face of trouble—"

"Why, that's the way to make it fly from yer," said Swift.

"Ah! to be sure it is," said the clerk.

"And if I can't give trouble the go-by with a broad grin, why, I does it with a drop of gin."

"I've tried both, but nevah succeeded with either," said the clerk. "You're pulling too near the shore, Swift."

"Then I'm just a-pulling where I wants to go, for I'm getting tired, and should werry much like to know how much furder you're going? Night will be with us soon."

"Oh! not yet; there's not a patch of it in the sky. Look up, Swift!" cried the clerk.

"It's werry dismal," said Swift, giving a momentary glance above. "Look at them 'ere clouds."

"They are travelling fast away to the west, and when the night comes she'll bring a bonnie moon with her, and make the water like silver. A lovely night, Swift, if you are fond of beauty."

"I likes a clean hearth and a good fire better than your moonshine."

"Ah! you wouldn't say that, I think, if you were a few miles further up the river, where the willows overhang it, and rest upon your oars and watch the fish play in the moonlight."

"That might do for children, Mr. Yapp, but it wouldn't do for me, I can tell yer. I declare they're lighting the lamps on the bridges."

"Then they are lighting them before they are wanted," said the clerk, increasing the rapidity of his rowing.

"Yes, but yer seem to forget that we have to pull back agin."

"Not I, Swift!" cried the clerk. "The rowing back, when we get a skin full of grog at the house I'm making for, will be the jolliest part of our entertainment."

"I'm a werry good-natured feller to take all this 'ere trouble to please yer!"

"By your face, mannahs, and habits, Swift, I could have sworn you would have made a good sailor."

"Not I!" said Swift. "I never could abide the sea! Terror firmer for me, where I can pull

up when I like, and smoke my pipe over a game of skittles or dominoes. A ship is a prison, that's my opinion, and sailors are transports. Freedom for me! I'm tied up too many hours a day already, and I shouldn't like to be night and day confined within the compass of a ship, and she under the strict eye of a cap'en. That 'ere wouldn't do for me at no price."

"While I should like it above all things," said Mr. Yapp. "I've a passion for the sea—"

"What the devil did yer get into a rag warehouse for?" retorted Swift. "D——n it! I would have squared things better with my likings than that."

"We can't control our fate, Swift. I've had no voice in my inclinations. By some unseen guardian or parent I've been moved hither and thither, while I've been kept as poor as a beggah."

"Lady Blaze has had some hand in that pie—that's my belief."

"And mine, too," said the clerk. "She will have no rest from me until I fathom the mystery of my birth. I'm quite certain now that my father is a gentleman."

"I should say so, too, if that ring was his'n. But then comes the question how did Lady Blaze get possession of your father's ring?"

"It shall all be made plain before I'm many days older."

"I don't think it's far from it. She's a wenomous woman, though, and hates yer deadly."

"But for what?"

"'There's the rub,'" as Hamlet says. Mind'ye, had I been you, I should not have been content to have remained in hignorance so long about my father and mother."

"Easy to talk, Swift."

"'Tain't so easy to row, though," said the warehouseman. "Are we pulling agin the tide now?"

"No, the tide is with us, but it is almost still, neither impeding or helping us in our progress. But I've been pulling against the tide all my life, Swift, and often and often wished it at an end."

"What! yer life?"

"Ah! my life; for what is life without peace and happiness? Many a time I've tried to suffocate myself with the bed-clothes, but nevah had the courage to complete it."

"That's your great fault, Mr. Yapp, want of courage. Now, if I had determined to lay hands on my life—which I believe to be a werry wicked thing—but 'sposing I had made up my mind to do it, the devil himself shouldn't have prewented me. But I certainly should not do it by suffocation—that must be horrid!"

"Drowning?"

"Oh dear no!" replied Swift, shrugging his ungainly shoulders; "I've a worser horror of that! Of all deaths—mind ye, I'm not in love with either of 'em—but of all deaths, I should hate drowning! But you are werry fond of the water."

"Not so fond as to drown myself in it."

"I should say not," said Swift, with a chuckle. "Yet if I loved the water like you, and wanted to end my life, I certainly should make a hole in it."

"I don't see that, Swift. I surely may like the water well enough without choosing it to die in."

"I said if yer wanted to commit sooicide."

"I know you did. Still it does not follow that because a fellah liked a boat on the rivah that the poor devil would select to be drowned in it if he wanted to make away with himself."

"Well, but don't yer see the hadvantage of it?"

"I do not; explain, Swift," said the clerk, who, during this long conversation upon anything and everything, was deeply thinking over the damned deed, for his own safety, he had resolved upon.

"Well, look'ee here. People say that the ghosts—do yer believe in ghosts, Mr. Yapp?"

"I do not, Swift, except those that are created from our own wicked deeds. You remembah the daggah scene in Macbeth, where he says—

"'There's no such thing;
It is the bloody business which informs this to mine eyes.'

He saw no daggah in the air, but his 'oppress'd brain' was so intent on murdah that it filled all space with the instrument he was about to use."

"Well, if you don't believe in ghosts there's a good many people as does; and they b'lieve that ghosts haunts the place where people die. So if that's true—and yer know we can't say it ain't—why then, if I was you—always and perwided you wanted to be a sooicide—as you are so fond of the water and boating, I should drown myself up by them willows yer have been talking about, then yer ghost could come and sit there and see the little fish at play in the moonlight, or yer might unmoor a boat and row yer ghostship all over the Thames."

"You are getting funny," said Mr. Yapp. "Then, by the same parity of reasoning—as you are so fond of skittles—you should hang yourself in a skittle-alley, and then, you know, in the dead of night you could come and have a quiet game at knock-'em-down by yourself. But, seriously, Swift, if you had to die, what death should you prefer?"

"Ah! there yer has me," said Swift; "but I think, on the whole, I should give preference to a cup of 'cold pison,' as the song says."

"Poison! eh? That would be too slow a process for me, and too agonising."

"Lord! death is always hagonising; and it is my opinion that, as neither of us are prepared to die, we had better say no more about it. We may be better men afore he knocks at our doors."

"You must soon repent and be bettah," thought Yapp, as he neared the spot where he had planned to strike the fatal blow, and take Swift's life.

"When death comes for me I hope he will find me in a nice feather bed, with things snug around me—"

"And your wife by your bedside—"

"That be d—d!" cried the warehouseman. "I want nothink more to do with Mrs. Swift. I've had quite enough of her. 'A bit of her mind,' as she calls it, would be the most wiolent death ever I could suffer. You must have mentioned her name only to hannoy me. I don't thank you for sich good nature as that. I'd scuttle the boat if she was here, and sing 'Oh, be joyful!' while she went to the bottom of this 'ere river."

"Why should I show mercy to one who is so much in my way when he himself would drown his very wife, and sing as she sank?" cried Yapp to himself.

The grey of evening was, indeed, now obscuring the daylight, and the lamps on every bridge showed brighter and cheerful as the darkness advanced.

Nothing now was to be seen on the broad expanse of water, and nothing to be heard but the plash of the oars of the two men, and the sound of distant railway trains whistling and careering along as if from spirit-land. Old Chelsea looked very picturesque, bordered with its avenue of trees, amidst which the lamps cheerfully shone, while the dull brick tower of Chelsea Church stood back in gloom like the dead amongst the living.

The reflection from the lamps on the bridges and the shore danced up and down with the movement of the water on the now grim river like sportive fairies.

On the right of the rowers, now like some black and blasted heath, was Battersea Park, at the end of which was the back entrance to a public-house, while its front was in the suburbs of Battersea.

"I've good news for you, Swift," said the clerk. "Look round there where that cluster of lights are, at the end of that dark hedge of bushes, it is a tavern, and there I propose to pull up and refresh ourselves."

"With all my heart!" said Swift, "for I'm getting dull, which is a werry unusual feeling with me. A cold somethink seems creeping all about me, and yet I'm as hot as a two hours' rowing can make a feller."

"You are unused to the work, that is it," said the clerk. "A glass of brandy and water will dispel all those feelings, and you will row back singing with your accustomed gaiety. We shall pull back in half the time, for the tide will be with us."

"There's a chill all over me, as if a feller's ghost was on his back. I'm not sooperstitious either, but I never had such a feeling of fear. Those infernal railway whistles seemed to upset my nerves, too—a thing I never knowed afore—and while my ghost seemed to riot about me, them 'ere whistles sounded like hell's demons let loose. Can't account for it nohow, for I've nothink on my mind but my old woman's temper. Blowed if I hardly know myself. Did yer ever have any of these hextraordinary feelings, Mr. Yapp?"

"Often and often, Swift," was the clerk's reply. "Depressions of the most suicidal character I am frequently the victim of. I have once or twice thought I should go mad with them. Indeed, these feelings are a species of madness."

"But I'm not mad!" cried Swift, indignantly. "I'm only haunted, like—can't make it out nohow—a sort of all-overishness. D—m it! I don't know what it is, and it ain't worth thinking about."

"Not a jot of it, Swift," said the clerk.

"A little brandy will make me walliant again. Pull out, Mr. Yapp, for I'm anxious for other spirits than cold ghosts."

"A few strokes more, Swift, and we run ashore. Steady—now leave her to me—don't pull—that's it—there we are," and they ran the boat close up to a flight of slimy stone steps, which led the way to a green arbour in the courtyard of the tavern.

The river was now covered with darkness, the bonnie moon refused to shine, and the few stars that were sprinkled over the face of the sky only served to show its angry looks.

The boatmen entered the bright little bar of the river-tavern, and Swift seemed to be himself again. He rubbed his hands, and laughed at his own folly in permitting a man of his strong mind to be scared by ghostly feelings.

"We have hardly time to sit down" said Mr.

Yapp, "so we'll regale ourselves at the bar, What say you, Swift?"

"Oh, I don't care where it is, so that we regale ourselves. So I mean to begin with hot brandy and water."

"The same for me. Two good stiff glasses, landlord," said Yapp.

The order was quickly executed, and Swift took a very hearty swig at it, and smacked his lips, and cried—

"That's jolly! That's the stuff, Mr. Yapp! Conscience, ghosts, spirits, devils, will all fly from a man arter a skinfull of this 'ere stuff!"

"How welcome a glass is after labour! Had we been guzzling all the afternoon we should have failed to extract the pleasure from it that we do now. Fill them again, landlord!" cried Mr. Yapp.

"It's a pity that you and I was not hacquainted afore, Mr. Seymour—I don't like Yapp, and that's the truth," said Swift, after the second glass, and getting into that *very* friendly condition which is always the first step to intoxication. "I'm getting that fond of yer, that, 'pon my soul, I likes yer. I should werry much like to have known Mrs. Yapp. She'll be Mrs. Seymour now. I wonder—hic-cup!—how she could have married yer with such a hugly name as Yapp? Yer must have had funny godfathers and godmothers to have invented such a name as that. Yer know Yapp rhymes with——"

"Papp. Yes, you have said that before. But good things will bear saying twice over. Drink, Swift, drink! There's no moon abroad, and a boat is not easy to manage in the dark."

"Yer don't catch me not in no boat to-night. I shall go home by the marrow-bone stage. And if I think proper I shall have a bed here. Oh! I can pay for a bed and a supper, and one for you, too, if yer'll only be good-tempered. Say yes, and strike the iron while it's hot."

"No suppah—no bed—until I get home," said Mr. Yapp. "Finish your glass while I just give a peep at the boat."

"I hope yer'll find that she's gone off without us," said Swift, lighting a cigar. "I shouldn't be sorry. But be it is as it may, I'll have a spree here or somewhere else. Would yer please to have a glass of anythink yer like with me?" he asked of the landlord, who was glancing at the newspaper. Swift found a ready customer in the tavern-keeper, and in the absence of the clerk the two exchanged sentiments over the inebriating grog.

Mr. Yapp went to the water's edge, and pondered by the boat, a part of which was in the water, and a part on the mud and stones of the shore. He looked round, then drew from his pocket a knife with a formidable blade.

"'Twill do," he cried, feeling the point, then gazing on it. "'Tis sharp—'tis strong. May this arm, this heart of mine, not fail me. I cannot breathe in security while he lives! I pity him—but he must die! He has no children to lament him, and his wife hates him! and I hate him! Knowing what he does of me, he is my mortal enemy. Poor fool! let him drink his fill, 'twill smooth his passage to the grave."

"Aye, Mr. Yapp! Come, I say—come and do yer share! No heel-taps! What are yer arter?" cried Swift, staggering down the steps.

"Back, Swift," said the clerk, in slight confusion. "I will join you in a minute. The demned boat had nearly got out on the rivah. Back, and order me another glass."

"Hi, hi, Mr. Yapp! All right, old feller!

The devil a bit if I'm afeared of ghosts or devils now!"

"What about your old woman, Swift?"

"D—d if I don't think I could face her now! Ugh! ugh! Didn't she go on about Mother Jones? You were a bit afeared on her—eh, Mr. Yapp?"

"She was very angry I must admit, Swift."

"I never seed her anything else since she's been Mrs. Swift. I only walued her at five pounds, and I find she aint worth five fardens."

"It is all a mistake to marry for money," said the clerk to Swift, while the latter stood on the first step of the flight, looking at Mr. Yapp as well as the darkness would let him.

"But you married for love, didn't yer, Mr. Yapp?"

"I did, Swift," said the clerk, who pretended to be busy with the boat.

"And love seems all a mistake, too, eh, Mr. Yapp?" cried out Swift. "For you are not werry happy."

"Very miserable, Swift," cried the clerk.

"Its my opinion both on us have made a mess on it," said Swift, withdrawing to the bar of the tavern, whither he was soon followed by his companion.

They drank deep, and when they left Swift found it rather difficult to walk steady, and it was somewhat dangerous his getting down the narrow flight of stone steps to the boat. He sang and shouted lustily, while the goodnatured clerk supported him by the arm.

"You needn't be so hofficious, I tell yer, Mr. Yapp. I'm not drunk, old feller! I mean to pull along the boat like blazes. But everythink looks d—d black. There's one thing, if I go overboard I can swim. Can you swim, Mr. Seymour?—Ah! that's the name for my money. Lord! fancy old Lady Blaze! and our governor has got the tidings of the haccount books by this 'ere time."

"It was a deuced bad act, Swift—"

"But it wasn't my hact—never forgit that," said the warehouseman.

"Oh, no," said the clerk, gnashing his teeth "but you have told me so before. That is my; trouble—but I think it will be all right."

"As right as a trivet!" cried Swift, jumping heavily into the boat, and nearly tipping it over.

"Steady, Swift, steady—there—there—now we are once again on the water."

"All right, Mr. Yapp," said Swift, fumbling with his pair of oars. "All right. Hiccup! Pull away, boy! Row, brothers, row—off we go!"

And off they did go, and soon got into the middle of the black river. Swift's back was turned on Mr. Yapp, the warehouseman little suspecting that in a few minutes he would be

"Sent to his dread account
With all his imperfections on his head!"

He sang snatches of songs, and talked away in the most frivolous manner, interlarding his silly conversation with an occasional oath. Mr. Yapp humoured him in all he said, and flattered him out of all propriety. Swift laughed—so did Mr. Yapp; Swift made a joke—Yapp followed on the same suit; Swift spoke in contempt and derision of his wife—Yapp ably supported him.

The clock of the Houses of Parliament struck ten in deep tones, which sounded sublime, yet melancholy on the water. Mr. Yapp cried the hour each time the clock struck.

"I'm a thinking we shan't make Lambeth by eleven o'clock. But I don't care if we git back in time afore the publics are shut up, for I means to have a parting glass with yer, Mr. Yapp."

"Oh, we shall be able to manage that," said the clerk, while he made his first step towards his dread, cowardly design on Swift's poor life, by drawing forth his pocket-knife, opening the blade, and holding it in his right hand.

"It's a werry churchyard sound has that 'ere bell," said Swift.

"Not so much as St. Paul's bell," said Yapp. "That sounds very sepulchral in the dead of the night."

"Oh, werry much so indeed!" cried Swift. "Them 'ere church-bells are not so cheerful as muffin-bells—eh, Mr. Yapp?"

"Far from it, Swift. And yet there's something very delightful to me in the sound of church bells. Do you know that song of Tom Moore's called 'Those Evening Bells?'"

"I never heard on 'em."

"A charming ballad," said the clerk.

"Give us a stave of it," said Swift.

"I don't mind; but it is rather dismal, and won't much enliven our journey."

Mr. Yapp sang, and his voice, combined with the pathos of the words and melody, sounded very sad, yet very beautiful, on the dark river, and seemed to impress and sober Swift, who here and there discordantly joined in. Strange and touching to relate, at the very lines where Mr. Yapp left off, and Mr. Swift joined in chorus, as it were—

"And when that I am dead and gone,
   Those evening bells will still ring on"—

the dastard clerk grasped his knife, and struck deep into the temple of his companion. Oh, it was a cruel blow! Poor Swift, while his life's blood spirted out from the place where the murderer's knife had entered, struggled round on his seat, and stared at the coward clerk, while the latter seized him by the throat, and so tightly, that the eyes of the murdered man were nearly forced from their sockets. With great difficulty the warehouseman cried, but cried in vain—

"Don't be a fool, Mr. Yapp! Don't kill a man who isn't fit to die! Give me time to pray!"

The clerk spoke not, and he gave his victim no time to pray.

Swift quickly died, and as he died he threw his head and arms over the boat, and they dangled in the water. The clerk, while the devil raged in him, took up the dead man's legs, and poor Swift was consigned to his river-grave.

In a minute Swift was dead; and in a minute Mr. Yapp was a murderer! But almost as soon as the deed was done, the clerk repented it. He had stained his hands with blood, and now his soul revolted at his crime.

"Foul deeds will rise,
Though all the earth o'erwhelms them to men's
   eyes;
For murder, though it hath no tongue, will
   speak
With most miraculous organ."

The clerk, before he had done the bloody deed, thought little of its seriousness. But now—as the body of Swift floated away from him, with its dead eyes staring to the sky—the murderer's feelings clothed his mind in darkness, and he shuddered at the crime he had committed. Unhappy man! As he gazed after the corpse, he would have given his own life to have recalled it to existence. But the dead man floated on —on—on! and as the body receded from his view, in his grief, resting on his oar, he cried—

"Come back, Swift! Let us be friends! Oh, don't leave me!"

It was a pitiful call! The "dull cold ear of death"—what so sealed against the human voice!

The ghastly corpse fairly out of the new-made murderer's view, the assassin took the bloody knife that lay at the bottom of the boat and flung it in the river. Then he turned the head of the boat towards Putney, not knowing nor caring now whither he pulled himself.

Sometimes he would rest on his oars in the middle of that dull river, and the tide would take him on after Swift. Then he would pull like mad back again.

"My God! what have I done? It was all needless. The man never threatened me even— and yet to slay him! Where am I drifting? Oh, demned coward! the waters are too good to drown thee!"

In his terrible frenzy he turned the boat again towards London, and pulled away—as swift as oarsman never pulled before—towards the body he had killed. The slow flowing tide favoured his operations, and he came again upon the upturned face of the dead. Poor Swift! his mortal remains floated on, but there was no peace in his distorted face. The immovable eyes still glared upon the moonless sky.

Mr. Yapp pulled the boat close by the body; but he was soon overpowered by the deed he had done, turned his boat round, and swiftly rowed away from it. The man's sorrow was intense. He had no conception that the shedding of blood was the awful thing it was.

Swift haunted him. He saw him with his ghastly eyes everywhere. His body seemed to cover the whole Thames; and, row as he would, that body seemed to follow him. He could not fly from it!

"What had he done?—what had he done?" were the painful questions of his mind; and he dared not answer them. Murder! Oh, it was a word with such terror in it that he could not speak it, though his wretched mind was full of it.

He had rowed many miles, but he felt no exhaustion. His mind was too deeply occupied with his crime to feel anything physical. The shore!—he trembled while he looked on it, for he imagined that Justice, with her officers, were there to seize him. Yet he must land, whatever fate awaited him.

Never was darkness so welcome as it was now to Mr. Yapp. Yet it was not deep enough to hide Swift from him. There he was, stretched out on the cold, dark river, his face grim with a horrible death.

"And these demned hands did it!" exclaimed the clerk, and the river and the shore seemed to echo his words. "'Give me time to pray!' and the devil within me would not give him a moment for a prayer! 'I did you no harm!' Nor did he. My cursed fear of him worked me to do a deed, which my wretched soul now torments me for! Dear children, I have now left you an inheritance indeed! Hide, hide yourselves from your father's shame! He has brought such a stain upon your names, that will never, never be washed out! I must land—I *must* see my children! Yet how can I face them! Their innocent looks will appal my guilty soul. I should be happier now were they both dead. Their mother, too!—she who has been the innocent cause of all my crimes! And yet I love her still. Ha'!" he exclaimed, looking round with a face of alarm. "Nothing—nobody! yet I swear something touched me on my shoulder! Swift said that dead men haunted the spot where they died; but he will haunt me everywhere!"

"Oh, wicked—wicked parents!" he continued, sometimes thinking, sometimes giving utterance to his dreadful thoughts—"wicked to leave me alone in the world without your help, without your care! These hands would never have had man's blood on them, had you not forsaken me. Your crimes have left your child to perish—and perish he will by the common hangman; and his blood and his crimes—whoever you are, rich or poor—be upon your heads."

The clerk looked round and about the dark waters, relieved only by the shimmering lights from the lamps on the bridges.

"Where is that body drifting? How can I escape? Murdah! Oh, it is too great a secret for one human breast to hold! I must reveal the deed—it is too overwhelming to keep to myself! My wife!—ah, yes—I'll tell her! Oh, no—that would be ungenerous, to make her a party to a murdah! She'd give me up, too—hang me! She has no love for me. Yet I must have some one to sympathise with me. Sympathy!—who *can* have any with a murderer? Let him be despised—cast into prison—hung out of sight! Let wife forsake him, and children tremble at his very name! Oh, Swift, Swift!—why did you not strangle me?"

These, and such as these, were the thoughts that haunted the mind of the guilty clerk. He was distracted—he was almost mad—with the position he had brought upon himself. Yet he reasoned the deed well out before he committed it—saw its advantage to himself. Swift living—that was his argument—I am his slave; Swift dead, all my guilt is buried with him. But he never dreamed that murder would haunt a man—track his steps like a bloodhound—lie down with him, clothe his dreams—and, waking, stand his accuser.

The clerk, without being able to direct his steps, or knowing distinctly where he was going or what he should do, pulled the boat to an obscure and unfrequented part of the river on the Surrey side for landing, and here, leaving the boat to its fate, he landed, and appeared to skulk by the people that he met.

As he neared Lambeth Palace, a man suddenly accosted him and asked him the best way to Hercules Buildings. Oh, what a shock for the man who was flying from murder. He thought the inquirer was an officer asking for Swift.

The clerk, without stopping, hastily told the man, who had so unintentionally thrilled him, that he did not know. Then, with his head low bent on the ground, and his hat—instead of being perched nattily on one side his well-formed head, as was his custom—was now pulled low over his brow.

All the features and characteristics of a gentleman seemed suddenly to have left him. He went down one back street and up another, always choosing the darkest, and avoiding every thoroughfare that was frequented or well lit.

We need hardly say that the murderer's mind was occupied with the same thoughts as those on the river. Now of Swift—now of his children—now of his wife, and now cursing himself for the bloody deed he had done.

In this truly wretched state of mind he walked about for hours, without feeling any exhaustion. At a small house in an out-of-the-way place in the Borough he went in, and called for brandy-and-water—and another—and a third. But it had not the effect that he desired, of drowning, even for a moment, the heavy trouble of his mind. He might as well have drank the water without the spirit, so powerless was it to obliterate the thing he was bitterly repenting.

Instinctively, and without designing it, he reached his home in the Camden Road, and here, as he stood before his house, his thoughts became more acute than ever. He turned down one of the intersections of the handsome road, and there, under the leafless branches of an old tree, he paused and wept.

Then he stole back again to his house, and he was a long time before he could bring his troubled mind to knock for entrance. How could he face his wife and children? Oh! he could not! and, beating his breast, he went to an old tree that was shrouded in darkness, leant against it, and shadowed out in his mind's eye the body of Swift floating down the Thames.

The measured tread of the policeman going his rounds disturbed the murderer's reverie, and he "moved on" before the officer reached him.

"I must either pull myself together and assume the style and mannah of other days, or give myself up as a murderah." This was the proposition he made to himself as he once more walked towards his house.

He appeared to have decided on the first plan for the present, for he went briskly up the white stone steps which led to the doorway, and knocked smartly and loudly—the knocking of a honest man asking for entrance into his own house.

George Mumford the page, never very alert to be disturbed, especially when he was toasting himself before the kitchen fire, and a table at hand with a feast of eatables.

Sarah, perceiving that George was in no hurry to move his outstretched limbs from the fender to let his master in, begged him to be quick.

"Do make haste, George! You'll make master knock twice, and you know nothing makes him so angry as that."

"That'll do him no harm, and it would me to be in a hurry after a full meal. My physician—aw—says that I—aw—must not exert myself too much—aw—for that I'm happoplektick, and that he wouldn't answer for my life."

The master knocked again, and louder than before; indeed, he had scarcely finished knocking, when the fat and lazy Mumford arrived and let him in.

"You are demned slow, George, in your attendance on the door!" cried Mr. Yapp, in his old tones. "You must be more alert, boy, or you won't suit me. Where is your mistress?"

"She is away at her father's, in Cross Street, Sir," replied the page. "And so is the children, too."

"What!—are you sure?"

"Well, I took them, Sir, so I don't think I'm mistaken," said the youth, with a knowing look. "Shall I take your coat, Sir?"

"Do so," said Mr. Yapp. "Wife and children gone," he muttered to himself, pulling off his coat, not knowing the damning stains that were on it. "Hum!—and did your mistress leave no message, no note for me?"

"Not with me, Sir."

"With Sarah, perhaps?"

"I'm quite sure she didn't. I saw her last; and then she said to me, 'don't wait up, I shall not return to-night.'"

"Hum—strange! But I'm not sorry," he again muttered to himself, going up the stairs to the drawing-room. "Bring up brandy and hot water, boy!"

When George returned to the warm kitchen, well lit with gas, and showing everything of domestic comfort and plenty about it, and thinking his master was "done-up" for the night, he said to Sarah, who sat by the fire mending a white stocking—

"Sarah, master looks very wild to-night; not drunk, you know—but wild-looking."

"What did he say, George, when you told him missus wouldn't be home to-night?"

"Hum'd and Ha'd. and seemed in a complete flutter and fluster. He didn't want me to see it; but I did see it. I think our wages is shaky."

"I shall insist on having mine to morrow," said the girl, looking up from her work.

"I think I shall insist on having mine to-night. Why should I wait for my dues? They've quarrelled—they've sold all their jewellery—and missus has gone away."

"That's all rubbidge," said Sarah.

"'Taint 'rubbidge,' as you will call it. You'll never get advanced in life Sarah, while you speak so unproper. Lord, there's his bell again! What can he want now? Past twelve—Lord, hark at the bell! But I shall take my time," said the page, walking leisurely out of the kitchen, with his hands in his pockets. "I'm not going to work after hours for any master, more especially for one who don't pay."

"Do make haste, George," said Sarah, when the bell had rung a third time. "You will get into trouble if you don't mind what you are about."

"If master is so impatient he must leave me, or I must him—which is one and the same thing," said George, quickening his pace, for his master, tired of ringing, came from his room, and with a loud voice called out for his page.

"Demn it, Sir! what is the matter with you?"

"I was fast asleep, Sir," said George; "it's past twelve, and I'm not in good health. And I'm in a little anxiety about my wages."

"What is owing to you?"

"Last quarter and part of this, if you please, Sir. And it would be very acceptable, for I want to bury my sister."

"Is she dead?"

"Oh dear, yes, Sir; I shouldn't want to bury her alive. That would be murder!"

Oh, how the master started at this unintentional hit at his guilty soul.

The page was alarmed at the change in Mr. Yapp, and the dreadful look that mantled his face.

"Please, Sir, I hope I haven't said anything to hurt your feelings. I hope you didn't understand me to say that I *had* murdered my sister."

"I hardly know; George—what—what I understood—get more brandy. My wife—your mistress—did you say you went with her to her father's?"

"I went with her first to Mr. Lambert's——"

"Who is Lambert?" inquired the frenzied clerk.

"Lambert, Sir, is a man who buys old jewellery, and gold and silver of any sort or kind. I should say he was a Jew, for he looked very much like one."

"And do you know what your mistress wanted with him?"

"I don't positively know; but it is my impression that she went there to sell her jewellery. I know she packed it up in her mahogany desk that usually stands on the table behind you, Sir."

"What! You are mad, boy!"

"And I must be blind, too, if I didn't see all I tell you. And what makes me think she sold the jewellery was this——"

George paused.

"Well? Go on! Speak, and speak quickly! Sold her jewellery?"

"You quite alarm me, Sir," said George, who never saw his master in such an excited state before.

"Demn it! tell me all you know."

"I will tell you all I know—I can't do more, Sir."

"You fool! you've too many words for me."

"I was always highly hedicated, and it takes a good many words to express my thoughts."

"Answer my questions, fool! or I will knock you down!"

"You had better not, Mr. Yapp," said George, rather pluckily. "I don't deserve so many insults—and I won't stand 'em neither. Pay me my wages, and I'll leave the place this very night."

"Where is your mistress?"

"At her father's."

"And my children?"

"At their grandfather's."

"Did you see your mistress give Mr. Perkins any money?"

"I did not, Sir; for when she got to Cross Street, she sent me back here after the children."

The clerk wrung his hands, and gazed wildly to the ceiling. Then he went to the mantelpiece, and leant his head on his hand, and audibly groaned. Rallying from this position, he emptied off his glass of brandy and water, and prepared himself another.

George, anxious to get from his miserable presence, asked his master if he might go to bed? He received no answer, and after a minute repeated the question.

"Do you know if she received any money from Lambert?"

"I do not, Sir. I was attending on a sick brother—"

"You said sister, just now."

"Yes, Sir—sister—I meant sister when I said brother."

"Did you see your mistress put the jewellery in the desk?"

"No, Sir—I didn't; but I saw her take it out on Mr. Lambert's counter. I noticed particularly the christening cup."

"My God! Oh! the wilful woman! Call a cab!—yet—no, no, never mind. Let her go—let her go! 'Tis bettah that she should. Get you to bed. Stay. Bring me another bottle of brandy. Has Cumbahland been here to-day?"

"Yes, Sir—and I gave him your note. He read it at the door."

"Well? What did he say? Did he see your mistress?"

"Oh yes—and stopped a long time."

"Ha! Now I'm bettah recouciled to—to—"

He did not finish the sentence. The boy went and returned with another bottle of brandy, and gladly left his master for that night.

And the wretched man passed the dismal night with his own dread thoughts—the glaring eye of the murdered Swift constantly before him.

CHAPTER XXXV.

SQUIRE SEYMOUR.—THE GIPSY WOMAN.—HOPES OF FINDING A LOST CHILD.

A FEW miles from Exeter there was an estate of unusual richness and dimensions. Acres and acres of wood, park, and pasturage stretched for miles in unbroken beauty.

Amidst this rich and productive country, Squire Seymour, the lord of the manor and village had built for himself a beautiful mansion in the best form and style of modern architecture. It was imposing in its aspect, and commodious in all its arrangements.

When Squire Seymour inherited the estate, the manor-house was of the Elizabethan period. He had no feeling for the antique, and picturesque as the old house was, he destroyed it, and at great expense built upon its prominent site the noble stone mansion that may now be seen.

The village of Wilby reposed in a quiet valley, and from the village many miles of delightful country had to be traversed before the manor-house was reached.

Up-hill and down-dale—well, and then you wouldn't find Squire Seymour's residence, for you must traverse hill and dale again, and then cross a heath of many barren and weird-like acres, and then many style-enclosed meadows and pasturages dotted with browsing cattle, and then ramble through long Devonshire lanes, perfumed with nature's sweetnesses, and gay with nature's wild flowers—before you come to the entrance to Wilby Park, which was well wooded and full of deer.

Entering this noble park, and at the end of a winding avenue stood the noble manor-house, with every possible convenience for a gentleman's use. Stables and kennels were not the least important feature of the building, for the Squire passed the chief part of his life with his horse and hounds.

Squire Seymour was very far from being a jolly man, or even an agreeable one, although he was fond of field sports. Since the death of his wife, some ten years since, he gave himself up a good deal to solitude, living alone, riding alone, speaking to no one.

He always wore a look of sorrow on his handsome and intellectual face; but it was not an unaccountable sorrow, for it was well known over the whole country, that he had lost an infant boy his only son. The villagers and his tenants forgave him many a hard word, and many a proud look, in remembrance of his loss, but while most sympathised with him, there were a few ill-natured spirits who said that his sorrow was assumed, and that the child had been put away by him, for that he had been jealous of his wife and suspected the boy—the missing boy—was not his own.

But there were only a few—a very few—who thus misinterpreted the Squire's sorrow, and amongst those was Roland Janson, the village blacksmith, who had lost the custom of the Squire for his clumsy performances in the operation of shoeing Mr. Seymour's horses.

Some little colour was given to this uncharitable opinion of the blacksmith's by the known fact that the Squire and his wife lived rather an unhappy life; but that arose from another circumstance, and had nothing to do with their lost son, who they both dearly and tenderly loved. Indeed there was little doubt at the time, that the mysterious loss of her child hastened the mother's death.

The Squire, too, when the little boy was found wanting, used every possible means to recover him. He offered large rewards, and rode night and day, from town to town, and village to village. But alas! all his efforts were vain and fruitless.

The lost child, when it was stolen was only a twelvemonth old; it had been left by its nurse for a few minutes playing on a sunny lawn, and when the girl returned, why lo! the child had disappeared.

With the disappearance of the child, also disappeared a Mrs. Walpole, a lady of considerable property who also resided at Wilby. This circumstance reasonably led to the opinion that wherever the lady was there would the child be found.

There was a deadly enmity between the Squire and Mrs. Walpole, and this confirmed the belief in her having stolen the child in malice.

On the heath, bordering the manor-house, was a gipsy's encampment, and about the time that the child was lost a gipsy woman of commanding figure and appearance was seen near by the spot. The Squire charged this woman with having stolen the child at Mrs. Walpole's bidding, and he had her tried before the county magistrates for the same. But although he could not substantiate the charge, and she was acquitted, the Squire always remained in the conviction that she was the thief.

Ever after, Squire Seymour became the formidable enemy of the poor gipsys, and behaved harshly to them, and would have hunted them from the heath they dwelt on had he the power; but the heath happened not to belong to his estate, and he could not order them from the enjoyments of their open-air home.

Never did the Squire cross the heath, but what he would manage to accost some of the gang of gipsys, and shake his whip at them, men, women, and children. And if by any possible accident either of them was caught on his estate, his servants were peremptorily ordered to hunt them away as if they were wild beasts of the field.

"You can just believe what you like," said Janson the blacksmith—a stalwart man, with a fire-burnt face—to a labouring villager, who stood by the postern of the smithy, while the hammer clanked on the anvil, and the bellows made the fire roar. "You can believe what you like about Squire Seymour's child. And I 'spose I might do the same, and no harm atween us."

"Lookee here, Janson," said the villager, "I doan't care about the Squoire more than you. But zounds! you doan't make me believe that he has made away with his own flesh and blood."

"Noa, noa, Giles, I doan't zay that, but I do zay that Squire knows where cheild is," said the blacksmith, his bare brawny arms pulling his bellows. "It's all make-believe,

MR. YAPP FLIES FROM HIS PURSUERS.

jist to cover the rumpages that used to take place in the house atween the Squoire and her leddyship that is in her grave—where he might be, too, vor all I keard."

"Waal, but lookee here, Janson, What do'er zay about Mistus Warlpole? She's gane, az well as the cheeld. And you know az well az I do that she owed Squoire a grudge."

"Waal, Giles, and doantee think that Mistus Warlpole was very ill-treated by Squoire?"

"I doan't know that she war, Janson."

"Hoa! how wudst loike a darter ov thoine to be jilted on her marriage-day?—answer me that, Giles,"

"I doan't know, I'm zure; but if my darter's lovyer loiked to change mind in church, all I can zay, better for gurl than change moind arter he's married."

"That be all very voine, but zome gurls, loike Mistus Warlpole's darter, went and broke her heart, cuz you know she loiked Squoire."

18

"Waal, and if Squoire zeed zumbody else he loiked better than Mistus Warlpole's darter, dang my buttons I doan't zee why he owt to marry her."

"Doan't be a vool, Giles," said the blacksmith. "If Squoire had zarved my darter as he did Mistus Warlpole's, I'd ha' hoided him—aye that I would. He broke her heart, Giles—doan't forgit that. And I zay, whatever Mistus Warlpole has done it zarves him right."

"The passon wouldn't zay so, Janson. ' Vengeance is moine, and I will repay it ' zaith the Lord.' "

"You go on zo jist cauz you work for Squoire," said Janson.

"And you go on zo agin Squoire, jist cauz you doan't. When you shoed Squoire's hosses, then you stook up for Squoire. Darned if Squoir beant a-riding this way now!" cried Giles, as he saw the lord of the manor, in hunting costume, on his favourite grey cob, coming rapidly towards the smithy.

The Squire knew very well that Janson was no friend of his, and, therefore, he was very severe if he knew any of his domestics or farm-servants associated with him. Directly Giles saw him riding toward where he stood, by the smithy door, he almost trembled, for the Squire was a very violent man, and there was a good deal of the old feudal lord's temper and arrogance in his composition. Poor Giles, although he had been arguing—if the humble conversation with the two villagers might be so dignified—with Janson in favour of his master, still he knew, that even if allowed an opportunity of explaining, it would not save him from his violence.

He sped like a fury through the stony village, and without reining up to the trembling Giles, he rode on shaking his long whip at him, loudly exclaiming—

"Why are you loitering there ? Go home !"

With hat in hand, the trembling labourer replied, although the Squire was out of hearing—

"Please, measter, I'se on my way whoam."

The smith left his bellows and came to the hatchway of his house, and laid his brawny, hairy arms on it, and looked after the galloping Squire, and then he said to Giles—

"I wouldn't have taken off my hat to zuch a hell-hound as he."

"Hoa, but you would though, if your vamily had depended for bread on him," said Giles. "But you are moighty independent." And Giles, with stooping shoulders, his hands under his smock, loutishly stalked off to his "whoam" up the village, his thickly-nailed high-lows leaving an impress in the dusty road at every step he took.

The Squire not many hours ago had read, in an old number of the *Times*, Mrs. Walpole's advertisment about her lost ring. The initials on the ring, and other particulars, confirmed him that this must be the ring he presented to Miss Walpole, his affianced bride, on the day preceding that his marriage with her was to have taken place.

This paper containing the advertisement he saw by the merest accident at the house of a county magistrate, where he had called after his day's hunting. He was overjoyed, and returned with all speed to the manor-house to prepare for a journey to London, and to Bolt Court, Mrs. Walpole's garret home.

On his way to his residence he crossed the heath, and saw a gipsy woman standing at her tent with a baby in her arms. He reined up before the woman, exclaiming, with up-raised whip—

"I shall find my son after all, you yellow-skinned witch !"

Then he set spurs to his horse, almost riding over the defiant woman, and stopped not until he reached his baronial residence.

CHAPTER XXXVI

THE CHANDLER'S SHOP.—ALTERCATION BE-
TWEEN MR. AND MRS. PERKINS.—THREAT-
ENED VISIT TO THE FORTUNE-TELLER'S.—
INEVITABLE RUIN.

AFTER the disposal of her counterfeit jewellery to Tom Brown's master, poor Mrs. Yapp, deeply chagrined and humiliated, and entertaining the deepest hatred of the husband who had duped her, made haste to her father's with the small produce of it—thirty-eight pounds twelve shillings.

She was in such impatience to reach her father's, with her sad suspicions that she had married a swindler, that the movement of the cab fretted her with its want of speed. Going along, she determined to send back Mumford, who rode with the cabman on the box, for her two children, let the consequences be what they might ; and she also determined never more to return to the husband who had forfeited all claims to her love, respect, or duty.

When the cab drew up to Mr. Perkins's shop of all-sorts, from a red-herring to a bachelor's tea-kettle, and from ha'penny dips to cream-laid writing-paper—the chandler was sitting in the little back-parlour talking over the money difficulties his son-in-law of mystery had plunged him into.

It must not be forgotten that before Mr. Yapp left his home on the day of Swift's murder on the Thames, he left notes for both Mr. Cumberland and Mr. Perkins. That note the chandler now held in his hand, and was discussing its disappointing contents with his spouse.

"I begin to think, Mrs. Perkins, that Mr. Yapp is a Jeremy Diddler, and that he has duped our daughter, and ruined us."

"I'm sure I don't think no such thing, Jacob," said Mrs. Perkins, full of her old faith in her showy, gentlemanly son-in-law ; "what he says is right enough—that until the mystery of his birth——"

"Bother his birth ! I wish he had never been born ! Begin to doubt that mystery is a bad thing to invest money in !"

"You *are* changing," said Mrs. Perkins.

"Changing ! Isn't it enough to make anybody change when his opinions have brought stark-staring ruin to his face ? Our mystery-mongering won't pay our bills. It won't do to tell the man, when he presents my acceptance due to-day, to hold it over until Mr. Yapp comes into his estate, or the ' unseen hands ' supply him with money. That bill must be paid, or we are ruined—absolutely ruined !"

"Well, it wasn't my doings as much as your own, Jacob," said his wife, woman-like, who actively supported him in all his doings, and at the sight of a failure turns round upon him by saying, "Well, it was your own fault ; had you listened to me it would never have happened."

"It doesn't matter one pinch of snuff whose doings it was, the result falls upon both of us equally—and equally, Mrs. Perkins, we are ruined, if that bill is not paid this day."

"Surely it can be renewed?"

"Surely it cannot. You don't know what you are talking about, Mrs. Perkins; and as for memory, you are entirely destitute of it."

"That always was your cowardly way to insult me when anything happened. What has my memory, I should like to know, to do with Mr. Yapp's bills?"

"Nothing—there! Nothing, I say!" cried the chandler, resting his hands on the elbows of his chintz-covered easy-chair, leaning forward and looking with dreadful ill-temper in his wife's face; "but when you talk of renewing—if you had any memory, you would have remembered that it had already been renewed three times!"

"I'll see the man myself when he brings the bill, and I'll be bound that I'll get him to renew it again," said Mrs. Perkins, pulling up her nose with a great deal of self-sufficiency, although quite ignorant of what she was talking about.

"Mrs. Perkins," said the chandler, again fixing his grey eye on her face, "I beg that you will say no more about a matter of which you are so entirely ignorant! Pray what has the man who brings the bill for payment to do with it? No more than that little girl you served just now with a Bath brick."

"Then, who has to do with it?"

"The holder of the bill."

"Well, and won't the man who brings it to be paid be the holder of the bill?"

Mr. Perkins could stand his wife's supreme ignorance no longer. He literally jumped from his chair, went into the shop, and slammed the glass-door so violently in the face of his wife, that it proved how strongly the panes must have been glazed in, or the four of them would have come smash to the floor.

Mrs. Perkins followed her high-passioned husband to the shop, saying—

"Look here, Jacob Perkins,—that is not proper treatment to your lawful wife, and I won't put up with it either!"

"You may do as you like about that," said the chandler, placing some bars of soap in a drawer. "I can't abide ignorance. I have tried all in my power to make you an intelligent woman, but you won't learn."

"Dear me! didn't you tell me that the holder of the bill was the person to whom the money was due?"

"I did. What of that?"

"Why, won't the holder of the bill be the person who presents it for payment?" said Mrs. Perkins.

"Certainly not."

"Oh, indeed! then I am an ignorant woman. Who is the holder of this cheese?" she pertinaciously asked, taking a cheese from the counter.

Mr. Perkins looked, but disdained to answer.

"Who is the holder of this cheese?" said Mrs. Perkins, repeating her question in tones that scarcely left the chandler room for escaping it. "Answer me, Jacob Perkins!"

"You are; but it don't belong to you for all that."

"It belongs to me while I hold it, doesn't it?"

"In that sense it does; but you dare not do what you like with it, because it is not your property," said the chandler, still busy with the bars of soap.

"And pray whose property is it?" asked Mrs. Perkins, still poising the round cheese in her two hands.

"Mine," was the gruff monosyllabic reply.

"Oh, bless my soul, Sir! I have yet to learn that what is yours is not mine."

"I was only speaking for argument," said Mr. Perkins.

"I beg that you won't get such arguments into your head any more, then. For I would have you to know, Jacob Perkins, that this business, and all belonging to it, is as much mine as yours, and a good deal more, for I have worked harder in it than you have."

"It was bought with my money——"

"Pish!—what of that? There would have been no business worth having hadn't I managed it."

"You may imagine the whole world is yours if it will make you happier," said Perkins; "but I can assure you that if you dared to take anything in it that doesn't belong to you, you would find yourself in the wrong box."

"I am not in the habit of taking things that don't belong to me," said Mrs. Perkins, indignantly. "What next, I wonder? This cheese belongs to me, though!"

"You would find it didn't, if I chose to interfere," said Mr. Perkins. "And what's more, as a wife, there's nothing in the world that belongs to you—not even the gown you've got on your back."

"You come and take it off, then," said Mrs. Perkins, in the highest resentment and dudgeon.

"I am only telling you the law," said her husband.

"Burn the law! What do you know about the law? I'll throw the cheese at your head if you aggravate me any more. Me got nothing of my own, indeed!"

"In law a married woman has nothing; her husband takes all, and is responsible for all her acts, except those called criminal. But all this nonsensical talk won't pay the bill due this day. It must be paid in hard cash, or we are ruined, Mrs. Perkins; and this business, that we have been quarrelling about, will be seized by our creditors."

A clerk from the bank—a gentlemanly-looking young man—here called with the acceptance, and presented it for payment. The bill was for one hundred and fifty pounds, and drawn by Mr. Yapp on Mr. Jacob Perkins. Mr. Yapp got the bill discounted by Mr. Cumberland, and pocketed all the money.

"There, Mrs. Perkins," said her husband, taking the bill from the clerk, and showing her a number of names endorsed on the back of it, "if this bill is not paid by me it will go back to all these people, until it comes to the hands of Mr. Cumberland, the first name on the bill. He will then demand the money from either me or Mr. Yapp, or both of us. Mr. Cumberland will be the holder of the bill until either of us pay it."

"Shall I receipt it, Sir?" said the clerk.

"You may receipt it if you like, Sir," said Jacob Perkins, "but I cannot pay it."

"Can't you renew it, Sir?" said Mrs. Perkins.

The bank clerk smiled at the woman's simplicity, and said—

"Oh, dear, no; the bill is not mine; I only present it for payment on account of the bank I serve."

"I hope you are satisfied, Mrs. Perkins," said the chandler, "I suppose now a stranger has told you, you will believe him in preference to your husband."

The clerk after leaving a notice paper when

the bill was lying for payment, left, smiling and looking eager to get home to the bank to relate to his fellow clerks Mrs. Perkins's simplicity in believing that he had power to renew bills that he presented for payment.

"There, Mrs. Perkins," said the chandler, throwing the notice-paper, left by the bank-clerk on the parlour table, and himself into the easy chair, and crossing his legs, "if that one hundred and fifty pounds isn't paid by four o'clock, it will become blabbed to my creditors, and I shall be a ruined man, and I and you will have to end our days in the union."

"You *are* meeting trouble half way. Union indeed!"

"I wish I could wake you up to the seriousness of my position. Everything I have in the world is mortgaged to its fullest, and there is not a thing in the shop but what I owe for. And I say again, that if that bill is not paid I shall be a ruined man, and our home will be in the streets or the union."

"Then I say that you have done more for Mr. Yapp than you ought to have done," said Mrs. Perkins.

"There now !" exclaimed the chandler. "As if you didn't know what I had done for him—fool that I was!"

"I think so too."

"Yes, you think so," reiterated Mr. Perkins, "now the mischief is done. Why didn't you tell me I was a fool before? Why didn't you tell me to pause when you were present and saw me hand over the mortgage money of my houses at Brentford to Mr. Yapp? Why didn't you tell me not to do it when I took every penny of ready money I had out of the bank, and lent him? Ah! Mrs. Perkins, you can talk now—now when it is too late, and we are ruined."

"It can't be long now before William comes into his property ; or at all events his unseen friend's wont let him be long without money."

Mrs. Perkins now began to soften; her eyes were being opened to the position of her husband through his liabilities for his son-in-law.

"What good will it be to us if he comes into an earldom, after we have perished in a work-house? I must and will have my money! I cannot and will not befriend him any longer. Maria and her husband must live as poor people until they become rich people."

"Well, I'm very sorry for it, Jacob; for you know William has been the best of husbands to our Maria, and such a father never was seen. He has bought them everything—"

"Oh, ha, yes—I know that—with my money. Very good of him to be sure, but I am quite able to spend all I had without the kind assistance of Mr. Yapp. Look at his letter. The devil him-self cannot tell what the young man means. Then he keeps away from me, too ; and I never can see him—he's never to be seen at home or abroad; and as for his coming *here*—as for his coming to Cross Street—he's a long way too proud for that. I must get the money and be fool enough to take it to him! Did it ever occur to you, wife, but it has to me, that we have been taken in—that he is no child of mystery, and that he knows as much of his father and mother as we do of ours?"

"Ah, but what about the fortune-teller?" suggested Mrs. Perkins. "She told us all that he would come into an earldom after the birth of a third child."

"But what if he never has a third child? Answer me that, Mrs. Perkins."

"I know nothing about the future—not I. It isn't every one that is gifted with that know-ledge."

"I begin to think that nobody is," said Per-kins, becoming, from his losses and money diffi-culties, a wiser man. "I shall see the old fortune-teller again and immediately on the subject. She must be interrogated very closely by me. If sne could tell Mr. Yapp that he was the son of an earl, and that he would inherit his estates after the birth of a third child, she can tell me who this earl is."

"I don't see it, Jacob," said Mrs. Perkins, who was anxious to stop his journey to Dolly Spittleberg's, for she was afraid that he would elicit from the juggling crone the visit and prompting made by her and her daughter.

"Don't see it? then you must be stone blind !" cried Mr. Perkins, thrusting his hands under his shop apron, and balancing himself back on the hind legs of his chintz-covered chair. "She ought to be able to tell me all or nothing."

"That is stuff, Jacob," said Mrs. Perkins, folding her arms and throwing her feet, encased in Florentine shoes, on the fender before a fire after her own warm heart, cheerful and agreeable. "I may know how to make a nice cake—and you know I do—but I cannot make a good pie."

"What in the name of goodness have your cakes and puddings to do with the mysteries of the future? You'll drive me mad, Mrs. Per-kins !"

"Don't holloa, Jacob Perkins," said the wife. "If I have married a madman, I don't want our neighbours to know it. You know your own business best, that's all I care to say, and all I will say. if you talk till Domesday."

"If you did it wouldn't pay this bill of your gentlemanly son-in-law's, and which your fool of a husband is liable for. I tell you, Mrs. Perkins, there's a big bubble somewhere, and the sooner it bursts the better. I've known poverty before to-day, and I'm quite philosopher enough to make its acquaintance again. But I think of you, more than myself. You are very irritating, very provoking, and sometimes in your tantrums very false, and give me a bad name and a bad character; but on the whole—the only proper and charitable way to judge of each other—you have been a dutiful, faithful, loving wife to me—"

"Yes, I have always endeavoured to be," interrupted Mrs. Perkins, bringing her apron to her eyes.

"One who has been economical, cheerful, and not at all exacting; who has given her husband his way in most things, and been assiduous and attentive in his business; who has been a good housewife, a good cook, and a good mother."

"Ah, that I have, Jacob," said Mrs. Perkins, still in tears, at her husband's good opinion of her, "and if our Maria was standing before us she couldn't say otherwise. I've worked night and day for her, bless her heart : and I hope and trust I've made her a lady ; and if—and if, poor dear—she has made a mis—mistake in her husband—"

"Oh, I've no doubt in the world about that," chimed in Jacob after his wife's speech and sobs. "He's terribly in debt to others besides me. None of the tradespeople paid—not even George Mumford's livery."

"Whoever told you so ?"

"The boy himself," replied Mr. Perkins. "Butcher, baker, tailor, landlord—Mr. Yapp is in arrears with everybody."

"You mustn't believe all Jarrge says," was

Mrs. Perkins' remark to this astounding intelligence. "That boy was always a notorious liar—his very mother, you know, will say that of him."

"That's true—quite true," said Perkins. "Still the boy couldn't altogether have invented; there must have been some foundation for it."

"A very small one I hope," said Mrs. Perkins.

"And I hope so too. But the boy has no motive in injuring his master, therefore I am inclined to believe that there is more truth in his statement than would please us. Poor, poor Maria! I very much fear my folly has betrayed her into a deplorable marriage."

"What folly? What have you had to do with it? You couldn't help it, you know. She liked the young man, and, come to that, we all liked the young man."

"No, I won't have that, I did *not* like him," said Perkins, the chandler. "I thought him a bit of an upstart from the first."

"Don't turn round upon the poor young man," said Mrs. Perkins, "don't, for Maria's sake. Poor thing! if all be true you tell me, she must be nigh broken-hearted. She always was a proud-spirited girl, you know, and God only can tell what her and our dear little grandchildren will do."

"We must think a little for ourselves, too," said Mr. Perkins, somewhat affected by the tender tones of his wife.

"Those sweet little children are ourselves, Jacob. They are the precious ones of our only child, and we must be kind and merciful to them, whatever their father may be. They shall never want, I know, while I have anything to give them—bless their little hearts!"

How lamentable that there should be such bad news in store for such a goodnatured, unselfish creature as Mrs. Perkins. How will she—how can she—bear to hear that the father of those little children she has been so affectionately expressing herself about, was now a thief and a murderer and that his wife and little ones might now be well ashamed to call him husband and father?

A good deal, too, must be said for Mr. Yapp. He, in his ignorance, it may be remembered, while severely reflecting on the diabolical murder of Swift, heaped all the guilt of his life on his father and mother, whom he wrongfully accused of disowning him and making him an outcast upon the world.

CHAPTER XXXVII.

A LOVE STORY.—WOMAN'S REVENGE.—A BROKEN HEART.

THE most guilty person of our tragedy was Lady Blaze. It was her revengeful spirit that really wrought the clerk's irretrievable ruin. Had not her fiendish passion of revenge instigated her to steal the child from his father's watchful eye and his mother's tenderness, in all human probability he might now have been a bright and useful ornament in society, instead of having outraged and flying from it.

All his crimes, great as they were, must now rest upon the revengeful soul of Mrs. Walpole. But for her it must also be pleaded in extenuation, that she had received from Squire Seymour a deadly affront—one that a mother rarely forgives, never forgets. Through her broken-hearted daughter he had aimed at the mother the most killing blow it was possible for one human being to inflict upon another without absolutely destroying life.

And, yet, oh! ten thousand times rather Mrs. Walpole would have preferred that the Squire had stabbed both her and her daughter to the heart than have offended so basely as he did against their pride, and trustingness, and love.

Some four-and-twenty years ago—oh, it had been a long, long grief!—Squire Seymour and Mrs. Walpole, a wealthy widow, were neighbours in the village of Wilby, and in riches and social station were quite equals. The Squire, at this period, was a young, handsome man, and had just inherited his father's extensive estate; while Miss Walpole, search the world through, could not be out-rivalled for beauty. Her mother, and for that all, were devotedly attached to the young lady, whom everybody thought was destined to become mistress of the manor-house; unfortunately for her, no one thought it so much, or relied upon it so much, as her own sweet self. Surely she had a right to be so reliant on the Squire's honour—for was not the marriage-day appointed?—was not the marriage-robe made?—was not the marriage-ring bought?—were not the bridesmaids engaged, and the guests invited?—and had not the bells rang in the morning of the, alas! inauspicious wedding-day, with as merry a peal from Wilby old churchsteeple as ever bell poured forth?

But yet so near, 'twas not to be! Robed was the expectant bride in her rich wedding dress, and the young lady was taking a sad, fond parting with her mother, preparatory to passing to another social state, when a letter was handed to her from the dastard Squire, intimating that the wedding could not go forth, for he had changed his mind.

Miss Walpole loved the Squire true and tenderly. She eagerly read his cruel, cruel missive, and she dropped dead at her mother's feet. The deadly disappointment had gone direct to her loving, sensitive heart! The bride-elect of Squire Seymour in a moment became the bride of death, and her mother the victim of rage and despair.

Never was there such a scene of misery and consternation as this. The dead daughter on the ground, with the Squire's cruel letter in her hand—the woe-begone mother—the wonder of the guests. Those six fair creatures—Miss Walpole's bridesmaids—lifted the dead lady from the carpet, and laid her on the couch, while the other bridal friends ministered to the solace of the now childless mother.

The blow was so sudden—the surprise so great—that there was no time to ask for explanation; and when Mrs. Walpole bent low to her fallen daughter, and exclaimed in agonising accents that she was dead—"Dead!" was the word of surprise on everyone's lips.

The mother took the letter laden with such bitter news from the hands of the lily-white corpse, and read, and read again; and while she read, the very room shook with the passion of her frame.

"Good friends, take this!" she exclaimed, "and read of Squire Seymour's shame." Then she took her handkerchief and buried her weeping face in it, convulsively sobbing—

"Oh, my child—my child! do wake again, for my sake! Her tender heart is broken—broken! Dear friends, leave me to my grief! You that so kindly came to share my joy, shall not be recompensed with my woe. Come round my child first, and take your farewells of her!"

The distressed mother fell into a chair at the head of the couch, and sobbed hysterically. The friends, bridesmaids and all, assembled round the lovely corpse—more lovely even in death than life. In her satin shroud she lay, her hands crossed on her bosom, and while all wept, she smiled.

A tall, elderly gentleman, in white waistcoat, and dress coat of the most admirable make, with hair and whiskers as white as snow, here silently approached Mrs. Walpole, whose head was still bowed on the end of the couch that contained the still-warm corpse of her darling child—love's martyr—and gently said—

"My dear Madam, permit me instantly to hasten to Squire Seymour for an explanation of his base conduct?—and communicate to him the dreadful results of it."

"If you regard me, Sir, do no such thing. Though it would bring her from the realms of death, I would not do it. Oh, Sir, respect a mother's pride. God bless her, *she* is dead! Mine will be a living death!"

"Believe me, dear Madam, it would be but right for you to know the Squire's reasons for this base conduct. Had you or your sweet daughter—whose fate we all intensely deplore, and whose memory will be ever cherished by us— ever received intimation of this guilty fickleness on the part of Squire Seymour?"

"Never, Sir. Therein lies its cruelty! He was too well loved by her,"—pointing to the corpse—"and for *her* sake I loved him also. But my heart is now full of hatred."

"Oh, be calm, Mrs. Walpole," spoke another visitor.

"Be calm!" she reiterated. "Be calm, and look there! Oh, no, no! It is cruel to ask it from me. Do me one favour—retire all of you, and let my grief find vent."

The company begged to remain with her, but she imploringly forbade it.

"To see you all attired in my daughter's honour, and she lying there in the cold grasp of death, mocks me, dear friends. Leave me, I beseech you! I have many prayers to say, and much to think about. Loneliness now and for ever will be my portion. It is no small addition to my grief to part with you; but, dear friends, I must now stand apart in the world. When the dead is buried out of my sight——"

She could not finish the sentence. Parting from her daughter!—Oh, no; though dead, the thought of parting she could not bear.

The beauteous bridesmaids came and knelt about the lovely corpse, kissing her hands and brow, and gazing with eyes full of tears on the dead being of their sincere affections. Poor young lady! she was deeply loved by all, and by none more so than those of her own sex. Pitiful painful—but the parting must be, and one by one they took their tenderest farewell, each praying in the inmost recesses of their souls for support from on high to the stricken mother.

Yet they were all soon to meet again—but in sable suits of woe; and Wilby bells, the echoes of whose marriage peals were still fresh on the ear of the mourners, tolled out in minute periods that all that was mortal of Alice Walpole was about to be consigned to the silent tomb.

Toll, toll the bell!—and while it tolled the mournful procession moved slowly across road and meadow to Wilby churchyard, and there,

amidst the tears of the villagers who had now gathered together with the friends of the deceased, and as the impressive service was read in choked utterance by one who knew and well regarded her, poor Alice was gently lowered in the dust.

As the villagers returned towards home, and as they passed the manor-house, the residence of Squire Seymour, some coarse yet honest remarks were made about him, and the women almost cursed him.

Mrs. Walpole could not be persuaded against following her daughter, and at the grave, to the surprise of every one present, she seemed less affected than the other mourners. Her grief was running into hatred and revenge for the slayer of her daughter. Oh! what a look, as she moved homewards with the other mourners, did she cast on the manor-house that her dear dead daughter was to have been the lady of. Inwardly she heaped the deepest curses on the Squire's head, and vowed revenge.

On the night following the funeral, Mrs. Walpole stole abroad and alone when all else were sleeping and the village was at rest, to Wilby churchyard. The moon was abroad, but it was ever and anon obscured by black clouds that travelled over it; and as she paused at her daughter's new-made grave, the turned-up mould about it smelling sweet, she was sometimes shrouded in darkness, sometimes well defined in the moonlight.

It was a summer's night, and the nightingale in the copse of an unfrequented, solitary meadow abutting on the churchyard, sang out delicious, plaintive grief, so much in harmony with the mother-mourner at her daughter's grave,

"Where all abandon'd to despair, she sings
  Her sorrows through the night; and on the bough
  Sole sitting, still, at every dying fall,
  Takes up again her lamentable strain
  Of winding woe; till, wide around the woods
  Sigh to her song, and with her wail resound."

Bending over the grave, and kneeling by it, Mrs. Walpole lost herself in holy grief, mingled with fiendish passions. Her terrible vows of revenge were deep and reached to heaven.

"He shall not live!" this was her first resolve. "O God! make me Thine instrument of revenge for this untimely murder of the sweetest of Thy creatures. She that knew no harm—thought no harm; whose soul was full of goodness, and whose young life was full of love, make me Thine instrument to avenge her death."

But the prayers of the avenger are never heard in heaven; and Mrs. Walpole felt, even while she vowed, that her prayer was an unrighteous one, and one that would never meet Almighty sanction and support.

Often and often would she pass the night, from the matin of the nightingale until the lark heralded the morn, still with unholy thoughts of vengeance burning in her soul and escaping her lips. Her life henceforth became a slave and a devotion to the passion of revenge.

Squire Seymour had never been asked for an explanation of his conduct to Alice Walpole, and therefore never ventured to offer one. But rumour said he had become suddenly smitten with another—a rustic beauty of an adjoining village, without money, connexion, or education. And for once rumour was right; for in less than two months from the death of Alice, he led to the altar of her own church, and amongst her own relatives, the daughter of one Mr. Fairburn.

who happened to be the cousin of Tom Brown's mother.

But the unequal alliance proved—as all wrong things do—a source of evil and unhappiness both to the Squire and his rustic bride. After twelve-months had worn away, and she had borne him a little boy, he shunned her society, and quietly treated her with neglect. But she happened to be an amiable girl, and locked up his cold treatment in her own heart, breathing no word of it to friend or relative.

Mrs. Seymour could not but often feel herself out of her position when she trod the baronial halls of her rich husband, and associated with his aristocratic friends. But she was not a woman to feel deeply, and as she showed no resentment, took no umbrage, to the Squire's frigid treatment, they lived a quiet but far from a comfortable existence.

As time wore on, Mrs. Walpole's grief became subdued, but her hatred to the Squire became more intense. She despised the ground he trod on, and for two years she deliberated how to wreak her vengeance on the man who had so mercilessly destroyed her daughter.

During this period she reared a handsome white marble tomb to her child in Wilby church-yard, on which she had had inscribed by the sculptor in gold:—

A Mother's Love
raises

THIS TOMB

In Memory

of

ALICE WALPOLE,

who was

Suddenly struck down by a blow

from

One in whom she trusted.

At length a cruel thought occurred to her to steal the Squire's child, a bonny infant boy of a year old. Child for child! The very thought gave her infinite delight, and she lost no time in thinking how it could best be done. She went off to London, where she had a residence at the West-end, and tampered with one of her female domestics by the name of Yapp, a widow, to go to Wilby, and live there until an opportunity was afforded her of taking the boy, and returning to London with it.

The old domestic, who acted chiefly out of sympathy for her mistress, whose daughter she knew and loved, and partly for a handsome sum of money on the consummation of the deed, was not slow in carrying out her mistress's wishes. To Wilby, well supplied with money, she went, and had not been there long until an opportunity offered itself, by which she could effect her purpose. She played her part well, and watched and prowled about the manor-house, until one day the infant boy was left alone upon the lawn, when, like a hawk, she pounced upon it, and fled at once to London with her prize—an inestimable one to the mind of Mrs. Walpole.

When the child was in the power of the revengeful lady, she shrank from it as if it had been a viper. She highly complimented the Widow Yapp on her admirable performance of her delicate yet fiendish commission, but begged her to take the babe from her sight, or she would not answer for what might happen; and the babe was at once placed out to be nursed by a needy woman, a friend of Mrs. Yapp's, in the neighbourhood of Kennington.

Here, under the name of Yapp, the boy grew to boyhood; then he was sent to a parochial school, and from school the humble situation of errand-boy was procured for him. Being a boy of some promise, quick at figures, and writing a good mercantile hand, he was speedily promoted to the post of junior clerk at the place where he commenced as a London errand-boy.

Of course he was often desirous to know of the woman who brought him up who and where his father and mother was. But he could learn nothing more than that she did not, nor did she know where the money came from that was sent by post for his support. Thus the poor boy could glean nothing about his parents; and he often blamed those who were racked and agonised about his loss, for their cruelty in separating themselves from him.

As he approached manhood, Mrs. Walpole conceived the dread idea of avenging her daughter's death by taking the life of the young man; and while this ghastly thought haunted her, she left her luxurious West-end establishment to the care of the Widow Yapp, and followed young Seymour from place to place, sacrificing every comfort, in order to be near him, while she trained her unholy mind to take his life. But it was well for her that she could not reach the enormity of so foul a crime; but she got her daily solace from the fact that her diabolical deed of stealing the child must have been a terrible source of agony to the tenants of Wilby manor-house.

CHAPTER XXXVIII.

AN ARRIVAL.—MRS. YAPP'S REVELATIONS OF HER HUSBAND.—A BOUNCEABLE BOY.

JUST as Mr. and Mrs. Perkins were toning themselves down to the inevitable ruin Mr. Yapp had plunged them in, a cab drove up to their shop, and the old folks at once recognised George Mumford, the page, sitting on the box with the cabman.

Before fat George had time to get from the box, the chandler and his wife were at the cab door embracing their daughter, who was heavy with grief, and her eyes red with weeping.

Mrs. Yapp hastened through the shop to the back parlour, the old folks on her heels imploring her to tell them whatever was the matter.

"Here, my dear, let me take your bonnet," said Mrs. Perkins, quite at her wits' end how to make enough of this unexpected visit from her daughter. "I and your father have been talking about you and your husband——"

"Husband! Oh, mother, my husband has been the ruin of us all! By what I know and what I've heard I fear that I have been duped into marriage with a very bad man."

"Maria!" exclaimed both mother and father, the former clasping her hands, and the latter looking with open mouth in his daughter's passionate face.

"I am with you now to return no more," said Mrs. Yapp.

"But let us hear, my dear, what it is all about," said her father.

"Aye, to be sure, let us hear," said her mother. "A lover's quarrel, I'll be bound, and nothing more."

"Indeed, it is very much more," said Mrs. Yapp. "Do not fail to understand me as quickly as you both can, that ever since I have been his wife I have been kept on the fruits of debt and knavery. But your bill, father!—that is my first concern. How will you manage to pay it?"

"I can't manage it at all; and if Mr. Yapp is what you say, why then, as I have been just telling your mother, I am a ruined man, and there is nothing before us but the union."

"Father," said Mrs. Yapp, bursting into tears, and throwing her purse of money on the table, "I have done my very best for you. In that purse is the produce of all my jewellery, including the christening cup belonging to my little girl, and the silver teapot you gave me. It being my own, I was determined to sell it to help you over your difficulties. And how much do you think I got for all of it?"

"Well, I'm sure I don't know," said Mr. Perkins, stroking his shining bald head.

"You had a fine lot, that's truth," said her mother.

"It was a fine lot!" exclaimed Mrs. Yapp. "A fine lot of rubbish and deception! Guess—what did I get for it?"

"A large sum, I daresay, my dear," said her father. "But you must remember, Maria, that there is a great difference between buying and selling. You know your husband——"

"Don't call him so, father. The name sickens me! I could have borne it, had I only been made to suffer! But that your hard savings should have been lost by his falsehoods, is more than I can think of without the greatest hatred to him."

"Take off your things, Maria, and tell me what I shall get for you."

"Nothing, mother, thank you," said Mrs. Yapp, throwing her muff and bonnet on one side. "I'm too excited for eating.—George!" she called to the page, who stood by the counter. The proud fat boy entered the parlour.

"Jarge looks well at any rate," said Mrs. Perkins. "I hope you have found him a good boy, Maria."

The page objected to the term "boy," and puffed out his cheeks in disdain, then fixed his staring eyes on his mistress to see what she would reply to her mother's question about his goodness.

"The farce is at an end, and I shall not make any complaints of him. I am sorry to say, mother, that he keeps up his old practice of lying."

George could have annihilated the whole of the Perkinses had had he the power. But he threw himself back on his old hypocritical dodgery, and said—

"You are rayther hard on me, mum. I know when I lived in Cross Street and associated with wicked boys I told a story or two, but I think if missus only considers a bit she must say that I wouldn't tell a lie now for all the world! I learnt a great deal of good while I was at Mrs. Yapp's, and it was a great blessing to me that I ever went there."

This bit of blarney worked miracles with the simple-hearted Mr. and Mrs. Perkins, and the latter said, with a sigh and a smile dimpling all over her shining face—

"Ah, I'm sure I'm very glad to hear that, Jarge."

The page's mistress said neither nay or yea to Mumford's deceit, and she bade him return with the cab and bring her two children back immediately.

"Would you like a bit of something to eat before you went, Jarge?" said Mrs. Perkins.

"Don't detain him now, mother," said Mrs. Yapp. "I am so anxious to obtain my children. He cannot possibly be hungry."

"I am rather hungry, mum—the air is keen this morning; but, of course—oh, dear, no—I won't delay if you wish it."

"I do, most particularly. You can get something when you go home, while Sarah prepares the children."

"Look here, Jarge," said Mrs. Perkins, putting about half a pound of old Cheshire in his hands and half of a half-quartern loaf. "Eat it in the cab as you go along. There, be off with you."

George blessed the old lady, and got a shilling from his mistress for tolls. He then jumped into the cab, and while he sat on one cushion, he placed his feet on another, and ate his bread and cheese with the most supreme happiness. When out of sight he ordered cabby to pull up, and he got out and lingered over a glass of old ale, in payment of which he changed the shilling given for tolls. After he had satisfied himself he came to the door, and said—

"Aw—cabby, will you have a glass of anything—aw?"

Cabby was always quick at attending to an "invite" of this sort, and the two fraternised over another glass of old ale.

"Aw—well, old fellah," said George to the many-wrappered cabman, "this will shell out a good fare to you—aw?"

"That all werry much depends on how much will be afforded for it," was the reply.

"We always pay according to Act of Parliament—aw," said the page, taking a Banbury cake from under a glass cover on the bar-counter. "The keen air makes me peckish—aw!"

"So it does me," said cabby, giving the page a gentle hint that he was open to an offer of something to eat. But the page's shilling wouldn't run to it, or rather he wanted it all for his own rapacious stomach, which made incessant demands upon him for supplies. The only reply George made was—

"I'm sure it must; why don't you treat yourself the same as I am doing? An empty stomach is the worst thing in the world. Look here, I'll show you a heart—give me another Banbury cake."

"I've got heart enough to order a cake, and stomach enough to eat one—but I've no money, young gen'lman, for luxuries. I only wish I had been a gen'lman's servant, like you."

"Well—aw—yes, a very good thing, no doubt, as things go. But my edication, and the family I come from, qualifies me for a cut above buttons. My mother is a lady——"

"Lord, I thought the boys said she kipt a mangle!" interrupted cabby.

"Boys will say anything in chaff," said George, with too much effrontery to blush. "But you ought to have too much sense to repeat it. I wish now I had punished them more than I did. You saw me knock two of them down with one blow, and then the others ran away."

"Oh, yes, I saw that," said cabby, who was, like Mumford, always a ready liar when he hoped to get something by it, and he was very anxious to get a crust of bread and cheese out of the page, and he was quite 'cute lad enough to see that it might be done by a "little flattery,"

THE CORPSE OF SWIFT BECAME ENTANGLED IN THE SHIP'S CHAINS.

so well recommended by King Richard the Third. Men find it more easy to flatter than to praise. At all events, flattery had the effect on Mumford so well expressed by an old author, that—

"Flattery is an ensnaring quality, and leaves a very dangerous impression. It swells a man's imagination, entertains his vanity, and drives him to a doting upon his own person."

The cabman's lying observation had all this effect upon the page, and he really began to think himself valiant and brave, and he exclaimed, bending his fist—

"Yes, I think I showed 'em all pretty well, not to make any mistake about me! Take a cake cabby; and I'll have another. I say, you can manage to bilk the toll, can't you?"

"By driving a little furder out of my way."

"Good! then we'll have this shilling to our own cheek. Another glass of ale for me."

"You'll excuse me," said soapy cabby, "but I don't think the shilling will run to no more. You've had two glasses and three cakes, and I've had one glass and one cake; and I think you'll find that jist the money."

19

"Aw—demn it!—never thought of that," said George; "but you are right."

"Oh, that's right enough. How will you manage about the change from the toll?"

"Don't see what you mean, old boy."

"Why, the toll is but tuppence—then you should have tenpence out for the missus."

"That shows you know nothing about haristocratic families. Change out!—ha, ha! that's a good 'un. Why, a servant of my standing wouldn't stop in a place a day if he was asked for change out."

"No wonder, then, Sir, that you looks so fat," said cabby.

"Aw—yes; but I look upon it as a waste of my time. My uncle was a general in the army, and he was very angry with me for not following his profession of a soldier. But there was too much restraint there for me. Besides, about that time, too, a young lady—a regular booty—fell hawfully in love with me, and hinsisted that I should not jine the army. Well, her friends were against the match; they said I was too young, and insisted upon its being broken off. Walker! says I. So I took this disguise—I'm in disguise, cabby—of a servant in the family where she regularly visits. There we meets, and carry on our little billing and cooing unbeknown to no one. When we are both one and twenty we shall come into large fortunes, and get married. And I shan't be sorry when the day arrives, for I'm rather tired of this kind of thing," pointing to his livery; "and what makes it more uncomfortable is, that my so-called master is jealous of me—aw?"

"What! with his wife?"

"Well—aw—yes! I knew her long before she was his wife—a very pretty gal—and I should have bucked up to her, but my friends thought I ott to look above her—aw—and no doubt they was right. A chandler's-shop daghter—aw! Oh, dear no—not to be thought on!"

"Do you mean to say," remarked the cabman, "that your mistress is the daughter of the shop-keeper I put her down at?"

"I does," said George.

"Why I understood you that she was the Duchess of Windermere," said the cabman. "But I thought it was all guff at the time."

"Why?"

"Because I didn't think Camden Villas would suit a duchess for a residence."

"Not exactly, would it?" said George, with a wicked smile. "You know, while I cracked up the position of Missus, I cracked up my own. D'ye twig?"

"In course I do. I saw through it all the time, you know, but I said nothing. But that ere boy, who said your mother kip a mangle—"

"Told a lie—and I hate a liar above all things. No one is ever safe with a liar. I'm glad I knocked him down."

"But you didn't knock that boy down," said cabby.

"Didn't I! Well, then, I meant to—so it's all the same, you know," said George, not at all pleased with the cabman's particularity about his deeds of valour, and brushing the Banbury-cake crumbs from his livery. "Well, we must hook it now, for missus is in a hurry to get her children. There's a hawful row at home—master's deep in debt—and missus is going to leave him. Hoorry! come on—except you're going to stand something."

"Me? Wonld if I could; but I can't afford it," said cabby.

"Well, lend me sixpence, and I'll have another cake, and take one home to Sarah, for she's a good sort, and rather sweet upon me."

"That's cool! Lend you money to buy cakes for yourself and your young woman!"

"My young woman!" exclaimed Bread-and-butter Bumford. "I'd have you to know that my young woman, as you hignorantly call her, is a lady, and not a domestic servant."

"Didn't you say that Sarah was sweet upon you?"

"But I didn't say that I was sweet upon her. Because a servant-girl falls in love with me, I'm not obliged to fall in love with her. I may flirt with her. I told you before—"

"Oh, there, as to what you tell me, amounts to nothing."

"What!" exclaimed the page, his large grey-green eyes staring on the cabman for his insolence.

"What you say one minute you contradicts the next, you do."

"I see, cabby, you're like the rest of the world—when a feller's money is gone, you turn agin him—aw."

"What's your money to me! You've stood a glass of ale—and for that I've got to bilk the 'pike. There, that's all I've got out on yer, so you needn't bounce. You're stuck-up—that's what you are!"

"Well, now you are agoing it!" exclaimed George, falling back on his old well-worn sentence when he could say nothing else. "I'm blest if I don't discharge you, and call another cab."

"Oh, as you like about that, after you have paid me my fare."

"And which you know I can't do."

"Then don't talk, but come on; for my time has to be paid for, remember. Sixpence every quarter a hour I stops here."

"You needn't be for ever a-going on about your fare," said the page. "This ain't the first time we've hired a cab! Cab! whew! I don't call that old humdrum thing o' yourn a cab at all! A Hansom for me—aw!"

"You're a handsome fellow, you are," said cabby, smacking his long whip.

"That thing ain't fit to take home my dirty linen," said George. "A feller ought to be paid sixpence a mile to ride in it. I hope none of my friends will see me as I ride along."

"I've seed some of your friends," said cabby. "A parcel of dirty street boys—errand boys They reckoned you up, Mr. Bread-and-butter Bumford! Ha! ha! ha!"

"Say that again, and I'll serve you as I did them," said George.

"And you served them out—by running away from them, like a cur with a tin kettle tied to his tail."

"What a crammer!" exclaimed George, than whom nothing more irritated to call him the coward that he was. "I was obliged to run, because you came and told me my missus was a-waiting for me."

"Yes; but there was quite time enough to have licked the boys, but you hadn't got the pluck. They'd have knocked you into the middle of next week hadn't it been for me."

"'Twas your hinterference that saved them," said George. "I was just going to pummel the lot of 'em when you came up. And you please never hinterfere with me again. I'm quite big enough to take my own part. If I'm not, it's a pity."

"Oh, you're big enough; but you're all bounce, and no pluck," said cabby.

"Here's a fine young porpus!" exclaimed a rough-looking man, coming up to the public-house door, to a companion as rough-looking as himself, while pointing to the page.

"He's fat enough for the Christmas cattle-show," said the other.

"I'm sure neither of you are very beautiful to look at," said the wounded page. "Two lunatics from Colney Hatch, I should say."

"You ought to charge double for him, cabby," said the first of the two men.

"If he was melted down, you could make a good many long-sixes out of his fat," said the other; and to George's deep chagrin they all laughed right heartily at this remark.

"You'd like to have in a week what I eat in a day," said the page. "But if you are poor men—aw—you needn't be blackguards. I haven't any change about me—aw—or I'd give you some, for a little beah—you common men. Now, cabby, drive on," he added, jumping into the vehicle, very glad to rid himself of his chaffing friends. But they were determined to give the young snob the last word, by calling after him, as the cab rolled off—

"Don't spill the fat, cabby!"

The page popped his head out at the cab window, and threateningly bent his fist at them.

Nothing further occurred to delay the cab's progress to Camden Villas, where, after it arrived, George pulled the gate-bell in the most violent manner, which made Sarah wonder whoever it could be. When the girl's eye caught George, she exclaimed—

"Well, I'm sure! It's much like your impudence to startle a person by ringing the bell like that! The least I could have thought was that it was master come home."

"Well, I'm your master," said George, cocking his hat on one side, and bustling through the slope of the garden which led to the kitchen entrance. "Get the two children ready immediately and forthwith," he added, as Sarah followed on his heels, while she could not help smiling at her fellow-servant's airs and "round-aboutedness."

"Who are you a hordering of?" said Sarah.

"You—there! Now just understand, once and for all, that I've had quite enough hinsolence to-day from one and another, and I'm not going to stand any of yours. I tell you to get the two children ready immediately and forthwith!"

"And I tell you I shan't!" said Sarah. "I'm not going to be spoken to like that by a puppy like you."

"Well, I'm sure! You're agoing it!"

"Please to speak properly, then," said Sarah. "I'm not your servant. Pooh!"

"Don't pooh at me! I won't be pooh'd at by a common girl like you!" exclaimed George, nodding his head so much that it was a wonder his hat, looped up with gold strings, had not tumbled off.

"And who do you call a common girl, I should like to know?" said Sarah, coming very close to the page, and looking rather alarmingly in his face.

"You are a common girl to pooh me for just delivering a message from missus."

"Missus would know better than speak to me as you did, you ugly know-nothing! And if you do it again, I'll give you a good punching, woman as I am!"

George looked at Sarah with as much surprise

as he might have done had the world been coming to an end.

"You punch me! No, nor your carrotty young man either couldn't do that!"

"He's done it before; and if I lift up my little finger to him he would do it again; and if he wouldn't I would, you overgrown glutton."

"There, now mind ye, you've been and gone and done it. Look out for squalls, young woman! I'll serve you out for this. And as for your baker feller—well—there—don't let him come in my way, that's all; for as sure as I'm a gentleman I should damage all the beauty you see in him, and which nobody else does!"

"Take care; I don't mind much what you say about me, but if you scandalises Mr. Woodhead, I'll tear your ogling eyes out of your head!"

Sarah here stooped, and armed herself with the little boy's hoop-stick that lay in the garden-path, and she shook it at George's head much in the same manner as a policeman would shake his staff at a troublesome person who wouldn't "move on."

George now saw that the game was going very much against him. He, too, looked round for a weapon of defence, for he plainly saw that the girl was in earnest, and was not to be daunted by his assumption or his abusive tongue. Nothing was at hand, and Sarah now had a great advantage in the possession of the hoop-stick. George saw this, and changed his tactics from the offensive to the pacific.

"You wouldn't be so hot-tempered with me, Sarah, I'm sure you wouldn't, if you had known the bobbery I've had to-day with one thing and another, and more with another than anything else."

"But that's no reason, George, that you should come home here and give yourself such unbecoming airs, and insult me and my young man, who never did you any harm."

"He has done me the deepest, cruellest, artfullest harm in the world," said the oily page in a lover's tones. "He has stolen your love and affections from me."

"You are too much of a sneak for me," said the offended domestic.

"Don't be so fond of calling names, Sarah."

"I learnt that habit from you, George."

"I'm not a sneak, Sarah, except it be after your heart," said George.

"Why I wouldn't have you if I wasn't engaged to Mr. Woodhead—that's flat."

"Why?—that's what I want to know."

"Now I'm not going over that nonsense again. You've had your answer, and that's enough."

"You do cut a feller short," said George.

"You talked about immediately and forthwith just now; but, upon my word, you don't seem in a very great hurry."

"Missus was in a greater hurry than me to get the children, that I can tell you," said George.

"Hurry is one thing, but civility is another. I'm not very slow when I know what is wanted of me. But for a person of your years and position, to pull the bell off its wires, and strut about like a young turkey-cock, and talk about immejetly and forthwith, and all that rubbidge—"

"Do say rubbish. I can't abear that a young woman I love so much should spoil herself by speaking uncorrectly."

"I shan't for you," said Sarah, striking him with the stick. "I shall speak uncorrectly if I like!"

"I've a real good mind to give you in charge,'

said Mumford, bending his fist at his demonstrative assailant.

"No more of your imperence," said Sarah, shaking the hoop-stick. "You're a false, cunning, lying, greedy, ugly, dressed-up monkey! There! that's what you are!"

"Well, you are agoing it! O you abominable woman! I'll give notice to missus this night that I will leave her service, for my life ain't safe with such an abusive, insulting, long-tongued, ill-tempered shrew! And the man who marries you—"

Up went Sarah's stick, and down it came on the extraordinary fat shoulders of the page. But the girl might as well have belaboured a jackass, for George was so well clothed in flesh that, strike as heavily as she would, the stick could not find the boy's bones.

"Come, I say, stow it!" exclaimed George. "I'll indict you for it at the Sessions, or my name ain't George Mumford! And then your doughy-headed baker will see what a vixen you are."

Sarah was at him again, and more violently than before; for she caught George over the head, which made him exclaim "Murder!" so lustily, that it brought cabby to the kitchen, and he gallantly rescued the page from the clutches of the desperate domestic.

When cabby first entered the kitchen, Sarah had hold of one of the page's wrists, and held him against the pantry-door, and was well belabouring him.

"Come, I say, young 'oman, what are you arter?" cried cabby, going up to her.

"She's a-murdering me!" cried George.

"You imperent hound!" said Sarah. "I'll teach you to carry a civil tongue in your head before I've done with you, you lying puppy!"

"Ain't she a-going it, cabby?"

"I can tell you that my fare is a-going it," cabby replied to poor George's question. "When are the children to be ready?"

"She won't get 'em ready," said George.

"Nor I won't," said Sarah; "and if missus was here I'd tell her the reason, plain and plump."

"Make no mistake in me," said George; but Sarah interrupted him, by saying—

"I *have* made a mistake in you; when I first came here I thought you a good boy; but I've found you false, cunning, lying, greedy, deceitful, and vulgar—"

"Vulgar! That's good! *You* call *me* vulgar! Well, I'm blest! I'll go after that," said the page.

"Come, I say, if the children are not got ready I shall drive back to Cross Street without 'em; for I'm sure there'll be a dispute about my fare."

"It ain't my place to get the children ready," said George. "Speak to *her* about it."

"Now young 'oman, do look alive. Don't you know that my cab's a-waiting?"

"Not I, nor don't care," said Sarah.

"Well, I say, young bloke," said cabby to George; "I can make nothing of the gal, you'd better dress the young 'uns yourself."

"And who do you call bloke?" cried George.

"You," said cabby. "Mind ye, you have just got out of trouble with the gal; don't get into it agin with me."

"Well, I'm sure! Who are you? Don't you think of coming over me the same as the gal. I'm forbearing with a woman, but with a man I'm an out-and-outer. Here," he said, doing a little scientific boxing, "this is my style."

"And this is mine," said cabby, throwing his arms and fists out in unmistakable earnest, and, to George's mind, frightfully strong. "Don't run away from it."

"Ah!" said George, not at all liking cabby's exhibition of his fighting powers; "we are only sparring for a lark. We'll have a glass of old ale, and then hook it back with the children. And if sulky sides," pointing to Sarah, who had seated herself by the kitchen fire, "won't dress them, why I will."

"Ah, well, get the children, and I will help you," said cabby.

"I ask you three times—one!—two!—three! —are you going to attend to the children and get them ready?" said George to Sarah; and the domestic replied with a mocking face—

"One!—two!—three!—No, I'm not."

"You hear that, cabby?" said George.

"I hear it—yes—what of that?"

"Because I want you to witness that the girl wont obey her mistress's orders."

"You can settle all these disputes when I'm gone. But don't keep me waiting, that's all. I've warned you enough that my time's a-going on, and I shan't abate a penny of my fare, so I don't deceive you."

The page fetched the children, a pretty boy and girl, from the nursery, where they had been playing ever since mamma had left home with the determination never more to return. But they were innocent of this—innocent, too, that their dear papa was a fugitive and a murderer. Had they even been told those dreadful things, God had so mercifully obscured their infant understandings to the ways of evil, that they would not, could not, possibly have realised their seriousness to themselves or their parents.

Cabby and George now set to work and dressed them up in the best way they could. The children seemed so delighted at the thought of going out with George, for they were well pleased with him; and it must be said for the page that he was very kind and entertaining with them.

But George showed little art in dressing them, and they had frequently to correct him. At length, with the little boy's hat placed on the girl, the feather hanging behind, and the little girl's silk mantle given to the boy, while his cloth cape was buttoned on his sister, the page carried one to the cab and the cabman the other.

After this George liberally drew a mug of beer for the cabman, and had a draught himself; then he cut a good, substantial slice of bread and ham to eat on his journey; and then the cab drove off, leaving Sarah in sulky mood and alone in the house.

"Pull up as well as you can, cabby, for lost time," said George. "Don't spare the hoss a sweating, and I'll make the fare all right. Now, then, off you go!"

And off they did go, and as fast as the jaded beast—which was not first class—could step out. George, on the way to Cross Street, made Master and Miss Yapp scream with laughter, for he played all manner of tricks with them, and made all manner of grotesque faces.

They were not very long in reaching Cross Street; and when the cab bowled up the narrow thoroughfare and pulled up at the chandler's shop, Mrs. Yapp, and her father and mother, came eagerly to the door and relieved George of his precious charge.

The children crowed again when they caught sight of their mamma; but Mrs. Perkins, in the fulness of her heart and affection for her sweet grandchildren, put mamma on one side, and took them both in her arms and carried them through the little shop to the parlour.

Mrs. Yapp paid the cabman his fare without dispute, and then she said to her page—

"Now mind, George, if your master asks for me and where I am, tell him; but if he does not ask, say nothing. I don't want you to conceal anything, neither do I want you to intrude my name on your master if he makes no inquiries."

"I quite understand, mum," said George. "And if Mr. Cumberland calls——"

"Well?" said Mrs. Yapp, while the boy paused.

"Yes, mum—if Mr. Cumberland calls and asks for you—eh, mum?—shall I tell him you are here?"

"Certainly not, Sir," said Mrs. Yapp. "Refer him to your master, if he calls. Whatever made you think about Mr. Cumberland?"

George's mistress looked searchingly in the face of her page, wondering at the mystery of his manner.

"Speak, Sir—what made you think of Mr. Cumberland?"

"'Pon my word, mum, I hardly know. I thought, perhaps, you'd like for Mr. Cumberland to know where you are."

"Why, pray?"

"Because I thought he always called to see you, and not master. He always asked for you."

"Pity, Sir, that your thoughts should be so idle. Had they been more in your work and less meddlesome with the affairs of others, I should have been able to give you a better character than I can possibly do now."

"I'm sure, mum, master thought the same as I do," said George.

"Indeed! Has he told you so? Ah, George, your looks tell me that you have been playing the spy and mischief-maker!"

"Well, Mum, master told me."

"Told you what? Speak!"

"To tell him when Mr. Cumberland called, and how long he stopped."

"The miscreant!" exclaimed Mrs. Yapp, between her teeth. "To place a spy upon me in my own house! A cheat himself, he thinks all the world like him."

Then she turned to George, and frowningly said—

"Out of my sight, you cunning rogue! and never let me see your face again!"

"It was no fault of mine, Mum; I was obliged to do what master desired me."

"Of course you were," said Mrs. Yapp. "But you were not obliged to try and ruin the character of your mistress! Go about your business, you rascal!"

"You are unjust to me, Mum," said George. "You should hear, Mum, what I have to say before you accuse me."

"Your looks accuse you," said Mrs. Yapp. "And were I to condescend to listen to what you have to say, I should only be giving you opportunity for more lying!"

"Lying, Mum!—whatever do you mean, Mum?"

"Exactly what I say," replied Mrs. Yapp. "I have often wondered that your master should have overlooked your faults so long as he did. But it is all explained now. Master and servant, you are a very fitting pair to live together; but let me tell you that your spying powers will have

for the future to be exercised on some one else than me. Begone from this door, Sir! I cannot bear to look on such a deceitful face. Begone!"

"If I only had my wages, I would never go back to the house again, that I'm sure I wouldn't."

"Go to the master who has so well employed you for them. You should be paid double, as you have had to do double duty—a spy upon the mistress, who has ever been kind to you, as well as page."

"Why don't you come in, Maria," said her mother, coming to the door with the little girl in her arms, while Jacob Perkins was nursing the boy on his knee at the parlour fire. "You will catch your death of cold standing in the draught of the doors. Now, Jarge, you make haste back home—or run over the way and see your poor old mother first."

"I'm almost dead, mother," said Mrs. Yapp, with her handkerchief to her eyes, sorrowfully walking to the parlour, followed by Mrs. Perkins.

George Mumford's mother carried on her industry with her patent mangle, opposite the chandler's shop, as the little yellow-painted board with an illustration of her gigantic mangle in the window showed. She was a tall, bony, clean, but very poor woman, and she laboured under the fond delusion that her boy George was the best and cleverest boy breathing. She knew he told lies—but what of that? Didn't every boy of spirit do the same thing? and her George was no worse than his neighbours. But the old woman liked her son for his ignorant pride and conceit, and still more that he looked down upon his mother and despised her mangle, which he was that spirited that he said he would rather starve than turn. Oh, he was such a good son, that when he was out of place he would sit by his mother's little fireside and eat bread-and-butter, if there was nothing better going, and look at his mother while she did the arduous labour.

Just as poor Mrs. Yapp left the shop-door, as her page with sheepish face was about to take his fat sides off, his mother espied him from her window, and she exclaimed to herself, stopping her mangle—

"Heavens above! Why, there's my Jarge, as I'm a living sinner."

Then, just as she was, in a clean but patched-up cotton gown, considerably torn and worn about the region of her flat, shapeless bosom, her long feet encased in a longer pair of tag-rag boots without laces, with much motherly eagerness she pulled up her draggling petticoats with both hands while she stepped across the running gutter before her door to her fat, proud boy, on the other side.

Before the page was prepared for this parental visit, he found himself in his mother's fond embrace; and, alas! for the temper of the son, his mother in her sprawling over-fondness knocked George's gold-laced hat into the gutter.

George tore himself from the poor woman's arms, stood back from her with a disdainful look, and exclaimed, while his mother picked up the hat—

"This is very hindecorous, Mrs. Mumford,"—at the moment his proud heart would not allow his lips to call her mother.

"Never mind the hat, Jarge," said the woman. "But you don't know how glad I am to see you."

"I don't like such gladness, Mrs. Mumford,"

said the page, his pride and passion still unaffected by his mother's affection.

"You don't know how glad I am to see you looking so well," said Mrs. Mumford, who formed but a sorry contrast to her over-fed son. "You are gitting more than ivir like your poor dear father, who was buried the day you was born."

"But what has that to do with my hat? You ought to have had more sense than to knock a feller's hat off."

"Come over the way, do, Jarge—come to your own home and have a cup of tea with your own mother," she said, suddenly kissing him.

"Don't!—don't it looks so!" said George, wiping the kiss away from his lips, and spitting as if something very disagreeable had got into his wide mouth.

"You nivir come to see your poor old mother, and you nivir write to her, and you nivir ask her to come and see you."

"I have no time."

"What do you do with your day out, Jarge?"

"Aw—the truth is, there are so many low people know me in this neighbourhood—aw—that I don't care to show a head here. I should lose charactah amongst my West-end friends. That is all—it is out of no disrespect to you."

"I'm glad of that, Jarge," said the mother, who, had she been as wise as she was fond would have given him a rap on his thick head, and told him to go about his business. But the more the youth puffed himself out as a grandee the more he won Mrs. Mumford's admiration. She thought him a paragon—a marvel—and a wonder; and so he was—of falsehood and conceit.

"No, I must go, mother," he said at length, allowing the word that stuck so long in his throat to pass his lips; and the young fool positively had the impudence to extend one finger to his mother, as it has now become the unseemly practice of people of station to those beneath them in the ladder of life.

"Oh, you mustn't go before you've had a cup of tea with me. Betsy Baker was asking after you last Sunday, and wondering that she nivir heard from you."

"Well, I'm sure! Betsy Bakah, indeed! Aw—you must tell her that she must please to think nothing more of me. I hope I'm a mile or two above Betsy Bakah!"

"Heavens above! but how fat you are getting, Jarge! I can't but help admire you!"

A female neighbour of Mrs. Mumford's here came up with a plate of sprats in her hand, holding her little boy by the other, and she offered to shake hands with the proud page, but he extended his finger to her.

"I declare, Mrs. Mumford, I hardly knowed your son, he has grown so fat and tall. And how do you like service, George!"

"Aw—well—seeing that I have two or three servants to wait upon me, and plenty to eat and drink, and nothing to do, I'm pretty comfortable, thank you. I hope you are the same, Mrs. Broom."

Poor Mrs. Broom shook her head before she replied—

"Seeing that I have to wait upon myself, a sick husband, a baby in arms, and five other children, with nothing to eat and drink but what I earn from charing, I'm pretty uncomfortable, as your poor mother knows. Jist like the world —some too much, and others too little."

"Now then, can't you leave my buttons alone, boy," said the page, snappishly, to the son of the woman with the sprats. "Don't you know it is very rude to touch a gentleman's clothes?"

At George's reproof the little boy quickly put his hands into his pockets, wondering whether he ever should wear such a beautiful coat. After the mother, too, had reproved her boy for his uncommon rudeness, she said—

"What a rich man Maria Perkins must have married for you to have two or three servants under you, George!"

"Oh, he's enormously rich!" responded the page. "But I think the servants are happier than they for all that."

"I shouldn't at all wonder, not I," said Mrs. Mumford.

"Oh, dear, no; it isn't always the richest are the happiest," said her friend. "I suppose you came home to see your poor mother?"

"No, I didn't," said George, pulling up his chin. "I don't want the whole neighbourhood to know it, but Mr. and Mrs. Yapp has parted. She is a Tartar and no mistake, and no husband could live with her."

"Heavens above! Jarge, you don't say so?" cried Mrs. Mumford.

"Well, I for one never thought she would make a good wife. She always was a proud stuck-up; didn't you think so, Mrs. Mumford?"

"I'm that astonished that I can hardly speak," was Mrs. Mumford's reply. "How many children has she got, Jarge?"

"Two. They are both over the way with their mother."

"Whatever was the rumpage about?"

"Say rumpus, mother, and I will tell you," said the particular youth.

"Rumpus or rumpage, it don't matter to me. But you always was a skollard. Do tell us, my dear son, what they have parted for?"

"She was jealous of me and master. She didn't like our being companions. Master wouldn't give up me, and she left."

"Oh, what a fool!" cried the woman, turning her sprats over. "Had her husband made a companion of a nice young lady, she might have flared, eh, Mrs. Mumford?"

"Why, yes. But my Jarge always was a favourite wherever he went—with men, women, and children."

"Ain't Betsy Baker fond of him!" exclaimed the woman with the sprats, laughing and shrugging her thinly-clad shoulders, as if she felt the cold; but her fondness for gossip defied heat and cold.

"What's good one day ain't good another," said George. "When I was a boy living at home here in this squalid street, Betsy Baker was all very well. But she won't do now at any price —aw—and so I have desired Mrs. Mumford to tell her. I really must bid you both good evening, for I have promised to smoke a cigar with a friend of mine at the Duchess of Windermere's. Ta! ta!"

As he was about to move off in this cold, contemptible manner, from his poor old mother, a couple of stout boys came up who had known him when he was errand boy at Townley's, and quizzed him from top to toe, and chaffed him immensely about his fat; and concluded by asking him what he was going to stand.

"You really stare as if you had never seen a gentleman before," said George, trying his old bounce over the boys; but it wouldn't do. When George styled himself a "gentleman," it became the cue to them for the loudest derisive laughter.

I say," said one with a cloth cap half over his eyes, "it would take a schoolmaster to count his buttons."

"It would take a strong rope to hang him," said the other.

"Hi! here, you policeman!" exclaimed George; "those two vagabonds are insulting me, and I give them in charge."

The boys laughed, and so did the officer, as he walked up to see what the stout page had to complain about.

"Now then, young fellows, let the boy alone, and clear off," said the officer.

"Boy! Policeman, who are you talking to?" cried George, drawing back.

"Don't hurt him, sir, he is my son," said Mrs. Mumford, coming to George's protection. But the gallant youth repudiated his mother's interference, and bade her go home.

"I think I'm quite big enough to protect myself from those prigs, or the peeler either, come to that," he said.

"Don't you be quite so bounceable," said the policeman. "Bounce won't do for me. If you move on, I'll take care those boys shan't molest you."

"Aw—thanks—thanks!" said the page, moving off amid the jeers of all who saw him. But before he had got to the bottom of Cross Street, his lanky, slip-shod mother, holding up her trapsing petticoats with both hands, came running after him for another kiss; and without consulting how far such motherly demonstrations would be agreeable to her son, she once more flung her long, bony arms around her son's apoplectic neck, and kissed him on both cheeks.

George was very much annoyed, and showed it by shaking his head, wiping his mouth, and cheeks, and spitting on the ground, intimating that his mother's fondness was as disagreeable as physic to him.

"I wish you wouldn't detain me in sich a filthy place as this. A woman of your years ought to know better. And if ever you meet me again, I beg that you will not let all the world know that you are my mother. It is injurious to me. Ta! tá!" he said, waving his hand, and crossing to the other side of Holborn, where he was soon lost, in the great crowd moving to and fro, from his mother's fond gaze.

CHAPTER XXXIX.

SWIFT'S BODY DISCOVERED IN THE THAMES. —THE DETECTIVES IN PURSUIT OF THE MURDERER.—A VISIT TO MRS. SWIFT'S.

BY St. Paul's great bell it was twelve o'clock, when the body of Swift was discovered by the captain of a Yarmouth boat lying off Billingsgate. The corpse of the murdered man, with those ghastly, unclosed eyes staring to the silver moon above, had been stopped in its onward course with the tide by getting entangled amongst the chains and moorings of the numerous craft that lay in repose at this busy part of the Thames.

The captain, without showing very much surprise, gazed awhile at the corpse, and then went ashore, to give information to the police. The same tide that had brought Swift's body to Billingsgate had also brought the boat in which the murder was committed, and which Mr. Yapp

left to its own guidance. There was the boat, with Swift's blood on and about the seat, gently undulated and rocked by the onward tide. The corpse and the boat lay together in the water under the bright beams of the moon, and ever and anon knocking against the keel of the Yarmouth fish-boat which had that morning made London with a cargo of fresh herrings.

It was not long before the swollen body was delivered from the water and in the possession of the police, by whom it was conveyed to a neighbouring workhouse for ownership. On searching the body there were a variety of odds and ends found on it, such as a latch-key, a large pocket-knife, a comb, one old glove, a red handkerchief, a few loose matches, a screw of tobacco, a half-smoked cigar, a linen money-bag, a blank bill-head of Bonthron and Son's, but not one farthing of money—for it should have been stated that Mr. Yapp, before pitching the body into the Thames, had rifled his pockets of the Bank of England notes paid to him by Lady Blaze.

There was now a great "hue and cry" about the murder on the Thames, and the detectives were soon at work to scent the murderer. They had not far to seek; the printed bill-head belonging to Bonthron and Son was the cue to the discovery who the man was that had been so romantically murdered.

The morning after the murder the newspapers were full of the "Murder on the Thames," and the placards set forth in the largest type, and the most sensational language the events connected with the finding of the body, with suspicions as to who was the chief actor in the great tragedy; while the pencil was at work graphically picturing forth the body entangled in the ship's chains, the blood-stained boat, as well as the body laid out for ownership at the dreary workhouse.

Two detectives, with the bill-head in their possession, were early at Bolt Court, but the place being closed, they dropped into the Lion, and gained many particulars about Messrs. Yapp and Swift; and from the description of the latter, they had little doubt but that he was the murdered man.

From Joe Bowers they also learnt where Swift resided, and thither they quickly went, and found that he had not been home all night. Mrs. Swift was then questioned by the officers if she had any idea where he was?

"Not I—nor don't care," said Mrs. Swift, who had let the sun go down upon her wrath, and had at this moment as much hatred towards her deceased husband as she had during the scene that had the day before taken place between them in the presence of Mr. Yapp at Bonthron and Son's. Then she said, looking impudently at the two strangers—

"I should like to know why you come here bothering me about my husband—the wretch!"

"We are officers in plain clothes, Mrs. Swift."

"And in plain faces. But for the matter of that I don't care who you are. I suppose you don't want to arrest me? If you do, here I am."

"A little civility, if you please, Mrs. Swift; you have had nothing but that from us."

"I can hardly be civil to any one who comes here after my husband," said the ungracious woman. "But if you want him, you had better step up to the second-floor back, and ask Mother Jones for him. I daresay she knows more about him than I do."

"You are excited, Mrs. Swift; angry, no doubt, because your husband did not return last night," said one of the detectives.

"Not I! I hope he will stop away altogether. I can maintain myself without his help."

"When did you see him last?"

"Yesterday morning," she replied. "And I don't think he will want to see me again in a hurry. Nor Mr. Yapp either. They are both of 'em a couple of thieves, and so I shall tell Mr. Bonthron when I see him."

"Do you *know* them to be thieves?—or do you merely speak in passion?" the spokesman of the two officers asked.

"What do you ask me this parcel of questions for? If you have to charge me with anything, why don't you say so, like men! You'll catch me in none of your traps, so you'd best not try. If you want anything with me, say so at once. Here I stand, a honest woman, and I should like to see the person who said otherwise." Here all Mrs. Swift's old pugilistic tendencies came up strong, and she placed one foot behind her and the other forward, pulled back her head, and thrust forth her lips, and kept her two arms by her side in the most rigid manner possible.

"My good woman," said the officer, "I wish you would be a little calmer, then you would soon arrive at the purpose of our visit. We are neither come to arrest you nor make a charge against you."

"Then what is it you want?"

"A few answers to a few questions relative to your husband."

"And don't I tell you that I know nothing about him? And don't I tell you that I don't want to know nothing about him any more?"

"Then we may presume that it would not be a terrible shock to your nerves if you were to hear that he was dead?"

"What's my nerves to do with you?" replied Mrs. Swift. "Now just look here, you two—both of you are strangers to me; don't you stop here and take up my time by asking me questions about my husband. This is my washing-day, or you wouldn't have seen me about quite so early this cold morning. What you've got to say, say; and let me get on with my wash. It's my turn with the kitchen copper, and I mustn't lose the chance of washing my clothes by gossiping here with a parcel of men that I don't know, nor don't want to, to answer questions about my dirty, drunken, rake of a husband. Let him go to Jericho for what I care."

"I am afraid, Mrs. Swift, that we shall find he has gone farther than that. Your husband, we are apprehensive, has gone to heaven."

Mrs. Swift laughed outright at such an apprehension on the part of the officers, and then exclaimed—

"Swift gone to heaven! That's the last place I should look for him in. You don't know Swift, that's now very clear. Heaven, indeed! My Swift in heaven! Lord-a-mercy! when he dies he'll go where he has often told me to go to, and where I shan't go because I know he'll be there."

The officers could not resist smiling as they looked at each other, while Mrs. Swift stood with her dress pulled up to her arm-pits, looking quite in earnest for an undisturbed day's wash, and very much inclined to be quarrelsome with any one who dared to interrupt her in her womanly purpose.

"When you last saw your husband, Mrs. Swift, what clothes had he got on?"

"Precious dirty ones—that's all I know," she replied. "Do what I would, I never could get him to be clean; he was so much taken up with drink, dominoes, and skittles, and that filthy hussy that lives on the second-floor back."

This last sentence was uttered quite loud enough to reach the ear of the lady on the second-floor back, and presently hasty footsteps were heard coming down the stairs, and then, as stealthily as a ghost, a far better looking woman than Mrs. Swift stood by her side, quietly demanding from her—

"And now what have you got to say about that filthy hussy that lives on the second-floor back? You're another, Mrs. Swift, and your husband was far too good for you; and here I am that says so, and I don't care the snuff of a candle nor the paring of a petater for you."

"Oh, if it wasn't for the law!" cried Mrs. Swift, grinding her yellow teeth. "But there," she added, throwing back her long neck, "you know you are not a bit better than you ought to be."

"As good as you any day in the week, and a good deal better," said Mrs. Jones, who, although she did not speak so loud as Mrs. Swift, there was an equal amount of vulgar passion in her speech, look, and action.

"You're a very trumpery woman, and Mrs. Winsey says the same," said Mrs. Swift.

"Oh, indeed! Thank you for nothing," said Mrs. Jones, adjusting a bit of a fringed red neck-tie, the bow of which had escaped round under her ear instead of remaining under her chin. "Mrs. Winsey says so, does she? Then now I walk my chalks to Mrs. Winsey's and see what she has to say about me." And with long strides, yet as quiet as a ghost, to the intense gratification of the officers she vanished up stairs to Mrs. Winsey's room.

"There, that's the woman you should have asked about my husband, if you want to know where he is to be found."

"Look here, Mrs. Swift, we are really on a very serious errand. We are investigating a murder."

"And what am I to do with that?" said the woman, in the coldest apathetic manner it was possible to conceive, more especially as the past conversation clearly pointed to the murder or death of her husband. But the mind of Mrs. Swift, at the best of times, was very obtuse; and when she gave herself up to obstinacy, as on the present occasion, no one could make her understand.

"Have you not heard of the murder on the Thames?" asked the officers.

"Not I! And what if I had? what is it to me, or what have I do with it?" she impudently asked.

"But surely you would not think it too much trouble to assist in tracing a murder?"

"But why do you come to me of all persons?" asked Mrs. Swift.

"Because of all persons we conceive you to be the most concerned."

"What! concerned in a murder? You must have more impudence than Mrs. Jones to tell me that!" cried Mrs. Swift.

"We presume that you would be concerned if it were proved that your husband had been murdered."

"What have you to with my feelings about my husband? You have done a pretty thing for my character, that I tell you, two policemen coming to my house about a murder!"

TOM BROWN SEIZED THE BRIDLE, AND IN THE FALLEN HORSEMAN DISCOVERED MR. YAPP.

"You still don't see the drift of our inquiries, Mrs. Swift. A man has been murdered on the Thames, and we have circumstances to show——"

"That I committed it?" cried the impatient woman.

"Certainly not; but to show that it is your husband who has been murdered."

"Why, you don't say so!" exclaimed Mrs. Swift, with slightly changed tones, looks, and feelings. The news the officers had communi-

cated to the wife in the gentlest manner possible had produced a little touch of nature even in the turbulent, unforgiving heart of Mrs. Swift; and she, who was so ready and so boastful about dancing on the grave of her murdered husband, was now shocked—though not much—to hear of his untimely end, and regretted that the last time they met they should have quarrelled.

"And pray who has been wicked enough to murder my husband?" she inquired.

"That is the point," replied the officer. "But

20

we have first to make sure that it is your husband that was murdered."

"Oh, you are not sure of it!" exclaimed the woman, assuming her old character of perfect indifference. "Then you may be sure that it is *not* he; for who would go and murder a penniless man like that, I want to know?"

"Is this his knife?" said the officer, holding up to Mrs. Swift the one that was found on the corpse. After the woman had turned it round and round and examined it, she said—

"I believe it is; but I ain't agoing to swear to it."

"That we don't ask you to do. Is this his pocket handkerchief?" holding up before her astonished eyes a red one with white spots.

"Aye, that it is! Ain't I washed it hundreds of times? and had he come home as he ought to have done it would have been in my bile now. But where did you find it?"

"That knife, handkerchief, and this comb—"

"And that comb I can swear to," interrupted the woman.

"Yes, very well; these things were found upon the dead body of the man who has been picked out of the Thames with a sharp wound in his right temple."

It was now unmistakably made clear to the woman's mind that her husband had been murdered, and she exclaimed, raising her apron to her eyes, but there were no tears—

"Poor Swift! Well he wasn't a bad sort after all. Hadn't it a-been for that Mother Jones and the drink, he would have been as good a husband as ever wore shoe leather. But Lord! it mightn't be him after all. Let me look at that handkercher again."

The officer held it up.

"Oh! there's no mistake about it!" she exclaimed. "If that was found on the body, that body is my poor Swift. I would swear to that hankercher! Where can I see the body?"

"We will take you in a cab to the workhouse where the body lies."

Mrs. Swift quickly attired herself for her melancholy errand, and she was soon in the presence of her dead husband, who, directly she saw, she exclaimed—

"Oh! that's my Swift! Those stockings he has on I only bought last week to keep his feet warm, and now they are spilt. Who has killed my husband?" she cried. "A cruel wretch, whoever it was! I'll see that Yapp about it instantly."

"Leave all that in our hands, Mrs. Swift. We beg you to keep quiet, and say nothing. Your husband was last seen with this Mr. Yapp you mention, and we will go back with you to Bolt Court and see whether he is now in his business, as he ought to be. You must attend the inquest to-morrow."

"What have I to do with your inquests? I have to go out charing to-morrow."

"Everything must give way to this matter."

The two officers, and the new-made widow, made the best of their way to Bolt Court, but Mr. Yapp had not made his appearance. There was a solicitor's clerk in possession of the premises, with Miss Bonthron, for after the receipt of Mr. Yapp's serious letter announcing the loss of his employer's account books, Mr. Bonthron, who continued very ill, sent immediately for his solicitor, and consulted him in the matter. The latter at once sent his clerk, accompanied by Miss Bonthron, to Bolt Court and interrogate Mr. Yapp further on the matter, for the

rag-merchant began to have his suspicions, and was in a perfect state of distraction at the loss of his account books.

The day went by, and Mr. Yapp never appeared, nor could the vigilance of the officers find out where he resided. It was singular how secret the clerk had kept his residence from the knowledge of every one.

There now arose inquiries for Lady Blaze, the garret tenant; she, too, could not be found. After the restoration of her ring, she took her trunk of valuables, and, late at night, left the house, leaving her odds and ends of furniture behind her.

The day passed and the following came, and late in the course of it the whereabouts of Tom Brown was traced; and through his master's purchase of Mrs. Yapp's jewellery, and she having presented her card, he was enabled to furnish the officers with the address of the man of whom they were in search.

Before this, however, the inquest on Swift was held, and a verdict of "Wilful murder against some person or persons unknown" was returned. Suspicion of course set in against Mr. Yapp; and after the officers had failed to find him at Camden Villas, £50 reward was offered for his apprehension. Large placards were circulated over the town, and at the police stations, wherein was given a full descriptin of his dress and appearance, especially particularising his fur great coat.

CHAPTER XL.

TOM BROWN AND HIS GRANDFATHER.—THE HEIR OF WILBY FARM.

IT was about the time that this tragedy was being played out that Tom Brown received a pressing invitation from his grandfather, the Devonshire farmer, to pay him a visit. The old gentleman was not well, and felt indeed in a declining state of health. At these periods when the sands of life are drawing to a close, we are given to reflect on the past, and to review our conduct to all men. The life we have led, for good or for evil, whether young or old, at the momentous moment of dissolution, stands before us, as it were, in a picture, and the evil we have done always occupies the foreground, and appals us with the serious shape it assumes, unrelieved by sophistry or special pleading.

Mrs. Brown's father now began to think that he had visited his daughter too harshly for the mistakes of her erring husband. She was gone—he could make no reparation to her—would that he could, he should have felt happier! While now that he felt death close behind him, he became concerned about his grandson, and addressed him the letter referred to at Mr. Lambert's from where the poor boy had previously written to him, giving him a touching history of his father's suicide and the fire that destroyed his mother.

This letter the cold-hearted farmer disdained to answer. Tom felt his grandfather's treatment acutely, but consoled himself with having done his duty in writing, and leaving the other to Providence.

About a week after Tom had despatched his letter, his grandfather, who was far stricken in years, the latter was seized with illness. Then the recital of Tom's letter came in review before him, and he felt self-accused of being cruel. At once he dictated a letter—for he was too ill to write—requesting an immediate visit from Tom Brown, and the boy was just prepared to start when the detectives came to inquire of him the residence of Mr. Yapp.

The sun was indeed now beginning to shine for Tom, who had for a long time known nothing but the most abject sorrow and trouble. His rich grandfather had relented in his coldness, and he grew largely in the esteem of Mr. Lambert, the rich diamond merchant, and his amiable daughter, in whom Tom reposed as in father and sister, and they in him as son and brother.

Tom's temporary parting with the good jeweller and his daughter at the railway was sad and mournful, and after the train departed all three felt the loneliness that comes over all affectionate hearts on losing those they love.

Tom had often been to his grandfather's farm when a very little boy; and although he had not been for years, still he retained a good remembrance both of the extensive farm and his grandfather. When he arrived, he felt himself at home—the orchard's, fields, the scenery round and about, and the old white gate at the entrance of the farm, were familiar objects to him—and so was the face of his venerable grandfather.

The boy was received at the station nearest the farm by a servant, and driven three or four miles in a gig to his grandfather's abode; a substantial house—surrounded by outhouses, piggeries, cow-sheds, stables, a picturesque watermill, and barns; while ploughs, carts, and other agricultural implements were scattered about the farm-yard, and the discordant cackling of geese, the screams of peacocks, and the loud crowing of bold chanticleer were to be incessantly heard.

Poor old grandfather, when Tom arrived, was swathed in flannel by the side of a large parlour fireplace, for the old man could get no natural warmth in his aged bones, and it had to be supplied by artificial means. The sight of the little traveller, who was in deep mourning for his mother, seemed to brighten up the thin old farmer, and he kissed his grandson and shook him long and warmly by the hand, and ordered the best of everything to be prepared for him.

The evening passed by Tom and his grandfather talking of Mr. and Mrs. Brown, the old man endeavouring by all means in his power to show Tom that it was his father's bad conduct that had been the cause of all the estrangement that had unfortunately arisen between them and him.

Tom said as many kindly and affectionate words as he possibly could for his father; and when the old man saw that his grandson was affected to tears by any reproach upon his parents, he forebore, and told Tom that he forgave his father, and that he was only regretting that evil circumstances should have arisen to divide them.

Then the old man spoke in the highest terms of Tom's mother, and the boy in his heart blessed him for it.

"Well, my boy," said the old farmer, with a serious look, "you have come in time to see grandfather die. I shall soon be in the company of your father and mother."

"I am very sorry to find you so ill, grandfather," said Tom, in unaffected accents.

"No doubt you are, boy; but you mustn't expect me to live for ever. I am past seventy-four, and I begin now to get tired of life and its labours. But your heart is too young to understand the ways of death."

"Oh! grandfather, I dread to hear the sound of the name of death."

"It is a name, boy, that we are always hearing, but somehow or other we never get familiar with it. But I have had my warnings, Tom, and like a good man must attend to them, and prepare to receive the destroyer of the body with a smiling face."

"I hope it will be a very long time before you die, grandfather."

"That cannot be, Tom. I'm overdue already, and must speedily return to the God who made me. You'll have to be master over the farm, boy. How say you—should you like to be?"

"Not through your death, grandfather. Besides, Mr. Lambert, who has been so good to me, wishes me to follow his trade."

"You must not think of it, Tom. You are my heir, and I must repose in you that you keep the old farm up, if it is for nothing more than keeping all the families employed on it that have been for many a long year. I have a numerous band of labouring dependents, and the farm must be held together if only for their sakes. The farm, too, with proper management should continue to be productive, as it has been to many generations of my family. And I'm sure I've left it better than I found it—for my poor father drank hard, and neglected and impoverished it. But by prudence and industry I have made it profitable, and shall die leaving my successor rich, and independent of the farm."

"I am too young, grandfather," said Tom.

"Your uncle Fairburn, who lives in the village, and whose daughter your mother's cousin, Squire Seymour, married, will be your guardian. He is a poor man, but a good one, I am happy to say."

"My mother's cousin, Mrs. Seymour, is dead, is she not, grandfather?" said Tom.

"Yes, poor girl. They stole her child, and although she lived ten years after that, she literally pined to death with grief; and I'm sorry to say the Squire did not treat her well, either."

"Was the child never discovered?"

"Never, nor ever will be. It is a very mysterious affair, and your uncle Fairburn has not been the same man since."

"Who stole the child, grandfather?"

"It is supposed a Mrs. Walpole, a lady as rich as the Squire himself, and who lived on Wilby Estate. But I can't say—I can't say."

"For what reason did she take the child?"

"Well, Tom, there was a reason, and a revengeful one it was You know that Squire Seymour played Alice Walpole false on her marriage day, and afterwards married your mother's cousin, who was a very beautiful girl. And it is said—but I hope it is not true—that when Miss Fairburn had a little boy, Mrs. Walpole stole it in retaliation for the Squire's dishonourable conduct to her daughter, who died broken-hearted. However, nothing of Mrs. Walpole nor the child has since been heard of!"

"How strange!" cried Tom, in tones of sympathy for the unhappy Squire.

"Well, it is strange," said the old gentleman, "that after so many years, nothing should have been heard of either—oh! that pain—that pain—it cuts me through and through! Reach me that bottle, my boy."

"I fear you have been talking too much, grandfather," said Tom, bringing a bottle of sedative from a black mahogany cheffioneer. The farmer with a trembling attenuated hand took the medicine Tom kindly poured out for him, and it gave him instant relief, when he went on with his narrative—

"However, Squire Seymour has now, thank God, got a clue where to find Mrs. Walpole; and it is my belief that where she is there will his son be found."

Then he told Tom all about the ring and the advertisement, and when his grandfather mentioned Bonthron and Son's, Bolt Court, Fleet Street, as the residence of Mrs. Walpole, Tom seemed transfixed with surprise.

"What is the matter, my boy?"

"Oh! how marvellous!" cried Tom. "Why that is the very place where I went as a London Errand Boy—and where, grandfather, I was so cruelly treated."

"And have you been a London Errand Boy, while I have been overflowing with wealth?" exclaimed the grandfather, in poignant tones. "You, my own flesh and blood, as it were, allowed to starve, while I had more than I knew what to do with! Oh! it is I who have been cruel!"

"Oh, no, grandfather—you did not know that we were so badly off."

"I did—I did know it. Your dear mother wrote to me, and I cruelly snubbed her. It haunts me now! it haunts me now! Oh, boy, never do an action that will give a death-bed pang. Virtue alone brings satisfaction to a dying man. Mind that, Tom—promise me, will you mind that, when I am no more?"

"Father and mother taught me that, grandfather," said Tom, "and I have always endeavoured to do what they taught me."

"I am very glad to hear it. Come to me, my boy, and tell me what your father and mother said about me."

"I never in my life ever heard them speak anything but affectionately of you, grandfather."

"I bitterly repent now that I had not been a better father to them. Oh! the curse of money. What is the good of it to me, now! Riches!—they only serve to make a death-bed terrible. To think, that because your father did not treat me well, I, who had thousands, should have allowed you to suffer so much misery! And you have been a London Errand Boy?"

"Yes, grandfather, and at the very place where Squire Seymour expects to find Mrs. Walpole," said Tom.

"And was there such a person living there?"

"There was a very mysterious woman living there, whom they called Lady Blaze."

The old gentleman asked for a description of her, and when he heard it, he cried—

"I have no doubt that is her," said Mr. Fairburn, "and if so, it is remarkable indeed."

"And it was thought by everybody that she was a lady living in disguise there, and it was further said, but no one could tell for why, that she lived there to be as near as possible to Mr. Yapp, who was Bonthron and Son's cashier."

"And how old was this Mr. Yapp?"

"I should think about four or five-and-twenty," said Tom.

"The very age of Squire Seymour's son, if he be living. Do you know the Christian name?"

"William," said Tom Brown.

"And that was the child's name," said the grandfather.

"But what about Yapp?" said Tom. "The son of the Squire would be called Seymour."

"That puzzles me, except Mrs. Walpole changed the child's name, in order that all clue might be destroyed."

"And I can tell you more, grandfather; this Mr. Yapp, I heard, never could find out who was his father or mother."

"That is the strongest confirmation of all," cried the farmer. "How much I wish the Squire had seen you before he went to London to seek Mrs. Walpole. But I'm sure, by what you tell me, and the ring she advertised as lost with the Squire's initials on it—I'm sure he is on the right scent, and I shouldn't be at all surprised, if I live so long, to find him come back with his long lost son."

The old invalid here expressed himself as being weary, and a respectable serving-man, at Tom's call, came into the room; and while the boy read a chapter from the Bible, the servant assisted Mr. Fairburn to bed, where, ever and anon during the night, he was awoke with racking rheumatic pains.

Tom, too, was very weary after his long railway journey from the Metropolis; and after wishing his grandfather good repose, he was shown to his bedroom by the serving-man's wife; and after fervent prayers for his grandfather's recovery, and for God's blessing on himself and his dear friends Mr. and Miss Lambert, he was soon asleep in his capacious well furnished bed.

———

CHAPTER XLI.

THE MURDERER ALARMED.—HIS DISGUISE FOR FLIGHT.—HE BRIBES THE PAGE TO SECURE HIS FLIGHT.

WHEN the daylight broke in upon the restless unhappy Mr. Yapp, the morning after his foul murder of Swift, it found him at a looking-glass in his bedroom with a razor in his trembling hand shaving off his moustache. It was the first step he took in disguising himself, for he felt that directly the body of Swift was found, that justice would be in pursuit of him, and a full description of his clothes and person would be circulated in the fullest public manner.

After this he went to his abundant wardrobe, and dressed himself in the oldest and most unfashionable attire he could find, and destroyed his identity in every possible manner, and even went so far, with a powerful dye he had at hand, to change the very colour of his hair. He further disguised himself for his flight from the hunters which he felt would early be in pursuit after him, by placing on his head a billycock hat which he was in the habit of wearing in his garden.

Just as he was ready for his start—hardly knowing, though, what road or route was the safest for him to take—one loud, decided knock at the door reached his ear. Oh! how it appalled him.

"Lost! Lost! They are upon me! Oh, Swift, Swift! you will soon be averged! Where can I fly for safety?"

His hand was on the window to jump out. Then another thought seized him—he would get on the roof of the house from the trap-door. That notion was as quickly abandoned as thought of. Then he clutched Swift's five-pound notes, and with them he would try and make his escape from his pursuers. Then the thought of suicide seized him. But in all his hurried designs he vacillated. He had nerve for nothing, and he stood in the centre of the room with a brain on fire, trembling, yet not daring to take one step in action.

He trembled with fear, and felt rivetted to the very spot of the floor he stood on. While thus paralysed in his movements he heard George answer to that one loud imperative knock, and he ventured to the door, and with a strained ear he eagerly listened to hear himself accused of murder.

"Is Mr. Yapp in?" asked a knowing-looking, tall, muscular man with very bushy whiskers, dressed in a green greasy great coat that reached to his heels, and well bespattered with mud of long-standing.

When the clerk heard this inquiry and his page's answer that he was, he was almost frenzied, and he again exclaimed — "Lost! Lost!"

"Well, if he's up I want to see him—if he's not up, don't disturb him, for I can wait."

"What is your business?"

"My business is with your master," said the man." "And I must wait till I see him."

"Then will you call again?" said George.

"Oh dear no; I must wait here," said the man.

"That you won't," said George, "without I know your business. D'ye think I'm agoing to let any one on the premises without I know what for. I'm not so jolly green as that."

"Well, I shan't go—there," said the man, who had got inside the front door.

"What!" cried George, bristling up as if about to thrust the man forth.

"Beware how you attempt to touch an officer in the execution of his duty," said the man.

"A hofficer!" exclaimed George, and when Mr. Yapp heard the word his blood ran chill, and had he not caught strongly by the door he must have fallen to the ground.

After George had recovered his surprise and had ceased to stare on the man, he rushed up the stairs, knocked at his master's open door, and abruptly exclaimed—

"Please, Sir, here's a hofficer wants you! and he won't go without you!"

"Oh! George," cried his master, pale as death, and trembling from top to toe.

The page was as equally surprised as his master to see him dressed so early and in so odd a manner, with a billycock hat on his head, and the colour of his hair changed.

"Come in here, George," said his agitated master, quite under the dreadful impression that the officer announced was on the business of the murder—"come into the room—don't be afraid of me. Now, boy, if you will get me out of the house without the man below seeing me, I will give you this—" holding up a sovereign.

George Mumford, while he looked with his greedy eyes on the golden bait in his master's hand, that shook like an aspen while he held it out, felt more puzzled than he had ever been in his life to make it all out. But the page's love of money soon aroused his ingenuity, which was something extensive in any crooked ways.

"How will you manage it, George?"

"I'd knock him down, Sir, if he wasn't such a whopper," said the bumptious page.

"Do anything—anything, boy!" said Mr. Yapp.

"I have it," said George. "I'll invite him into the parlour to wait until you come down, and when he's in, I'll turn the key on him, when you can slip out through the garden."

"Good! Be quick! be quick, then!" cried Mr. Yapp.

"I'll take the sovereign first, if you please, Sir," said George, having his eye on the tempting reward.

"There—and you have earned it with my best thanks, George," said Mr. Yapp, anxiously listening to the operations of his page after he had left him with the dreadful officer.

Immediately he heard the key turned on the man, Mr. Yapp rushed like mad down the stairs, through the garden, and seemed to breathe again when he had escaped from the officer, who eventually proved to be only a sheriff's officer in possession for arrears of rent.

CHAPTER XLII.

GEORGE MUMFORD'S ALARM AT DISCOVERING BLOOD ON HIS HANDS.—MR. YAPP TRAVELS EXPRESS.

DIRECTLY after George Mumford had recovered his surprise at his master's inexplicable flight from the house, he unlocked the door of the room in which for the moment he had imprisoned the sheriff's officer, and impudently told the man that, as he did not choose to explain his business, his master declined to see him, and had gone out for the day.

"And that don't matter to me, young man," said the officer. "I don't pertic'lerly want your master nor your missus; but I want the furniture, if they don't pay the rent in three days from the date of this warrant. And for those three days I don't move from the house."

"Crikey! here's a pretty go!" cried George. "How much rent is owing, Master?"

"Three quarters last Christmas," said the man, "and, as far as I can see, there ain't more than enough here to pay it, with my expenses and all."

"I can tell you one thing, old feller," said the bumptious page, "you don't move a stick afore I has my wages."

"Stuff! the sheriff has nothing to do with that."

"We'll see about that. If the sheriff takes the things by force afore my wages is paid, I'll have the sheriff up afore the Lord Mayor."

"Don't be a fool," said the man, squatting down in a silk-covered arm-chair.

"Mind'ye I won't be called a fool by you," said George, with his hands in his pockets, and thrusting his thick head, with a very short crop of hair, impudently forward. "You needn't be bounceable, if you are a man in possession." And before the tall officer could reply, the page started off in an excited frame of mind, if he had any, to alarm Sarah with the news that her overdue wages would be lost, that her master had absconded, and that there was an execution in the house for the rent, and that her clothes would be seized; but he never said one word about the sovereign his master had given him.

"I shall make up a nice little bundle for myself," he said, "and I should advise you, Sarah, to do the same."

Then George, in the most frantic state, ran

upstairs and downstairs—(even passed the pantry without going in for a pick—a most unusual thing,—then he traversed the kitchen in the wildest state imaginable.

"Now, Sarah, make up your mind—what will you take?"

"I shan't touch a thing, and let them touch a thing of mine if they dare," said Sarah. "I shall summons them if they don't pay me."

"How can you summons when master has run clear away?"

"That's all rubbidge," said Sarah. "Besides, I know where to find missus."

"And so do I, but that's no good to either of us," said George; "for she ain't answerable for master's debts. But I'm not going to argue, I'm going to pack a bundle; and if you're not a fool, you'll do the same. Do it, Sarah, or you'll be ruined—quite ruined!"

George's dreadful excitement completely bewildered the girl, and she became "that flurried" that she also quickly paced up and down one side the kitchen, while George occupied the other in the same manner.

"Look after yourself, Sarah; I mean to," said George, walking to and fro."

"But the man won't let you take nothing out," observed Sarah.

"Let him stop me if he dares!" cried George, bending his fist. "Master's gone out in his old clothes, and I'll go out in his best, or my name ain't Mumford! That fur coat of his'n is worth all my wages, and I'll have it!" he cried, scampering up the kitchen stairs to the hall, and taking the coat to the kitchen, where he laid it out on the table preparatory to packing it up. While doing this, his hand received a stain from the blood of Swift that was still wet on the sleeve.

When the page saw the blood on his hand, he made such a dreadful face that he quite frightened Sarah.

"D'ye see!" he screamed, extending his hands, "d'ye see! Sarah? Ha! They'll take me for a murderer! Look at the blood, Sarah!"

The girl gazed with horror on the page's blood-stained hands, and screamed so loudly, that the sheriff's officer ventured below to see whatever the matter could be; and directly he entered the room, the page cried—

"D'ye see, Mister! Blood on my hands! Blood from master's coat! Oh! be a witness, or they'll hang me for murder!"

"I'll leave the place this instant," said Sarah, "or I shall be hanged too!"

"Oh! don't leave me, Sarah," cried George.

"If you'll excuse me, I think you are both frightened about nothing."

"I'm sure my master has committed a murder, and he bribed me with this sovereign to lock you up while he escaped But I'll have no blood-money!" he exclaimed, dashing the coin on the table. "I'll take you both to witness that I leave the sovereign there. Oh! get some hot water, Sarah, and wash my hands. I can't abear myself with blood on 'em. Make haste! make haste!"

"There may be blood on a man's coat without his having committed a murder," said the officer. "Where's Mrs. Yapp?"

"She's gone to her father's," said Sarah, while George rubbed and scrubbed his stained hands, over which he made many wry faces.

"Your master's about as much committed a murder as I have," said the officer. "It isn't likely he would have hung his coat with blood on it in the hall if he had."

"Why did he give me a sovereign to lock you up? Why did he cut off his moustache? Why did he go out without the coat which he always wears? Why did he dress himself in old clothes and his garden-cap?"

"I can't say, I'm sure," said the officer.

"Then don't talk," said George, pertly.

"Don't you be uncivil," said the officer. "It won't make me no better or worse whether you or he have committed a murder, as long as you don't murder me," he added, with a laugh, "and that you certainly won't do if I can help it."

"Come, old feller, now what do you advise me to do?" said George, more pacifically.

"Well, I should say it would be a very serious thing to charge your master with murder just because you find blood on his coat," replied the sheriff's officer.

"It ain't just for that—there are other curious things—and you must put that and them together, and then where are you?" said George.

"Well, I should say if you know where your missus is, you'd better go and state your fears to her," said the officer.

"And so I will," said George. "I'll have my breakfast, and off I goes to Cross-street."

Then the page, and Sarah, and the officer sat down to the morning's repast; and while George and the latter ate heartily, the poor girl was so concerned about the horrors of the morning, that she could partake of nothing more than a cup of tea.

CHAPTER XLIII.

GLIMPSES OF A LOST FATHER.—TOM BROWN RECOGNISES MR. YAPP. — THE CLERK'S FLIGHT.

ABOUT three hours after Mr. Yapp escaped from Camden Villas, firmly under the impression that the officer who had called at his house for him was to arrest him on the charge of murder, he found himself, without intending it, on the Great Western Railway, driving by express towards Plymouth. He had no special purpose in this journey more than any other, and he was flying he knew not whither.

But while he fondly thought he was flying from justice, he felt that he could not fly from himself. Swift sat with him in the train, face to face; and even when he closed his eyes, the image of the murdered man was deplorably palpable to his senses.

He took a second-class ticket to Plymouth, without at all knowing what he was to do there, or why he went there. Whilst in his agitation and pondering what to do, he found himself at the Paddington station, and the express train just off for Plymouth was the only reason that could be assigned for his taking that route.

Little did the passengers who travelled with him think they had a murderer side by side with them; but while all noticed his taciturnity and his gloom, no one thought him other than a gentlemanly young man.

On his journey he got out at each refreshment station, and drank as long as the stoppage of the train would allow him; but it brought to his troubled mind no obliviousness, and the damning murder was the companion of his thoughts.

Arrived at Plymouth, the extreme destination of the train, for some hours he wandered about the streets, and at night found himself upon the esplanade of the Hoe, face to face with the great grand sea, which in its roar and rock-dashing billows seemed to invite him to destruction.

For three days he hid about the famous seaport of Plymouth, not knowing what step to take for his safety. He was afraid to take ship for distant parts, for it was his impression all ships going out would be well watched for him.

During his stay here, he read with a groan in the newspapers of the reward offered for him, and his description. He became more uneasy, more unsettled than ever, and after that, everyone he met with he suspected to be a detective. Plymouth was the first place he had read or heard of the reward being offered for his apprehension; he began to loathe it, and at once, and on foot, without knowing where he was going, he took the road to Exeter, which he made in a couple of days, sleeping but once on the journey. At whatever house, either village or roadside, he dropped into, he heard nothing but of the dreadful murder on the Thames.

When he reached the city of Exeter, the people there seemed in greater commotion about the murder than ever. The first night he arrived there he took a bed at an obscure house; and while standing at the bar of the public-house, two men were talking about the murder, and while his own name was being mentioned freely, one said to the other—

"I have heard that the murderer has been traced to Plymouth."

"Ah, then, they'll soon nab Master Yapp," said the other.

The murderer's heart sank within him.

"Traced me to Plymouth!" he immediately exclaimed. "Then I am too near my pursuers. Off again, or I am lost! I'll take horse back to London! Oh, Swift! Swift! how much I envy you your death! Let them take me—hang me, for I'm sick of life!"

After thus musing with himself, he went abroad in the city, telling the landlord he wanted to call on a friend, and that he would return in an hour.

Having plenty of money in his pocket, he quickly hired a strong grey steed; and without the remotest intention of returning it, he left a deposit for the hiring, mounted the horse, and rode off out of the ancient city into its lovely picturesque suburbs.

Sometimes he would ride wildly, as if some one was pursuing him, then he would slacken, as if he had said, "I'll fly no more, let them take me!"

At length he reached the village of Wilby, the principal owner of which was his own father, Squire Seymour. But this, of course, he had not the remotest knowledge of. Having ridden so far and so long, he pulled up to the village hostelrie to bait his horse and refresh himself.

At the house he heard news indeed! news of his father! at least, from what passed in conversation between two villagers; and what he had accidentally gathered from Mrs. Walpole, he believed to be his father.

Janson, the blacksmith, and an agricultural labourer, over their cups together, were talking about Squire Seymour having returned from London without finding the child Mrs. Walpole had stolen from him.

"Seymour!" he cried to himself, when Janson mentioned it, "the very name Mrs. Walpole, unintentionally called me by!"

Then he turned to the talkers, who were lounging against the village little bar, and said—

"And how long since was the child of this Squire Seymour stolen?"

"But I say he has not been stolen, Sir," replied the pig-headed blacksmith. "It's my opinion there has been foul play at the Manor House, and that Mistus Warlpole had no more to do with the child than you had."

"Well, I'm a stranger, so I cannot say anything about it," said the fugitive clerk. "But how long ago is it since the boy—the child was a boy I think you said?"

"Ees, zur; and a voine little feller he waz," said the labourer. "Now let me zee, Janson—it must be two-and-twenty year come Midsummer since the boy dizappeared from Wilby."

"And how old was the boy when he was missed?" inquired Mr. Yapp.

"Only two years, zur."

"Another link in the chain. That makes about my own age," mused Mr. Yapp to himself. Then he inquired where Squire Seymour lived, and if he was rich.

"He lives about two miles from here; and he be rich indeed. But he would give all he had to find his zon, that I am zure."

After this conversation, he paid his score, and rode in the direction of the Manor House, which, when he reached, he reined up before it. hid from sight only by a few tall elms. While he stood at rest upon his horse he poured out upon himself the bitterest self-accusations.

"How can a murderer-son face his father? Oh! he would curse his son rather than embrace him,

Befor he finished his soliloquy, a slight branch from one of the elms fell suddenly upon the high-spirited horse, and the reins hanging loosely on him, he started and bolted like lightning through the Squire's park, flew over the heath, and threw his rider about a quarter of a mile from the farm of Tom Brown's grandfather.

Unfortunately for Mr. Yapp his foot became entangled in the stirrup, and he was dragged hurriedly along the road, and his head knocked against the gate of the farm, by which, at the moment, was standing Tom Brown.

The boy sprang forth, and heroically seized the frightened horse by the bridle; and, to his great astonishment, recognised Mr. Yapp, his old, but cruel, master, in the fallen and wounded horseman.

CHAPTER XLIV.

MR. YAPP FINDS HIS FATHER.—DEATH OF THE CLERK.—LADY BLAZE SATISFIES HER REVENGE.

"MR. YAPP!" cried Tom Brown, after he had made sure that it was him, and released his foot from the stirrup.

The wounded man groaned, then gazed on Tom Brown, but spoke not. The youth left the horse and knelt by the side of the thrown man, and again called upon his name.

The dying man then gazed upon the youth again, and faintly said—

"Ha! Tom Brown! There stand you,—and there Swift!"

The poor boy looked round in terror at the name of Swift; but seeing no one again turned his attention to the dying man, and said—

"Where is Swift?"

"Why there he stands by your side! and

both of you stand there to accuse me! I killed him, as I thought, yet there he stands! Forgive me, Swift!—forgive me, Tom!"

Tom Brown, in great excitement, went into his grandfather's house and consulted with the inmates on what was to be done. His grandfather was too ill to go to the gate, but advised Tom to send one of the servants for the doctor, and another for Squire Seymour, to see if it were his son or not, and in the meantime to let the servants bring Mr. Yapp into the parlour.

"Oh, do not move me, for I am dying! and the very road is too good for my deathbed! Before I close my eyes in death, I ask your forgiveness, boy. Do forgive me! The murdered Swift—yet he stands there—there—by your side! Oh! speak to me, Swift!"

"There is no one there, Mr. Yapp," said Tom Brown.

"Don't tell me so," he excitedly cried. "There he stands bleeding from the temple—and now he floats away upon the water."

The Squire here rode up, and Tom Brown told him that the gentleman who lay groaning on the road was Mr. Yapp, of whom he had but yesterday spoken to him about. But the Squire had had such information concerning the dying man that left on his mind no doubt but that it was his long-lost son that was now lying before him, and moreover that that son was a murderer.

"Here is Squire Seymour, your father," said Tom, to the dying man. Mr. Yapp as much as he was able extended his hand, and the words, "Forgive me, father," faintly escaped his pallid lips.

"Oh, my son!" cried the father, "what have you been guilty of?"

"Murder, father!" gasped the wretched dying man. "Oh, forgive me!"

"I do, my son, freely," said the agonised Squire, kneeling and clasping his son's hands in his. "You have been the victim of evil circumstances, and a martyr to a wicked revengeful woman. *She*, Mrs. Walpole, God will make her answerable for all."

"I dare not cast my guilt upon another. I have deeply transgressed, father, and to God alone must I look for mercy!" He groaned, as if about to expire.

"Get a tumbler of wine, boy," said the Squire to Tom Brown. The latter was not slow to do the Squire's bidding, and the father held the glass to his son's lips, and he drank off the whole of it, and for a minute or two rallied, and feebly said in broken sentences—

"Father, I have two little children—help them—be a father to them—let them take my place in your affections. They are far more worthy."

"On that point you may die happy," said the father. "I have seen them, and love them. And your wife——"

"Yes, take care of her," said Mr. Yapp, but not with the same warmth as he spoke of his children.

"And this poor boy. I have wronged him, father; he will tell you how, for I have not strength. Protect him."

A woman superbly dressed here suddenly came upon the scene, as well as some villagers who had been made aware of the accident. It was Mrs. Walpole, otherwise Lady Blaze. She had heard in London of young Seymour's guilt; and her revengeful spirit rejoiced in it. She was glad that the hangman was in pursuit of him, and hearing that the Squire was in London, she took the opportunity of once more visiting Wilby, where the news of the accident of Mr. Yapp's fall from his horse soon spread to one and all.

"Child for child!" cried Mrs. Walpole, extending her finger, on which sparkled the diamond ring Swift stole from her.

"Oh, you wicked, cursed woman!" exclaimed the Squire.

"You now can feel the wrong you did me. I vowed then to be revenged, and my revenge is satisfied. This ring," (taking it from her finger) "I swore to keep until my vow was fulfilled—now take it from me, for I hate it as the gift of one whom I loathe!" She cast the ring to the ground.

She spoke wildly but eloquently, and her tall, commanding figure, with her magnificent face, gave even a sublimity to the scene.

"Thank heaven! my child died innocent—yours lies there—a murderer!"

"For which *you* are responsible," said the Squire, in bitter tones. "But spare me now, I entreat you. Ha! my son—he's dead!" he exclaimed, as one loud, deep, expiring groan rose upon the air. "He's dead!"

"And I am satisfied," said Mrs. Walpole, walking away in quiet dignity, leaving the Squire bending over the dead body of his son.

———

With the death of the ill-starred clerk our story is at an end.

The detectives, when they found Mr. Yapp, found only his dead body, on which an inquest was holden, and then he was interred in Wilby churchyard.

Not many days after this, died Tom Brown's grandfather, leaving his grandson the farm and all he possessed, which was something considerable.

More than this for the good boy, it became known to him that Mr. Lambert desired, when he increased in years, that he should marry his daughter, who Tom prized far more than riches.

The Squire at once sought out the children and widow of his unfortunate son, and he brought them to the Manor House, and they eventually inherited his large estates; while old Mr. and Mrs. Perkins were reimbursed all the losses they had incurred on their "Child of Mystery."

The furniture at Camden Villas was all sold off, and George and Sarah turned adrift to seek new situations.

George soon found one at a small photographer's; and, from his great rotundity, he became so well known about the neighbourhood, that his master had his likeness placed in the mahogany-case at the doorway as a specimen of his skill in taking likenesses.

Tom Brown was the beloved of all who knew him, and the people of Wilby looked forward to the happy day when Wilby bells should merrily ring for his union with Miss Lambert, the daughter of the rich diamond-merchant.

THE END.